S0-AVZ-138

POSTING TO
ST PETERSBURG

JEFFREY REID

Trafford
PUBLISHING

Order this book online at www.trafford.com/05-1410
or email orders@trafford.com

Most Trafford titles are also available at major online book retailers.

© Copyright 2007 Jeffrey Reid.
All rights reserved. No part of this publication may be reproduced, stored in a retrieval
system, or transmitted, in any form or by any means, electronic, mechanical, photocopying,
recording, or otherwise, without the written prior permission of the author.

Sandra Dyer: Editor
Hannah Gordon: Cover Designer
Laura Grace McFarland: Authors Assistant

Note for Librarians: A cataloguing record for this book is available from Library
and Archives Canada at www.collectionscanada.ca/amicus/index-e.html

Printed in Victoria, BC, Canada.

ISBN: 978-1-4120-6499-6

*We at Trafford believe that it is the responsibility of us all, as both individuals
and corporations, to make choices that are environmentally and socially sound.
You, in turn, are supporting this responsible conduct each time you purchase a
Trafford book, or make use of our publishing services. To find out how you are
helping, please visit www.trafford.com/responsiblepublishing.html*

*Our mission is to efficiently provide the world's finest, most comprehensive
book publishing service, enabling every author to experience success.
To find out how to publish your book, your way, and have it available
worldwide, visit us online at www.trafford.com/10510*

 www.trafford.com

North America & international
toll-free: 1 888 232 4444 (USA & Canada)
phone: 250 383 6864 ♦ fax: 250 383 6804 ♦ email: info@trafford.com

The United Kingdom & Europe
phone: +44 (0)1865 722 113 ♦ local rate: 0845 230 9601
facsimile: +44 (0)1865 722 868 ♦ email: info.uk@trafford.com

10 9 8 7 6

Thank You

To all the wonderful friends who give me such
unstinting support and encouragement.

CHARACTERS

Ambassador Lord Malvern and Lady Malvern

Monty Montague

Prince Boris Barinsky

Princess Natasha Barinskaya

Count Sasha Dolgurky
Countess Nadia Volonskaya
Their servants Mr Basov, Mr Bibikov and Andrei

Countess Tatiana Golvinka

Baron Max Hertzburg
Baroness Gisela Hertzburg

Baron Llov later Betskoi
His servant Mischa

David, Lord Mountforte

Servants Percival and Smithers

Raveski, Count Panin

Prince Potemkin

Count Nikolai Kolcluley

Countess Elizabeth

Count Dmitri

Countess Sophie

Madame Amelia Barteneva

General Suvorov

Herr Shuffel

CHAPTER ONE

IT WAS 28 APRIL 1791. Lady Malvern had finished dressing, and now sat in her private sitting room waiting for her husband to arrive. She tossed back her drink and leaned forward on the sofa to help herself to another. How many vodkas had she had? It was fortunate that no one would smell her breath, and the cold air on the way to the ball would soon clear her head. She refilled her glass as she thought what a wonderful evening lay ahead.

Then for no apparent reason her mind drifted back to when she was seventeen and passionately in love with John Severn. The rage, when her father learnt that they wished to marry. He had forbidden her from ever seeing him again. She still remembered how he had stormed and raved, shouting angrily, 'Well-bred or not, the man is a ne'er-do-well.' She had been broken-hearted.

True, Severn had fulfilled her father's prophecy, but life would have been much more fun if she had married him. Sighing slightly, she recalled how the heir to the then Lord Malvern had appeared on the scene and how her family had determinably pushed her into marrying him.

Her father had proved prophetic when he stated that Malvern's pup was an up-and-coming young man who would go places. Well, he had. British Ambassador to the Russian Court of Empress Catherine was a plum posting. He was honourable, clever and ambitious, but so dull, with no sense of humour. Still, he loved her. But she knew that even after all these years he was still nervous of what he called her 'indiscretions.'

Shaking off her melancholy, she finished her drink and decided to help herself to another. Just then her long serving maid came back into the room. She frowned as she saw her mistress about to pour herself another drink. Almost immediately, however, her expression softened as Lady Malvern asked, 'Martha, is His Lordship nearly ready yet?'

'No, M'lady,' she answered; 'He will be about another fifteen minutes. He only returned from a meeting an hour ago.'

'That's all right then,' Lady Malvern replied, settling back comfortably on the sofa and taking up her drink. 'What does the young Lord Mountforte look like? Both his parents were good-looking.'

'It is hard to say, your Ladyship; I only saw him very briefly and that was by chance as he arrived to meet his Lordship.'

'By chance?' Lady Malvern asked with a charming but somewhat disbelieving smile. 'What is he like?'

'Well, Lady Margaret, from my brief glance he is good-looking and has a fine figure. I do know the Russian servants were surprised and pleased to find he speaks excellent Russian.'

'Yes, his grandfather buys a good deal of timber from Russia, and apparently insisted on young Mountforte learning the language. His Lordship says it will be a great asset for the Embassy, despite French being the language of the Court.'

At that moment Martha's husband, who was Lord Malvern's valet, tapped on the door. He stepped inside and addressed Lady Malvern. 'His Excellency is ready now, Your Ladyship.'

Lady Malvern rose gracefully from the sofa. She was a large-boned woman and inclined to plumpness, but like many large women she had a natural grace of movement and manner. Both Martha and her husband were proudly aware that their mistress was regarded as one of the best-dressed women in St. Petersburg, even if her taste was sometimes startling to the more conservative members of society.

'Thank you, George. Off we go.'

George and Martha had a code they used with Lady Margaret if the ambassador was in a bad mood, and George now commented, 'His Excellency has had a difficult day, M'lady.'

Lady Malvern sighed. Well, she would simply have to cajole him into a better frame of mind, for she fully intended to enjoy herself tonight. 'Thank you, George.'

The two old retainers followed as she glided out to join her husband, who was waiting at the head of the staircase.

'Good evening, Malvern. Have you had a good day?'

'No,' grunted her husband, offering his arm to descend the stairs.

'This staircase is the loveliest I have ever seen,' she remarked soothingly as they began to descend.

'Vast, too vast,' muttered her husband in a none-too-mellow tone.

Halfway down the stairs the watching servants saw Lady Margaret stop to talk to one of the footmen. Despite her husband jerking her arm impatiently, she persisted in asking the footman how his very-pregnant wife was faring. The Ambassadress was interested in everyone and her caring attitude was one of the reasons she was so popular.

As she moved on down the stairs she took in the young man standing awaiting them at the bottom. So this was young Mountforte. Martha had not exaggerated when she had said he was good-looking. He would set many a young girl's heart fluttering. Once it became known that his grandfather was the extremely rich and reclusive Earl of Highgate, and that Mountforte was his sole heir, every woman with an unmarried daughter would set out to catch him.

As they reached the foot of the stairs her husband turned and introduced the young man. 'Lady Malvern, this is my new secretary, Lord Mountforte.'

David, Lord Mountforte bowed and took the hand she extended, kissed it, and gave her such an attractive and open smile that for a moment she was quite taken aback.

'I would not have recognised you; your parents were great friends of mine. You were just an eleven-month-old baby when they visited us at my father's London house a couple of weeks before they drowned. What a terrible tragedy! Did you not go to live with your grandfather immediately after that?'

'Indeed I did, Lady Malvern. I have heard much of my parents, but I have no memory of them.'

'Well, well,' Lord Malvern broke in somewhat tersely. 'We had best be on our way.'

He signalled a footman to beckon the sleigh that had been waiting at the gate until they were ready. The sleigh, which was emblazoned with Britain's coat of arms and drawn by three matched dark bays, drew up to the great double entrance doors to the Residence. As the party entered the sleigh the Ambassadress's skirts billowed forth like the topsail of a ship. For someone so large and stately she appeared extremely supple. Her hair was brushed up on one side, leaving her right ear uncovered. In it she wore a huge diamond and emerald earring, while its twin was fastened to her left bosom. The diamond looked brilliant even among the many other jewels she wore.

Once they were all in the sleigh, bundled up in furs, muffs and gloves against the cold, they set off at a fast trot.

'How very fortunate you are to have arrived at just this time,' Lady Malvern said. 'Tonight you will be a guest at the grandest ball you will ever attend.'

'I am told it is to honour the Empress and to celebrate the capture of Ismail.'

'Yes, it was a marvellous victory for Russia and gives them command of the mouth of the Danube and much beyond. Knowing Potemkin, the ball will be sensational for he is unbelievably talented and equally unbelievably extravagant.'

'He can well afford to be extravagant,' snapped the Ambassador. 'He has the Empress always ready to bail him out.' Turning to the young man, he continued, 'Potemkin is a great and talented man, even a genius, but he treats the Russian Imperial Treasury as his own. His palace put him so much in debt that the Empress bought it from him then immediately gave it back to him as a gift.'

Putting her lips close to David's ear, Lady Malvern whispered. 'Potemkin was the Empress's lover for years and even now they are extremely close. It is strongly rumoured by some, that they secretly married.'

They fell silent as they drew nearer the palace, and the horses gradually slowed to a fast walk as they began to catch up with others heading in the same direction. The closer though they drew to the palace the harder the horses were to hold and it took all the driver's skill to control them.

The air was sharp and crisp. The palaces, mansions and shops on the Prospect looked enchanting with snow lying over and around them. To David they looked like the choreography for a wonderful children's fairytale. In many of the windows he observed people, young and old, staring out at the vast assortment of carriages as they passed by on their way to the palace. Every so often a horse would misbehave and there would be shouts and curses, or a conveyance would collide with another, causing a bad-tempered commotion.

As the driver eased their sleigh closer to the palace the streets were lit with flaming torches and the air began to thicken with the smell of smoke and horse dung. Finally, they reached the vast, colonnaded building. It was stunningly lit, and they had ample time to observe it as they waited in the confusion at the entrance, where several carriages had converged at once. It was nearly forty minutes before the Ambassador's party was able to move from the entrance, up the grand stairs to where Prince Potemkin was receiving his guests.

As they slowly climbed the stairs they began to hear the strains of an orchestra coming from the ballroom. The splendour of the palace was overwhelming. As they passed through the huge entrance hall they glimpsed marble, gold, painted domes and ceilings, porphyry, malachite, huge stone vases and urns, and wonderful lapis lazuli furniture. The acrid smell of the outdoors was replaced by the fragrance of scented wax candles and the perfume of ladies as they jostled along with their partners, some politely and others more vigorously.

When Lord and Lady Malvern finally reached the Prince, he greeted them warmly and after a few words the Ambassador introduced David.

'Mountforte has just arrived from Britain,' he explained. 'He is my new First Secretary.'

The Prince, a noted anglophile, cordially greeted Lord Mountforte and after a short pause he added, 'Perhaps if you are free next Thursday morning you will join me here for coffee. I shall be delighted to see you, for I look forward to hearing the latest news from England.' Then, after a further brief word with Lord and Lady Malvern, and a smiling nod to David, he turned and greeted his next guests.

As they moved into the ballroom the Ambassador seemed pleased.

'Very interesting,' he commented. 'We will talk on this tomorrow. He is hard to get hold of, and your meeting could be very fortuitous. Potemkin is a great visionary and highly cultured.' Adding dryly, 'Though a great womaniser, he is after the Empress, the most powerful figure in Russia.'

David had been thrilled to receive the invitation from the Prince for apart from being aware of his importance, in the brief few moments he had spent with him, he had been struck by Potemkin's impressive presence, and beguiled by his undoubted charm.

They entered the magnificent ballroom and Lord and Lady Malvern moved to join some friends who were standing to the right of an impressive marble statue of Venus de Milo. David followed, gazing at his surroundings with awed fascination. He knew the hall they were standing in was the biggest in Europe. At 21 metres high, 74 metres long and 15 metres wide, it could easily hold several thousand guests.

Lady Malvern paused, and moved closer to David. 'The palace is reputed to cover over 197,000 square metres. Further, there is a winter garden of the same size, with paths, hillocks, heated pipes and immense hidden stoves that have allowed an exotic tropical garden to be developed.

To David the vast room seemed a fabulous paradise.

The ballroom was ablaze with beautiful bejewelled women and elegant men in every form of dress, many wearing decorations. Some were resplendent in uniforms, others were in Court dress, while yet others like the Pasha of Khotin and the Emir of Bokhara, robed in gorgeous national dress. Russia's empire was now vast and St. Petersburg, the heart of the empire, was a major cosmopolitan city. The empire encompassed so many different nationalities and religions that any major function was a marvellous tapestry of colour. There were chieftains, khans, emirs, pashas and hetmen, all in striking national dress and adorned with magnificent jewels and orders.

CHAPTER TWO

AS THEY STOOD GLORYING IN THE BRILLIANT SCENE BEFORE THEM A FOOTMAN APPROACHED, BOWED TO LORD AND LADY MALVERN, AND INFORMED THEM THAT PRINCESS EKATERINA DASHKOVA WOULD LIKE THEM TO JOIN HER PARTY. Lady Malvern promptly murmured to David, 'The Princess is a great anglophile whose son was partly educated in Edinburgh. There he made friends with the prodigious Benthams, who are now working for Potemkin. The Princess's son is now too serving under Potemkin in the Crimea. Dashkova is very influential and makes a good friend.'

Following the footman across the huge room, the Ambassadress continued speaking rapidly. 'The Princess is the niece of one of the other powerful men of the Court, Count Simon Vorontsov. Her sister, despite being very ugly, was the mistress of Empress Catherine's late husband when he was Grand Duke, but this is not something to mention these days.' When they reached her side the Ambassador introduced Lord Mountforte, and the Princess introduced him in turn to her friends. These included Madame Valeria Rimsky, an elderly man the Princess introduced as Count Ivan Shuvalov, and Count Nikita Panin. The latter, David later learned, was an enemy of Prince Potemkin and had formerly been Russia's Foreign Minister.

Just then Madame Rimsky, who was commenting on the guests as they entered the ballroom, said, 'Here come the Barinskys,' and added for David's benefit, 'That's Prince Boris and his wife, Princess Natasha.'

As he turned to follow the direction she was pointing with her fan he saw a tall, handsome man crossing the room, with one of the most beautiful woman David had ever seen leaning on his arm. The Prince was smiling and nodding to people on all sides, but the Princess kept her eyes straight ahead and acknowledged no one. David was fascinated. Not only was she hauntingly beautiful, she appeared so fragile that she would have floated away had the Prince not held her arm.

However he was not the only person who was struck by Princess Natasha.

'Prince Barinsky is so gentle and kind to his wife,' one of Princess Dashkova's friends murmured. Count Panin took up the theme, commenting to David, 'It has greatly surprised me, because before Barinsky met his wife, the former Countess Dolgurky, he was regarded as a ruthless and callous womaniser, just like his late father. To put it bluntly, he was a cad. Frankly, it is amazing to see how he has changed into such a courteous and considerate husband.'

Madame Rimsky interrupted. 'I don't know how, Prince Boris puts up with his wife's lack of even the minimum of civility to the people around her. Look how she treated her grandmother, Countess Volonskaya, and her own younger sister, Countess Tatiana Golvinka. She has not said more than hello to either her grandmother or her sister in nearly two years, in fact not since a month or so after she married Prince Boris. Countess Nadia has twice called at her granddaughter's residence in St. Petersburg. On both occasions the major-domo told her the Princess wasn't home, yet the Countess knew for certain that she was. Apart from the humiliation,' Madame Rimsky continued, 'it has been heartbreaking for the Countess, and for her other granddaughter, Countess Tatiana, who was completely snubbed when she went up to her sister at one of the rare functions the Princess attends these days. It was dreadfully mortifying for Tatiana, although she tried to pretend it had not happened but too many people had witnessed the snub. Natasha never goes out without her husband and when she does go out she says virtually nothing. It is extraordinary when one remembers what she used to be like. Yet look at her, no woman in the room can compare with her for beauty. Her fragility has only enhanced her looks.'

Princess Dashkova, who considered herself a beauty, bristled visibly at Madame Rimsky's remarks. Her friend rattled on, 'I've heard that Natasha never visits her little seven-year-old son by her first husband, even though he is said to be very sick. As a result, I have lost all respect for Natasha, whom I once greatly admired.'

Princess Dashkova cut in, 'I believe all the untimely and, not to put it too strongly, odd deaths in her family must have badly affected her and caused a sort of breakdown. One must remember what a close and loving family they had been. These deaths, I am sure, have resulted in her being the way she now appears. Remember what a lovely young girl she was: well-educated, a gifted musician, and an amateur painter. What fun she was when she was married to Count Dolgurky. Those wonderful balls they gave and those splendid house parties held at their country estate.'

Madame Rimsky nodded in agreement, and began to reminisce about the enormous time and effort Natasha used to devote to charity. 'I acted on two committees with her and it always surprised me how practical she was, and how understanding of other people's problems. I would never have believed she would turn out like this.'

Count Panin nodded in agreement, saying his wife had also served on committees with the Princess and had thought highly of her. Then, turning to Lady Malvern, who had made no comment, he said, 'You are friendly with Countess Volonskaya. Does she ever mention Natasha?'

'Rarely,' the Ambassadress replied, 'and only briefly. I never bring up the subject myself.'

David, still watching Princess Natasha, asked, 'What do you mean, odd deaths in the family?'

Shuvalov, who had been listening quietly, now said, 'There has been a series of tragedies. First her beloved brother Sergei Golvinka was killed in a mysterious hunting accident. No one knows where the shot came from. This shattered the family, since he was a much-loved son, grandson and brother. He was only twenty-two, and had just become engaged.'

'Yes,' Count Panin chipped in. 'Sergei had just become engaged to Princess Maria, a charming girl and so suitable in every way.'

'And so in love,' Madame Rimsky added. 'She has been pining for him ever since, and there is talk of her entering a convent.'

Shuvalov continued. 'The Golvinkas are extremely rich. His son's death caused the old Count to draw up a will leaving everything to his two daughters, with the proviso that until they were 25 they could only have the income and no capital. Of course, if at that age they were married, as expected, control would revert from the present trustees to their husbands. They will also inherit their grandmother's fortune. She inherited enormous wealth, and greatly enhanced it through shrewd investments.'

Princess Dashkova intervened to say, 'Not just shrewd investments but also extremely competent management of her estates.'

'Then about six months after the death of his son Sergei,' Count Shuvalov went on, 'the older Count died in an accident.'

'What was the accident?' asked David, totally engrossed.

'Well,' continued Shuvalov, 'his horses bolted and the coach he was sitting in shot off the end of the bridge into a canal. The Count might have been able to save himself but the bolts on the doors were jammed and he couldn't get out, so he drowned. Neither the coachman nor the footman's bodies were found.

'The Golvinkas had some of the finest of horses. They were bred at the Count's mother-in-law's stud near Moscow and were always well-trained. No one knows why they bolted or why the coach doors jammed. It was rumoured that the footman and the coachman were suspected but neither could be found, despite a reward being offered for news of their whereabouts. Anyway, why would they want to do it? There was no motive.

'It was extremely suspicious,' Shuvalov said, shaking his head. 'The death of a much-loved father so soon after the loss of a beloved brother had a disastrous effect on the two girls and indeed on all the family.'

'Then, of course,' said Princess Dashkova, turning to David, 'came the final blow with Sasha Dolgurky's death.'

'Good Lord, how did he die?' David asked, shocked.

Princess Dashkova replied, 'when he was staying on his estate he often went out at dawn to shoot rabbits. Unless he had guests who wanted to come, he only took his dogs. One morning he didn't return for breakfast and when they went to look for him they found him dead. He had accidentally shot himself. It was devastating.

I firmly believe this is the reason for Natasha's breakdown and why she behaves the way she does.'

Madame Rimsky said coldly, 'It still doesn't explain her callous lack of care for her own son. Prince Boris is apparently the only one who takes any interest in young Count Alexei, even though he is only his stepson. The little boy must have been about five-years-old when his father died. Nadia and his aunt, Tatiana, adored him. But Prince Boris says his doctors advised him to keep Alexei in the Ukrainian climate, where the air is very good for his health. So they have not been able to see him. It is really very difficult for the Prince, who has twice gone to see Natasha's grandmother to apologise for her refusal to receive them.'

Count Panin pensively added, 'I have never been able to find out where Prince Boris got his money from before he married Natasha.' He shook his head in frustration. 'I know he had none, because his father had gambled it all away. Then suddenly Boris came into a lot of money.'

Dismissing Panin's musings Madame Rimsky said, 'I do think Prince Boris is a wonderful husband. It can't be easy humouring a wife who has dismissed her old, trusted servants and surrounded herself with new staff. They are so grim they look almost like gaolers.'

'How did the Countess come to marry Prince Barinsky?' David asked.

'On the rebound from all the tragedies, I think,' Panin said promptly. 'Barinsky was always present to offer help and advice. Natasha was shattered, and even though he was a relatively new friend, he was always there and she began to lean on him for support. Personally, I had the feeling sometimes that he was very pushy and was trying to shut her old friends out. I often think that if Nadia hadn't been in France with Tatiana, attending her property in Bordeaux, when Barinsky was hovering around Natasha, the wedding would never have taken place. It was such a rushed and peculiar wedding. No one was invited and then they immediately disappeared on their honeymoon. Nadia was shocked when she came back to find they were married. She did not like him. It is only since he has been so good to Natasha and so sensitive and apologetic to Nadia that she has come to reluctantly appreciate his kindness and understanding.'

'In that case, it is fortunate she was not here to forbid the marriage,' said Madame Rimsky. 'For now Natasha's become so impossible, refusing to go out and not speaking, he is probably very sorry Nadia didn't come home in time to stop the wedding. His patience and tolerance of his wife's behaviour seem inexhaustible. He must love her very much.'

Suddenly a blare of trumpets sounded as the musicians struck up to announce the arrival of the Empress. David stared; he had never seen a more glorious sight. First a guard of officers appeared, magnificently uniformed, with wonderful breastplates and headdresses. These were the Chevaliers Guards, and all were noblemen. The

Empress herself was elderly, but very regal and superbly gowned and jewelled. Prince Potemkin met her at the door, where he knelt and kissed her hand.

The orchestra struck up an anthem and all stood at attention. The Chevaliers Guards, who had presented arms at the playing of the anthem, now marched down the centre of the great room. A cavalcade of elegantly dressed gentlemen- and ladies-in-waiting followed, forming a stately procession before and behind the Empress. The guests bowing and curtseying to the Empress caused the hall to appear to be full of swaying rainbows as the candlelight flickered on and lit up stunning jewels and decorations.

A massed choir, previously hidden, now burst into an anthem of praise for the Empress's achievements, the words and music written by Potemkin himself. The Empress bowed her head graciously, waved and smiled as she passed down the hall. She had a particularly warm, intimate smile that made whoever caught it believe it was solely meant for them. Now and then she stopped briefly as she recognised someone and gave them her special attention.

As the Empress and her escort passed into the winter garden the guests again began to circulate. David found that Lord Malvern was introducing him to the Prussian Ambassador, Baron Hertzburg, a stern, handsome man of about sixty, and then to the Ambassador's wife, Baroness Gisela Hertzburg. David caught his breath. What a contrast! The Baroness was a ravishing beauty who looked about twenty-four with the soignée style of a truly sophisticated woman plus an enchanting accent. Within minutes he could feel the impact of her latent sensuality. His blood quickened, and he hoped no one noticed his agitation. The Baroness was as charming as she was elegant, and after a few minutes conversation she said to Lord Malvern, 'You must bring Lord Mountforte along to our soiree tomorrow evening if he is free.'

Before the Ambassador could reply, David burst out that he was free. He then felt a fool for showing such uninhibited enthusiasm, quite apart from speaking before the Ambassador had had a chance to reply. His candour, however, appealed to the Baroness, who smiled sweetly and said she was sure his presence would brighten the evening.

As the Ambassador led the way to the winter garden David wondered if he might receive a reprimand, but Lord Malvern seemed unruffled, merely remarking, 'I think from the Baroness's smile you have created a favourable impression.' He went on, 'They are a very able diplomatic couple and exceptionally charming hosts.'

They had now entered the vast winter garden, and once again David was staggered by the size and magnificence of his surroundings. The garden was filled with perfume and resplendent with massed plantings of bulbs, roses, citrus trees, palms, grapes and pineapples, as well as other more exotic species.

The organisation involved in staging such a ball must have been colossal, David mused. He was amazed at the Russians' competence for he had understood that this wasn't a talent they had in abundance. When he said as much to Lord Malvern the Ambassador nodded. 'Potemkin employs a large number of foreigners and it will have been some of these people who have created all this. The Prince, rather like the Empress, is adept at employing the right people, and they both generously reward these key people. Potemkin has many envious detractors and enemies who deride his achievements but everyone, enemy or not, who visits the Ukraine and the Crimea comes back confirming his unbelievable success in building a Black Sea fleet, and impressive cities, palaces and cathedrals.'

They watched now a short ballet performed for the Imperial Family, after which the guests followed the Empress into a vast room hung with fabulous tapestries depicting the life of Esther. In the centre of the room was a full-sized golden elephant adorned with diamonds and rubies, with a live blackamoor on its back. Standing around it were Ottoman pashas, resplendent in their national dress. These were rulers who had been captured when Potemkin's forces took Ismail.

The Empress retired briefly to examine the winter garden more closely.

Dancing then began, and continued until well after midnight, when supper was served. It was incredible, thought David, that so many guests were all able to be seated at tables. At 2 a.m. the Empress left, surrounded by her gorgeous entourage and escorted out on Potemkin's arm. As he handed her into her carriage Potemkin again fell to his knees and kissed her hand. The Empress's departure was as magnificent as her entrance — the guards saluted, trumpets sounded, and swords and sabres clashed. As her carriage drove away the orchestra broke into a melancholy lament.

The Barinskys left shortly after the Empress, he still bowing and smiling, while the Princess looked straight ahead, her beautiful face unutterably forlorn. For some inexplicable reason David felt drawn to the Princess although he couldn't fathom why since they hadn't exchanged a smile or a word. In fact, she hadn't appeared to notice anyone. She fascinated him and he badly wanted to know more about her. Perhaps he would meet her husband at a diplomatic function. He looked a pleasant enough chap.

Meanwhile the ball continued in full swing for another three hours. Lady Malvern was popular and well known and once she had introduced David around he found himself in great demand as a dancing partner. The ball took on a note of hilarity that had not been possible while the Empress was present, and a number of the guests had to be helped to their carriages after drinking too much wine.

It was very late by the time the Embassy party left as Lady Malvern loved a party and knew she could stay in bed until midday. Not so David, who was on duty at ten the next morning. Watching Lady Malvern moving around, greeting acquaintances and chatting to friends, David could see how well-liked she was. She also had, he discovered, a risqué sense of humour that appealed to him.

As they finally left the palace, David thought what a marvellous and astonishing night it had been and what a splendid introduction to Russia: a ball the magnificence of which he was sure he would never see again, an invitation to the palace of the most powerful man in the land and another invitation, to a soiree the following night at the Prussian Ambassador's residence. Already he felt his blood warming up in anticipation. Never had he seen so many beautiful women in one night. He must remember the details so he could write and describe it all to his grandfather and send it in the next diplomatic bag.

He was certain Russia was going to be the most exciting of postings. He was very lucky his grandfather had managed to secure him this appointment through his friendship with Lord Malvern's family.

When the sleigh stopped outside his lodgings, a short distance before the Embassy, he said goodnight to Lord and Lady Malvern and expressed his thanks for their generosity in including him in the party. As he prepared for bed his last thoughts were of the ravishing Baroness Hertzburg and they were far from platonic.

CHAPTER THREE

THE NEXT MORNING THE AMBASSADOR CALLED DAVID IN A BARELY SUPPRESSED RAGE. David wondered nervously what solecism he had committed and was relieved when he found he was not the cause of the Ambassador's anger. Lord Malvern informed him in the strictest confidence that the Austrians had secured a copy of part of Britain's and Prussia's secret negotiations with the Ottomans. At present neither he nor the Prussian Ambassador knew how they had come by the information. This was an extremely serious matter for it could inflame both the Empress and Potemkin and turn them against Britain.

The Ambassador muttered, 'I personally can see nothing wrong with Russia taking and holding the Ottoman fort of Ochakov on the Bug River, no matter how much it increases Russia's power in Ukraine. Russia is very pro-Britain under Empress Catherine, Prince Potemkin and powerful magnates like Count Simon Vorontsov. We have large interests in Russia and our trade is huge.' He went on for David's benefit. 'Ever since Richard Chancellor, in 1553, impressed Ivan the Terrible and gained almost a monopoly over Russian trade with England, English – and now British – interests have flourished and continued to expand in Russia. All this could be lost if Prime Minister Pitt continues to intrigue against Russia over Ochakov with the Prussians, Ottomans, Poles and French.' It was apparent to David that the Ambassador could not understand who was advising the normally cautious British Prime Minister to support the Ottomans.

'I do not have proof,' Lord Malvern continued, 'but I am told that Prince de Ligne is suspected of bribing someone at the Prussian Embassy for information on the negotiations and has passed it to the Austrians, who have in turn, I believe, passed it to the Russians, who are currently, as you know, their ally against Prussia and the Ottomans.

'The French are also involved and despite supposedly being an ally of ours they are deliberately causing trouble.'

Having let off steam, Lord Malvern now relaxed enough to discuss how the Embassy was to launch a diplomatic counter-crusade. One possibility was to enlist pro-British allies like Count Simon Vorontsov who had been Russian Ambassador to Britain, to help him restore any loss of prestige Britain might suffer because of the leaked papers.

'The Prussian Embassy has begun an investigation to find out if any of their staff have turned traitor. Meanwhile, Britain currently buys most of the timber for our vital shipbuilding from Russia. Stupidly several British Members of Parliament are already publicly saying that Britain should withhold some of its Russian timber purchases and switch the orders to Poland, thus limiting Britain's dependence on Russia. These statements are not helping the position of our merchants here and of course they have nothing to do with the Ochakov problem. However, even though we in the Embassy may not agree with Prime Minister Pitt on this matter, we have to faithfully carry out his policy,' he concluded, sternly emphasising his sentiments by glaring at David forcefully.

CHAPTER FOUR

BARONESS HERTZBURG DELIBERATED IN FRONT OF THE MIRROR WHILE HER MAID DRESSED HER FOR THE EVENING'S SOIREE. Here she was, twenty-nine, with a husband of sixty-five. He was a courteous but cold man, though Gisela admitted that he was generous and tolerant. She reflected on how she had changed in the years since, as a naïve, shy young girl, she had arrived in Russia as the new Ambassador's wife. Now, an invitation to any of her receptions was keenly sought after, and people would almost fight to be invited to special functions such as her birthday party for the King of Prussia.

Still, her life was a disappointment. She had wanted to marry Paul Osterman, her second cousin, although now she recognised this would have been a mistake, as he had become a drunkard. They had been in love at the time and hoped to become engaged in a couple of months when an unexpected suitor appeared. Her father was deeply in debt and although Paul was moderately wealthy, he could not compete with her new suitor, Baron Hertzburg. The Hertzburg wealth came not only from land, but included huge revenues from their Swabian and Rhine coalmines.

The Baron's first wife had died several years earlier and he had recently been appointed to represent Prussia in Russia. This, in these troubled times, was a key posting. But to be effective, he needed a wife. Therefore, aware that his acquaintance was in serious financial difficulties and having met Gisela, he offered to clear all Count Gortha's debts if he would give the Baron his oldest daughter's hand in marriage. The Count willingly agreed without consulting Gisela. She was grief stricken, for she was just nineteen and the Baron fifty-five, and she was very much in love with Paul. Her father announced that the marriage would take place in two months, although in fact the Baron had taken ill and it was five months before she was married. As the years had passed she had gradually grown accustomed to her marriage, which was outwardly glamorous, but inwardly dull and unexciting.

Her husband had turned out to be an astute diplomat and had proved very successful in his Russian posting. The family property in Prussia was maintained by his son, a shy, studious man who was four years older than Gisela. To her utter bewilderment the Baron had never slept with her. At first she suspected that he kept a mistress but this was not the case. When she was twenty-three he had made it clear by subtle hints that provided she carried out her ambassadorial duties suitably and was discreet, he would not query her private life. Until then she had never taken a lover but later allowed herself to be seduced by a very attractive 38-year-old Hungarian. She had had two other lovers at different times.

Although happily aware that she was coveted by most men and envied by many women, she still wasn't content. Yes, she liked being an Ambassador's wife and had surprised herself by becoming adept at assisting her husband who now shared all his diplomatic secrets with her. That was fascinating but it was not enough.

Above all else she wanted children, children of her own on whom she could lavish all the love that welled up inside her. Her husband never visited her bed and now that her last amour, the Polish Welensky, had returned to Cracow she would have to look elsewhere for the love she sought.

The dashing young Englishman, Mountforte looked attractive and possibly something of a challenge. That tantalising, untouched appearance, a very sensuous mouth and an air of unconscious arrogance all added to his allure. It would add some spice to her life to see how long it would take to seduce him. She had never attempted to seduce anyone before. There had never been any need being well aware she had that indefinable something all men wanted, all men except her husband. Idly she wondered if she should, just for fun, try and seduce her husband. But no, that would end up spoiling their relationship, which apart from the disappointment of having no children, now worked very harmoniously.

Gisela decided to wear a ruby and pearl set of tiara, necklace, earrings and bracelets and as the maid clasped them on they gleamed against her flawless magnolia skin and lustrous black hair. Once the maid had finished, Gisela stood up and looked keenly at herself in the long mirror. Yes, she was a wholly desirable-looking woman. Tonight she would set about discreetly beginning the pursuit of Lord Mountforte. The thought brought a sparkle to her eyes and unconsciously her body took on a more sensuous stance.

Just then a footman knocked at the door. 'The Baron is ready and the guests are about to arrive, Baroness.'

Gisela picked up an exquisite ivory and gold fan and went to join her husband at the top of the stairs to greet their guests.

CHAPTER FIVE

THE POTTED GARDENIAS LOOKED BEAUTIFUL AS THEY SPILLED DOWN THE STAIRS UNDER THE HUGE CHANDELIERS. Their scent almost blotted out the perfumes of the ladies climbing the stairs. In the ballroom behind them the orchestra struck up a Tyrolean air and soon a bevy of footmen began passing around drinks.

As she greeted her guests, Gisela kept an eagle eye out for Lord Mountforte. Finally, the British party arrived. Lady Malvern was in fine form while Lord Malvern was looking a little worn, but Mountforte looked young and virile. That chiselled, strikingly handsome face with its dashing smile was devastating. A flame shot through her body.

Vaguely she heard her husband greet Lord Malvern, then mutter, 'We have not yet discovered who has betrayed the negotiations, but yes, it is that suave, two-faced Prince de Ligne who has passed them to Austria.'

Gisela watched obliquely as Lord Mountforte followed the Malverns upstairs. After welcoming him, she softly asked, 'Will you keep the third dance for me?' She saw his eyes light up with pleasure.

'I will be delighted ... and honoured,' he stammered.

Gisela noted that Lady Malvern had overheard the quiet brief exchange and was giving her a speculative glance. She reminded herself that she must remain utterly discreet.

David, meanwhile, entered the ballroom with a spring in his step as he thought yet again what a marvellous place St. Petersburg was.

His euphoric mood was steadied when Lady Malvern stopped to point out someone she called Countess Nadia Volonskaya, stating she was a great anglophile. David looked across and saw a beautifully preserved, finely-featured lady of about seventy-five. Her expression wore the slightest air of disdain and her face, despite its fine bone structure and high Slavic cheekbones, had a tinge of severity about it.

Lady Malvern commented, 'She is considered one of the Grand Dames of St. Petersburg but I find her very pleasant.'

Just then the young girl beside the Countess said something and she smiled, her face suddenly becoming astonishingly warm and beautiful. David noticed that she moved her hands with great elegance, rather like a very polished dancer.

'Who is the lovely girl by her side?' David asked.

'That is her granddaughter, Countess Tatiana,' Lady Malvern replied. 'She is just eighteen and only came out earlier this year. She is the younger sister of Princess Barinsky. Once they were such close companions and friends, despite the difference in their ages, and this estrangement has been a bitter blow to Tatiana.'

David was immediately interested, as anything to do with Princess Barinsky aroused his curiosity. But the Ambassadress continued to talk of her sister.

'Look at all those men around her. She has many keen suitors, because not only is she a beauty, she is a fabulous heiress like her sister, and will have even greater wealth when her grandmother dies. Countess Nadia has enormous estates in Smolensk and around Moscow, and now, through her friendship with the Empress and Potemkin, a vast estate in the Crimea. With your grandfather's interests in timber you could find the Countess interesting because she has one of the largest forests in Russia, just outside St. Petersburg. She is something of a legend in the business world. In the Crimea, I am told she is moving with great speed and insight. Already she has her factors planting grain, grapevines and oranges, she has brought in sheep from England and France, and has begun to establish beef and dairy herds.'

The Ambassadress seemed very keen to have him take an interest in the Countess and her granddaughter and he was indeed curious to know more about this family that had suffered such tragedies. As they slowly moved toward the Countess they saw Tatiana rise as one of the men offered her his arm and led her toward the dance floor.

'I am told,' Lady Malvern continued, 'that the Countess has moved faster than all the other aristocrats except Potemkin in developing her estate there. She is said to have bought or transferred three thousand serfs to the Crimea and all within the last twelve months. This has further endeared her to the Empress and Potemkin, since by investing heavily in her estates she has shown she is convinced Russia will win against the Turks and hold the Crimea. She is known as a very liberal serf owner and this seems to have paid off. Their conditions are good, and they are provided with schools and hospitals.'

'The Countess is among those aristocrats who believe in educating their serfs. It is amazing how successful this education, is for among the serfs on her Smolensk and Moscow estates you can find trained plumbers, carpenters, musicians, painters and agriculturalists. This has created a lot of goodwill and also considerable prosperity on the properties. All her estates are said to be highly profitable and the family is certainly well served and respected by their serfs.'

Lady Malvern reached the Countess and after greeting her warmly she immediately introduced David. The Countess extended him a slim, elegant hand to be kissed and then enquired, 'How do you like St. Petersburg? And what is the latest news from Scotland? I have a distant cousin by marriage who came from Scotland some twenty years ago and married my kinsman Alexei Obelensky. I am sure Countess

Obelensky would look forward to meeting someone who had come so recently from Scotland.'

As she was speaking her elegant face became animated and her voice was most attractive. Despite her age, David was charmed by her. When the dance finished the granddaughter returned to her side and Countess Nadia introduced David. Tatiana curtsied and smiled at him and he kissed the hand she held out.

'With your beauty you certainly will not be short of admirers, Countess,' David said.

To his surprise, instead of modestly accepting his compliment Tatiana immediately retorted, 'Ah, but are they admiring my beauty, admiring my fortune, or a little of both? How would you determine where their real interest lies, Lord Mountforte? As a man you must know.'

She spoke with a mischievous smile and a laugh in her voice but David, unused to a young girl being so frank, especially with a stranger, was startled at her outspokenness. Despite her beauty and undoubted elegance she was very forward for a girl of eighteen. He hesitated before replying, 'I have no idea how you could determine the case, never having been in that position myself.'

Incorrigibly, Tatiana said, 'But rumour has it that you too are wealthy and with even greater expectations.'

The old Countess looked up sharply and said something he didn't catch in Russian to her granddaughter who looked suitably chastised. But as the Countess turned to continue her conversation with Lady Malvern, Tatiana smiled cheekily at David and said in an amused whisper, 'Have I upset you?'

He replied in a tight voice, 'Of course not.' David concluded privately that beautiful or not she was very spoiled. He was quite shocked that a young girl of eighteen should speak in a style more suited to that of a married woman. For the first time since he had arrived in Russia he felt uncomfortable, rather suspecting that she was inwardly laughing at him. Certainly her eyes were dancing with mischief, and he began to wonder what on earth she would say next if her grandmother was not there to restrain her.

Just then the orchestra struck up a polonaise and Tatiana was immediately surrounded by men wanting to partner her. To David's amazement she thanked them loudly then said solemnly that she would if she could but Lord Mountforte had just arrived from Scotland and had beseeched her to give him the next dance. She felt she could not disappoint him since having only just arrived in Russia, he knew no one. At this her suitors variously looked downcast or sent angry looks toward David. With a lightning glance at him, Tatiana took his arm and led him onto the floor before he had time to think.

She then remarked, 'You should now smile because you have bested your rivals and have in your arms one of the richest heiresses in Russia, and an acknowledged beauty to boot.'

When David, rather stiffly, told her she had no right to behave the way she had she simply laughed. 'I couldn't let you go away offended with me.'

As they danced she continued to chat and laugh, even though David did little more than grunt. He was annoyed that this chit of a girl had taken control of the situation. Well, he would soon put her in her place. But he had to admit she was a lovely dance partner and he was partially mollified, acknowledging that they made an eye-catching pair.

When the dance finished Tatiana curtsied and thanked him mockingly, while he bowed and escorted her back to her grandmother. The Countess added to his discomfort by commenting, 'You make a very attractive couple on the floor.'

Tatiana promptly responded, 'I am sure we did. That was probably why Lord Mountforte insisted I dance with him,' at the same time flashing him a teasing look.

David was staggered at her audacity and decided she was obviously counting on him being too much of a gentleman to contradict her. Before he could say anything she again thanked him prettily and said she looked forward to seeing him at her grandmother's house, as she was sure she would invite him to visit. The latter remark was accompanied by a questioning glance at her grandmother who immediately said, 'I will certainly do so.'

Tatiana retained her innocent expression as she said goodbye and David was certain that only he caught the brief glance of triumph she managed to shoot him. He suspected she was enjoying teasing him and she had certainly beaten him this time around, but he was determined to redress the balance the next time they met.

As he walked away he saw Prince Barinsky on the other side of the ballroom but there was no sign of the Princess. David immediately forgot about Tatiana as his mind conjured up a vision of the poignantly beautiful Natasha, but despite a searching glance around the room he could not see her.

Finally the third dance was announced, and David eagerly sought out Baroness Hertzburg, who slipped smilingly into his arms. As David clasped her, a shaft of desire shot through his body, leaving him shaken. She smelt wonderful, looked beautiful and for a moment David was tongue-tied. But not for long as she led the conversation, asking if he was enjoying St. Petersburg and whether he missed Scotland, and how long his posting to Russia was to last. He rapidly unwound, and the fifteen minutes on the dance floor flew by. He was now totally bewitched and was desolate when the music stopped. There was no chance of any further conversation, however, as the Baroness was immediately surrounded by guests vying for her attention.

Although he returned to the dance floor none of the later dances meant much to David and he constantly found his eyes seeking out the Baroness and trying to see what she was doing. Meanwhile the Baroness, well aware of the impression she had made, later sent a footman with a note asking David if he was free to join her for the ice-skating competitions that were to take place the following Saturday. This gave him an opportunity to seek out the Baroness and tell her he would be delighted. He left the soiree shortly afterwards, walking on air and feeling he was the luckiest man in the country.

The Baroness was also feeling pleased with her scheme. She had enjoyed talking to him and was sure that once he lost his shyness with her he would be a very attractive and interesting companion. Certainly, if he did become her lover, she had never had one so young and seemingly untouched. She went to bed eagerly anticipating her next meeting with David. The Baron was leaving for Moscow the following day and would be away for a month: apart from the few society functions she was expected to attend she would be completely free.

Yes, Saturday was going to be interesting and quite possibly the beginning of a stimulating affair. An unexpected delicious sensation quickly warmed her body. The only problem was how to get him into bed without tarnishing his image of her, for she suspected he thought of her as something of an innocent. She would have to come up with some scheme, and on that titillating thought she drifted off to sleep.

CHAPTER SIX

THE FOLLOWING THURSDAY DAVID SET OFF TO MEET PRINCE POTEMKIN ONLY TO FIND HE WAS WITH THE EMPRESS AT THE HERMITAGE. David was asked to come back at three that afternoon. Returning to the Embassy, he told Lord Malvern what had happened and was again advised to listen carefully to the Prince for any indication of the Russian reaction to the Ochakov negotiations. The Ambassador was extremely concerned and as yet had been given no clue as to how the Empress and Prince Potemkin had reacted when they received the stolen documents.

'Mountforte,' he said, 'you are to report back immediately after you leave Potemkin's, no matter what time and whether or not you have any news. While you are with the Prince, you are to express complete ignorance of the Ochakov situation. It is most fortunate that you received this invitation from the Prince when you had only been here three days.'

At two thirty, David put aside his work and set off again. When he arrived he was immediately shown into a splendid audience room where a dozen or so men were sitting or standing around talking. The Prince greeted David, and at once introduced him to the others. David tried to remember their names so he could inform Lord Malvern, but it was hard to retain them all. However, he did remember some.

Potemkin began to talk to David of the Benthams, who had come from England and had helped the Prince build the Black Sea fleet for Russia. The Prince was very complimentary about the brothers, commenting on how able and progressive they were, and how versatile Samuel Bentham had been in the Crimea. Just as David was beginning to relax, however, the Prince switched tactics.

'Why,' he suddenly demanded, 'is Britain supporting the Ottomans behind the scenes and working with Prussia against Russia's interests? Almost everyone of consequence in Russia is an anglophile, trade between the countries is huge, and British investors are a very significant influence in Russia.'

The other men fell silent as they listened to Prince Potemkin berating the British. As the Prince continued his tirade he became passionate about Russia's right, indeed, he said, 'Russia's duty is to expel the Ottomans from Europe. Is not Russia the guardian of the Slavs in the Balkans? The other Christians too must be freed from Ottoman tyranny.'

Although intimidated by the Prince's stance and inwardly quaking, David managed to keep his voice steady as he replied, 'As you know, Your Highness, I have only been in Russia less than a week and therefore have not been privy to any of the Ochakov negotiations. I can, however, report that to my certain knowledge everyone at the British Embassy, from the Ambassador down, is a committed supporter of Russia. I too, witnessing the greatness of Russia, admire its expansion and have been touched and impressed by the warmth of Russian hospitality.'

Prince Potemkin, who was a tolerant and generous man, relaxed somewhat and responded, 'Lord Mountforte, you are obviously going to become a most successful diplomat.' He then began to talk enthusiastically about what he was doing in the Crimea. He spoke of building towns, ports, churches and hospitals, and opening up land to people who would work it properly. He was bringing in people from overseas to help populate the land. He had formed fighting regiments from the Cossacks and he also spoke of his Black Sea fleet. David was soon swept away by his vision and could scarcely believe what he had already accomplished.

By the time David left he was totally convinced of the Prince's genius. He was also well wined and dined and feeling slightly inebriated. He would have preferred to have gone straight home to bed but remembering the Ambassador's instructions, he thought he had better go and see him if he was still up. It was by now very late and when he reached the Embassy he stopped outside, wondering if it would be better to come back at breakfast time. However, light was gleaming from the library windows, so he went to the main entrance. The door was opened immediately, and he was greeted by the major-domo, 'His Excellency is expecting you,' the man said as he led David to the library.

Lord Malvern, tired and red-eyed, was sitting writing at his desk. He looked up and remarked, 'I was expecting you earlier. Was it a good meeting?' He suddenly squinted hard at David. 'You are not drunk, are you?'

'Not exactly, Your Excellency,' David replied.

'I'm relieved to hear it,' the Ambassador returned. 'I do not want a drunk for a secretary. Well, what did you hear?'

As David relayed what had happened, and the Prince's comments, Lord Malvern relaxed a little. It was clear he was thankful to learn that while the Prince was very upset at the attitude taken by Britain's Prime Minister and genuinely bewildered as to why Pitt should be adopting this stance, there was no hostility toward Britain's representatives and their interests in Russia. David was commended on his handling of the situation but also received a none-too-delicate hint, accompanied by a cold glance, that he should restrict his drinking when on duty.

The next day was a busy one at the Embassy. Montague, the youthful Second Secretary who had been away in Moscow, returned. This was David's first meeting with him and he immediately liked him. David had now taken over his predecessor's work and Monty seemed able to help him with anything he didn't yet know. Monty was an excellent 'Number Two' and the longer David worked with him the more he came to appreciate his considerable skills. He was well liked by all the Embassy staff because of his good nature and his willingness to help anyone.

David gradually learned that Monty's father had died when he was fourteen, leaving his widow and Monty's younger sister with very slender means. An uncle had helped Monty into the diplomatic service and he was hoping to achieve a position where he could eventually contribute to his mother and sister's income. It was apparent they were a close-knit and happy family. Monty, though, didn't seem to realise how long he would have to be in the civil service before he would be able to contribute a significant sum to his mother and sister. As for supporting a wife, that would have to wait until much later, unless she was rich.

A couple of days later the Prussian Ambassador, deeply embarrassed, advised his British counterpart that the Ochakov papers had been stolen from his Embassy. They decided to meet, with their First Secretaries in attendance, to discuss what strategies they could adopt to minimise any potential disaster.

A meeting was arranged for the following day, to be held at the British Embassy. When the Prussians arrived it was with a mixture of anger and shame that Baron Hertzburg revealed they had found the traitor in their camp. It had turned out to be young Herr Shuffel who had got into debt at a gambling house owned and presided over by an unprincipled Baron Llov. Apparently Shuffel had lost a great deal of money and the debts were only cancelled when he produced the information Baron Llov demanded. When interrogated, Shuffel stated he believed the information was sold at a profit to the Austrians. Shuffel was being sent back immediately to Prussia.

After discussing the situation, the two ambassadors decided the best tactic was to deny all knowledge of the plans and try to persuade everyone to believe the French were fabricating evidence with the Austrians. Baron Hertzburg commented that he should have left for Moscow two days earlier, but because of this matter he had delayed his trip and instead would be leaving the next day.

He would be away for about twenty days but Lord Malvern should feel perfectly free to contact either his wife or his First Secretary, Captain Lamsdort, in his absence. They could send any urgent messages to him in code, as he was confident the code had not been broken.

Unlike his friend Monty, David was untroubled by financial constraints. He had rapidly found himself a large and attractive apartment near the Embassy, had engaged a cook and a general manservant and also was looking for a good valet. He had decided to buy a sleigh and a well-sprung fast travelling coach and have his family's coat of arms painted on the doors. This would mean purchasing at least four good harness horses. Until he bought a sleigh and a coach he was reliant on the Embassy's conveyances, or had to hire transport.

CHAPTER SEVEN

THE DAY OF THE ICE-SKATING COMPETITION CAME AND DAVID WOULD HAVE LIKED TO HAVE OFFERED TO PICK UP BARONESS HERTZBURG, BUT AS SHE WAS TAKING A PARTY IT WOULD NOT HAVE BEEN APPROPRIATE.

The day was clear and sunny and the stark nakedness of the trees etched wonderful patterns against an azure-blue sky. In his eagerness, David arrived early and he looked around the grounds while waiting. The park was full of people dressed for the cold with coloured scarves and boots poking out from coats of heavy cloth, leather or fur, forming a striking contrast to the snow that was lying on the ground. The band was already playing and the centre was full of people skating. The atmosphere was one of a carnival and the scene could have been a painting had it not been full of movement. Already, David thought the day glorious.

After about twenty minutes he spotted the coach of the Prussian Embassy pulling up at the stands. The Baroness, accompanied by four other guests, proceeded up the stairs to her box. David moved swiftly across and was greeted warmly by the Baroness who then introduced him to Count and Countess Schumann and Prince and Princess Alexi Orlov. The Schumanns were a delightful couple. They were old friends of Baron Hertzburg's from Germany, and had been disappointed to find that their host needed to go to Moscow during their visit so would be staying on till he returned.

The Orlovs were also pleasant and refreshingly open in their views on everything from politics to farming while making no secret of their dislike of Potemkin. This apparently stemmed from a long standing feud that had begun years ago when Potemkin had usurped Alexi's brother Gregory Orlov as the Empress Catherine's favourite. The Orlovs had been among the prime movers to install Catherine as Empress and resented the fact that Gregory was no longer the favourite.

'The Empress has been munificent in her generosity to them though,' the Baroness whispered to David when she was unobserved.

As the skating was now about to start, it was explained to David that everyone was eligible to enter the competition, with the competitors being gradually weeded down to ten in each section. There were events for mixed doubles, single ladies, single men, and acrobatic competitors. After twenty-five minutes the music stopped and the judges selected ten competitors to continue to the next round. These ten then continued skating until the winner was selected. It was a delightful way for everyone to enjoy themselves and a marvellously colourful sight.

To David's delight the Baroness asked if he would partner her in the doubles and he readily agreed. Once on the rink he found that the Baroness was a classically graceful skater of no mean ability and he was glad of the skating he used to do over Christmas and New Year in Scotland. However, the Baroness was a far better skater than he was, performing dazzling turns and brilliant figures of eight. Then the band played a polonaise that was sheer heaven as their hands and bodies touched. Every now and then she would spin away from his arms, then speedily glide back again and he would twirl her around, feeling a tantalising thrill the odd time her soft cheek briefly touched his. Her scent was intoxicating and kindled the passion building up in him. He had never before experienced such a depth of passion or such erotic feelings.

They were not picked among the ten competitors to continue although David knew they could have been had he proved as talented as she. When he said as much to her she only smiled and touched his cheek with her gloved hand, saying, 'I have enjoyed our skating together much more en masse as we were not the centre of attention.'

David flushed with pleasure at her words and especially her touch. Then, adding even more to his happiness, the Baroness asked, 'Would you mind if, in private, I called you David and you called me Gisela?'

David, elated said, 'Of course.' He began to want Gisela all for himself, her touch, her scent, and most of all her body. He began to imagine a closer association between them and found himself resenting her husband. Such an old man who seemed a cold fish had no right to have such a young and glamorous wife. Deep down he knew this was unfair and caused simply by jealousy on his part.

The doubles competition was eventually won by a brother and sister team. It was a popular win and when the pair was presented with the cup there was a huge round of applause.

Wen the music resumed, everyone who wished to skate went back to the rink. Maddeningly, everyone now had to skate solo as the women were being chosen. Gisela skated around David, darting to and fro like a butterfly, so he followed suit, at one stage chasing her round the rink as both burst into laughter. When he caught her he felt sure she must have let him since she was much the better skater. The horn blared, signalling that all but the ten finalists should leave the rink. Impulsively he swept her up into his arms and skated off to the other side of the park. This caused some astonishment among those who noticed the elegant wife of the Prussian Ambassador being swept along in the arms of the dashing First Secretary of the British Embassy. However such was their pleasure that neither David nor Gisela cared. Gisela was in ecstasy enjoying the strength of his arms and the smell of his body, while David was vibrating with the intensity of his feelings.

As David let her down, Gisela, frightened by the feelings he aroused in her, began to wonder whether she should continue her pursuit. There was something desperately appealing about David and she certainly didn't want to have an affair she couldn't control. It would be fatal to fall seriously in love outside her marriage. Desiring a man was one thing, loving him was to court danger.

Just as these thoughts were running through her mind David impetuously took her in his arms, bent and gently kissed her. Gisela knew she should stop now and distance herself from David if she wished to maintain a peaceful, ordered life. However, as she had made no protest to the first kiss, David kissed her again but with more passion. Lightning shot through her and she saw sparks. It was at that moment that Gisela was lost. Blindly she wanted David. It was an ardent desire she had never before felt for anyone.

As they climbed the stairs to her box Gisela was breathless, as if she had been on a marathon run. Some of the women who had seen David with the Ambassadress in his arms were plainly envious but she saw the Schumanns look at her strangely. When the Orlovs returned shortly afterwards Alexi gave them both a knowing look. David, however, was in a dreamlike state totally unaware of any undercurrent except one between Gisela and himself.

Alexi broke a somewhat pregnant silence by announcing that one of the finalists in the ladies' competition was Tatiana Golvinka. Sure enough, when David returned his gaze to the rink there was Tatiana. She looked stunning in a dark fur coat and hat, with a scarlet scarf and boots, and was literally skimming around the ground. She had a fur muff over her hands, and every so often she would remove one hand from the muff and move both hands in the air. She gave the impression of a joyous nymph, particularly each time she made a brilliant leap landing gracefully back on the ice.

Aware of the slightly strained atmosphere in the box, Gisela rushed into conversation, saying, 'When I first came to St. Petersburg, Tatiana's sister was married to Count Sasha Dolgurky. Some of our happiest times in St. Petersburg were at the receptions and parties the Dolgurkys gave. I admired and liked them both and I cannot believe how Princess Natasha has changed since the deaths in her family and her marriage to Barinsky.'

The Orlovs agreed, saying they too had been great admirers and friends of the Dolgurkys. Like everyone else, however, since her husband's death and her marriage to Barinsky they had never received any recognition from Natasha, even though they had written to her. Alexi added that he was amazed at how devoted Barinsky was to Natasha, as he had been regarded as a rather bad hat before his marriage.

Here the Countess Orlov, clearly highly affronted by Natasha's present attitude, commented tartly, 'Many young men were wild before their marriage. Barinsky has made a point of apologising for his wife's rude treatment of us. He indicated that she has had some sort of breakdown.' She went on, 'I simply cannot understand how Natasha has cut herself off from her son. She used to adore him. I never would have believed it if Prince Barinsky hadn't told me himself. He said he was deeply worried about it and it has seriously damaged the little boy's health. The doctors suspect he has tuberculosis. To keep him out of his mother's way and for the sake of his health, Barinsky has sent the boy to the Crimea. The climate around the Black Sea is very beneficial for those with tuberculosis.'

The Countess's attention returned to the skaters. 'Look at Tatiana talking to old General Fitzland. I must say, I think Tatiana is growing up into a great beauty. In a couple of years' time she will be every bit as beautiful as her sister.'

Gisela agreed, remarking, 'I think Tatiana has the same wit and warmth Natasha had when I first knew her.'

To no one's surprise Tatiana came first in the single women's skating contest and again a strong round of applause greeted her when she received the cup. As they were watching they saw Prince Barinsky go across to congratulate Tatiana and stay chatting for a few minutes. Natasha was nowhere to be seen.

David was slightly surprised at the favourable comments his companions had made about Tatiana. He had expected at least some remarks about her being rather spoilt but on the contrary everyone seemed to praise her warmth, charm and the modesty she retained despite her beauty and wealth.

Gisela asked the Orlovs, 'Is there any truth in the talk of marrying her to Prince Karl of Sweden?' Orlov replied that the Empress and Potemkin wanted to cement ties between Russia and Sweden, and that a marriage between the wealthy and beautiful Countess and Prince Karl would greatly assist that cementing.

'However, I understand that although Prince Karl and Sweden are keen, privately neither Tatiana nor her grandmother are happy about such a match. Karl is a noted marionette. Of course, if the Empress decrees it Tatiana will have to marry him but Nadia is a long term friend of the Empress and a close friend of Potemkin. I believe she has managed to persuade them not to force the issue, at least not yet.'

Countess Schumann then remarked, 'The Prince wasn't very popular when he visited Prussia last year, too pompous, and so conscious of maintaining rigid etiquette.'

While Gisela's experience as a diplomat's wife enabled her to maintain the conversation while her mind was elsewhere, she could think of nothing but David.

With the ladies presentation over, everyone was again invited onto the ground while the ten men were chosen. This time Gisela could not help herself and she openly flirted with David. David responded to her in a frankly amorous way. He was on fire and all thoughts of Gisela being a married woman were forgotten. He simply pictured the two of them together. His career, the Baron, and his grandfather were meanwhile of no concern. He was wildly in love and as he and Gisela skated he began to believe she returned his feelings. They spun round and round each other and with every spin they embraced briefly and then spun apart again.

As the judges announced the ten finalists, David and Gisela returned to the box. Gisela was left in no doubt that the Schumanns and the Orlovs were aware of how they felt, and she received strong hints from Countess Schumann that she did not approve. The Orlovs pretended that they observed nothing but she imagined how they would gossip about the situation later with friends.

It had begun to snow heavily, so Gisela suggested that the Orlovs should join the Schumanns and have tea at the Embassy. Then, despite the sexually laden atmosphere and much against her better judgement, she found herself asking David to join them. An hour later they all were taking tea and discussing the day.

While they were talking a footman brought in a note for the Baron and handed it to the Baroness.

After scanning the note Gisela passed it to David, saying, 'I think you had better deal with this.'

David read it in his turn. The writer said that Mr. Montague, from the British Embassy, had been gambling with an Ivan Segure and they had both lost heavily. In an aside Gisela told him that her husband had placed an informant at the gambling place, called the Golden Eagle, where Herr Shuffel had lost his money. The Baron believed it to be crooked.

'I will take it up with Monty,' David said quietly, 'as I know he is not wealthy.'

Gisela was taking the Schumanns and Orlovs on to a play at the Grand Duke's that night so when David was taking a reluctant farewell, Gisela gave him a key to the Embassy's side door. She described how to find her bedroom but asked him not arrive until after 3 a.m. when all the household would be asleep. She would leave her bedroom door, on the first floor, ajar with the light on. After a hurried but passionate embrace David left his mind alive with wild and rapturous thoughts of the coming morning.

CHAPTER EIGHT

At two thirty he arrived at the side gate, unlocked it with the key Gisela had given him, and slipped in. He almost collided with the night watchman, who was in a drunken slumber a couple of yards away from the gate. Tiptoeing rapidly across the lawn, he found the side door, opened it and stole inside. There was no one in sight so he swiftly crept up the stairs. At the top he turned to the right and saw a door slightly ajar, with light shining from it.

Slipping through the doorway, he shut the door carefully behind him and turned to find Gisela in bed. She looked exquisite, with a silk sheet covering up to her waist and her breasts fully exposed. For a moment her face was expressionless as she studied his, then it was slowly transformed to become the most radiant of smiles. His heart pounding, head spinning with emotion, he crossed to the bed. Bending he lingeringly kissed her, then swiftly he began to undress. Trembling with rising passion, his fingers seemed all thumbs as he undid his buttons. His desire for Gisela intensified until he was near choking with passion and lust.

Gisela observed his back as he peeled off his clothes. When finally he was naked she was shaken with the intensity of her feelings. She tensed in bed, trying to control herself as she waited to caress his superbly sculpted body. Then he turned and she almost gasped at his size. His erection ran straight up, almost to the centre of his stomach. He paused, then with his eyes holding hers, paced slowly over to the bed, and just as slowly pulled the sheet down off her. For several seconds his gaze lingered on her, savouring the sight of her naked body, with its perfect breasts and erotic thicket of hairs between her legs. For an uncontrolled moment he nearly thrust down and buried his face in it.

He climbed onto the bed, kissed her, and gently ran his tongue and lips over her face, ears and neck. Gisela began to sensuously explore his body until she reached and clasped his throbbing member. Tenderly at first, almost worshipfully, David touched her breasts with his tongue, then took a nipple into his mouth and sucked. They began to make love, first gently and then passionately. His desire was enhanced by the dense, silky texture of her skin and the fragrant scent that emanated from her body

His passion built up and up, reaching an intensity Gisela had never before experienced, and she responded with unrestrained and rapturous desire. He was so different from her previous lovers, whom she now dimly realised had only sought their own pleasure. David was young and ardent, but he wanted to share his passion and pleasure. She couldn't feel enough of him, inside her or out. David thrust into her at first slowly and deeply and then began to drive faster and harder and they finally climaxed together.

Later – sweaty, satiated and exhausted – they parted, feverishly promising to meet again that evening. It was 5 a.m. when David reluctantly slipped away just before the servants rose to begin their duties.

Now began a time that for David was filled with heady and marvellous days. He floated on a cloud. Just thinking about Gisela often caused a stirring in his loins that he couldn't control. No work was too difficult; in fact nothing was too difficult as long as he could see Gisela at least once a day. They made times to meet in his apartment, and on each occasion when they first came together they would kiss and she would melt into his arms. Slowly and sensuously they would undress each other. They touched erotic points of each other's body before, naked and often clasped together, they would fall into bed. Their foreplay only heightened the pleasure they later aroused. Then they would lie together and talk of what the future held. Gisela was less anxious to discuss this as she saw the obstacles in their way, whereas David in the first flush of their romance believed all could be overcome. They talked of his career, his grandfather and her husband.

One day, just before the Baron returned from Moscow, Gisela asked David if he had spoken to Mr. Montague about his gambling. David had completely forgotten, but he said that Monty had not been looking well lately and apparently had a bad cold. When Gisela told him their informant had seen him gambling again with Ivan Segure, David promised to speak to Monty the following day.

Gisela was an enchanting mistress, not that David thought of her in such terms. Instead, he thought of her as his future wife. Gisela had a beautiful body, a wonderful sense of humour, and an exceptionally well-informed mind. She described St. Petersburg and its denizens in humorous sketches, bringing the people they knew so vividly to life that the next time David met them he saw them in a totally different light. Thanks to Gisela's impersonations, sometimes funny, sometimes pompous, sometimes sad, he now knew their foibles, strengths and weaknesses.

For Gisela, life had never been so happy. She had managed to persuade David to give up his wild scheme of running away together and to wait a while. Now she began to wonder how she would handle the Baron.

But in the midst of their romance, tragedy struck.

CHAPTER NINE

THE DAY AFTER GISELA REMINDED HIM ABOUT MONTY'S GAMBLING, DAVID ASKED HIS FRIEND IF HE COULD HAVE A WORD WITH HIM. They went back to David's apartment for lunch, and while pouring drinks David asked outright about the gambling rumour.

Monty, looking pinched and drawn, seemed enormously relieved when David made it clear he knew about his gambling. He had been going to speak to David on the following Monday and possibly ask a favour. However, firstly he had to attend the den tomorrow night as he and his friend Ivan Segure both believed the gambling club was crooked, and they wanted to prove it.

'What makes you think that?' David asked.

'We found out that Baron Llov doesn't own the gambling house, but only has a ten percent share. The rest is owned by another man Llov fronts for. Ivan and I want to find out who he is. We have been tipped off by one of Llov's servants that the two men will be meeting in the Baron's office tomorrow night at ten thirty. Apparently Saturday is the night the owner normally collects the money. We plan to arrive at nine thirty, play for a while, and pretend to leave around ten. Ivan has bribed the servant to let us into a box room next to Llov's office before the mystery owner arrives.'

By now David was extremely concerned for Monty. 'How did you come to go to a gambling den?' he asked.

Monty confessed he had been taken to the house originally after a bachelor party where he had gotten drunk. Since he seldom drank very much, he believed the drinks must have been doctored. Neither he nor Ivan could remember getting to the den, or the gambling part of the evening. However, the next day they were presented with notes detailing substantial losses that Baron Llov said they had incurred during the night. The notes carried their signatures but neither could remember signing anything and they believed they were forgeries.

Monty had been shattered, because the only way he could cover his debts was by selling the one valuable piece of property his father had bequeathed to him outright. This was a diamond ring worth over £2000. His father had intended that he should sell it when he married, but Monty, determined to make his own way in the world, had told his sister he would sell it and give her the proceeds as a dowry when she married. Now, selling the ring was the only way he could see of paying his gambling debts. But worse was to come.

Still trying to understand what had happened, he and Ivan had gone back to the den another night. They remembered nothing of the former night they had spent there so, in desperation, they decided to try their luck. They were both careful, and they won over 150 roubles between them. Foolishly, they allowed this to whet their appetites, persuading themselves that perhaps fortune was on their side and they could win back enough to cover their previous losses. By the end of the evening they were 1900 roubles down. Ivan, a second son, was as worried as Monty. He knew it was going to be difficult to ask his father for the money as his father abhorred gambling, believing it to be the ruin of many of Russia's best families.

'The Baron called us into his office that night and asked us to pay up every rouble we owed immediately. I said there and then that I couldn't, and would need at least a month to raise the money. The Baron refused, and told me that unless I found the money immediately he would expose me as a gambler who welshed on his debts. That would be the end of my career. Ivan was in the same situation, if he was exposed his reputation would be ruined.

'We discussed the whole affair,' Monty continued, 'and we both believe we have been cheated. I went back the next evening to ask again for time to pay, and the Baron put a dreadful proposition to me. If I got copies of certain documents from the Ambassador's safe, my debts would be forgiven. I refused outright, but the Baron has given me twenty-four hours to think it over.

'Meanwhile Ivan discovered that Llov wasn't the real owner of the gambling den, and the servant told him about the owner visiting Llov tomorrow night.'

'What do you intend to do?' David asked.

'I will never betray my country. If we haven't found out anything tomorrow night I was going to ask you to lend me the money until I could sell the ring.'

Monty looked nervously at David, who could see clearly that he was under a huge strain.

'Of course I will advance you the money,' he said, 'but I would also like to come with you and see if I can help.'

From what Monty had said, David suspected young Stuffel had probably been trapped in the same way.

Monty's relief was so transparent that for a moment David thought he might burst into tears. He managed to compose himself, but jerkily rushed to explain that he would expect to pay interest on the loan, at the same time fulsomely expressing his thanks.

'I will certainly not be charging interest on any money you borrow,' David assured him, 'so please do not mention that again. Anyway, you probably have no debt at all, but we need to prove that.'

'Now, to practical matters, can I come with you?' he asked, cutting short Monty's continued protestations of relief and gratitude.

It seemed there was no way they could smuggle David past the bribed servant, who, already fearful, had only been persuaded to help because he desperately needed money for his family. Finally it was agreed that David would hide in one of the outbuildings at around ten thirty. This would be after Ivan and Monty had gone upstairs and been hidden. They would hopefully find out the identity of the real owner when they emerged from their hiding place, and with luck would flush out a corrupt gambling and spy network. They would carry pistols, and David would be similarly armed. If there was any trouble he could surprise Llov and his men, who would not be expecting another armed man outside.

David sent a brief note to Gisela, explaining the situation, and next evening set off for the gambling den, with a groom. About a quarter of a mile from the den he stopped and dismounted, telling the groom to hide the horses and wait for his return. He then jogged off into the darkness.

Monty had explained where there was a low part of the wall near the stables, and David found this and climbed over without difficulty. He peered around to get his bearings and take in the building, which was about six hundred yards away. The windows on the ground floor were brightly lit, while upstairs there seemed to be just one room with lights. This could well be the office Monty had told him about, and where the mysterious owner would meet with Llov. There was a tree growing alongside the window. It had a straight trunk for about twelve feet, and David suspected it would have no footholds. However, this did not perturb him, as he had often climbed similar trees as a boy. There was a branch near the upstairs window that might enable him to see in if he could get across and climb the tree. About a hundred yards away from him were the stables, where he could hear the gentle whickering of horses. He would make for there, and hide until the gaming house owner arrived. He might even be lucky enough to see his face.

Just as he was creeping toward the stables he heard the clang of a bucket and a stout figure dimly appeared in the dark, talking to himself and heading towards the back of the house. David froze and waited until the figure was out of sight, then ran silently toward the stables. There was a light emanating from the big double wooden doors, and he stopped in the shadows and cautiously peeped in to make sure there was no one there. The light came from a lamp in the tack room, which was straight ahead, but there did not appear to be anyone else present.

At that moment, however, he heard someone approaching. David quickly slipped into an area off the tack room, and found himself in a space where hay and other feedstuffs were stored. He dropped down behind a stack of hay, hoping he was hidden from view. He heard someone enter, and from the sounds made it was clearly the same person he had seen a few minutes ago. He was obviously upset over something, as he was grumbling to himself. The light flared briefly as he lit another lamp, then he carried it off to a distant part of the stables, his grumbling growing fainter as he moved away. David decided to wait where he was until the mystery man arrived, and then try and climb the tree. So he could see out, he quietly made a small gap in the hay through which he could command a frontal view.

It was then that he had the eerie feeling that someone was watching him. He peered cautiously through the hole, and was suddenly shaken to find a pair of eyes staring fixedly at him from the left. He was about to draw his pistol then realised, to his great relief, that they were the eyes of a cat. He breathed deeply and tried to relax. When he looked again he could see it was a cat with kittens, curled up in a nest in some straw that lay between him and the door.

He was just wondering whether he should change his mind and make for the tree at once when out of the darkness he heard the sound of a trotting horse approaching. The stableman must have heard it too, because suddenly there was a bustle of activity and David saw him move out to wait at the stable door. Tense with a mixture of apprehension and excitement, David stealthily raised himself to get a better view. Just then the horse and rider rode into the stable light. His heart racing, David watched as a tall man, heavily cloaked and head covered, slipped off the horse. To his astonishment, David saw that he was masked.

In a harsh but cultured voice the rider instructed the stableman to have the horse fed and ready for him to leave in an hour. Then David's heart nearly stopped. The biggest wolfhound he had ever seen appeared in the doorway. He stayed as if frozen, scarcely breathing, as the dog suddenly stiffened and began to sniff the air.

'What is it, Karl?' the masked man asked, promptly drawing out a pistol.

Knowing the dog had smelt him, David pulled out his own pistol and tried to think how to cut down two men and a dog before he was shot himself. Eyeing the dog's stance, the masked man, pistol at the ready, commanded, 'Find, Karl!'

The dog sprang forward, its teeth barred. As David rose his pistol to fire there was a flurry of sound as the cat, thinking the dog was after its young, leapt out and raced for the doorway in an attempt to draw it away from the kittens. The dog seemed to spin in midair then raced after the cat, oblivious to its master's fierce commands to heel. David steadied himself and waited, pistol drawn, for what would happen next.

It was unexpected and sickening. The masked man put away his pistol and again called the dog. This time the wolfhound responded, and David watched as it came into the light. But as it saw its master pick up a whip the massive animal cringed and went down on the ground about ten yards away. The man flicked the whip threateningly against his riding boot, again calling the wolfhound in a menacing voice. Slowly the dog crawled towards its master, its whole being pleading for pity. The man stood waiting implacably, continuing to flick the whip.

David, who had feared the dog before, was now sick with apprehension for it. The man forced the dog to crawl right to his feet, where it rolled over in total and abject subjection. Then the masked man began to beat it methodically. It was the worst beating David had ever witnessed, and it was made even worse by the obvious enjoyment the man was taking in inflicting it. It took all David's control and his concern for Monty, to stop him shooting the man dead. The dog writhed and whimpered, but made no other sound until the savage beating stopped abruptly and the whip was thrown to the stable hand, who cowered motionless nearby. Then the man strode off. The dog, one leg dragging and obviously broken, its body wracked with pain, limped behind its master, all thought of its earlier quarry wiped from its mind.

The stableman slunk off towards the back of the stables. David found that the fear he had experienced earlier had totally left him, overtaken by the intense revulsion he felt for the masked man. Stepping out from his hiding place, and finding no other sign of human life, he ran to the tree. He had little trouble shinning up the trunk but it was painstakingly slow and risky easing himself out along the branch. By the time he was about four feet from the window the branch was becoming dangerously fragile, so he lent slightly to the left, endeavouring to see inside. Before he could get a glimpse into the room he saw a grim-looking man pull across a curtain, and any chance of a view was lost. He felt weak when he realised that if the man had not been looking back into the room as he drew the curtain he could have seen David and shot him dead without any questions.

Unbeknown to David, disaster was about to strike.

Ivan and Monty had successfully been smuggled upstairs, and were now in a cupboard built into the wall between the office and an adjoining room. Here they could hear everything said in the office, and if they opened the door slightly they would be able to see the real owner as he left.

All initially went to plan, and they could hear the unknown man giving orders to Baron Llov. The Baron was to squeeze a young Rontsov for money they knew he didn't have, and at the same time encourage him to continue gambling by suggesting he win his losses back. At no stage, apart from the first punt, which was merely to tempt him, was he to be allowed to win. As Monty and Ivan listened, their belief that the gambling was rigged was confirmed. Monty caught his breath as the unknown voice continued, telling Baron Llov that it was vital they force Montague to steal the Embassy papers. Prince de Ligne had told him the Austrian government would pay a fortune for them.

Monty could scarcely wait to see the owner of the voice, as it continued to make its demands clear to the Baron. Among other orders he was commanded to entice a youngster from the French Embassy into the gambling house.

At this point Baron Llov demurred, saying, 'Surely after the Stuffel affair, most Embassy staff will be prohibited from coming here?'

'Not at all,' the voice replied. 'Look, that simpleton Montague has come here again, and he must know about Stuffel.'

'Perhaps the Prussian Ambassador has hushed it up and told no one,' the Baron persisted.

'Not Hertzburg, he is too honourable not to tell his ally, Lord Malvern,' said the voice contemptuously. Certainly they will not have told the French, however, despite them currently being allies. The French, Llov, are notorious for putting their own interests first and creating havoc for others, allies or not, whenever it suits them.'

Llov responded nervously, 'I don't think we should keep operating the gambling den for much longer. I know it has been wonderfully profitable but too many young aristocrats have lost large sums here and I believe people of consequence are beginning to talk.'

The voice reluctantly said, 'You are right, Llov, Panin is becoming suspicious. Make plans to disappear at the first sign of serious trouble. Just walk out at that stage and leave everything as is.'

'Where will I disappear to?' asked the Baron, 'and how can I keep in contact?'

'First go straight to the Crimea. I have a house in Kiev. Give me some paper and I will write a letter now authorising my housekeeper to let you stay there for an indeterminate length of time. If you do have to go you will need a new name, as we do not want anyone to associate you with this place.'

There was a pause, then he continued. 'You had better become a Polish explorer looking at the new territory Russia has recently won from the Ottomans. I'll call you Yakov Bestoi. At the first sign of danger leave here immediately and go straight to Kiev. I'll contact you later on. You must avoid any connection with me in St. Petersburg.'

Monty and Ivan heard the two men sketch out a cover story in case anyone should enquire too deeply into the past of Baron Llov or Yakov Bestoi. Finally the man announced that it was time he left.

By now Ivan and Monty were keen to know the identity of the mystery man whose name had never been mentioned, and as they heard the office door opening they began to stealthily open their cupboard door. Despite the cramped and dusty conditions the two men had managed to remain silent throughout the conversation, but now Ivan tried desperately to stifle a sneeze. He managed to turn it into the softest of sounds, but it was enough to make the Baron and his patron whirl around, both reaching for their guns.

Although Monty tried to pull the cupboard door shut, Llov seized it and swung it open. The two men outside were briefly stunned as they took in the sight of Monty and Ivan crammed in the cupboard. Monty, in his turn, gasped as he recognised the second man, who was now half unmasked. He knew instantly, both Ivan's and his life were lost unless they could immediately escape.

Yelling to Ivan to run, he rushed at the two men with such violence that he shoved them aside. He heard Ivan thundering behind him, but his friend only managed to reach the top of the stairs before he was shot dead. Monty, twisting left and right to avoid being an easy target, made it halfway down before he was shot in the shoulder. The impact of the bullet caused him to stumble on the stairs and the next two bullets missed him. He managed to regain his balance and was just rounding the corner of the staircase when a further bullet struck him in the neck. Blood gushed out, and the young man was dead within minutes.

Outside, David heard the shots and could only pray that Monty was safe. He leaned closer to the window in desperation, and just managed to make out a voice saying, 'Both dead. Good. One of the servants must have been bribed to bring them up here. Find out who it was. I'll wait here until you bring him up.'

Fifteen minutes later they had found the servant, interrogated him and, despite piteous pleas, cut his tongue out and then slashed his throat. The three bodies were put into sacks and one of the Baron's serfs was told to have the coach brought round and the bodies put into it. They were then to be taken and quietly dropped into one of the smaller canals off the Neva.

Although David could make out only snatches of the conversation it was clear that Monty was dead. Stricken, he began to swing and slide as fast as he could down the tree, at the same time trying desperately to think what he should do next. Then, as he touched the ground, something hit him on the back of the head and he passed out.

The object had been wielded by the serf who had gone to tell the coachman to harness the horses. As he was returning to get the bodies he had seen a movement in the tree. Picking up a cudgel, he had crept stealthily closer, seen a man descending the tree, and hit him on the head. The serf then rushed in to tell Baron Llov about the new intruder.

The Baron and his business partner, fully aware of Montague's connections, were making rapid preparations to leave. Without bothering to inspect the new body they told the serf to sew the intruder into a sack and throw him in the canal with the other three. Still unconscious, he put David into a sack, and all four bodies were loaded into the coach. Two servants jumped in with them and the coach set off to find a quiet part of the Neva in which to dump them.

CHAPTER TEN

DAVID – QUICKLY RECOVERING CONSCIOUSNESS WITH THE JOLTING OF THE COACH – BECAME AWARE OF HIS SITUATION, AND HEARING THE SERVANTS TALKING UNDERSTOOD THAT HE AND SOME OTHERS WERE TO BE THROWN INTO THE CANAL. If they found he was alive and conscious, he knew they would kill him before throwing him in the river. He suddenly received a vicious kick, which he thought might have broken a rib, and a groan rose to his throat, but he managed to stifle it. After lying absolutely still for several minutes he at last managed to grasp the dagger. He carefully extracted it from his boot, keeping his other arm motionless as it lay along the length of his body.

It was around 4 a.m. when a suitable spot was found, with no one in sight, and the Baron's servants quickly began to drop the sacks into the canal. The first sack was thrown in, then the next. As David felt his body hit the water he immediately began to saw at the string that had been used to tie up the sack. He knew he could only hold his breath for a few minutes, and the water was bitterly cold. The bottom of the sack had been weighted with stones so he sank immediately. He concentrated on trying to open the sack, the effort helping to keep him from freezing. Once he had cut through the top, the rest was easy and the weighted sack fell cleanly off him.

David was worried that the Baron's men would see him appear, but he had no alternative other than to swim up and pop his head out of the water. Fortunately, by the time he rose to the surface the serfs were just getting into the coach, anxious to get away. David heaved an enormous sigh of relief but remained as still as he could, gently treading water, knowing that if they heard any sound they would come back.

By now the icy water was beginning to affect him, and once the coach was well away David clambered out of the canal. Fortunately he was able to get his bearings fairly quickly, and he began to run through the back streets to his apartment. Although he was shivering, the run had helped to warm his body sufficiently to keep him from freezing. By the time he arrived home it was just on 5 a.m., and his manservant was already up. He couldn't believe his eyes when he saw His Lordship soaking wet and totally bedraggled, but he immediately laid out dry clothes for him and began to heat water.

As soon as he had bathed and changed, David went to the Ambassador's Residence to tell him about the horrifying events of the night. The two men then drove directly to the headquarters of the Secret Police, whose responsibility it was to investigate crimes involving any overseas embassy.

The police accepted the matter as urgent and immediately an officer and men were sent to the gambling den with David and the Ambassador. They found the caretaker and asked to be taken to Baron Llov, but were informed that the Baron had left at about five thirty that morning. The caretaker added that he did not know where the Baron had gone, but that the housekeeper might. They woke the housekeeper, but she said she didn't even know the Baron was not at home, and she certainly did not know where he had gone or for how long. The police then asked for the coachmen and the two servants who had gone out with the coach earlier that morning, but not one of them was to be found. The coach was in the stable but there were no horses. It appeared the three men must have gone with Baron Llov.

Lord Malvern and David left the police still questioning the remaining staff and went with another officer to the canal. David showed him the spot where at least three other bodies were thrown, and the officer said he would have the area dragged that morning. He agreed there was no current of any strength so the weighted bags and their contents would almost certainly still be there.

They then returned to the Embassy, where they had the task of informing the rest of the staff. Everyone had liked Monty, and when they were told of his death and some of the circumstances surrounding it a wave of horror and depression seeped through the building.

David told the Ambassador about Monty's suspicion that Baron Llov didn't own the gambling joint, but simply fronted for some powerful personage. This person not only ensured the tables were crooked, but used the gambling to get young men into debt, then forced them into illegal acts of treachery in order to clear their debts. He told Lord Malvern how Monty had refused to betray his country, and had been going to ask David for an advance until he had sold the diamond ring he had been keeping for his sister's dowry.

They were both aware what a devastating blow Monty's death would be to his mother and sister.

David privately decided to send some funds to Mrs. Montague and pretend it was money that was owing to Monty. He then sent a message around to Gisela to inform her of the events of the night.

Around midday, the Secret Police reported that they had recovered three sacks, each containing a body, and asked for someone from the Embassy to come and identify them. David went and identified Monty and Ivan, but he did not recognise the third man. However, as he was dressed in the livery of the gambling den he assumed he was the servant Ivan had bribed. He looked ghastly with his mouth open and his throat cut, making David's stomach turn over. He only just escaped vomiting.

The police later reported that the Baron had not returned, and they had no knowledge of where he was. However, with all the horses gone from the stable, they surmised that he might have slipped out into the countryside. They were rigorously pursuing clues.

The Polish Embassy advised that there was no such title as Baron Llov in Poland, which meant the man known as the Baron was a con man as well as a fraudster and murderer. The gambling tables were inspected and, although it took some time to find them, every one had hidden artifices and mechanics which could alter the legitimate play.

The Chief of the Secret Police later visited the Ambassador and assured him that they would not rest until they had found the fraudulent Baron and tried him for murder, among his other crimes. The Ambassador was not so optimistic about the Baron being caught. He had left so speedily that it was as if he had already been prepared to go at a moment's notice. None of the servants at the gambling den had been paid and when the safe was opened, there was nothing inside.

The next day St. Petersburg was agog with the news of the murders at the gambling den. Everyone had his or her theories. When Lord Malvern met Panin and Barinsky at the Club, Panin commented, 'I am amazed the police weren't aware of the activities of this scoundrel and murderer, Llov, earlier. That gambling den has been operating for more than two years.'

He added, 'I now hear all the gambling tables can be altered to suit their operators and that no gambler has any chance of coming out winning if the operators and Llov don't agree.'

Barinsky snorted. 'Like you, I cannot understand how the authorities have let this gambling den operate for so long. I thank the Lord I stopped gambling, after I married my wife, otherwise I too could have been one of the men sucked in.'

Count Panin said rather sarcastically, 'You have always been too dexterous to be sucked in, as you put it, by a charlatan like Llov.'

CHAPTER ELEVEN

When Gisela arrived at David's apartment that night she was pale and drawn, having become quite distraught upon realising how close she had been to losing David. She flung her arms around David as soon as she entered the hall, and continued to cling to him for some time, babbling endearments and kissing him passionately. David had never seen her so distressed, and adored her all the more.

Several days later, on the return of Baron Hertzburg, Lord Malvern took David around to the Prussian Embassy so that the Baron could learn first-hand what had happened. David told Hertzburg as much as he could of the story, from when he had climbed the tree, been thrown in the Neva, returned to the Embassy and identified Monty for the police.

David, normally so straightforward, found himself avoiding eye contact with the Prussian Ambassador for he felt ashamed of cuckolding a man who had always been so courteous to him. He wished Gisela would let him tell the Baron about their love for each other so he would not feel such a hypocrite. He made up his mind to speak to her as soon as they were next together. He was also fretting that now the Baron was back he would see less of Gisela. This was another reason for them to declare themselves.

Lord and Lady Malvern received a letter from Countess Nadia Volonskaya expressing her sorrow at the death of Mr. Montague, and the Countess also sent a letter to David in a similar vein. David also received one from Tatiana, expressing her condolences over Mr. Montague's horrific death but rejoicing that he, David, had survived. She said how heroic he had been to cut his way out of the sack, and that she hoped he would call to see her and her grandmother soon. However, she said he must come within the next three weeks, as after that they were to visit her grandmother's estates in the Crimea.

Tatiana was very excited about this visit as she had never been to the Crimea before, and she added that she was looking forward to seeing all those romantic Cossacks and fabulous khans and emirs. They had also been invited to Prince Potemkin's estate in the Kuban. His estate was vastly bigger than her grandmother's: indeed, it was bigger than many countries. Her grandmother's was still large, she wrote, as it was possible to ride over it for several weeks without leaving the estate.

David wrote back thanking the Countesses for their kind letters, and asking if he could call on them one day the following week. His manservant, who delivered the letter, was asked to wait, and was then handed a letter to be given to Lord Mountforte. This was an invitation to dine with the ladies the following Thursday.

David was glad to accept, as he had only that morning found out that Gisela was going away with the Baron to Berlin for eight weeks. He could not envisage how he would be able to stand eight weeks without her. Besides, he had come to like the old Countess, finding she was witty, kind, extremely cultured and also a shrewd businesswoman. She had some knowledge of the East India Company, in which his grandfather had a substantial interest, and also of the Levant Company. Although she had no money invested in either company she was intrigued by what David's grandfather was doing. He enjoyed discussing these matters with her, and had found that her comments were always interesting and often apt. He had sometimes taken to mentioning them in his letters to his grandfather when he thought they might amuse or interest him.

When talking of the Crimea, the Countess had explained that she hoped as the towns of Nikolaev and Odessa were developed, the grain from the Crimea, would one day be exported overseas through these cities. He had told her his grandfather also had interests in ship-building in Liverpool and interests in merchant ships that sailed to the Levant and India. This intrigued her, and she said that when his grandfather paid him a visit she would like to meet him. David had replied that unfortunately his grandfather was now a virtual recluse in Scotland and seldom left the old castle. He went on to explain that the Earl had become reclusive since his son, David's father, and David's mother both died on a ship that had sunk in a storm in the Bay of Biscay when David was just two years old.

David found Tatiana a charming hostess, and consequently she rose considerably in his estimation. He now found he didn't mind her mischievous teasing, although he still did not like it when she unexpectedly said things such as that she had seen Baroness Hertzburg and David skating and had thought how beautifully they skated together. Then, after a pause, she murmured that she supposed they would do everything beautifully together.

He knew she could not know about his love affair with Gisela, but she made it sound as if she did. She never said these things in front of Countess Nadia, but when she did say them he would catch a glimpse of eyes dancing as if they held a secret. It made him slightly uncomfortable. After making these odd remarks she would once again become the most delightful of hostesses and make the whole party laugh and sparkle.

The first time he had met Tatiana, she had startled him by pretending to her suitors that Lord Mountforte had earlier claimed her for the next dance. Now used to her teasing, he readily came forward to claim her hand. Once she had whispered in his ear, 'I wonder if I had, how do the English say, a plain face, whether I would have so many adoring suitors?'

He had laughed and replied, 'Yes, because you have all that money.'

Unexpectedly, she had become rather quiet and replied pensively, 'Too much money can be almost as big a problem as too little.' She went on to say, 'That awful Swedish Prince is still trying to pay court and it is taking all Grandmother's considerable skills to keep him at bay. Grandmother and I devoutly hope the Empress won't insist on my marrying him for Russia's sake. It is like a cloud over my head. I will go into a convent rather than marry him.'

She had heard that David would one day be one of the wealthiest men in Britain, and she asked him, 'Do you have any problems like me? Would your King force you to marry for the sake of your country?'

David had laughed and told her, 'No, in Britain, the only people whose marriages the King arranges are for his children, and he is having problems in that quarter with his son, the Prince of Wales.' This led to a long and entertaining conversation.

He found he had begun to enjoy being with Tatiana. She was very amusing, and he would feel very sorry for her if the Empress decreed she must marry a man she didn't like. It must be depressing having a threat like that hanging over one's head. Tatiana said that maybe she would elope before a marriage to the Prince could take place or, laughing, that perhaps she would slip away on the next ship that was leaving for Britain and go and stay with his reclusive grandfather.

David had laughed heartily at this, but later amused himself thinking that the old Earl would probably enjoy having Tatiana stay. She was so full of life. He chuckled over the fantasy of the Earl and Tatiana living in the castle in Scotland. It was a fascinating thought, but it would never happen.

CHAPTER TWELVE

FOR HER PART, WHILE GISELA HAD TOLD DAVID THAT SHE WOULD MISS HIM WHILE SHE WAS AWAY, PRIVATELY SHE BELIEVED THAT IF DAVID WERE TO LEAVE HER NOW SHE WOULD DIE. Her former lovers had meant nothing to her in comparison. She had enjoyed their passion, but had unconsciously known that she had always been the giver. This had not worried her at the time, because she had simply wanted to pour her frustrated love on someone. But when David had come into her life, everything had changed dramatically.

He meant everything to her, her entire existence had changed. Sometimes she felt a deep compunction about cuckolding her courteous and generous husband. At other times she fell into almost irrational despair contemplating a future with David in which he was cut off from his career, his country and his friends. Would he still love her or would he come to resent her? She couldn't bear that.

She was very conscious that she had changed over the past few weeks, and she was anxious that the Baron should not notice. In the past she had played the role of wife and Ambassadress beautifully, with style and tact, but now she knew she sparkled and radiated a glowing warmth. No one other than her trusted maid knew that she slipped off to Lord Mountforte's apartment whenever they both had a spare hour or more. It was not just the deeply erotic physical passion she felt for David that kept her enraptured, but an overwhelming love. Anything he wanted, she wanted for him.

When they had first gone to bed together David had been touchingly tender but now he was in complete control. She had never experienced youthful ardour before since both her previous lovers had been older men. While they had played expertly with her body, their own satisfaction was their paramount concern.

Once David had overcome his initial heady passion he became a caring and very sensuous lover. He always wanted her to enjoy every moment of their time together. He only had to enter a room and, no matter how many people were there, she would feel her nipples start to tingle and her body begin pulsating with wild emotions. At other times she felt as if she would faint. Just his hand brushing her breasts or caressing her thigh would cause her almost to explode with desire.

After they had made love they would lie back in bed and talk while still nuzzling and caressing each other. It would then often be only a matter of moments before their passion would re-ignite and they would reach for another climax. The only world she wanted was the one that existed in his arms.

What worried her now was the fact that David hated deceiving the Baron, who was always so courteous toward him. David was too highly principled for deception, and he urged her to obtain a divorce and marry him. Gisela did not like deceiving the Baron either. Although she had never understood why he did not come to her bedroom, he was a good husband in every other way. He always treated her with the greatest of consideration. She had a lavish allowance, and he never questioned her spending. He never forgot her birthday, and he always gave her generous and carefully chosen gifts. He expected her to be dressed by the leading dressmakers and was openly appreciative whenever something stunning was created for her. No, he was a fine man and he didn't deserve to be deceived.

She looked out the window at the trees, which were just coming into leaf. They had that lovely light green, fuzzy texture which they would keep all week until the leaves matured a little. She loved spring. Perhaps it would be best to have this time away in Prussia. She could try to rationalise the situation without the influence of David's presence beside her, constantly urging her to run away with him. It was impossible to think clearly when he made the impossible seem possible. No, over the next few weeks she must resolve what to do with her future.

Would the Baron divorce her? She didn't think so. If she told him about David he would have every reason to do so, but would he? It would harm his career and make his position at the Prussian Court very difficult, despite his good relations with the King. He wouldn't like the scandal. Indeed, would she? If she was honest she had to admit to herself that she would not enjoy the dreadful alienation that would be the lot of a married woman who had run off with another man.

A divorced woman was excluded from so much. She would be estranged from the Court, the Embassy and all the functions she graced and enjoyed now. Most of the great private homes would be closed to her, and even her closest friends would avoid her out of embarrassment. But she knew she could face all of this if she could have David and keep him happy. The question was, would he be happy? In the long term, she doubted it.

Firstly, it would ruin his career. Governments were such hypocrites that they would hardly retain a man who had run off with a married or divorced woman and lived with her as husband and wife. Secondly, what would his grandfather say? David assured her the old Earl would come round because he would not be able to help loving her once they met, but would they meet? He was already a recluse and he could well refuse to meet her. Would he threaten David by cutting off his allowance? She had no money of her own, and if she left the Baron he would naturally end her allowance. David had a very generous allowance from the Earl and a reasonable income from the property he had inherited from his mother. But she knew this was nothing like the fabulous fortune the old Earl intended to leave David, only part of which was entailed. In the end, however, she knew if David pushed her hard enough she would leave the Baron, hope for divorce, but go with him whether she got it or not.

What really concerned her was whether their love would be strong enough to withstand the snubs and restrictions they would undoubtedly suffer. She was convinced she could endure it, but could David? He said they could live in Italy, where the conventions were not so strict, but deep down she didn't believe he could live forever without going back to his Scottish and English heritage. So long as David was happy and loved her, she believed herself to be capable of giving up all she had. It always came back to that nagging question: would he be happy?

David being so vital a person would want to continue his diplomatic work. If that wasn't possible, he would want to live on and manage his estates. While she felt she could endure the cold treatment they would receive, and the lack of the social life she so enjoyed, she thought David would become resentful on her behalf. That would be futile. Would he then, like his grandfather, become a recluse? In addition, she was six years his senior. Would he cease to love her, and begin to secretly regret giving up his career for her? Of course he would continue to treat her with his natural courtesy, but if he ceased to love her she would sense it and that would be more than she could bear.

She must reach a decision while she was in Prussia. She could not afford to keep putting it off. For one thing, she knew that if she didn't reach a conclusion soon David was quite capable, in a fit of high-minded passion, of approaching the Baron with his confession. Her other lovers had taken delight in the secrecy needed. But for David, so open and so principled, the need for secrecy somehow tarnished their relationship. He wanted their relationship to be known and acknowledged by one and all.

Her thoughts were interrupted by a knock at her door, and a footman advising that the Baron was waiting in the hall and their travelling coach was ready to depart. She signalled her maid to bring down her small travelling case.

Downstairs, the Baron greeted her warmly, kissed her hand and expressed the hope that they would have an enjoyable journey. 'I hear that although spring is just starting in St. Petersburg it is well under way the closer we come to Berlin. We will come across some slushy mud for a day or so out of St. Petersburg, but then the roads are expected to clear and the weather improve. I have sent staff ahead to the hotels and taverns where we will stay, to ensure they are suitably clean and prepared.'

She realised yet again, as she thanked him, how very thoughtful her husband was. At certain destinations they would be staying with friends, which was why some of the trunks in the coach contained elaborate gowns and her maid held a case with some of her jewels in it. She was looking forward to staying with the Potockis. Countess

Sophie, who was said to be one of the most beautiful women in Europe, had led a life far more hazardous than the one she was contemplating for herself, yet Sophie had achieved the position of the wife of one of the richest aristocrats in Poland. At the age of twelve she had been sold by her Turkish mother for one thousand ducats to the Polish Ambassador. She was married at fourteen to an aristocrat, had been mistress to numerous men, and finally caught the elderly Count Felix Potocki. There were rumours that the Countess was having an incestuous affair now with her stepson, Yuri Potocki. It should be an illuminating visit.

Their departure from St. Petersburg was reasonably smooth. The coach jolted on its way until about two o'clock, when they reached the tavern where lunch had been ordered ahead for them. The Baron seemed in high spirits, and now that Gisela was contemplating leaving him she wondered if she had appreciated him enough in the past. She didn't love him, but she did admire him, and he had the means to provide her with a lifetime of luxury, position and consideration. There were many women who would greatly appreciate even half of what she had. Then her mind returned to David and she thought that if he had not come into her life she would never have felt the rapture that sometimes totally engulfed her.

God, how would she survive eight weeks without seeing him? She had said she would write to him, but that he was not to write to her in case someone spied on her incoming mail. Privately she knew there was no chance of this, as the Baron was too honourable. But she needed to have time to think through her dilemma without being influenced by his tempestuous letters.

After lunch they set off again with fresh horses, as the Baron had had horses sent ahead so their travel on the roads could be as quick as possible. Over the next few days they were perpetually on the move, spending the nights in hotels and taverns en route. Gisela rather enjoyed the journey. The coming of spring was apparent all around them. It was lovely seeing the green again and the flowers beginning to peep through after so much snow.

Her husband was an interesting travelling companion, and she wondered why she had not been aware of that before. Was it because she had been too in awe of him? Her affair with David had caused a slight feeling of guilt within her, which perhaps made her more perceptive of her husband's feelings. Whatever it was, she was enjoying her time with him far more than she had when they'd travelled together in the past. They even made jokes together. What an enigma he was, she thought.

Two weeks later they arrived at the Potocki residence, and Gisela thought how like the Russians these Polish magnates were in the overwhelming splendour of their palaces, furnishings and indeed their way of life. The old Count and his young Countess came out to greet them. The Baron and Count Felix were longstanding friends, having served in a military campaign together, which had led to a strong feeling of comradeship. Gisela's first impressions of the Countess were how beautiful she was, and how elegant her dress and manners were, but later she thought that her eyes were hard and she had a clearly manipulative demeanour. She felt sorry for the old Count. They were, however, treated to the most lavish of hospitality during their four-day stay.

One evening while they were resting before dinner Gisela asked her husband, 'Max, what do you think of Countess Sophie?'

'I think she is very beautiful,' he replied. 'But in my opinion she is hard-headed, greedy and totally self-interested.'

'That was my impression,' Gisela said, 'but she is exquisite.'

'Just so long as you do not let yourself look too long into her eyes. They are the true giveaway of her character,' Max replied.

Gisela thought of the rumours that the Countess was having an affair with her stepson right under the Count's nose. Gisela thought this disgusting, but she felt she couldn't mention it to Max since she too was guilty. Away from David, and in a place like this, Gisela was beginning to feel rather sordid. She again decided she must resolve her position while she was in Prussia. She knew she would never have any rational thoughts while she was in St. Petersburg with David.

The more she worried, the more she thought she would ask the Baron for a divorce. Surely he would understand. After all, he had been so likeable and so human on this trip. She couldn't understand why she had never noticed it before.

Later, as she lay in bed, she craved for David. She longed for him to be lying alongside her and caressing her. Whether the Baron agreed to a divorce or not, she would go and live with David. She would take the consequences and even risk the possibility of losing David's love. But surely he would always love her? She tossed and turned, unable to sleep as she tried to resolve her dilemma.

Finally it was time to leave the Potockis, and they set off on their way to stay with another old friend of the Baron, Princess Izabela Lubomirski, at Lancut, a truly fabulous palace. When they arrived they were warmly greeted by Princess Izabela, who made Gisela very welcome, but was obviously most pleased to see her old friend the Baron again. Gisela was struck by how fond of the Baron his friends were.

They stayed four days, during which the Baron enjoying some shooting, but the talk was all about Russian intentions towards Poland and how strong the Prussia-British alliance was. The Princess was extremely well-informed, but it was clear she thought Poland had little chance of remaining independent. She was making strategic moves now to ensure that her family and her vast fortune remained intact.

Gisela found the discussions fascinating. Her hostess was also a very amusing and outspoken woman, and as a consequence the visit was a scintillating one. She was sorry when the time came to leave.

The horses, having rested for the last four days, were eager to go and set off at a smart pace. The rest of the journey passed without incident. The mornings were crisp and fine, and the days warm and sunny.

Gisela loved seeing the farmers and peasants out ploughing the fields and planting their crops. But by the time they finally reached Berlin she was feeling tired and dishevelled, and she was greatly relieved to find that when they reached their home everything was in order and the staff well prepared to receive them. Max really was the most understanding and considerate of husbands, she thought.

The following day the Baron paid a visit to the Foreign Office and saw the minister, then had an audience with King Frederick, with the Foreign Minister in attendance. The King appeared well pleased with the Baron's report. He was particularly interested in his comments on the discussions he had had regarding Poland with the Potockis and the Princess Lubomirski, whose views the King always found acute and to the point. As the Baron was leaving the King informed him that a reception for the Swedish Crown Prince was to be held at his palace, Mon Repos, and that an invitation would be sent to the Ambassador and his wife. This meant that Gisela and Max would have to stay in town until after the reception, but meanwhile they could make plans for visits to the Baron's estates in the country and to Gisela's family.

Although Gisela had always loved her mother, she had privately feared and disliked her father. Now, however, for the first time she was looking forward to seeing all the family again. She was a woman of consequence now, the highly regarded wife of the Prussian Ambassador to Russia, and as such she no longer had any need to fear her father. But all her confidence fled as she reflected that in a few weeks' time she would no longer be the Ambassadress, but rather an estranged woman about to be divorced for adultery, perhaps even considered a wanton woman who had run away with her young lover and ruined his career and her own life.

Gisela suddenly felt sick, but as the feeling passed she decided she would spend as much time with her mother as possible and let her see how much she loved her. She even wondered if she could discuss her problem with her mother, but then realised it would only distress her. Even though her mother loved Gisela, she would never oppose her husband and would strongly urge Gisela to stay with the Baron. No, she would just show her mother how she loved her and say nothing. Let this be a happy visit, since it could be her last. Indeed, it may be the last time she would see her mother at all.

It seemed that the more she thought about running off with David, the more the treacherous consequences revealed themselves. Even if her mother wanted to see her daughter again, Gisela's father would never allow it. His pride in his daughter would be destroyed and he would disown her if she left the Baron. While she cared little for what her father might think, it was her mother's thoughts that concerned her. Again she wondered if she should tell her and seek her blessing. But what if her father found out that his wife had known their daughter was planning to run away and she hadn't told him? She was certain he would make her mother's life not worth living.

There was no one from whom she could seek advice. Perhaps if she had been a Catholic she could have gone to confession and sought help, but on reflection, the church would probably have her locked away in a convent with her father's blessing, considering her an unredeemable sinner.

The reception for the Swedish Crown Prince was a grand affair, as King Frederick the Great had exquisite taste and was a great lover of music, some of which he composed himself. He was also an accomplished flautist. The reception was more restrained than those at St. Petersburg, largely because the King didn't much like women. The ladies were dressed very conservatively, and Gisela noticed many of them looking enviously at her stylish dress and beautiful jewellery. She felt rather overdressed, and said as much to Max, but he simply replied that she outshone everyone and had nothing to worry about.

The King greeted her pleasantly and, to everyone's astonishment, remarked on how lovely she looked, saying loudly that he wished more of the ladies would take as much care with their appearance as the Baroness clearly did. This caused some consternation among the women, and much whispered comment. Several women who Gisela knew vaguely later asked her who made her clothes, and were disappointed when she gave them the name of a St. Petersburg dressmaker.

Two of the King's musical compositions were played and the orchestra performed a number of other pieces, but there was no dancing. The Swedish Crown Prince seemed rather dull, and Gisela thought how much more fun the Russian receptions were, with the ballet and music all interspersed with dancing. If only she were back in St. Petersburg now, dancing with David. The evening ended much earlier than it would have in St. Petersburg, and when the King retired Gisela and Max left and returned to their townhouse. The Baron had decided they would leave early in the morning, for his northern estates.

The next morning Gisela again felt unwell, and thinking back over the last few weeks she realised that it was possible that she was pregnant. On the one hand she was shocked and horrified, while on the other she could not help feeling joy at the thought of finally having a baby. Then the terror settled in.

The Baron would disown the baby and make her have an abortion.

The Baron would simply divorce her.

No, the Baron would not divorce her, but she would be sent to the countryside in total seclusion, have the baby, and then it would be sent to an orphanage.

These thoughts raced through her mind as she tried to think what she should do. Should she write immediately to David? No, she had better make sure, and she also needed to find out what the Baron's reaction was.

Slowly, she reached the conclusion that there was no way she was going to abort or give away her baby. She had always wanted children, and she was going to keep it. What was the best way to do this? Tell David, tell the Baron? The Baron would have to know at some stage, but when to tell him? Tell him here where her family would hear all about it, or tell him in St. Petersburg where she would have David's support and strength? Would David be pleased that she was to have a baby? Of course he would. Would he be thrilled with a baby born out of wedlock? He would be so happy he would accept it. But would his grandfather?

What about David's future? They would have to go into exile in Italy. What would David do? He would be bored without a career or estates of his own to manage. Perhaps he could sell his mother's estate and invest in an estate in Italy, or could he? What if the estate was entailed to a legitimate heir and could not be sold? Oh God, how she wished she was back in St. Petersburg. There was so much that needed to be considered.

Above all, she must remember how glad she was to be having a baby. Through all the pressures and stress that would come from now on, she must hang on to that fact. She was going to have a baby of her own, keep it, and pour all her love into it.

What if the Earl disowned David? Should she quietly sell some of her jewels and slip away, find somewhere in the country to live? Bring the baby up by herself, later telling the child her husband had died in an accident or war? But the Baron didn't deserve such treatment, nor did David. What should she do?

Somehow she went through the motions of dressing and preparing to leave for the country. Much later, as she sat silently in the coach, her thoughts in turmoil, she became aware that the Baron was speaking to her. 'What a success you were at the reception last night. I was so proud.' When she did not respond he said, 'you are very quiet, my dear. Are you feeling well?'

She murmured something about being tired, and he arranged some cushions around her as the coach bumped its way towards his estates. By the time they arrived it was late afternoon and Gisela really did feel tired and ill. She excused herself and went upstairs to her room, later sending a message to the Baron asking him to forgive her if she did not join him at dinner.

All night she tossed and turned, finally falling asleep around six and not waking until ten. When she did come downstairs she was told the Baron was in the study with his son, going over reports on his estates and the coalmines his son administered on the family's behalf. Gisela decided she would take a walk in the garden, hoping the fresh air and scent of the flowering bulbs would cheer her up and clear her head.

To Gisela's surprise the Baron's sister, Countess Bertha Esterman, suddenly appeared and came across the lawn to join her. Gisela had not realised she was in residence. She did not know her sister-in-law well, but had enjoyed her company when she had visited St. Petersburg with her husband several years earlier. Bertha greeted her warmly, saying, 'How lovely you look. I have so wanted to see you again to say how grateful the family and I are for the happiness you have brought Max.'

Gisela tried to suppress her surprise at this statement. Perhaps she had made Max content, but not, surely, happy. Bertha continued, saying that in all his letters Max said what a wonderful wife he had, and how without her he would not enjoy St. Petersburg and would want to come back home to Prussia. Gisela was quite stunned at the Countess's comments, for she saw that the Countess was quite sincere.

Bertha went on to describe how the family had never liked Max's first wife. 'She was a private disaster. She would not entertain, and was always complaining, always nagging, and then she fell into ill-health and died. It affected his career; no one liked her, not even her parents. But he was marvellous to her. The family never understood how he put up with her.'

'But you,' said Bertha, 'know what a wonderful nature he has. We are all so grateful he has found the happiness with you that he never had with his first wife.' She smiled warmly at Gisela. 'My dear, I just wished to take this opportunity to express the family's and my gratitude.' Then she added, with a twinkle in her eye, 'You really are enchanting.'

As she smiled and thanked Bertha, Gisela recalled that neither her husband nor his son had ever spoken of his first wife except in passing, and she had never had any idea that her stepson liked her. Perhaps both Max and his son were basically shy people. She now remembered Bertha telling her this when she was in St. Petersburg, but at the time she had not taken any notice of her comment.

'Max writes quite poetically about you these days.'

Gisela's thoughts were in a whirl. When they went in to change for lunch, she found herself wondering how she had misunderstood so many signposts in her life. She was completely flummoxed.

Dinner that evening was an extremely happy affair. Max's son was clearly delighted to see his father and, to her surprise, Gisela herself. The Baron was equally pleased with Justin's handling of the estates and coalmines, and announced that he was going to increase his allowance. When she went to bed that night Gisela had no idea what to think. She missed David terribly and was confident he would find a way out of her dilemma, but now she felt she could not bear to hurt the Baron or humiliate him in any way. By the time she finally found sleep, she had resolved nothing.

CHAPTER THIRTEEN

THE NEXT MORNING AT BREAKFAST, THE BARON SUDDENLY ANNOUNCED, 'I AM GOING TO MAKE OVER ONE OF MY ESTATES IN SILESIA TO GISELA. She will inherit an ample income for life from the family fortune, plus a townhouse in Berlin, but I wish her to have additional independence and her own estate will give her that. Unless you decree otherwise, dear, the estate will be managed along with my other estates, by Justin, but the revenues will be sent wherever you wish them to be banked.'

Gisela, stunned at this announcement could scarcely refrain from bursting into tears, while Bertha and Justin looked delighted. To Gisela this was salvation. Now, no matter what happened, she would be able to have her baby, and support it and herself in comfort. She decided then and there to say nothing about her pregnancy until the estate was in her name, so no one could take it away from her when they were shocked at her news.

Max then told her the estimated annual revenues of the estate and she couldn't believe how generous he had been. For most of that day she wandered around in a daze, sometimes wildly happy, at other times oppressed by a feeling of guilt over how she had treated Max. After agonising all day, gradually her sense of honour prevailed. She could not let her husband go ahead and transfer the estate to her without telling him she was pregnant. The decision made she would tell him after dinner but would not tell him who the father was, neither would she agree to an abortion. She would keep her child, but he could decide about the divorce or separation.

Although the days were lovely the evenings were still cold, and after dinner the family sat chatting around a fire as they drank their coffee. When they had finished their coffee Gisela asked, 'Max, could I speak to you alone for a minute or two.' She smiled at the others as she excused herself.

'Certainly,' the Baron said, smiling easily. 'Come into the library where we can talk.'

Gisela had drunk several glasses of wine with dinner, to give herself the courage to talk to him, and when they reached the library the Baron made it as easy as he could for her to tell him what she wanted. Finally she blurted out her dilemma in a manner that was totally unlike her normally gracious way of speaking.

'I'm pregnant. I have just found out. Will you give me a divorce? I don't deserve the estate.'

His face went white as he absorbed her words, and then he said, 'Relax, my dear. We will talk this through.'

He sat in silence for a minute or two while Gisela, perched on the edge of her chair about to flee, waited in trepidation. Then, to her amazement, instead of raging, he said, 'I will not give you a divorce. I will recognise the child as mine. If it is a boy I will settle an estate on him as I would on any younger son. If it is a girl I will give her the same size dowry as I would my daughter.'

Gisela was overwhelmed, and burst into tears of pent-up emotion and relief. Once again she was stunned by her husband's magnanimity, and she stared at him in wonder. Then her mind flew back to David, whom she loved, and who was the real father of her child.

The Baron, watching her intently, saw the range of emotions passing over her face, and gravely said he too would like to explain something.

'Do you remember just after we become engaged, how I became seriously sick with a fever?' Gisela nodded, and he went on, somewhat hesitantly, 'When I recovered from the illness I found I was impotent. I believed it was only temporary, and my doctor assured me I would recover. That was why the wedding was slightly postponed.' Speaking slowly and sadly now, he went on, 'My potency has never recovered. That is why I have never visited you in your bedroom. I should have told you as soon as I knew but I kept hoping for some miracle, and then it was too late. I love you passionately and I have ached when I saw how much you needed some physical love. I know I have treated you with reserve, but it is only because I didn't want you to know what had happened.

'I kept on hoping to recover my virility. It never happened, but I knew how you longed for a child. I had seen it when I watched you playing with a child or holding children. It caused me great sadness and I felt a terrible futility. That was why I hinted that, provided you were discreet, you could take a lover. I hated the thought of it, but since I knew I couldn't pleasure you I had no moral right, I believed, to deny you this.'

Gisela listened spellbound, amazed at how understanding and generous her husband had been, and shocked at how much he must have suffered.

'You are a wonderful wife and Ambassadress, and apart from my lack of virility, I have been a very happy man.' He reiterated how much he loved Gisela, and she could hear that his voice carried a plea for love. She was profoundly moved, and despaired to think what a great spirit he had and how small hers was.

'What do you want me to do?'

'I want you to have the baby, but you must give up Lord Mountforte.'

She was appalled. She had never once mentioned Lord Mountforte to him. She had not believed he even suspected. She felt unworthy and sordid.

'Yes, I have known since I returned to St. Petersburg from Berlin. You may see him at formal functions, but never again alone, and he must never know the child is his.' Then, through stiff lips and a mask-like face, he asked, 'Would you like to think it over tonight? We can discuss it again after breakfast tomorrow?'

Gisela nodded dumbly, hesitated, then went across and softly kissed him on the cheek. Confounded, he looked up at her in silence, and a blush slowly coloured his pale cheeks. Overcome, she turned and rushed out of the room.

As she lay in bed that night she was torn between feelings of gratitude for the security the Baron had offered her child and the fact that she couldn't bear to lose David. She knew she would not be able to meet him, even in a crowd, and ignore him. Why, if she so much as touched his hand or arm she immediately felt a sensation shimmer through her body. Yet the Baron too had suffered, and no one could have been more magnanimous than he had shown himself to be.

The next morning, rather than face her sister-in-law and stepson at breakfast and listen to their pleasant chatter, she asked to be sent breakfast in bed. She needed to be by herself to try to decide once and for all what she should do. The Baron had offered her everything except a divorce, which she knew would ruin his career. Most women would jump at his offer, but the thought of losing David was agony. And to live with David without obtaining a divorce would ruin both their lives. She hated the thought, but David was only twenty-four, and unless he was caught on the rebound he would at some later stage make a happy marriage. But she was certain that his marriage could never be as gloriously happy as she knew theirs could have been under different circumstances.

She was aware that she was already beginning to give up David in her mind, and it was making her feel almost suicidal. If it were not for the baby, she would be ready to commit suicide, knowing she would never see and be with David again. She would have to talk to Max again. She sent her maid to ask the Baron, if he were available, to come and see her in her boudoir.

When some fifteen minutes later Max arrived, she noticed how pale he was, and she thought he looked as if he had not slept either. It touched her deeply that this good man was suffering through no fault of his own. As the Baron perched on a chair across from her, she said, 'I cannot decide what I am going to do. However, Max, I am overwhelmed and filled with gratitude at your offer of accepting the child as your own.'

While she had come to recognise the true worth of her husband just in time, she was not sure she could give up David, and she knew without doubt that David too would love their child.

As if reading her thoughts Max replied, 'I will not divorce you, and even if I did, you must know that Mountforte's career would be ruined. I also believe from what I have heard of the Earl that he would do his best to disinherit his grandson. That too would dramatically change Mountforte's future. While he may still want to run away with you, what would he feel like in a few years' time? If he was disinherited by his grandfather, how would you feel later? Have you thought of that?'

Gisela nodded. 'I have, and the more I think of it, the more I see the risk to David and his love for me.'

They talked for several hours, the Baron rationally and persuasively, while Gisela was torn between love, honour and duty. Finally, after much pain on both sides, Gisela said, 'I will remain with you, but I must be allowed to see David once more when we return to St. Petersburg. At that meeting I propose to explain to him that I will never see him alone again. I promise you I will never tell him about our child.'

She then saw clearly the stress the Baron had been under, because his voice broke as he said he would do everything in his power to see that she never regretted her decision. Once he let his guard down he looked so vulnerable that she wondered how she had ever thought him stiff and formal. She yearned to offer him something in return, and astonished herself when she said, 'Now you have told me about your impotence you have nothing to be ashamed of, and perhaps you should start visiting my bed. Even if we cannot consummate our marriage we can perhaps comfort each other.'

It was the Baron's turn to be overwhelmed by his wife's generosity, and later he asked hesitantly if he might join her that evening. Instead of feeling repugnance Gisela felt curiously happy; she was giving love to someone who needed it and who deeply and honourably loved her. Yet her whole being was tearing itself apart with the anguish of knowing she would have to completely sever her ties with David. It seemed small consolation that her child would be legitimate and that David's career would not be ruined. She was stricken and exhausted, her emotions stretched to breaking point.

Over the following days she gradually began to recover, and she realised that her sister-in-law and her stepson really did like and admire her. Their affection provided a counterbalance to the pain she felt over losing David, and she found that once she relaxed in their company they opened up to her. She began to notice and enjoy aspects of their characters she had never taken the time to appreciate before, particularly the dry and charming sense of humour they shared.

In some ways it was good that she was not able to meet David immediately. Despite her pain, she appreciated seeing another side of her husband, a warmer side that she had never experienced before. He came to her bed gratefully, and they gently caressed each other. To her, it was like having a much-loved teddy bear, but to Max it was the realisation of a marvellous dream. She now knew she could ask Max for anything and if it was in his power he would give it to her. But he had given her quite enough, and she did not ask him for anything else.

Still, she yearned for David's touch, the scent of his body, the swish of his hair, the talks, the jokes they enjoyed after making love. Sometimes she became moist between her legs just thinking of him and then she felt she couldn't go on and would go mad. It was times like these she determinedly tried to thrust aside any thoughts of David and concentrate solely on her future as a mother and a much-loved wife. She thought how desperately she wanted the baby, and spent more and more of her time planning what she would do if it was a boy or if it was a girl. It was the excitement over the future of her life with her child that really kept her from being grief-stricken to the point of insanity.

One day Bertha commented, 'I haven't seen Max so light-hearted and spontaneous since before his first marriage. It's wonderful to see him like this, and I can never express my gratitude and happiness over what you have achieved.'

Gisela knew Bertha was very close to her brother and that they corresponded regularly. She had also been told that Max had always provided Bertha with a large private allowance, making her financially independent of her husband. Gisela also watched Justin begin to relax more around Max, and realised this was the first time her stepson had seen his father as anything other than a generous but remote father. Max was joking, laughing and even playing charades in the evenings. In fact each person's relaxation and happiness threw an aura of gaiety over the household as they responded to each other. Everyone was happy and only Gisela had a recurring pain in her heart when she thought of David.

In the second week of their holiday on the estate, the Baron announced that Gisela was pregnant. Bertha and Justin were both overjoyed. Suddenly Gisela realised that Justin must have had a very solitary childhood, and she was glad to see he was genuinely happy for her. She hoped it would be a girl, but if it were a boy, Justin said, he would take great pleasure in teaching him to ride, shoot and fish. All of which, Gisela knew, he was good at, like the Baron.

That night the Baron organised a celebration dinner where everyone, including Gisela, who was overwhelmed with gratitude at Bertha and Justin's response to the news, joked and generally made merry. Gisela warmed to see how happy Max was, and realised without any doubts at all that he would be a genuine, loving father to her child. From now on she resolved to think of the child as the Baron's, even to herself. They both liked animals, and sometimes in the mornings they would go off and ride. During these rides Max was so solicitous of her that she laughingly told him she wasn't anywhere near as fragile as he thought. It made no difference; he still took the greatest care of her. She found it very touching, and deep down she was aware of a growing sense of security. She would lose David, but it was in his best interests, and certainly in the best interests of her child. Thinking along these lines, she began to understand what compensations and wonderful security she had.

One day Max received a message from the King's Secretary ordering him to return to Berlin for an audience with the King in two days' time. Would Gisela like to come with him and stay at the townhouse? Gisela could tell he wanted to have her with him but wouldn't say so. She decided that although she was very happy in the countryside she would go with him, and suggested that Bertha and Justin should be invited to come too. They happily accepted, and everyone was delighted.

Max then decided they should give a dinner dance party in Berlin. He consulted Gisela and Bertha on who they would like to ask, and Justin was asked to invite some of his friends. When Gisela said they should ask some delightful young girls for Justin he blushed but seemed pleased, and again Gisela reflected on what a likeable person he was. She decided he had locked himself away for too long looking after the Hertzburg fortunes, and it was time he had some fun. Perhaps she could help him find a wife. Max then proposed they should give a ball. It would be the greatest ball of the Berlin season. Bertha and Justin were secretly amused knowing the Baron was really giving the ball to show off his beautiful wife to Berlin but they knew if they told Gisela it would upset her and she would become nervous so they kept their thoughts to themselves. Gisela pointed out that the ball season was over, but the Baron, full of enthusiasm, insisted everyone would come back for their ball. Once he had made up his mind to do something he was a great organiser, and everyone and everything began to hum around him.

Gisela was also a great help, having successfully organised many functions at the Embassy. The Baron now decided that the ball would be on a Russian scale — a ball such as Berlin had never seen before.

Initially Gisela was a little apprehensive. She had not come out in Berlin until after her marriage, and she scarcely knew Berlin society. Gradually Max's enthusiasm began to infect her, however, and she was soon helping to plan on a scale she had never before envisaged. This also took her mind off David, and in that way it was oddly restful. By the time they left to return to Berlin the guest list exceeded 500. The final plans would be put in effect when they reached Berlin, from where the invitations would be issued.

Baron Hertzburg's audience with the King went well, and as it drew to an end the King asked what steps were being taken to apprehend the so-called Baron Llov. The Baron told him he had made inquiries to no avail, but since the murders had taken place the Russian Secret Police had taken up the search. The King then asked if there was any indication of who Llov was fronting for, and when told there wasn't, said he would give the Baron two of his trained spies to take back to Russia and set them on the scent. They would officially be designated as additional secretaries. The King also expressed his regret at not being able to attend the Ambassador's ball, but he said many of his relatives would be attending, and were looking forward to it.

The Baron then decided it would be useful to interview Herr Shuffel, so the next day a rather nervous Shuffel appeared before him. However, when he found that the Baron only wanted a description of Baron Llov, and any other details he knew about him, he relaxed and eagerly related all he knew. It was not much, but there was one crucial detail. Shuffel said Llov had a darkish birthmark, about the size of a grape, below his left ear, and there was also a slight nick in his right earlobe. When Llov's temper was aroused, which he thought happened easily as he had seen it twice himself, the birthmark quickly turned a strawberry colour and acquired a sort of glow. Hertzburg thanked him, and said he would like him to come in the next day and describe Llov to his two new secretaries.

The day before the ball, Max brought home a package for Gisela and asked her to open it. When she did, she found a dazzling tiara, earrings and necklace. The stones were large emeralds, surrounded by small, skilfully cut diamonds, all set in gold. Whenever the diamonds were touched by light they seemed to illuminate the emeralds, which glowed as if they were alive. The workmanship was superb, and Gisela was enraptured. How glad she was to have brought some of the latest, Russian-designed gowns with her. She wanted to look dazzling at the ball.

On the night of the ball the Hertzburg mansion sparkled as it had never sparkled before. A marvellous fountain had been installed in the entrance hall, and the jets of water were arranged so that they kept live, waxed roses tumbling in the air. There was a wonderful scent of jasmine, roses, gardenias, freesias and tuberoses from the Baron's hothouses, and the hall was decorated to represent a tropical garden. There were even budgerigars and canaries flying round the top of the plants behind fine netting. There were elegantly arranged candles throughout, and several clusters of candles hidden behind coloured glass, which gave off a lovely, tinted light.

As the guests left the hall and mounted the stairs to the landing where the Baron, Gisela and Justin were waiting to receive them, they passed on every third stair a pair of blackamoors standing perfectly still. There were eighteen in total, and each held a flaming torch. They were naked from the waist up, and wearing gold and scarlet breeches below. Everyone gasped and wondered where the Baron had acquired them. Max had in fact brought in some of the servants from his estates and had them polished black. To the Berliners they were sensational, and everyone believed they were genuine blackamoors. With the ballroom decorated in Moorish style and adopting some of their customs it became a spectacular evening which people were to talk about forever.

Max and Gisela were thrilled at the evening's success.

Many of his friends commented on how St. Petersburg and how his marriage must be suiting him, as they had never seen him in such high spirits. Bertha also said she had never seen her brother so happy, telling Gisela that she really believed he had loved planning the ball, and imagined he would give many more receptions in Berlin once he returned permanently from Russia.

Two days later they returned to the country, while Justin stayed in town to complete the transfer of the Silesia estate to Gisela. He would then be going to Swabia to check on the family's interests there. As she said goodbye to him Gisela added that she hoped for two things. 'Firstly, I hope you have found someone you like enough to take an interest in among the young ladies at the ball.'

Justin flushed, then slowly grinned and said, 'Yes, I have.'

'That's wonderful,' Gisela replied. Then she added, 'Secondly, I hope you will pay us a visit in St. Petersburg and try to stay at least a month.'

He was obviously delighted at Gisela's invitation, and said he would love to come. He explained to his father however that it could not be for several months, since there was too much to do on the estates at present.

It was now a long time since they had first set out from St. Petersburg, and they only had a few days left before they were to return. It would take them several weeks to travel back to St. Petersburg and they were still awaiting instructions from the Sovereign as to who they must visit on the return journey. He was very anxious to know how much support the Russians had among the Polish magnates. It was they who really decided Poland's fate, short of a war. The King, a Machiavellian diplomat, wished to know which way they were leaning and who was wavering.

While awaiting the royal summons, they enjoyed riding and fishing together, and Max did some shooting with one of his neighbours. Bertha had gone back to join her husband on their property in Northern Prussia, but before she left she had promised to visit them the following year in St. Petersburg.

Gisela had only seen her parents briefly, when they had stayed for a few days at the mansion in Berlin. Her mother looked tired, Gisela thought, but just as sweet as ever, and she was very happy to see her. Gisela had brought her mother a very fashionable Russian sable coat, which she was thrilled with. While Gisela no longer feared her father, she still did not like him. This was partly because he was so selfish and hard on her mother, but also because he had now become a proud, boastful father. So impressed was he with Gisela's style and position, and the fact that the Baron openly sought her advice, that he had became almost obsequious. She was glad when he left them, but very sad to see her mother go. She begged her mother to try and visit her in St. Petersburg, even suggesting that her mother might travel back with them and stay for a couple of months. Her mother said she couldn't leave her husband for that long on his own, but she did say she would love to see St. Petersburg, and that she would talk with Gisela's father about them both visiting the following year. With that Gisela had to be content.

Finally, the King sent a message to the Baron requesting him to come to an audience in two days' time. They returned to Berlin, knowing they would be leaving Prussia to return to St. Petersburg within a few days. The King was exceedingly frank, and told the Baron that his aim was to undermine Russia to the extent that the Russians would have to agree to return the Danubian Principality to the Ottomans, to have Austria cede Galicia to Poland, and to allow Prussia to take the Polish towns of Thorn and Danzig. The Ottoman Sultan had agreed to ally himself with Prussia with the objective of regaining the Crimea. England was also backing Prussia, and Prussia was now to threaten Austria if it did not make peace with the Ottoman Porte.

Baron Hertzburg was impressed with the Sovereign's strategy but knew his position as the Prussian Ambassador to Russia would be challenging in such a difficult political climate. The King concluded the audience by giving the Baron a list of the Polish magnates he was to visit on his return journey to St. Petersburg. He was also sending with the Baron several couriers who would bring back his reports to King Frederick as the Baron left each of his Polish hosts. This was how urgent the Sovereign judged his mission to be.

The Baron was ordered to leave Berlin for St. Petersburg within the next forty-eight hours. When they left they took six coaches and twenty servants, including the King's couriers. In addition to the normal coach horses an additional forty were taken as relay changes. The Baron set a cracking pace, which he maintained all the way to St. Petersburg, apart from when they stopped to stay with the various Polish magnates. Now that summer was coming the roads were easier than when they had been travelling in early spring. The fields that were being ploughed on their way to Berlin were now covered in healthy and abundant crops. By the rivers ducklings could be seen, and once in a while a couple of cygnets.

The King's request of the Baron was to ascertain what the true position of the Polish magnates would be in the event of a war between Prussia and Russia. Max had already reported to the King on his visits to Count Felix Potocki and to Princess Izabella Lubomirska, but now he found out through another branch of the Potockis that Princess Izabella was negotiating with Potemkin over a major property. In addition, being an old friend of Queen Marie Antoinette, the Princess's inclinations were to support the Russians and Austrians if she supported anyone. This information now clarified where Princess Izabella stood.

They also visited Prince and Princess Radziwill at Nieborow, a grand house where Princess Helena was engaged in laying out vast gardens. The Baron found that the Radziwills, like many other Polish magnates, regarded their enormous estates as quasi-independent. In private, and sometimes not too privately, they regarded themselves as superior to the Polish kings. They lived in great splendour, on a similar scale to Princess Lubomirska and the Potockis.

The Baron believed the Radziwills' first concern would be with their own position, and that it should be noted that Prince Michael Radziwill had been one of those who had recognised the first partition of Poland in 1772. Gisela liked the Radziwills, but considered them to be totally unscrupulous in their efforts to retain their position.

They visited another branch of the Potockis at Radzyn Podlaski, where again the lavishness was on a scale that Gisela had thought only the Russians were capable of. Baron Hertzburg believed that these Potockis, who also considered themselves virtually independent rulers, would support the Russians at a pinch. They also visited the Sanguszkos at Lubaktow and the Bielinskis at Kozlawka, both of whom lived on a royal scale and would look to their own interests first. There were two leading families, however, about whose position the Baron was very clear — the Czartoryskis and the Branickis.

He wrote to the King stating that the Czartoryskis were completely nationalistic and would only ever act in what they believed to be Poland's best interests. Prince Adam and Princess Izabella Czartoryski's two sons were in St. Petersburg to ensure the Czartoryskis and their family never again supported a nationalist uprising. The family would strongly resist any partitioning of Poland. The Braneckis, however, were openly pro-Russian, and would support any position Russia took while Catherine was Empress.

Max went on to state that he was convinced that Poland would never again be a strong country while all these 'little kings,' as he called them, had their own kingdoms inside the Polish state. He believed that while Poland continued the tradition of electing kings it was not possible to have a central government of any strength. The election caused too much intrigue and unrest. In Russia, for instance, a member of the nobility could ultimately lose his lands if he offended the Czar or Czarina, whereas in Poland, because of the electoral system, there was no such fear to keep the nobles in check.

His recommendation to the King was to deal with the various magnates individually. However, he also recommended keeping clear of the Czartoryskis and Branickis, the former being wedded to the idea of a strong, centralised Polish Government and the latter because the strong-willed and capable Princess Branicki was a niece of Prince Potemkin. As long as Prince Potemkin lived and the Empress Catherine reigned, her sympathies, and therefore her husband's, were aligned totally with Russia.

Gisela was amazed at how determined and powerful many of the Polish magnates' wives were and how much they owned in their own right. It had been an eye-opening journey and she was staggered by the wealth these magnates had accumulated and retained in a country that had suffered uprisings, invasions and partitioning.

CHAPTER FOURTEEN

Back in St. Petersburg, David was disconsolate, missing Gisela and resenting not being allowed to write to her. As an attractive man, however, who was known to be in line to become an Earl and inherit one of Britain's greatest fortunes, he was much sought after. Now that summer had almost arrived, there were also more outside activities, and he was busy overseeing an English trainer race two horses he had imported from England. He hoped to make a name for himself in racing this season. But all this activity only temporarily distracted him from thinking of Gisela.

He was kept relatively busy at the Embassy and worked in harmony with the Ambassador, whom he found left him alone to do his job once he had decided David was competent.

About a week after the Hertzburgs had left for Berlin, Lord and Lady Malvern and David received an invitation to a dinner party at the Countess Nadia's. All three were delighted to accept. The Countess was a noted and gifted hostess whose company they all enjoyed, while her St. Petersburg palace was one of the great non-royal palaces.

The Ambassador suggested to David that if he had a chance to talk to the Countess at length he should ask her about the Crimea and Ukraine, as he would himself. She is a great friend of Prince Potemkin, and now possesses significant land in the south. Britain needs to know more about the area and the Countess could be a very useful source of information.

When they arrived at the palace, which was just off the Neva, on the Fontanka Canal, they found that the palace and the area around it were both lit up by blazing torches. David estimated there must be over two hundred torches.

The Countess and her granddaughter greeted the Ambassador's party warmly, and the latter whispered to David that they had caught him at last. She then laughed and added that perhaps as there were more families presently away from St. Petersburg and therefore fewer beautiful women available, he had more time on his hands. For a moment, from the way her eyes sparkled at him, David suspected she was referring to Gisela, but then he decided there was no way she could know about their relationship and was merely teasing him.

As they entered the salon they were introduced to the other guests. Running his eye around the room, the Ambassador quietly observed to David that it was a powerful and influential group the Countess had asked to dinner.

The talk before dinner was mainly to do with music, poetry and the arts in St. Petersburg, and David was once again struck by what an extraordinary country Russia was at heart. It was vast, and becoming even more so as Potemkin conquered more territory. It was still barbaric in many ways, and hugely undeveloped, but it had great potential and was now a formidable military power. Formerly it had been a power only on land, but it was now also a major force on the sea. It had several great cultural cities, in a sea of generally backward countryside.

It was a very enjoyable evening and David found the company's conversation on the whole very stimulating.

When dinner was announced, the Countess rose, took the arm of the British Ambassador, and led the way into the dining room. David offered his arm to Tatiana, who remarked, with that familiar glint in her eye, that wasn't it nice that every lady wasn't travelling outside St. Petersburg. He agreed, but warily wondered if she knew anything or was simply guessing.

The dining room was as splendid as the salon. There were wonderful candle sconces on the walls, with a massive candelabrum in the centre of the table and two smaller ones at each end. The cut glass and silver setting on the enormous table were superb. The walls were hung with embroidered pale-green silk, and flung over the polished, inlaid wooden floor were some of the most vibrant rugs David had ever seen. He was told they came from Afghanistan, Persia and Constantinople.

They had hardly sat down when Count Panin asked the Countess Nadia about what was happening in the Crimea. David was surprised at Panin's question, but Tatiana told him that her grandmother, unlike Count Panin who remained an enemy of Potemkin, was a great friend of the Prince. She had befriended him when he had first come to St. Petersburg as a young man, the son of minor gentry, at a time when she was an honorary lady-in-waiting to the Empress.

It turned out that the Countess Nadia was fully cognisant with all that was happening in the Crimea, and that she greatly approved of what Potemkin was doing. Princess Repnin, who was sitting on David's left, said very softly, 'The Countess is in favour of Potemkin's policies because he has granted her large estates in the Ukraine, and right in the south of the Crimea she has been granted an estate in Soudak where the land is said to be exceptionally fertile.'

Tatiana heard this and replied, rather heatedly, that it wasn't so. 'Grandmother has been granted the land, like certain other nobles, because she prepared a plan for Prince Potemkin proposing what she would do with it. Prince Potemkin wants to civilise the whole area, and if someone's plan to develop our new country meets with his approval he will give them the land.'

Suddenly the Countess said, 'Lord Malvern, I am leaving at the end of the week to visit my southern estates. I shall be away about nine weeks. Would Lady Malvern and you like to accompany me?'

Lord Malvern's face lit up with pleasure, then fell immediately. 'I am afraid that in two weeks' time I must entertain Prince Poniatowski at the Embassy,' he replied. The Prince was one of the key Polish aristocrats. Therefore, it was with a feeling of frustration that he declined the Countess's invitation.

Just then something Tatiana said made those around her laugh, drawing everyone's attention to that end of the table. As Malvern glanced over at her his eyes rested for a moment on Mountforte. Of course, Mountforte was the solution. The opportunity for England to learn first hand what was going on down there was too good to miss.

He turned back to Countess Nadia and asked, 'Would it be possible for Mountforte to go with you?'

'Certainly,' replied the Countess, 'it would be delightful for Tatiana to have someone near her own age accompanying us.'

David was somewhat surprised that the young Tatiana was accompanying her grandmother, and must have made his feelings apparent, for Countess Nadia promptly added that it was essential for Tatiana to come with her. 'Tatiana must learn all she can about the estates she will one day inherit. My father took me everywhere with him when he could, which I believe was one of the reasons I became so involved with business. Tatiana already reads all the reports on the estates that I receive, and next year I am going to give her one of the smaller estates to administer on her own.' This, she added, was the best way to teach young men and women to look after their inheritance and indeed improve it.

Lord Malvern's mind boggled. He couldn't for the life of him imagine Lady Malvern or any of the young women of his family administering any of his property.

After dinner they retired to the music room, where there was an array of instruments including a piano, a harp, and an organ. They enjoyed some music with Princess Repnin on the harp, while Tatiana played the piano and sang. David was impressed that Tatiana not only played well, but also had a truly sweet, clear soprano voice. Lady Malvern, who had had a little more to drink than she needed, and was being watched fairly carefully by her husband, then said, 'Lord Mountforte has a wonderful voice. Would you like to hear him sing?'

'We certainly would,' Countess Nadia said immediately. Tatiana suggested he pick something from the array of sheet music, and offered to accompany him.

David made a mild demur, but was quickly overruled. Running his eye through the music he was surprised at the catholic tastes of his hostess and her granddaughter. They must receive music from all over the world. He chose a Scottish air, which Tatiana accompanied on the piano with considerable skill.

He loved singing and, quickly forgetting the other guests, he nostalgically conjured up his Scottish homeland. When he finished, there was loud and genuine applause. Unfortunately the applause woke Lady Malvern from the sleep she had dropped into, and on wakening she apparently thought she was at the theatre. Seeing so few people, she momentarily believed everyone else had gone, and appealed to her husband for them to leave before the doors were shut on them. Then she spotted Panin, who had just stood up to arrange a cushion on his chair. 'Have you been to the loo?' she asked. 'I heard you had a problem.'

Count Panin, who did indeed have a problem, became most uncomfortable, but was saved from answering by Lord Malvern's rapid intervention. With a furious look at his wife, the Ambassador explained, 'My wife has had several busy nights and is rather overtired.'

Lady Malvern caught the words 'busy nights' and glanced over at her husband. 'You had the busy nights and the chamber pot, not me,' she said with some force. No one was certain what she meant by 'busy nights and the chamber pot' and Lady Malvern looked as if she was about to elaborate. However, the Ambassador, his face scarlet, now jumped up stiffly, muttering excuses, grabbed his wife's arm very firmly and helped her to her feet.

He hurriedly thanked the Countess for her hospitality, said goodbye to the other guests, and was just leaving when Lady Malvern asked in a loud whisper, 'Why are we going so early, is something wrong? I always thought you liked Countess Nadia. *I* do.' Then in a louder voice, she added, 'Is it Panin? I know you say he has half the spies in Russia in his pocket but ...'

Before his wife could say any more the Ambassador in a rage nearly pulled her arm out of its socket as he hastened her out the door. Lady Malvern cried out in pain and exclaimed, 'You are hurting me; you do not know your own strength when you drink too much.'

This last remark so infuriated Lord Malvern that, on reaching the pavement, he practically flung his wife into the coach. David, who had made his own hurried farewells, shot after them, but said nothing as they settled in the coach.

'I cannot understand why the coachman made me run for the coach,' Lady Malvern said angrily. 'There are no robbers or assassins around, are there?'

Lord Malvern savagely told her to shut up, at which his wife's face and posture took on a look of hurt dignity, and apart from the odd burst of hiccups she said nothing for the rest of the ride. David was sorry for Lady Malvern, for whom he had considerable affection, but there was nothing he could do to ease the situation.

The seething Ambassador then turned to David and informed him sharply that he was to prepare to leave at the end of the week for a nine-week visit to the Crimea with Countess Nadia. David was startled, as he had not realised the Countess was to be away for so long. He had been counting the weeks until Gisela returned, and wondering how he was going to stand not seeing her for so long.

'Is it really for nine weeks?' he asked.

'Yes, nine weeks,' snapped the Ambassador, 'and you are to write me regular reports on all you see, plus any other relevant information you pick up.'

David worked out that by the time he returned from the Crimea Gisela would have been back in St. Petersburg for at least three weeks. He knew he couldn't last that long. The mere thought of her aroused him.

'I don't know that I can afford to leave my work for that long,' he told the Ambassador.

Lord Malvern wasn't usually an irritable person, but he was still stressed by his wife's behaviour, and was not at all his normal self. 'I will be the judge of what work you need to do. What do you think happens if someone dies on the job? It is left and dealt with later.' Then, in what David considered an unnecessarily sarcastic tone, he added, 'Or do you think you have become indispensable to the Embassy in the short time you have been here? Well you haven't: you will go. Don't you understand how fortunate you are? It is in His Majesty's interest that you go and find out all you can.'

The Ambassador's face looked like thunder, and David wisely decided not to pursue the matter any further, or at least not immediately. Normally a trip of the sort proposed would have elated him. Now, with the prospect of it lengthening the time before he saw Gisela by three weeks, it was sending him into depression.

The next morning the Ambassador called him and said he was to go and see Countess Nadia regarding arrangements for the journey. He added that, if possible, while in the Crimea he was to try and see Samuel Bentham, who was out from England. Bentham's brother was due to arrive shortly. David was to glean all he could from Bentham, who was involved in much administration for Prince Potemkin. The Prince seemed to trust Bentham completely. Lord Malvern added that David should not try to break that trust by asking Bentham to spy. Bentham, an honourable man, would be unlikely to act as a spy, but if David was shrewd he could learn a lot just through conversation with him.

The British Prime Minister was very anxious to have all the information they could send back to him. The Ambassador clearly saw this trip as a marvellous opportunity to learn more of Russia's strength and weaknesses in the Crimea. David realised he would have to go since his request not to certainly wouldn't be granted and would only invoke the Ambassador's anger.

David decided to take his valet, Percival, two of the grooms from his stable, and the late Monty's manservant, Smithers. He had come to St. Petersburg with Monty, and had he not found further employment in Russia, would have had to find his own way home and seek a new position in London. To David's satisfaction, he had turned out to be like Monty, earnest, totally honest, loyal and hardworking.

So David prepared to see the Countess, and let her know he would be taking four servants plus a coach he had recently acquired, along with some good horses.

On reaching the Volonski Palace he was immediately shown into the library, where the Countess was addressing a distinguished-looking man. Tatiana sat in a chair next to them, listening. Tatiana immediately rose to greet him, extending her hand in the most charming way for him to kiss. She looked lovely, in a simple but elegant silk dress.

The Countess then welcomed him, and introduced him to Mr. Barsov, whom she said controlled her finances. They had just been discussing the trip, what funds would be sent ahead and what funds she would take with her. Barsov then took his leave, and the Countess mentioned what an excellent man he was. 'He was born on our property and he and Bibikov, who administers overall control of my estates, are worth their weight in diamonds.'

David asked if the two men were accompanying the Countess on the trip south. 'Only Bibikov,' she replied. She then asked David about his travel arrangements. 'I had planned on taking two menservants, two grooms and a coachman, plus three riding horses and nine coach horses,' he replied.

The Countess nodded approvingly, and said, 'I will be taking four coaches and a number of wagons, since I need to take so much down to these relatively new estates. Bibikov has been instructed to send men ahead with relay horses. I have bought two thousand more sheep and one thousand head of cattle, which are expected to arrive from France and be unloaded at Nikolaev, and from there be driven slowly to my Soudak Estate.'

She went on, 'Prince Potemkin has secured five thousand Tokay vines from the Emperor Joseph of Austria, and they are apparently flourishing, so I asked an old friend, Count Miklos Esterhazy in Hungary, if he could find some Tokay vines for me. He has sent me two thousand plants this week. They are being sent ahead with my gardener, Williams.'

'That's an English name,' said David, who was frankly astounded at Countess Nadia's energy and organisational skills.

'Yes,' Tatiana said with a wry smile. 'We are all infatuated with English gardeners; both the Empress and Potemkin employ them. The vines should be planted by the time we reach the Soudak Estate.'

David was becoming aware that there was much more to Tatiana than he had originally thought. Until recently he had regarded her as a witty but slightly frivolous beauty. He still often had the sensation that she was teasing him, but as he listened to her and watched her with Countess Volonskaya he began to realise that in years to come she might easily be a copy of her grandmother.

Countess Nadia told David that she had heard from travellers who had been south recently. Then she wished him well, adding, 'Don't hesitate to visit me before we leave if you are in any doubt about the trip.'

Tatiana saw him to the door. 'How glad we are that it is you and not Lord Malvern who is coming with us,' she said with a very sincere, straight face. David was flattered and must have shown it. Then she burst into laughter and said, 'Grandmother said, "Thank God Malvern cannot come and it is young Mountforte instead, otherwise, judging from what Lady Malvern said, we would always be stopping the coach for Lord Malvern and a chamber pot.'

David didn't know whether to laugh or not, but Tatiana looked so amused that he could not help himself. For the next few days he was immersed in his work. He wanted everything as up to date as possible before he left for the Crimea. He also checked on his riding and carriage horses, and assured himself they would be in perfect condition for the journey. As he became more and more excited about the trip he had an inspiration. He decided to purchase two wagons and several more horses to pull them. Firstly, this would enable him to take as much horse feed as necessary. Secondly, as a surprise for Countess Volonskaya, he bought two superb Ottoman tents, plus rugs, carpets, sofas and cushions to furnish them with, as well as some Turkish lanterns to light them.

Three nights before he was to leave, the Empress was to give an Imperial ball at the Hermitage. On learning that David had been invited, Countess Nadia asked him to join her party after he arrived, an invitation he was pleased to accept.

On the night of the ball, the square in front of the Hermitage was ablaze with flaming torches as a variety of carriages squeezed their way to the entrance to offload their passengers. As David stepped into the hall he faced a beautiful double staircase of white marble, called the Jordan staircase. On every second step stood gloriously uniformed guards, standing perfectly steady and holding unsheathed swords upright in their hands. David wondered how long they could stand like that without moving.

The entrance and staircase were lit by fabulous chandeliers, wonderful wall sconces, and by footmen holding flaming torches. It was an impressive sight, though not as lavish as the ball, given by Potemkin for the Empress.

As was usual on these occasions, all the guests, both women and men, were beautifully bejewelled, and the Russian orders on many of the men's dress looked extremely distinguished and colourful. David joined the throng as they climbed the stairs, moving slowly up to meet the Empress. When he finally arrived before the Empress and his name was announced by the major-domo she greeted him with great charm and David saw why so many people cherished their relationship with her. He then stood to one side to await the arrival of Countess Nadia and her friends.

Suddenly there was a quieting of the hubbub and David looked over to see Prince and Princess Barinsky bowing and curtseying before the Empress. He heard the Prince say, 'We seldom come out, because of the Princess's health, Your Majesty.'

The Empress turned to the Princess and said, 'Natasha, you have been away too long. The Court misses you. When are you coming back to Court? I am very sad to hear you have not been well; can I send my own doctor to see you?'

In reply Princess Natasha only smiled wanly, but at the mention of a doctor the Prince thanked the Empress, and said, 'We are very happy with the doctor Natasha already has, Your Majesty.'

'Well,' said the Empress, touching Natasha lightly on her chin and lifting her face so she could see her better. 'I hope you are fully better very soon, my dear. I have known you since you were a child. If I can help in any way, you only have to ask me.' With that the Empress turned to the next guest and the Barinskys moved on, passing behind a huge porphyry jardiniere on their way toward the ballroom.

This was the closest David had ever been to the Barinskys. The Prince was handsome and distinguished looking, but the Princess was flawlessly beautiful, and unbelievably fragile. She seemed to float rather than walk, and he again had the impression that had the Prince not held her she would have wafted away. In David's eyes she appeared an exquisite but utterly grief-stricken Madonna. He felt an urge to protect her, but from what? She had a doting husband, and judging by the conversation he had just overheard, the Empress cared for her as well.

As he moved toward the jardiniere he heard the Princess cry out softly that she couldn't go on this way, she just couldn't. Then there was a slap, followed by a gasp, and a silken but vaguely menacing voice said, 'You will go on like this. Remember Alexei?'

David was puzzled. There was something familiar about Barinsky's voice, but what was it?

The Princess replied, so quietly that David had to strain to hear, 'I never stop thinking of Alexei, as you know only too well.'

The Prince said, 'There then, there will be no more nonsense. We will go in for half an hour.'

Sounding desperate, the Princess pleaded, 'Please let us leave now. My grandmother is bound to be here and I cannot take any more.'

David heard another slap, a small cry, and a minute later the Prince and Princess emerged from behind the jardiniere and entered the ballroom. Fortunately they did not look behind them, or they would have seen David, who stood rooted to the ground.

While still puzzling, he heard Tatiana's voice at his elbow. 'Here we are, don't you think Grandmother and I look stunning? I know one shouldn't ask, but I also know you won't say so unless I do ask.'

Countess Nadia laughed merrily and said, 'What a little minx you are, Tatiana. Now what can poor Lord Mountforte say?'

David stared. Both women looked lovely. Countess Nadia had fine, patrician features that were slightly lined with age. She was extremely elegantly dressed, sumptuously jewelled and carried herself wonderfully. For the first time, he realised where a great deal of Princess Barinsky's beauty must have come from. As for Tatiana, she seemed to glow, and looked enchanting. So long as one excused her forward manner, he reminded himself, her precociousness disturbed him less and less.

He smiled and said to Countess Nadia, 'I could not wish to be seen with two more distinguished and beautiful ladies.'

The Countess returned his smile and thanked him before turning to speak with some friends who had appeared beside her. Tatiana took the opportunity to whisper, 'How deceitful you are to lie to my grandmother, I am sure there must be someone you think far more beautiful than either of us.'

What a knack Tatiana had for annoying him, David thought. Just when he had managed to put Gisela out of his mind for an hour or two, Tatiana would say something that not only irritated him, but conjured up visions of Gisela, either at the ball or lying in his arms. He could feel himself beginning to stir. Damn it, Tatiana was spoiling the evening for him. He decided to ignore the remark, only to be told by Tatiana. 'Don't look so cross, otherwise all the guests will think you do not like me.'

David replied, 'If you keep on talking like that I won't like you.'

To his amusement, she replied with a look of pretended astonishment, 'What, not like a great beauty who is also a fabulous heiress? Surely everyone will think you wanting in the head and also badly in need of glasses.'

He could not help laughing, and had to admit that she made fun of herself as regularly as she made fun of him.

Countess Nadia rejoined them, and Tatiana mischievously put her hand on his arm as they moved on into the ballroom and found the table reserved for them. They were soon joined by the rest of the Countess's party, which included Prince and Princess Peter Bagration, Prince Dmitri and Princess Golitzyn, and Prince Pavel Dashkov. After greetings all round, the latter began to devote most of his attention to Tatiana. David, meanwhile, could not help being conscious of a feeling of elation. He was very aware that as a First Secretary he was extraordinarily lucky to meet so many of the country's most influential people on a social basis, and so soon.

After a few minutes Prince Pavel asked Tatiana to dance, Prince Golitzyn asked Countess Nadia to dance, Prince Bagration asked Princess Golitzyn to dance, and it was left to David to invite Princess Ekaterina Bagration to dance.

The Princess turned out to be charming. As they took the floor she remarked, 'I hear you are going to the Crimea with Countess Volonskaya. You will love it, particularly the south. I am writing to my husband's cousin, King Hercules of Georgia, to suggest that he invite Countess Volonskaya to visit Georgia.'

David's heart sank. This would normally have been a wonderful opportunity, but he thought if the Countess accepted it would be even longer before he saw Gisela. However, he tried to feign enthusiasm, as the Princess went on to describe the beauties of Georgia to him. Then, to his embarrassment, she began to make subtle sexual overtures to him. As the polonaise ended, she said with a very flirtatious look that he must visit her soon. She would send him an invitation. Feeling slightly embarrassed and hoping no one had observed them, he escorted her back to the table, but made sure he did not sit beside her.

Unfortunately, the next dance he had was with Tatiana. Once on the floor the outspoken Tatiana promptly said, 'Be careful of Ekaterina. Her mother, Countess Skaoronskaya, is a great-niece of Prince Potemkin's, and he is very fond of her.'

David still could not accustom himself to Tatiana's outspokenness and pretended he did not know what she meant. Tatiana said, 'Don't be silly. I am talking of Ekaterina Bagration, with whom you have just been dancing, if you can call the way she moves dancing.'

David reflected that he had never before met a girl like Tatiana. He was also embarrassed that she had noticed Princess Bagration's blatant movements, and now wondered who else had. He certainly did not want any rumours to reach Gisela.

As if she was a mind reader, Tatiana said, 'Don't worry; everyone knows Ekaterina is a nymphomaniac. Poor, heroic Prince Peter. So valiant in battle, but he cannot control his own wife.'

David was further dumbstruck when she went on, 'Prince Peter has many friends in St. Petersburg, so be careful, he would make a dangerous enemy.' She then went on to describe various duels and deaths following adulterous affairs.

By the time the dance ended, David didn't know whether he was annoyed, impressed, amused or grateful to Tatiana. However, of one thing he was sure, he had to avoid Ekaterina. He sat down, and had just turned to talk to Countess Volonskaya when he saw the old lady stiffen and her face become a mask. He looked up and saw Prince and Princess Barinsky coming toward them. The Prince was smiling charmingly, but the Princess's face was taut and David almost thought he could see tears glistening in her eyes.

The Prince bowed and greeted everybody cordially, while Princess Natasha curtsied, but remained aloof and mute. Countess Volonskaya smiled at her granddaughter, but only received an inclination of the head, which David thought very rude. She did appear to be under a tremendous strain, but then, he noted, apart from Barinsky, everyone appeared to be under a strain.

Barinsky then said, 'My wife is not well, and we are just leaving, but I wonder, Countess Volonskaya, if when we go to the country next Tatiana could come to see us? I think it would be good for Natasha.'

Natasha swayed as if she might faint, but the Prince's hand shot out to steady her. Countess Volonskaya replied, 'We are shortly leaving for the Crimea. However,' she said very slowly and deliberately, 'if Natasha wants Tatiana to visit we can discuss it when I return.' Then, with the faintest hint of an appeal in her voice, and addressing both Prince Boris and Natasha, she said, 'While we are in the Crimea I would like to visit my great-grandson, Alexei.'

Prince Barinsky paused, looked at his wife, and said, 'wouldn't that be lovely, my dear? He is always wanting to see people of his own blood and they never have time to see him.'

For a moment it looked as if Princess Natasha was going to say something in reply then, as if summoning up the last of her strength, she merely whispered, 'I have to leave,' and almost ran towards the door. Her husband gave an expressive shrug as he looked at his wife's back. 'I am sorry,' he addressed the Countess, 'but we have had to move Alexei to Baden-Baden because of his health.' Then, before the Countess could say any more, he bade them all a quick farewell and strode swiftly after his wife.

No one looked at Countess Volonskaya. After a moment, however, the Countess recovered and said, 'Natasha was such a lovely child in every way, and remained the same until Sasha died. From there on I do not know what went wrong. She must have had a breakdown. I myself had never liked Barinsky much, but look how wrong I have been. He is proving a most considerate and kindly husband. This estrangement between Natasha and everyone else grieves me greatly.' For a moment the sorrow she felt ravaged her face and David thought she looked about a hundred. Then she lifted her head and gazed straight ahead. 'No one knows what is in store for them in this life.'

Tatiana had sat silently throughout this conversation, never taking her eyes off her grandmother. Her face was pale and terribly intense, but when Prince Pavel asked her again to dance she got up and joined him on the floor. David asked the Countess Volonskaya if she would like to dance. She smilingly agreed, but he felt the joy of the evening now meant nothing to her and that she would rather be at home nursing her grief in private.

After a little while the Countess said in a semi-confiding tone, 'Natasha and Tatiana used to be very alike, beautiful, clever, high-spirited, lovable and very, very kind-hearted. Tatiana is just like Natasha was at her age and oh, how I loved them both. Yet despite all my love, wealth and influence, it seems I can do nothing for Natasha.'

David was tempted to tell the Countess what he had overheard the Barinskys saying earlier, but he had heard so little, and it was probably out of context. Anyway, he couldn't see how it would help. Perhaps he might mention it to Tatiana later. The ball wore on, but despite Tatiana's attempts to brighten the evening, all the gaiety had gone because of the sadness everyone had seen in Countess Volonskaya's face, and in that of Princess Barinsky. They all knew Countess Nadia was simply waiting for the Empress to depart so she too could leave.

Finally, there was a blast of trumpets and it was announced that the Empress was retiring. All the guests stood. The guards saluted, and the guests curtsied and bowed as the Empress and her entourage made their way down the ballroom. Shortly afterwards Countess Volonskaya announced that she too was tired and would like to be excused. The rest of the party drifted off to other friends or, like David, left for home.

Prince Pavel tried to persuade Tatiana to stay, saying he would see she was properly chaperoned, but Tatiana was determined to go with her grandmother. David noted with some interest how Tatiana got her own way without appearing to. 'I will see you to your coach,' he told the two women.

As David returned to his apartment, he could not help thinking about the Barinskys and what he had overheard, but no matter how he puzzled he couldn't work out what was going on with the couple. The next morning, as he was walking to the Embassy, he saw Tatiana coming up the street. She seemed to be trying to avoid him, but halted when he called out. When he caught up with her, he noticed she had been crying. 'What's wrong, Tatiana?' he asked.

For a moment he thought she was not going to tell him, but after a moment she said in a tight voice, 'You saw what happened last night when my sister and her husband came to our table. Well, this morning, as I always do on a Wednesday when in St. Petersburg, I went along to the orphans' charity to find out what they needed for next week. A list was given to me and I discussed what I could give, then I headed off to Grandmother's to arrange it. Natasha used to do it before.

'Well, I was just coming out of the orphanage building when I looked up and saw the Barinsky carriage. The curtain drew back and my sister beckoned me to come over. I was so pleased because Natasha had always been a wonderful sister and we used to be such friends. Natasha hasn't spoken to me for nearly two years, so I was happy and excited. Imagine then, when I reached the coach, and before I could even speak, Natasha whispered in a frantic voice, "Don't you dare visit Boris on his estate; I don't ever want you to go there. Never be alone with Boris anywhere." Then she shut the window and pulled the curtain across. That's why I am upset,' Tatiana explained.

'I don't know why she is jealous of me and doesn't want me to see Prince Barinsky. I was only going, if Grandmother let me, to see Natasha. I have never liked Prince Barinsky, though I have to try now because he is so good to Natasha and little Alexei.'

Tatiana looked as if she would burst into tears again and David, who had never seen her like this, asked her to come back to his apartment for some tea. It was only a five-minute walk away, he told her. Tatiana agreed. 'Yes, I'd like to do that as I can also repair my face, which I am positive looks a perfect mess.' In fact, David thought she looked rather touchingly vulnerable, but he didn't say so.

When they reached the apartment, David told one servant to make tea and another to go round and bring some cakes from a shop famed for its pastries. Tatiana touched up her face, and then joined David for tea.

'Neither Grandmother or I can understand Natasha. She was such fun. Everybody loved her. She wasn't just frivolous, but headed or sat on the committees of several charities. She adored her first husband, and he her. They both loved their son, little Alexei, too. We cannot understand her now. We have always loved her.

'Apart from the huge income paid into her bank account by our father's trustees, Grandmother also pays Natasha the same allowance as she pays me. Yet she never speaks to us, doesn't want to see us, and doesn't even want to see the son she used to adore. We feel desperately sad about it. We have so much, but in the midst of all this wealth and luxury, we have this terrible ongoing loss of Natasha and Alexei. The three of us are the last of Grandmother's direct descendants and she is in despair trying to discover what has made Natasha like this.

'Prince Boris has asked us over but then Natasha just won't come down from her room and we sit there making small talk while he goes up to try and persuade her to see us. But she has never come down.'

David then told Tatiana what he had heard the Prince say at the entrance to the ball. 'I didn't know what to think of it, but I felt there was something familiar about the Prince that I couldn't place,' he said.

'I don't know what it could mean, and I don't know why the Prince would seem familiar to you,' Tatiana replied.

After that she admired the Wedgwood tea-set he had brought from England and said how elegant he had made his apartment. 'It is so very comfortable for a bachelor,' she added.

Since Gisela had chosen some of the furniture and furnishings for him, David was rather stuck for words. Then, just as they were about to leave, Tatiana stopped and said, 'Oh, what a lovely vase. Funny, I remember seeing Baroness Hertzburg buying one just like that. I had thought at the time that there was only one of each item in that shop. Doesn't that teach you to be careful; even in the most expensive places they can deliberately mislead you? I hope the Baroness doesn't see it. If ever she visits, you must hide it.'

David's thoughts were in turmoil. Did Tatiana know he was having an affair with Gisela? He never knew how to take her. She said things so innocently, yet there was always something enigmatic in her look. As soon as the Baron returned, he was going to see him and ask him to give Gisela a divorce. If the worst happened and he wouldn't divorce her, he would take Gisela away and they would simply live together.

He did his best to hide his feelings as he saw Tatiana to her carriage. She thanked him with her usual charm, and said how much she looked forward to seeing him on the morrow. As David went toward the office he wondered if his relationship with

Gisela was common knowledge; he certainly hoped not. He had no idea what Lord Malvern would say. He wished yet again that he could write to Gisela. It was all so frustrating. If only Gisela were here.

He thought back to his encounter with Princess Ekaterina, and hoped King Hercules did not invite Countess Volonskaya and her party to Georgia. She, being so intrepid and vital, would almost certainly accept, and this would probably mean an extra month on top of the nine weeks he was already committed to. If it wasn't for Gisela he would be overjoyed at the opportunity, and if only she was on the trip he would accept any number of invitations.

When he reached the office he found that the Ambassador had put together a list of things he wanted Mountforte to try and get information on. Among other things, he wanted to know what fortifications there were on the Rivers Bug and Dnieper, and if there were many additions to the fortress on the Don. David wondered if the Ambassador had an atlas. Surely he could see the huge mileage between the Don and the Bug, and the distance he would have to travel up the three rivers to find out anything. The Ambassador also seemed to have forgotten that David had been invited along to accompany Countess Volonskaya, and his movements would be limited by her wishes.

He tactfully pointed this out to Lord Malvern, who simply replied, 'This is information the British Government needs urgently for their planning if there is a war with Russia in conjunction with their present ally, the Ottomans. Therefore, Mountforte, you must find out as much as you can.' Then he added curtly, 'You are here to work, you know, and are not on an extended holiday.'

'I will do my best,' David replied, although personally he felt it was very underhanded to expect him to spy on his hostess's land with the intention of supplying his government with information that might help defeat Russia.

In fact, he thought it ridiculous to be planning a war against a country where the major political figures were so pro-British and the trade was so prosperous. The country was swarming with British-born experts, soldiers, gardeners, architects, merchants, naval officers, even people like Sutherland, Potemkin's personal banker, who was the most influential banker in Russia. He knew that deep down the Ambassador felt the same. Still, they were both under orders and must obey them. It didn't make him feel any happier.

CHAPTER FIFTEEN

THE FOLLOWING DAY WAS SUNNY AND WARM, AND DAVID ARRIVED AT THE MEETING PLACE ON THE OUTSKIRTS OF ST. PETERSBURG TO FIND THE TWO COUNTESSES IN RIDING COSTUME. This was a surprise. He had expected to ride on and off during the trip alongside the coach. While he had imagined Tatiana might also ride sometimes, he had not expected Countess Volonsky to be riding a horse. She saw his surprise, and told him she still rode round her estates. Unless the weather changed for the worse, which she did not think was likely, she would be spending as much time on horseback as in the coach.

The women were astride two spirited grey geldings that put his best riding horses to shame. When he commented on their quality Tatiana told him her grandmother had bred them at her Tula stud, just outside Moscow. They were bred from two Akhal-Teke mares and a stallion her grandfather had got from the then ruler of Tadzhikistan. This breed was famous for its endurance and stamina. They were better than Arabs, according to Tatiana, and could carry a person for longer than any other breed. The stud now had fourteen mares and three stallions, she said, plus foals and yearlings, and there was great demand for their progeny. If they had a fault, it was that sometimes they had a weak back, but Tatiana told him that the Countess had, by careful selection, bred that fault out of the stud's bloodlines.

David had not known that the Countess had a stud, let alone a famous one, of which Tatiana was clearly very proud. 'Grandmother has another stud where she breeds carriage horses and draught horses. She has even imported six Suffolk Punches from England and is crossing them with a Polish breed.'

By now they were ready to leave and they all mounted their horses, the two women assisted by their grooms. The wagons had been sent on the day before, and only the coaches remained. Both the ladies were accomplished horsewomen, sitting as if they were extensions of their horses, while at the same time managing to look very fetching. After a couple of hours' riding he was also openly envious of the Countess's horses. Noting this, Countess Nadia suggested that after lunch he should ride one of the Akhal-Tekes.

The Countess explained that they would be heading for Novgorod first, on to Smolensk, then down to Kiev where Count Finsky had a palace he wished to sell. She was considering buying it. She had never seen the palace, but now that she had a large estate in the Ukraine and estates further into the Crimea she really needed a place of substance to stay when she came to visit. David asked if she meant to keep returning regularly. 'Oh yes,' the Countess replied. 'I shall need to spend around two months of the year there.'

Several members of the Countess's staff had been sent on ahead to check the accommodation and ensure everything was ready for her, and the party stopped for lunch at an inn where her own servants had prepared the food. They were to stay that night at another inn, also prepared by their servants and so on until they reached Kiev in a few days, where they would be staying with friends.

The weather remained fine and they made steady progress. While the inn they slept at was not terribly good, the Countess's servants had cleaned it and provided mattresses, sheets, pillows and cover, so they were able to sleep the night in comparative comfort. That evening, David was surprised to hear Countess Volonskaya say they would be leaving the inn at eight sharp. The servants were to breakfast at six, and Tatiana, David and herself at seven. Everyone must be ready to leave on the dot of eight. The servants did not seem at all surprised at these orders, and he gathered this was the way the Countess always travelled.

After riding all morning, the Countesses had both ridden in the coach after lunch. David had ridden all day and was too tired to think, even of Gisela, when he went to bed that night. The following morning he arrived down to breakfast sharp on seven o'clock, to find Tatiana and the Countess already at the table. They both appeared in very good form and were looking forward to the day. Everyone was prepared for their early departure, and in fact they set off at 7:45, the Countess wishing to make good time. The two women were again dressed for riding, and one of the Countess's grey geldings was saddled and ready for David.

The countryside was not very interesting as it was not good farmland, and little in the way of crops was grown other than flax and hemp. There were oats and barley, but these crops were not very productive. Later, when they reached Novgorod, once the wealthy eastern terminal of the now fading Hanseatic League, they were to find that the city was unable to grow enough to feed its population even in a good year, and had to import food from other parts of Russia.

On the third day, David prepared a surprise. The Countess had groaned the day before that she had had bad reports of the next inn they were to stay at, although her servants were going ahead to do the best they could. David called her foreman and the others who were going with him and told them what he wanted to do. Then, very early the next morning, those who were to prepare the inn set off with two of David's servants and two of his wagons.

When the main party left a few hours later the Countess, who noticed most things, asked, 'Why are you missing two wagons, David?'

'I sent them off early, as it will help to keep the dust of the convoy down,' he replied glibly.

'How very thoughtful of you, David,' the Countess said.

By now the three of them had formed a very companionable group, and David enjoyed being called by his Christian name. The Countess always rode in the coach after lunch and sometimes Tatiana went with her, but other times she rode with David. He enjoyed his conversations with her, and was certainly learning a great deal about Russian history and politics.

Once the Countess told David that she wanted to look into building a couple of barges to bring the produce of her estates up the Dnieper River to the towns on its banks and stop off at Kiev before returning south. This would provide a greater population for marketing her produce and should bring more profit. Prince Potemkin had promised to introduce her to Samuel Bentham, who in addition to building a navy for the Black Sea, had also built barges for Potemkin. The Prince believed that Bentham would be able find someone to build what she wanted.

That afternoon the weather turned cold, so David joined the two in the coach, where they enjoyed games of cards to pass the time. Finally they reached the inn where they were to spend the night. The Countess looked out and was briefly baffled, as she couldn't see her servants, her carriages, or indeed anything of hers. Then one of her servants appeared on horseback and said they had found a better inn about two miles along the road and bid them to follow. The Countess was surprised at the servants' initiative, and said as much to Tatiana and David. 'I do hope they are right,' she murmured.

About twenty minutes later the rider turned off the road and they entered some rough pasture. Countess Nadia thought this extraordinary, and Tatiana said, 'I wonder if the servants have been drinking. Who on earth would build an inn so far off the main road?'

Suddenly Tatiana noticed a group of tents and pointed them out to the others. At first David pretended bewilderment but shortly owned up and said that they were his contribution to the journey. The Countesses were to have one tent for themselves, while David had the second tent, in which one quarter was set up as his bedroom and the rest was furnished as an Ottoman dining and sitting room. A third provided sleeping quarters for the staff.

The main tents were splendidly spacious and wonderfully furnished. The vibrant colours of the silken hangings, carpets and cushions gave off a lovely glow when the candles were lit. The Countesses loved them and were utterly delighted. David was intensely proud, for the tents looked even finer than he had hoped. They both praised him and he was particularly pleased when Countess Volonskaya said, 'I will always take tents with me now when I go on a long journey. Why have I never thought of it before? Where did you procure them from, David? They are a marvellous idea.'

David had also asked his servants to shoot some wild duck and small game, which the Countess's chef, Andrei, had worked his magic on. It was a very happy evening, as enough ducks and other game had been shot for all to enjoy. David admired the attitude of the Countess's servants, who were always helpful and friendly which said much for the manner in which the Countess treated them.

Everyone slept well and in great comfort, and the following day they set off a little later than usual as no one wished to see the beautiful tents dismantled. Finally the tents were carefully stored away, after which the wagons were sent on to Smolensk. This, Countess Nadia told David, was one of Russia's oldest cities, and it had some very ancient buildings which were much admired. 'At different times Smolensk has been tossed around like a baton,' the Countess went on. 'It was seized by the Grand Duchy of Lithuania, then reverted back to Russia, then in the time of what was called the "Troubles," Poland seized it.'

'However, it is now back for good,' said a patriotic Tatiana. 'Russia reclaimed it over a hundred years ago.'

The town was on the key route to Warsaw and the West. The river was navigable here and much river traffic flowed to and from Smolensk. The city was one of the biggest producers of linen, and a considerable producer of vodka. The surrounding forests abounded in birch, spruce, pine and oak, and as a result the town boasted a large timber industry.

The countryside had been changing as they travelled south, and there were now more hills and valleys. In the valleys cattle grazed and there were crops of rye and oats, plus potatoes. The latter, fairly recently discovered in South America, were now being planted as a profitable crop.

David and a couple of the servants took to riding ahead at times in order to shoot something for dinner. Once Tatiana joined them, and by now he wasn't surprised when she turned out to be an excellent shot.

By mutual agreement they decided that since the tents were so much more comfortable than the inns and taverns they would use them every night. This meant the wagons were always sent off a couple of hours ahead of the main party. The Countess said they would be staying in Smolensk for two full days, as she and her steward, Bibikov, wanted to see what the prices were and what the demand would be if she sent produce up from her Crimea estates. She encouraged David to accompany her to the markets, and then invited some of the key merchants back to the tents to discuss business further. The merchants, who were already rather in awe at dealing with a Countess and not her bailiff, were stunned by the sumptuous tents.

'Dealing with a Countess is practically unheard of and I tend to get the better part of a bargain, but of course Bibikov looks after the dealings once I have established them.'

The interest she took in everything was incredible, and David noticed that Bibikov usually let the Countess take the lead in any negotiations. If he had not seen it with his own eyes, he would not have believed an aristocratic lady of enormous wealth would be dealing with merchants personally. He could scarcely wait to write to his grandfather, who he knew would be fascinated.

Each evening before bed he compiled a report on the day's observations for the Ambassador. The trip was becoming more and more enjoyable and he was thoroughly relishing the company of the two Countesses. It was now only at night that he thought of Gisela, but then he ached for her. Fortunately the strenuous days on horseback meant sleep came much more easily than it did in St. Petersburg.

One morning, when they were on the outskirts of Smolensk, he sent Smithers into the city to purchase a new halter for one of the horses. The man seemed a long time coming back and David was just beginning to wonder what could have delayed him when he came riding up at a fast trot. He jumped down quickly and told David that he had seen Baron Llov.

'How did you know it was him?'

Smithers explained that on one occasion when Mr. Montague had gone to the gambling den he had taken Smithers with him in case there was trouble. Mr. Montague had told him there was no way he would agree to certain demands that were being made of him by Baron Llov. Smithers didn't know what these demands were, but he had waited in the hall downstairs. He said Llov had come downstairs with Mr. Montague, and he had clearly heard him say, 'In forty-eight hours or else.' Mr. Montague had replied that he needed more time, but Llov had shouted, 'No!' His shout had startled Smithers, who had swung round to see if Mr. Montague needed help. It was then that he had seen Llov close up. He had been fascinated when he saw that under his left ear he had a large birthmark that seemed to be glowing. He also noticed that there was a slight nick in the lobe of the Baron's right ear.

Well, today he had seen Llov coming out of a tavern. He knew it was him without a doubt because although the birthmark was obscured behind a white scarf, tied around his neck, he quite clearly distinguished the nick on his earlobe. Anyway, he had already recognised Llov's face. He tried to follow him, but unfortunately Llov was accompanied by a tall, savage-looking manservant. He believed he had not been seen, so he followed Llov through several alleys to find where he was going, but then Llov disappeared. As he began searching to find which door he had gone in he was suddenly seized from behind and slammed against a wall. It was Llov's manservant, who must have observed him trailing them. The man hit him and asked why he was following them. When Smithers denied that he had been following them the manservant hit him again, threatening him not to come spying around again or he would deal with him for good.

After David had heard Smithers's story he went to the Countess and told her what had happened. After talking it over with Smithers, they decided that, since only he knew what the Baron looked like, they would send him back into the city to try to find him. But this time he would be accompanied by David's valet Percival and one of the Countess's men, Raveski, so he would have support if he came under threat.

The men were to be as unobtrusive as possible and go first to the tavern where Smithers had seen Llov emerge. They were to make discreet enquiries, and if possible find out where he was living and what name he was going under. David was sure he would not be using the name of Baron Llov. Once they had found out the name, the Countess and David would go to the Governor of the Oblast, who lived in Smolensk, and have him arrested.

The three men mounted up and rode into Smolensk. Over lunch, the Countesses and David discussed the tragic events leading to Monty and Ivan's deaths and all three were keen to bring the pseudo-Baron to justice. Around five o'clock Raveski and Percival arrived back looking totally haggard, and leading Smithers's horse. They handed their horses to a groom and proceeded to tell their story. On arriving in the city they had stabled their horses near the inn, and decided that Smithers would go in first by himself, have a drink and then tactfully ask some questions. The others would wait outside for fifteen minutes and then walk in casually, without acknowledging Smithers, order a drink, then watch what happened.

When they went in, to their surprise there was no sign of Smithers. They noticed stairs leading to an upper level, so they said they wanted a room for the night and asked if the inn had one available. A barmaid told them they did have rooms, so they asked if they could see one. She then sent them upstairs and told them to take their pick, as all the rooms were available. Upstairs there were four doors, all shut. They opened the first, which revealed an indescribably filthy room. When they opened the second, to their horror they found Smithers. His eyes had almost popped out of his head, his tongue was severed, and blood was still trickling from the cut at his throat. He could only have been murdered in the last few minutes, yet they had seen nobody come down the stairs since they had entered the tavern. They reasoned, therefore, that the murderer must still be in one of the other rooms.

With their knives out, and in great trepidation, they opened the other two doors, but there was no one there when they heard a bang from the roof outside. They rushed back to the room in which they had found Smithers and saw that the shutters were open, giving them a bird's-eye view of the roof below. A large man, who they assumed must have been the Llov's manservant, was scaling down the wall. He must have been hiding in the room beneath some old sacking that was lying at the back of a mattress.

As they listened to the men telling their tale they were all horrified, especially David, who had come to know Smithers well and respect him. The men were sent off for a meal, and it was decided that Bibikov would then return with them to reclaim the body. The only thing to do then, David told the Countess, was to bury Smithers in the Christian cemetery. He asked her if there was likely to be a Protestant minister there, as he knew Smithers was a member of the Church of England. The Countess said there was bound to be one, since Smolensk was a cosmopolitan city, and there were a number of English merchants in the hemp trade there.

Meanwhile, they decided the best way to apprehend the so-called Baron was to advise the Governor of the Oblast what had happened. Unfortunately they only had Smithers's description of the Baron, since no one else had seen him. Apart from the appalling tragedy of Smithers's death, there was also the fact that both the British and the Prussian Embassies had to find out the real owner of the gambling den and the only way to find that information was through Llov.

They found it extremely frustrating being so close to uncovering the mystery and then losing the trail. After talking with the Countess, David decided that before going to the Governor he would go back into the town with the two armed servants and see what he could find out. So, as soon as the men had finished eating, the three of them rode into Smolensk. When they reached the tavern Percival waited outside with the horses while David and Raveski entered. David went to a table, while Raveski sat at the bar and ordered a drink. When the barman came to David's table to take his order he asked for a vodka, then asked if the man knew the whereabouts of Llov, and described his appearance. At this the barman replied coldly that he did not know anyone of that description.

David clinked a gold coin on the table, but although the man eyed the coin covetously, he still maintained he did not know the man described and David could see he was too scared to say anything. He finished his vodka in a gulp and walked out, followed shortly afterwards by Raveski.

Just then a young girl darted out of the tavern holding a baby in her arms. Looking around furtively, she rapidly approached David and nervously said that if he gave her the gold coin she would tell him the name of the man he had described. David looked at her and the baby and saw how poorly dressed they were. He promised her two gold coins, a fortune to her, if she told him the name. She said the man's name was Betskoi, and that he was always accompanied by a large, evil servant called Mischa, whom everyone feared. That was why the barman, her husband, would not tell him the man's name. She too was frightened, but they were desperately poor and needed the money.

He was about to ask her where Betskoi lived when she suddenly turned and rushed away. David wondered what had frightened her, until he turned and saw an elegant man, followed by a large servant who fitted the description Smithers had given him. The elegant man must be Llov, David decided. As the man was about to pass him he said, 'Baron Llov, how are you?'

For a moment Llov faltered and the massive servant took a step forward as if to seize David. Then Llov noticed the two armed men who were with David, raised a hand to halt his servant and said quietly, 'You must be mistaken. My name is Betskoi, not Llov.' He then bowed and began to move away, but David called out quickly, 'May I have a word with you?'

At that Betskoi stopped, 'I only have a moment, but yes, certainly.'

David then said, 'The Secret Police in St. Petersburg are seeking a Baron Llov, but if I am able to find this man, and if he will tell me who the real owner of a certain gambling den is, I will ensure that Llov receives a pardon and also 500 roubles.' He then said that he was staying in a group of tents three miles outside Smolensk on the South Road.

David noted that his opponent's eyes flickered when he mentioned the pardon and the money, and for a hopeful moment he thought Llov was going to confess. Then the steeliness returned and he repeated that he did not know Llov. It had been an interesting conversation, he said, but he was unable to be of assistance. As he turned to go David remarked that it was an unusual coincidence that Llov had a mark on his right ear just like the one on Mr. Betskoi's ear. Mr. Betskoi agreed that it was certainly interesting, and passed on into the tavern.

A few moments later, as they were mounting their horses, a scream rang out from the tavern. Llov's servant thrust the door open and the young woman informant was flung out onto the street. As she began to run David tried to stop her, but sobbing, she fled down the street and disappeared into an alley. There was no point in going after her. They knew they would never find her.

There was also no use in trying to speak to Mischa but David considered there was a good chance that Betskoi, or Llov, whatever he was called, might well approach him after thinking over his proposal. So they rode back to the tents, where they found Tatiana and the Countess anxiously awaiting their news. It was now late, and as soon as David had tidied himself they sat down to dinner, during which David told them what had occurred.

After a lengthy discussion they decided that they would contact the Governor first thing in the morning and give him all the details. David had the feeling, however, that Betskoi would either contact him to discuss the idea of the pardon and reward, or he would leave Smolensk that night. He said Betskoi had given him the impression that he was tired of fleeing and having to hide.

After dinner they were playing cards when Percival came in and whispered to David that Llov was riding up between the tents. David asked if he was alone, and was told that he was. He asked Percival to bring him in immediately he dismounted, but that he and two others were to stand ready and armed outside.

A few minutes later Llov entered, his person covered by a black cloak. On removing the cloak he turned out to be elegantly dressed, but not for riding. He explained that he was clothed in this way because he had had to give his servant Mischa the slip. Although Mischa was ostensibly there to protect him, he was really in the service of the man whose name they wished to know. Llov was certain that if ever he tried to betray that man, Mischa's instructions were to kill him.

He added that he had wanted to accept the offer David had made earlier, but he had not been able to with Mischa there. The servant had become even more watchful since their meeting, but Llov had pretended he was going to sleep and had left Mischa to enjoy himself in the tavern. He had seen Mischa head off about twenty minutes later, after which he had quickly got his horse and had ridden out as fast as he could.

Now, he said, he was prepared to give them the name they wanted providing they agreed to a few conditions. He asked if they were going to Kiev, and if so, if he could travel with them. Secondly, he wanted to know how long it would take to secure his pardon, and finally he wanted 1,000 roubles. David said he believed the Embassy would secure him a pardon almost immediately and would pay the price he asked. They would take him to Kiev if they could have his former patron's name.

David and Llov shook hands, and then Llov warned him that the name they wished to know would shock them. At that he made a choking sound and slowly collapsed to the ground. As they all rushed to his side he seemed to be trying to say something. David bent over but all he could make out was what sounded like 'Mischa.' Then Llov gave a brief gargling sound and died.

They were all shocked at his sudden death, but also puzzled, since there was no sign of why he had died. David called to the servants who were on guard outside, but they too, had also seen nothing suspicious. It was only as they picked up the body to take it to one of the wagons that they saw blood dripping from his back. When they turned the body over they were dumbfounded to find a knife embedded in his back. He had been murdered.

It seemed his servant Mischa must have been suspicious, and instead of going to the tavern as Llov imagined, simply tricked him into believing he had gone to the tavern. Instead he must have followed him, suspecting he was going to betray his master, and stabbed him before he could do so. It was apparent he had thrown the knife from some distance, since the servants had been unaware that anything had happened. By now it was too late to try to find the assassin. It was pitch black, being no moon, and he already had a ten-minute start on them.

The Countess and Tatiana's faces were pale from shock, but despite this they immediately became practical as they discussed with David what needed to be done. They would have to let the Secret Police know, and give them a description of Mischa. It was decided that they should report to the Governor in the morning and send a courier taking separate reports of the events to the British Ambassador and the Secret Police in St. Petersburg. After that, the Countess said, they should press on to Kiev.

By now David looked upon Tatiana rather like a younger sister, and the Countess Nadia almost as his own grandmother. Their experiences over the last few days had brought them all closer, and they acted as if they were one family. When the morrow dawned they breakfasted and then the three of them set out for the Governor's palace, arriving at about eleven o'clock. The Countess was received with great courtesy and David noted that the Governor was slightly in awe of her. While he did not know her personally he obviously knew much about her, and he was only too pleased to do anything he could.

After hearing their story the Governor said he would immediately put his men to work on catching Mischa, and would arrange for reports to be sent to the police in St. Petersburg. They told him they had already sent a courier with a report, but he said he would follow this up with another. They also discussed the burial of Smithers's body, which the Governor said he would arrange as he knew the Protestant pastors. He would send his people to collect the body.

He then invited the Countess and her party to stay and have dinner with his family that evening, adding that he and his wife would be delighted if they would stay the night. The Countess thanked him but said regretfully that they would be leaving immediately after their meeting with him. The servants were already packing and the tents were being dismantled.

David, meanwhile, was terribly discouraged to have got so close to finding out who was the real owner of the gambling den and then to have lost the chance. Countess Nadia was also frustrated, and a little disturbed. She maintained that when Llov had said they would be shocked when they found out the name of the owner he had looked at her in particular, although Tatiana and David did not agree with her. She had been trying to think who it could be, but simply couldn't come up with a likely name. In an effort to distract her grandmother and ease the tension, Tatiana began making suggestions about who she thought it could be. Since this included people like Count Panin, she soon had them in fits of laughter, particularly as she attached outrageous motives to each of the names she came up with.

It was on this note that they arrived back at the camp, where they were pleased to find that the wagons and coaches had all left, on time, four hours earlier. Just one coach was waiting, in case the Countess decided not to ride that day. They expected to take a week getting to Kiev, where they were to spend at least a further week with Count and Countess Kolcluley, who were old family friends of the Countess's family. In fact, Count Nikolai Kolcluley had been a great friend of her late son-in-law, and his son, Dmitri Kolcluley, and two daughters were great friends of Tatiana and her late brother. Neither Tatiana nor she had seen Dmitri for over eighteen months as he had been serving in the Crimea with Potemkin. They had seen a good deal of the girls earlier in the year, however, as they had been up for the ball season in St. Petersburg, where the Kolcluley's had a lovely, Palladian-style mansion on the Fontanka Canal.

The week-long journey from Smolensk to Kiev was uneventful, and they lived surprisingly well. In the evenings, David would always – joined occasionally by

Tatiana— go out shooting duck and other fowl. They always ate well because Countess Nadia had brought along one of her excellent chefs, who conjured up superb meals using the provisions they had brought with them, food they bought on the way, and whatever was shot. The chef, Andrei, seemed to be enjoying the challenge of cooking on the move, and each morning he would meet with the Countess and they would plan the day's meals.

It seemed that from the moment David had first had the tents erected, and Andrei found that they would not be staying in inns any more, he had taken on an extra zest for life. Tatiana said she had never seen him so animated, and believed he loved travelling on the road and enjoyed the challenges it created. Certainly he had no complaints, and he and Countess Nadia could often be heard laughing as he described what he had to improvise with that day.

David was interested in the relationships between the Russian aristocracy and their servants and serfs. For example, if the Countess's maid, Anna, thought her mistress was doing too much she would not hesitate to say so. If she thought the Countess was sitting in a draught she would immediately, despite the Countess's protestations, bring rugs or a shawl, or shut the window, and she would often scold. The Countess's steward, Bibikov, would do anything for her, but he was not afraid to argue with her over what was the best breed to raise on such and such an estate, or to tell her she had overdone it if she walked too far. For her part, the Countess was always concerned for the well-being and happiness of her people. Pick good people, she would say, and they will look after you, and you in turn must look after them.

David was also surprised at how many elderly servants and serfs the Countess had living in retirement on her estates or in her town palaces. This was based on the family creed that when they were young, the servants looked after you, and when they were old, you looked after them.

Tatiana's maid, Marie, was twenty years older than her mistress, and had been with her since Tatiana was nine. Marie still quite often treated Tatiana as if she was still a child of nine, reproving her, laughing with her and scolding her, but always with the utmost devotion. The affection between master and servant was really all-embracing. David basked in this warm atmosphere, where no respect was lost on either side: each knowing their place, but everyone feeling secure.

The scenery became more picturesque as they neared Kiev, and sometimes if there was a river near at lunchtime David, Tatiana and some of the servants would bathe in it. The horses also loved splashing around on a hot day and were fun to watch, some swimming out into the deeper part of the river and then returning, others standing in the shallows and using their hooves to splash the cooling water up onto their stomachs. Tatiana's dog Minnie would often be brought out to gambol with her pups, and she entertained them all with her antics.

Sometimes in the evening the servants would catch a lot of fish in a net or on lines and they would all have fish for dinner. Andrei could do wonders with fish, adding whatever herbs were available to create a delicious scent to the tempting flavours of the cooked fish. There were also plenty of hares around the area they were now travelling through, and from time to time Andrei would add them to the menu.

It was in many ways idyllic, with little to be concerned about. In the afternoons David would often join the ladies in the coach, where they would chat and play cards. During the day he was usually so busy he did not have time to think of Gisela, but at night he was often overcome with thoughts of her, and tossed and turned as his body ached for her. At other times he was so tired that the moment his head touched the pillow he went to sleep, and he didn't wake until around six in the morning.

One evening there was great excitement, as David had shot a large boar which was wonderfully cooked by Andrei, and everyone had generous helpings of it.

Finally, seven days after they had left Smolensk, they arrived in Kiev. It was late afternoon and the sun was fading but it still touched the lovely cupolas of the churches and the softly coloured facades of the government buildings, palaces and mansions. Countess Nadia, a great admirer of the city, commented proudly, 'Kiev is the heart of Russia, and has some wonderful old buildings. We will go to the cathedral on Sunday and you will see how splendid the churches are, and you will be enthralled with the marvellous choir. It is recognised world wide that base voices trained in Kiev are the finest for timbre and depth.'

A rider had been sent ahead earlier in the day to advise Count Kolcluley that they expected to arrive later that afternoon, and when they did arrive two girls of about Tatiana's age rushed out, calling welcomes to the Countess and Tatiana. The servants also ran down to greet the coach, open the doors and lower the steps. The Count and Countess Kolcluley appeared on the veranda and called to the girls to come back and not be such hoydens, but it was clear that their calls were half-hearted. The girls kept on chatting and laughing as the Countess and Tatiana emerged from the coach, and there were kisses all round. Countess Nadia introduced David, then they all moved inside, leaving the servants to sort out the baggage. They were then shown upstairs to their rooms, and informed that tea and other refreshments would be awaiting them in the conservatory when they were ready. The two girls, Sophie and Daria, went with Tatiana while she changed, laughing and swapping the latest news.

David slipped off his riding clothes and changed into pantaloons, shirt and jacket, then went downstairs where he was warmly welcomed again by the Count and Countess. They offered him refreshments, and the Count immediately started questioning him, asking how long he had been in Russia, how did he like St. Petersburg, how was the trip, and if he enjoyed working at the British Embassy. He went on to express the hope that the British Prime Minister was not serious about going to war with Prussia, Sweden, Poland and the Ottomans against Russia. 'We are all anglophiles here,' he said. 'And Russia is a bulwark for Christianity. I can't understand what Pitt is up to.'

At this stage his wife intervened, saying, 'Nikolai, leave the poor boy alone and let him have his tea in peace.'

The Count laughed and said apologetically, 'I am sorry. Of course, we have plenty of time to discuss matters at our leisure over the next week.'

The Countess then said that their son, Dimitri, was expected home that evening or the following morning. He had four weeks' leave pending the return to the Crimea of Prince Potemkin. 'Dimitri is expected to be made a major shortly, even though he is only twenty-four,' the Countess said proudly. The Count obviously shared her pride in their son, saying how well he had performed in Russia's last battle against the Zaparogian Cossacks. 'These Zaparogians are a very tough fighting force,' he said. 'There are 20,000 of them living on their own — they are never allowed to have women living with them, so that there are no outside distractions.'

The Countess, however, expressed her worry over Dimitri, because he had been told he was being transferred to General Suvorov-Rymmksky's command. 'Everyone knows,' she said bitterly, 'that Suvorov has no concern for his men's lives, so long as they win whatever fight they are engaged in. With Prince Potemkin it is quite different. He is famous for taking care of his men and has instructed all his officers to do the same, but even though Suvorov is under Potemkin's command it makes no difference to him whether his men survive or not, just so long as he wins the battle and gains the glory.'

The Count began to remonstrate gently with his wife, but at that moment Countess Nadia appeared. She, of course, wished to hear all about Dimitri and his accomplishments, which both his parents were delighted to discuss. They had just got into the Countess Elizabeth's worries about her son's new commander, when laughing over something Sophie said, Tatiana, Sophie and Daria appeared making a charming picture of three lovely, spirited and animated young girls. Immediately the conversation became light-hearted, with much laughter and jokes as they all caught up on each other's activities since they had last met several months earlier.

Dinner was a happy affair with lots of reminiscences. Countess Elizabeth kept a very good table and each of the courses was delicious. As David accepted a large helping of the fifth course Tatiana whispered to him that there were fifteen more to come, and that he had better be careful as she didn't want him splitting his trousers when they all went riding tomorrow. Then she laughed and said it was only because she wasn't a very good seamstress. Perhaps her maid could mend them. By now David was well used to her teasing, and he laughed and assured her he would do some press-ups that night in his bedroom to take the weight off. When she repeated this to Sophie there were peals of laughter from the girls as they began to tease David.

Suddenly a voice cut through the conversation. 'Hello, everyone, starting dinner without waiting for me?'

Countess Elizabeth leapt up and rushing round, flung her arms around the young man, then promptly burst into tears. Dmitri chuckled and said, 'I hope these are tears of joy.'

'Of course, darling,' Countess Elizabeth replied, as Sophie and Daria rushed up and tried to fling their arms around their brother. The Count stood up at the head of the table and beamed broadly while awaiting his turn. Finally Dmitri disengaged himself, shook hands with his father, kissed him three times, then kissed Countess Volonskaya's and Tatiana's hands. He was then introduced to David, shaking his hand warmly.

David saw a good-looking, clean-cut young man with a very engaging smile and a warm personality. He couldn't help thinking what a very pleasant family the Kolclulcys were. Soon smiling servants had prepared another place for Dmitri, and his family were all talking at once asking what was happening down south. The household staff meanwhile hovered round the table, straightening this and that, clearly wanting to hear all his news. There was no doubt about his popularity, and David was not surprised when a few minutes later the family's elderly nanny tottered into the room to put her arms around his neck. Dmitri jumped up and embraced her in a gentle bear hug that delighted the old woman. 'Is it true you are home for four weeks?' she asked.

His mother broke in to ask the question that was uppermost in her mind. 'Do you think Suvarov will take any notice of Prince Potemkin's instructions to look after his men?' she asked her son.

Dmitri laughed and said, 'Please, Mother, let me eat this delicious dinner. I have had a long, tiring ride over the last few days, and awful food, and I have been dreaming of your wonderful meals. I promise I will tell you all you want to know tomorrow.'

His mother positively glowed at this reference to her meals, telling the servants to put more on his plate and getting up time and again to make sure he had all the condiments. Dmitri smiled with tolerant affection as his mother fussed over him, gently teasing her as she did so. He then complimented the girls, saying how pretty they all looked, which immediately caused them to respond by saying what a flatterer he was. Or was it, they asked, because he had been stuck with his soldiers for so long and hadn't seen any ladies for months?

'It's not that,' he replied, 'but I have seen none to equal you.'

Glancing absent-mindedly at Countess Volonskaya, David thought he detected a look of wistfulness on her face and he wondered if she was thinking of her dead grandson. As if she knew she was under observation her mood changed and her face took on a genuine look of happiness as she again began participating in the conversation.

Dmitri was one of those gifted people who were able to make everyone feel part of a party. Quite effortlessly and probably, David thought, unconsciously, he made sure no one was left out of the conversation for any length of time. When the cook's youngest daughter, a child of six, peeped round the door to catch a glimpse of her hero, Dmitri spotted her and leapt up, swept the giggling child onto his shoulders and became a horse she rode laughing around the dining room. When her mother appeared she started to remonstrate, but it was clear that she was thrilled at the attention her daughter was receiving from their dashing young master. As he slipped her off his back Dmitri announced that when little Anna grew up she would be the toast of the town. Anna, not understanding the expression 'toast of the town,' wailed that she didn't want to be toasted. She wanted to marry Count Dmitri. Amid the general laughter Dmitri gently picked up the little girl and cuddled her, whispering that he would be an old man and she a great beauty by the time she was old enough to marry. But, he promised, she would have lots of handsome young men wanting to marry her.

Later that evening it was decided that a picnic should be planned for the following day. The servants were told to prepare food and to gather all the other essentials such as rugs, cushions, chairs and fishing rods. They would picnic on a grassy bank of the little river which fed into the Dnieper, where Dmitri knew there was good fishing. Dmitri had only been home for three hours and he was already the life and soul of the party. David decided it was no wonder he was rising so quickly in the army.

It was obvious that Dmitri and Tatiana were good friends, and at one point Dmitri asked her how many proposals she had received during the season. He was sure she must have been inundated with them, he teased.

'Well,' Tatiana replied with a laugh, 'I am not sure how many proposals I received for myself, but I certainly received a goodly number for my fortune plus myself.' Everyone joined in the laughter, and it occurred to David that the Kolcluleys and Countess Volonskaya would very likely be extremely happy if Dmitri and Tatiana were to marry. He also sensed that underneath his teasing manner Dmitri was serious about his question. They would clearly make a delightful couple, so he was not sure why he suddenly felt as though someone had poured cold water over him. He came to the conclusion that he just felt a little left out since he was not truly part of either family.

Countess Elizabeth then turned to Countess Volonskaya and said, 'We haven't liked to ask before, Aunt Nadia, but it is rumoured that the Empress wishes Tatiana to marry the Swedish Prince in order to strengthen the ties between Russia and Sweden.

'There is some gossip to that effect,' Countess Nadia replied. 'The Empress has not spoken to me directly about the matter, but I have managed to let her know my own views privately through my friend Countess Bruce, who as you know is the Empress's closest lady-in-waiting.'

Count Nikolai said, 'May we know your views, if it is not impertinent to ask?'

'Of course, as old friends you may certainly ask,' said the Countess. 'I have indicated I would like Tatiana to marry for love, and preferably a Russian.'

Both the Count and Countess had appeared slightly anxious during this conversation, and they now visibly relaxed. David could not help but notice that Dmitri's face also lightened.

'However,' Countess Elizabeth persisted, somewhat hesitantly, 'what if the Empress is persuaded by her ministers that the marriage is in Russia's interests, Aunt Nadia, and she commands it?'

'Well then, of course,' said Tatiana's grandmother, 'we have no choice but to obey.'

Tatiana stood up abruptly and said, 'He's dreadful. I've seen him, but fortunately he hasn't seen me. He's dim-looking and everyone I know who has met him says he is stiff, formal, unintelligent and has no sense of humour.'

'Well, his father and his uncle are certainly intelligent,' said Count Nikolai, 'though I don't like either.'

'Anyway, when he sees me he won't like me and won't want me.'

'Don't be silly. Why wouldn't he like you?' several voices asked at once.

'Because, said Tatiana, 'he will see me like this.' And with that she took a fine linen handkerchief from her little bag, tore it in half and stuffed a piece each both cheek, pushing out her face. She next took from her bag a piece of cotton and stuffed that between her bottom row of teeth and her lip, giving her a very unbalanced look. Then she suddenly began to walk in an extraordinary, tortured way across the room, which gave her the appearance of having a major deformity. Everyone began to laugh and clap, as she was so changed that she looked not only deformed but ugly as well.

Amid their laughter she took out the handkerchief and cotton, saying if that didn't put the Prince off she had been cultivating the appearance of having a fit of epilepsy and a dribble. She followed up with a demonstration that was greeted with helpless laughter, and Tatiana, enjoying their response, drew the scene out.

She then confided, 'The secret is to find out if he is intending to propose before he has seen me and then to make sure he sees me in my disguise, as it were, before he does propose. I'll guarantee if he sees me like that he not only won't propose, he will be convinced that the Russian Court has tried to hoodwink him.'

'That,' said Dmitri, laughing, 'could then cause Sweden to start a war against Russia. Perhaps history will not only record Helen of Troy starting a war, but Tatiana of Russia.'

Soon after this they withdrew to bed, but before they went Dmitri asked David what guns he had with him. When David told him he said, 'I had thought you might need the loan of a gun but you certainly don't with that arsenal. Perhaps you could be interested in a day's bear hunting?'

'Certainly,' David replied, thinking what a generous fellow Dmitri was, since he was fairly sure he would really rather stay and enjoy Tatiana's company. After setting a day for the hunt, David then made off to catch Countess Nadia before she prepared for bed. He had been thinking, and decided to ask her what she thought of surprising the Kolcluleys with a party in the tents. The Countess thought this a marvellous idea, and immediately entered enthusiastically into the planning. David would have the tents erected in secret somewhere along the riverbank, while she would talk to her chef about food for a party, and back David up when he suggested a boat trip to the Kolcluleys.

David's idea was to find a boat to take everyone downriver, then at a set place someone would spot the tents a little back from the riverbank. At that stage, pretending surprise, he would stop the boat and take them all up to investigate.

They managed to catch Tatiana before she went to bed, and she was delighted at the idea. It was purely by chance that none of them had mentioned the tents to the Kolcluleys — fortunately, there had been too many other things to talk about, especially with Dmitri's arrival. The more they discussed it the more excited they became about the tent party, and when they finally parted for the night they were still bubbling with ideas.

CHAPTER SIXTEEN

BREAKFAST WAS NOT UNTIL NINE THE NEXT MORNING, WHICH GAVE DAVID SOME TIME TO CATCH UP ON HIS REPORT TO THE AMBASSADOR. He was conscious that he would be able to find out a good deal from Dmitri about the south, but remained firm in his resolution that he was not going to abuse the Kolcluleys' hospitality by spying, whatever the Ambassador expected. If he was observant he could learn all he needed by just listening to everyday conversations. He despised the thought of deceiving these trusting and hospitable friends, which was what they were rapidly becoming.

At eleven they all set off with much merriment and whoops of glee for Dmitri's picnic spot. The servants had already gone ahead, and when the party arrived an hour and a half later everything was laid out and looked delectable.

Before they ate, Dmitri, David and the three girls went for a swim. They played a light-hearted game of water polo, the girls against the boys, but David observed that Dmitri was being just a little too attentive to Tatiana, who was clearly enjoying the attention. After they came out and had dried themselves, they joined the others for another delicious meal concocted by Countess Elizabeth's chef.

After lunch everyone lay around sunbathing, although the girls had large hats covering their heads and tops that covered their arms and necks. No girl from the Russian nobility wanted to have a brown-tanned skin.

Later the Count joined the younger members of the party in fishing, while Countesses Nadia and Elizabeth returned home in one of the pony carts that had brought them. The fishing was good, and Dmitri was congratulated on his excellent choice of a fishing spot. He and David had planned their bear-hunting trip for the following day, if the weather held, but David could see Dmitri would really prefer to stay around and see as much of Tatiana as he could. He therefore suggested that since Dmitri had only arrived home the day before it seemed a shame to lose a whole day away from his family so soon. Why not postpone the bear hunt until he next returned to Kiev, David proposed, and after a few polite protests Dmitri happily agreed.

The following day Countess Volonskaya wished to go and inspect the palace she was considering buying. It proved to be rundown but sound, as she had expected, with very little major work needing to be undertaken. While it would have to be completely redecorated and furnished, the Countess said she and Tatiana would

look forward to that and would spend some pleasurable time contemplating how
to furnish it once she had bought it. She decided to offer a lower price than was
being asked, as property currently seemed quite cheap in Kiev, with not many buyers.
However, she was confident that as the Crimea and Ukraine opened up and were
developed, property in Kiev would rise in value, although any increase was likely to
be a while off.

If she bought the palace, she told her friends, she would come down for several
months every eighteen months. The Kolcluleys were naturally delighted. They also
had an estate in the Ukraine, but they were amazed when they realised how fast the
Countess Nadia had moved. They then began to discuss what each was going to
do or was already doing on their estates. The fact that Countess Nadia already had
Tokay vines on the way to her property in the south completely staggered them. How
did she get Tokay vines? They knew Prince Potemkin had been able to acquire his
through the good offices of Emperor Joseph of Austria, but how had she acquired
hers?

It was quite clear that she was much further advanced on her new estates than
anyone else they knew of, apart from Potemkin, who was so far ahead that he had
even set up a glassworks on one. He was an amazing man. Dmitri described him as
a genius, stating that there was no country as well led at present as Russia, under the
combined leadership of the Empress Catherine and Prince Potemkin.

After a while, Dmitri, his father and David moved into Count Nikolai's den,
where they could continue their discussion while leaving the ladies to their own
pursuits. Dmitri talked of the cities Potemkin was building and of how a merchant,
Mikhail Faleev, who was a great favourite of the Prince's, was, under his instructions,
fast building a major city called Nikolaev on the River Bug. Cities and towns were
springing up like mushrooms everywhere, agriculture was being promoted and
manufacturing pushed. The Black Sea fleet was being added to, and the Cossacks,
after being defeated by the Russians, were now being formed into Cossack regiments,
which Dmitri thought might one day form the backbone of the military. They were
a naturally warlike people, he said, and he recounted some colourful stories of their
horsemanship. There were still some Cossacks in rebellion, who savagely raided the
odd settlement, but most had been defeated or won over.

The army had suffered severe losses of manpower, Dmitri said, but Potemkin
was much loved by the soldiers because he always tried to care for them. He himself
greatly appreciated what Potemkin was trying to do for the men, and he tried in this
matter to emulate the Prince, but there were many officers who still treated their men
shockingly. It was obvious he hero-worshipped Potemkin.

Count Nikolai interrupted to say, 'Isn't Potemkin very extravagant? Doesn't
he travel with something like sixty musicians, his own chief gardener, Gould, an
Englishman who has about two hundred assistants with him and creates gardens

almost miraculously wherever Potemkin wants them? Isn't he also building vast palaces for himself as soon as these towns are built?'

It was apparent even to David, with his short time in Russia, Count Nikolai had been listening to the stories that Potemkin's enemies had been spreading, and equally obvious that Dmitri did not like his father believing them.

'True,' said Dmitri firmly, 'but he is now Viceroy of all the south and that includes the part of the Caucasus that Russia holds, the Kuban, the Crimea and Ukraine. It is a vast area, and in this area he is building cities, towns, and all with churches, hospitals and music conservatories, as well as encouraging universities to be built and establishing municipal and government buildings.'

'I know of no other man like Prince Potemkin. Fortunately the Empress has recognised his genius and given him her full backing. As a result the Russian Empire is expanding at an incredible rate, comparable only to when we were under Ivan the Terrible. But remember that the Russian political climate then was much more autocratic, not liberal as it is now. The Empress is a much more humane ruler and her punishments not as harsh.'

After three years serving Potemkin, Dmitri's judgements were well-informed. He said he was aware that the Prince had many enemies at the Court in St. Petersburg, some of whom were good men like Count Simon Vorontsov, who disagreed with Potemkin on policy and principles, but most were simply jealous. They resented his power and wealth, and above all his closeness to the Empress. David found the whole discussion fascinating, and he admired the robust manner in which Dmitri defended his hero.

The Kolcluleys had arranged fancy dress party to be held the next night, so after dinner they all went to bed early thinking of their costumes. The theme of the fancy dress was early historical figures of Russia. The next day everyone was busy either sorting out and making their costumes or seeing to the decorations and food and wine for the dinner. There was lots of laughter as each tried to keep secret what they were going to wear, and they all tried to find out what characters the others were going as.

That evening they all assembled in the receiving hall half an hour before the guests were due to arrive. Count and Countess Kocluley were dressed as a Kievian prince and princess, while Countess Nadia looked stunning as Princess Olga, the first Russian of note to convert to Christianity. Sophie and Daria looked lovely, wearing the wonderful old Russian embroidered headdresses, called kokoshucks, and the loose-fitting dresses the Russian women used to wear. Oddly enough, these dresses were coming back into fashion, as now that her health wasn't so good the Empress found them more comfortable than tightly laced gowns. Tatiana came as a coquette, and amused everyone by her affected manner as she played the part of trying to be a lady, then lapsing back into that of a common tart. David was dressed as an old-fashioned coachman and looked distinctly appealing, but the star of the evening was Dimitri. He was dressed as the Tartar Khan who in the twelfth century had despoiled Moscow. His dress was splendid, multicoloured and bejewelled. He seemed to have as much jewellery on as his sisters, and when he jumped in the air and waved his scimitar wildly around his head like a whirling dervish he made a very striking sight. He looked so handsome and virile that David knew he would have been jealous if Dmitri hadn't been, underneath all his glamour and wit, such a modest and decent fellow.

The guests began to arrive and the mansion rang with shouts, laughter and music. When the dancing began David saw Dmitri immediately go up and invite Tatiana to dance, and dance she did, but not in the manner of a coquette. They made a striking couple, she in her vulgar but colourful dress, with ostentatious red glass beads swinging about in the polonaise, and he in his gorgeous Tartar dress. David asked Countess Nadia if she would like to dance, and after suggesting he might prefer to dance with a young lady more his own age she said she would be delighted. She was a gifted dancer and obviously enjoyed a polonaise. While they were dancing David remarked what an attractive couple Tatiana and Dmitri made. The Countess agreed.

'I want Tatiana to have a happy marriage,' she said, 'and Dmitri is such a fine young man. He would make a wonderful husband, and our families have been friends for several generations.'

David couldn't help but feel a little jealous of Dmitri, on whom the stars seemed to be shining. He thought of the difficulty of Gisela's and his position. Why did she have to be married when he met her? Would the Baron give her a divorce? How would his grandfather take the news that he was marrying a divorced woman, or even perhaps living with a married woman?

The Countess interrupted his musings to say that his mind seemed far away and she'd give him a rouble for his thoughts. David smiled and apologised, saying his thoughts had flown and he was just enjoying dancing with the best dancer in the room. 'Ah,' said the Countess, 'that may have been the case some years ago, but now my granddaughter easily outshines me. Look at her now.'

Tatiana was being spun round and round by Dmitri. Watching them David became convinced that he was spinning her faster and faster so she would begin to fall and Dmitri could then catch her in his arms on the pretence of saving her. He was amazed at how long she could keep going, but suddenly she put her hand on Dmitri's shoulder and stopped. David felt quite relieved, and positive that while Dmitri laughed with Tatiana he was still disappointed he had not had to catch her.

Both David and Dmitri moved around dancing with the various girls, and David danced in turn with Sophie and Daria. They each whispered little jokes to him and teased him, saying some of the girls were very interested in him. The guests were a very convivial group and David liked them all. Several of the young men were, like Dmitri, officers who were on leave awaiting Prince Potemkin's return. Over dinner David chatted with them about their experiences in the Crimea and learnt a great deal. They all to some degree resented the people who were criticising Potemkin, stating that the criticism was unjustified and only caused by jealousy. The Prince, they said, was much loved in the Crimea because of his concern for his men and their families, and because of his vision.

David received some very flattering attention from several of the young ladies, and there was general disappointment when they learnt he was leaving in a few days' time. Countess Nadia told several friends that they would be staying with the Kolcluleys on the way back, although she wasn't yet sure when exactly that would be, and it would probably be only for a night.

It was a most enjoyable evening, and only slightly marred for David when he overhead Countess Elizabeth whisper to her husband that she did hope Dmitri would propose to Tatiana soon. Did he not think they looked very happy together, she added.

In the morning they had a long, leisurely breakfast as Countess Volonskaya had told her hosts the day before that David was going to take them all downriver on a horse-drawn barge and give them a luncheon. Everybody was looking forward to this and so after breakfast, amid much laughter, they climbed into the carriages that were to take them to the jetty in the town where the barge was moored.

The barge looked very old, and in truth it was, although David had had it thoroughly cleaned. There were many jokes along the lines of its river-worthiness and whether they would sink, or be taken by pirates. Once they were all aboard, the horse was instructed to 'Walk on' and away they glided. The current was with them, and although it wasn't very strong it meant the horse really wasn't required, though he would be on the way back. David and Dmitri took turns at a rather unwieldy tiller.

The scenery became greener and more attractive about twenty minutes out of town, and soon they saw a variety of different water birds, some with their young, on the river or on the banks. It was a very restful journey and Countess Elizabeth kept saying how surprised she was that they had never thought of doing this before. She insisted that they would certainly do so again, and thanked David for giving them the idea.

Just before they reached the spot where he knew they would see the tents, David said, 'Should we find a suitable place on the bank to disembark and have lunch?'

Everyone agreed, then Tatiana said, 'Is that a tent I can see on the bank?'

'I can see what looks like the top of a tent,' Dmitri said. 'I wonder what it is doing there. How strange it looks, just like an Ottoman tent.'

'Perhaps the men should go and see,' Countess Volonskaya said. 'It would be dreadful if the Ottomans have outflanked our army.'

'Don't worry, Aunt Nadia,' said Dmitri. 'They wouldn't have a show of being here. I'll go and see who it is.'

By now, however, everyone wanted to go, so the horseman was ordered to stop and have the horse pull the barge into the bank so they could all get off. As they climbed up the bank Countess Elizabeth exclaimed that there were two large tents. How lovely they were, she said. Everyone became even more curious as to whose tents they were and why they were here. Suddenly, a Borzoi dog rushed out like an arrow. Dmitri lunged at it, thinking it was trying to attack Tatiana, but missed. The dog then leapt up on Tatiana, greeting her with obvious affection. Dmitri, suddenly suspicious, said, 'What a well-fed dog, and so friendly. Are you sure it is not your Minnie?' Then Sophie and Daria saw some young pups coming out from behind the tent and exclaimed how sweet they were. At this point Tatiana could not help bursting into laughter, and she and the Countess Nadia explained to the Kolcluleys about the tents.

They were absolutely stunned, particularly when they saw the servants, several of whom David had dressed as Turks. Everyone admired their costumes, and when they entered the tents they exclaimed over and over how beautiful they were, and how elegantly and comfortably furnished. When Count Nikolai heard that they had not been staying at taverns but in the tents instead, he exclaimed that it was a marvellous idea. Countess Nadia gave all praise to David, saying it was all his idea. They now loved sleeping and dining in the tents, she said, and whenever she was travelling in summer she would now always use tents, unless she was staying with friends like the Kolcluleys.

At that stage David invited them into the second tent, where drinks were served while the food was being set out in the other tent. There was much chatter as they sat down on the sofas and cushions in the tent the two Countesses used as their bedroom.

'I wonder,' said Sophie, 'that you ever deigned to stay at our house when you could have been luxuriating in these.'

Dmitri agreed that the tents were wonderful, adding that he thought they must be based on a Turkish design as he had seen some a little like this before and after the Battle of Ismail. His mother promptly asked him to please not talk of wars today and thereby upset her. She was enjoying the tranquillity of the day and did not want to be worried, as she always was when she thought of her son as a soldier. Everyone agreed, and Dmitri said he was sure the Ottomans had tents for peace as well as war.

'Never mind,' said his mother. 'Not another word about the Ottomans, Turks, Tartars, or whatever they're called.'

As they were enjoying their drinks Count Nikolai asked David how long it took to erect the tents and set them up. David told them that once the servants had learned what to do they were erected in less than thirty minutes.

'Marvellous,' said the Count. 'but what about the wooden floor on which the rugs and furniture are placed?'

'That is easy, as the wooden floors are in panels and simply placed together,' David replied.

Lunch was announced, and the party rose and moved back to the other tent, where a sumptuous meal was now laid out. Andrei had excelled himself. Everyone said, though none of course had been there, that they felt they were dining with the Sultan in Constantinople. Andrei was brought in, and everyone applauded his superb luncheon. Andrei beamed and beamed, unused to so much gratifying attention.

It was a delightful day, and everyone in their different ways, and for slightly different reasons, wished this idyll could go on for many, many more days. Still, they were confident that they would see much of each other in the future. David was included in all their future thoughts, and they in his.

After lunch, still laughing, teasing and joking, they slowly made their way back to the barge, which the horse then pulled back to the jetty in town. The two carriages were waiting and they drove home, stopping on the way to take another look at the palace Aunt Nadia was proposing to buy. The Kolcluleys were pleased because it was quite close to their mansion and they could all envisage much pleasure in the future. For some unfathomable reason everyone felt tired after the day's outing, so an early, light dinner was arranged and by ten everyone had retired.

The next morning they all went to St Sophia, the beautiful old Kiev cathedral. David and Tatiana, who had never been there before, both loved the wonderfully peaceful and harmonious atmosphere. David didn't understand the service, which was in Old Russian, but commented later that he still felt a sense of peace just from the atmosphere and the well-nigh unbelievable singing. Never had he heard basses with such depth and timbre, and never had he heard such wonderful sopranos, who were positioned above the main entrance door and, to David, truly sounded like angels. The others felt a swell of pride at his words since David, despite being a friend, was still a foreigner.

A slight feeling of sadness permeated the rest of the day, since the Countess Nadia's party was leaving the next day and they would all miss each other's company. 'Still, we will be back for one night, at least, in a few weeks' time,' said Countess Volonskaya, 'and then it won't be long before you all return to St. Petersburg for the next season.

'And Dmitri,' she added, 'you must take some of the leave due to you and spend it with your family in St. Petersburg where we can share the pleasure of your entertaining company.'

Everyone agreed and looked pleased at this thought, especially Countess Elizabeth. Dmitri briefly showed his feelings for Tatiana as he gazed at her before turning to thank her grandmother. Tatiana, David noted, gave nothing away apart from a genuine smile for everyone.

They again had an early night, as Countess Volonskaya wanted to leave by eight thirty in the morning. After briefly slipping outside, Dmitri arrived back to find that Tatiana had gone to bed, having pleaded a headache. Calling goodnight to everyone she had added, 'Tell Dmitri I look forward to seeing him in the morning, but I must go, my headache is getting worse.'

Countess Elizabeth was most sympathetic, asking, 'When did it come on? You were so sprightly up until now.'

Tatiana said that occasionally a headache came on suddenly, and the only cure was to lie down. David didn't believe her, as he had never heard of these headaches before, and he thought he saw a puzzled look flit across her grandmother's face. He wondered if Tatiana was simply trying to avoid Dmitri, yet they had seemed so happy together.

When Dmitri returned and found Tatiana gone he looked disappointed, but quickly became the life and soul of the party again, until they all decided it was time they too retired for the night. David thought no one could help but like the dashing but kindly Dmitri. The day before Count Nikolai had proudly told him of the two medals his son had won in the last two battles Russia had fought. One was for his part in the campaign against the Tartars, and the other for his valour in the battle of Ismail. He said, he never talked much about Ismail for while proud of the victory, Dmitri thought there had been too much savagery with the women and children. Dmitri, was a chivalrous soldier with a high code of honour. Sometimes his mother and he thought it too high, and that Dmitri wasn't concerned enough about his own safety.

The next morning as they were finishing their breakfast, at around eight o'clock, a servant announced that Madam Bartenev was here and wished to see Countess Volonskaya.

'Good heavens,' said the Countess. 'I haven't seen her for years; in fact I thought she had died. Please show her in.'

A tiny figure appeared in the doorway and Countess Volonskaya rose quickly to embrace her, saying, 'Amelia, my dear, what a lovely surprise! I haven't seen you for well over, let me see, it must be fifteen years.'

The old lady replied, 'I've become something of a recluse, Nadia, since my husband died, but I just returned from the country last night and only then did I hear from my steward that you were in town. It was too late to call then, and knowing you of old I thought you would leave early. I am so glad to catch you. You look so well, my dear,' she said, 'and as usual causing a stir wherever you go. Everyone knows you are here. You are the glamorous, fabulous Countess Volonskaya, but it has always been so, hasn't it, my dear?'

Nadia said, 'Nonsense,' and began to describe to the others how her old friend, Amelia Bartenev, was once one of the great beauties at Court and could have had the pick of any of the eligible bachelors. She chose instead a charming, scholarly professor and retired from social life, other than seeing a few old friends. Until her husband died she had lived happily ever after, as they say in fairytales. Amelia denied ever having been a beauty, but was obviously very pleased to hear Nadia, a great beauty herself, describe her in this way.

Their departure was delayed as Countess Elizabeth set up another place at the table for Madam Bartenev. As she was about to leave, around an hour later, Madam Bartenev asked her friend, 'And how is your great-grandson, Alexei, faring?'

Sadly the Countess said that she never saw him, as he was in poor health and had to stay in the country. He was never brought to St. Petersburg, and so she had not seen him for two years.

'When I decided to come to the Ukraine and Crimea, Prince Barinsky, his stepfather, told me that Alexei had been taken to Baden-Baden a couple of weeks earlier to see if they can cure him there.'

'Did you say Baden-Baden?' Amelia asked.

'Yes. Barinsky told me so just before I left St. Petersburg. He said what a shame it was that I had missed him, because Alexei would have loved to have seen me.'

'That's extraordinary,' said Amelia, 'because my steward's cousin is married to Barinsky's bailiff. She has a rather hard time with her husband, I gather. He saw his cousin yesterday and gave her some clothing. Barinsky is a very difficult man, and has always been mean.' She then turned to the Kolchuleys and said, 'I am related to the Barinsky family and never liked them, but being related, I can say what I think about them.'

'What has this to do with Alexei?' asked Nadia.

'Oh, didn't I say?' Amelia replied. 'Well, yesterday, knowing you were here, Pavel, my steward, asked his cousin how the boy was. She said he was holding his own, but that it's not much of a place for a little boy. And it really isn't. I remember going there as a child over sixty years ago and it was damp and mouldy, a sinister-looking fort, which is what it originally was. It was built by the Poles when they held this area eons ago.'

Nadia was now looking quite agitated, and asked, 'Do you mean that Alexei is still at this place near here?'

'Well, yesterday he was,' said Amelia.

'Where is it?' asked Nadia, suddenly becoming very stern. Apparently by carriage it was about six hours to the fort, but by horseback it was possible to travel cross country and it would probably only take about two and a half hours.

'How many servants are there?' Nadia asked, to which Amelia replied that she believed there were four.

Nadia had now taken over the conversation, and she asked Amelia to say nothing to her steward or anyone else until she sent word. She then said they were going to the old fort, which was called Branka, straight away. Turning to David, she asked him if he would come with her and Tatiana. Dmitri offered to assist, saying he knew the way to Branka, and the Countess accepted gratefully. She then said that she would leave one travelling coach with the Kolcluleys and pick them up later, if they didn't object. Tatiana's and her maidservants would also remain, but she would send the rest of the entourage on towards her estates in the Ukraine on the understanding that she would join up with them as soon as possible. Then she suddenly added that six of her guards were to go with the servants and six would remain to escort her. She asked for her best horses to be saddled for Tatiana, David, herself and the guards, and as a last thought told her foreman to bring Minnie with them, as she was sure Alexei would love to see her. For a moment there were tears in her eyes.

They were all astonished at the way the Countess had taken charge so swiftly: as Amelia was to say afterwards, she should have been a general. As soon as the horses were brought around and the guards assembled, she flung her arms around old Amelia and said, 'Thank you, my dear, you have no idea how wonderful it has been to see you. I believe you may also have helped me solve a problem that has been worrying me for nearly two years.'

She then said goodbye to the Kolcluleys, who wished her luck and told her to take care. Tatiana and David said their farewells, then the four of them mounted up and, accompanied by the guards, set off. Once outside the gate, the Countess set the horses to a fast trot. They knew her horses could keep up this pace all day. For around twenty minutes Dmitri, Tatiana and David said nothing, waiting for the Countess to speak. Finally, she said that she couldn't understand what was going on. Prince Boris had definitely told her that Alexei had been sent to Baden-Baden to see some doctors there. Why would he say that if Alexei were still here?

The Countess then began to wonder aloud if her early impressions of Barinsky had been right. Tatiana chimed in, saying she had never liked Barinsky, and still didn't. She had always felt there was an aura of evil around him and that he didn't tell the truth. The Countess responded that that was what she used to think until he married Natasha. Outwardly, at least, he had appeared devoted to her. Since their marriage she had seen very little of Barinsky, except at the odd reception, or the couple of times he had visited her to apologise for Natasha's refusal to receive any of the family.

Dmitri mentioned that although he only knew Prince Boris by sight, he was disliked among the young officer corps. He had the reputation of being a bully, and there were also rumours of his cheating at cards, which he thought was why the Prince had resigned his commission. These were only rumours, however, because Barinsky was at least ten years older than him, and so it was only hearsay.

By now they were all feeling disquieted and unconsciously pushed their horses faster. The terrain had become somewhat hilly, and Dmitri led them into a defile between two hills. It widened out into a lovely valley where here and there stood little groups of thatched peasant houses. According to Dmitri, this land had in the past belonged to the Barinskys, before Prince Boris's father, the old Prince, had gambled it away. A merchant called Zorich now owned it, but Dmitri had never heard of him visiting the valley, only his steward.

After another half an hour or so they began to climb a gentle hill, then they came across a rough road that Dmitri said led to the fort. Soon they breasted the hill and saw below them a small, swampy valley. On the top of the next hill was a grim-looking three-storey tower that Dmitri said was the old fort Branka.

'What a dour-looking place,' David couldn't help remarking, and Tatiana agreed it looked an odd place to keep a little boy. When they rode down into the valley they found the ground was so swampy that if they moved off the rough road their horses' hooves sank up to a foot in mud. There seemed to be mosquitoes everywhere too.

The Countess's silence and the stern look on her face made the others hesitate to speak, even among themselves. Once through the swamp they kept to the road, which wound its way up the hill so the fort disappeared from sight for a time. Then, over the next rise, it loomed above them. It must once have been a formidable bulwark against any enemy, but now it was much neglected and looked from the outside to be barely habitable.

Minnie bounded round a curve in the road and set up a hare, then rushed off after it, barking madly. Tatiana, who had been looking up at the fort, saw a little face appear at a window on what looked like the third floor.

'Look, Grandmother,' she said excitedly. 'See that face? It could be Alexei.'

But the Countess had been soothing her horse, which had shied and turned skittish when Minnie barked unexpectedly, and by the time she turned back the face had gone.

The party rode up to the fort, now filled with anticipation. The massive door had opened as they approached, and at its entrance stood a man with a gun. Fearlessly, the Countess rode straight up to the man and said she was Countess Volonskaya and she had come to see her great-grandson. She demanded that the man tell her who he was.

The man replied that he was bailiff to Prince Barinsky, and his name was Joseph. Then he added that no one was allowed into the fort without a letter authorising them to enter from Prince Barinsky. The Countess replied that this was nonsense and certainly did not apply to the family. The truculent Joseph, who by now had been joined by another villainous-looking man, reasserted that no one could enter the fort without authority from the Prince. He began to shut the heavy doors, but they took time to push shut and both David and Dmitri, plus two of the guards, jumped off their horses and seized the entrance. The guards then overwhelmed the servants, but not before Joseph had shouted out to someone behind him. The guards tied up the two men, and the rest of the party moved into the fort.

There seemed to be no one about, but eventually they found a woman hiding in the kitchen, which itself was in a filthy state. She denied any knowledge of a boy, despite Tatiana saying she had seen a boy at the window. They continued to search the fort, and although there were signs in one of the bedrooms on the third floor that a little boy had lived there, no boy was found.

The Countess, who was now inwardly frantic with fears for her great-grandson, was just about to order the guards to extract the truth from the two captive servants when Minnie, having lost the hare she had been chasing, came running up the stairs to rejoin her mistress. All of a sudden Minnie began scratching and whining at a door behind the Countess that was so skilfully concealed they had not noticed it. They tried to open it but it appeared to be locked from the inside, and it was too stout to be broken down, even when the men ran at it. Meanwhile Minnie kept whining and barking, trying to get in. Everyone was now wondering if Alexei was behind the door, and if so was he dead, or was he locked in with a jailer?

David decided to go and find an axe, but when he got down to the kitchen he had another thought. Taking hold of the woman they had encountered earlier, he said that if she did not come up and tell whoever was in the locked room upstairs to open up he would lock them all up until the door was opened. The woman then confessed that Alexei was there, but they dare not let the boy leave the fort or Prince Barinsky would kill them all. David promised to protect them from the Prince, provided the boy was alive and that they would bear witness against the Prince, who David said would then go to jail. The frightened woman was not totally convinced, but saw no alternative but to go up with Lord Mountforte.

When they reached the third floor the woman went to the door where the others were standing and shouted out that Anna was to open the door and let the boy out. A guttural, unintelligent flow of words came from behind the door. Fortunately, the woman from the kitchen seemed to understand what it meant and repeated that Anna was to open up. The door then opened quickly, almost knocking over Tatiana, who had been standing quite close. A large, shambling woman with a retarded-looking face broke out, pulling a slight-looking, gagged boy with her.

Everything was forgotten as they looked at the boy. There was perfect silence for a moment, then Countess Nadia threw her arms around him, wailing 'Alexei.' She kissed the boy, and then, with tears running down her face, she began gently to remove the gag. No one had seen the Countess cry publicly before. It briefly paralysed the group, before Tatiana was also hugging and kissing the little boy with tears streaming down her face as well.

Meanwhile Minnie had also been trying to kiss Alexei, and she suddenly gave a great push and ended up with her paws on his shoulders and nearly licked him to death. Alexei had at first clasped his skinny arms around his grandmother and just hugged her, laying his head on her breast, saying nothing. Then, as he became somewhat more composed he hugged his Aunt Tatiana, who lavished hugs and kisses on him, then he wrapped his arms around Minnie, who his grandmother said had found him. Then Alexei shyly thanked the men and looked back at his grandmother.

Meanwhile the Countess had been observing his shabby clothes and how underfed he was. She decided they must do something immediately about getting him some food or he would be too weak to ride back to Kiev with them. She turned to the woman from the kitchen and asked what food there was in the house. She then told her to go and quickly make some soup, and to instruct the other woman to make a fire in the warmest room downstairs. Both servants seemed happy to get away, and the rest of the party followed them down to the room in which the fire was to be lit.

One of the guards was ordered to watch the two women, while the other three were told to go to the two guards who were with the menservants, tell them to find some transport, and to take the men back to Kiev. The other three guards were then to wait, as two of them could bring the women in later and one would ride with the Countess's party.

Once the fire was going and the broth brought in for Alexei, his grandmother quietly began questioning him. No, he said, his stepfather had only come and visited the fort once since he had put Alexei here. He thought it was about six months ago, because it was winter. No, he had never left the fort or seen anyone since he had been here, other than the servants. No, he had never seen any doctors. No, his mother had never been to see him and he knew she wouldn't. When asked why this was, Alexei answered that when his stepfather was taking him from the St. Petersburg house his mother had been sobbing and had tried to hang on to him. His stepfather had hit her and told her she would never see Alexei again. Quietly, Alexei said he had told his mother that if she tried, or went to her grandmother, he would have Alexei killed.

He said when Barinsky came down to the fort it was only to cut off his finger to take back to his mother who, Barinsky said, wouldn't do as she was told. He held out his left hand and they saw that the finger next to his little finger had been cut off at the first joint. The end of the joint was splayed and looked slightly deformed. They were to find out later that this was because nothing had been done to stop the finger bleeding, other than wrapping a dirty cloth around it. Just for a moment, the old Countess looked as if she was going to faint. Tatiana, crying, rushed over to cuddle the boy as he sat on his great-grandmother's knee. David and Dmitri swore oaths and didn't even think of apologising. No one could quite believe what had happened to this little boy of seven, who quietly related his story.

No, he had had no tutors in the eighteen months he had been there. Yes, he had been allowed out in the back courtyard for an hour at a time, though only when it rained, but he didn't like going out there because he had to stay in his wet clothes until they dried on him.

The more they listened to him, the more they marvelled at how he had remained sane. He did have friends, he told them. Two birds would come every morning and every evening to his window and stay for about thirty minutes. He would talk to them and give them some of the black bread he had saved for them from his lunch. The other friend was a mouse that used to come in at odd times during the day, and they would play with some small pieces of wood Alexei had picked up in the courtyard.

This was all said without any emphasis or self-pity, and it was frightening to see this self-restraint and discipline in such a young boy. It seemed incredible that half-starved he had not broken down under the duress he had suffered.

Suddenly he said he knew that since his mother could not come, his grandmother would one day find him and come and save him. Finally the strain seemed to break through and he burst into tears. Nadia and Tatiana could not restrain their own tears as they hugged the little boy, while Minnie tried vainly to lick him.

Then the Countess seemed to pull herself upright, and said it was time they left the fort and set out back to the Kolcluleys. Since it was too far for Alexei to ride in his present condition, she asked David and Dmitri to take turns at letting him ride with them. They agreed readily, and Dmitri said he would take Alexei first. A few minutes later they were all mounted and had set off for Kiev.

They had only been riding for about fifteen minutes when the rest of the party heard little Alexei laughing. It seemed incredible that he should have such spirit after all he had been through, and they were all grateful to Dmitri for using his particular gift for making people happy. Alexei was so happy riding with him that it was agreed that he should ride all the way with Dmitri.

As she rode, the Countess's thoughts swung back and forth between joy at having Alexei back, hatred of Barinsky, and love, remorse and fear for Natasha. Long before they reached Kiev, she announced that she would send one of the guards as a courier to her steward, Bibikov. He would take a letter advising Bibikov that for family reasons she had to return immediately to St. Petersburg, with instructions about what he should do. The courier would leave Kiev that night, as soon as she had written the letter. He was to return as quickly as possible and bring a groom up with two teams of coach horses. She would leave her maids at Kiev until the horses arrived — she and Tatiana would do without maids until they got back to St. Petersburg. She would take the second coach's team of horses along with her as well as a change for her coach so she could make the best speed.

Another guard was to be sent straight to her stables in St. Petersburg and have grooms bring down more horses to provide a change. They would meet up at a place that was two days out from St. Petersburg. The guards were told that when they reached Kiev they were to go and buy sufficient torches so that the coachman would be able to see the road if she wanted to travel by night. David offered to ride ahead and arrange for Barinsky to be apprehended, but the Countess said she would rather wait, as she was worried about what would happen to Natasha. They would all return to St. Petersburg together, and then she would confront Barinsky. She added, however, that she would be grateful if David was there at the confrontation.

Although none of them had mentioned Princess Natasha, they had all been thinking about the agony she must have been going through. David now told the Countess about the conversation he had overheard at the ball, which he now understood only too well. Tatiana was full of remorse at how badly she had misunderstood her sister when she had hissed to her from the coach not to go to the country and never to be alone with Barinsky.

The Countess vowed that Barinsky would pay for all he had done, and she began to think of all the wonderful things she would do for Natasha when she arrived back in St. Petersburg and brought Natasha to her palace. She imagined the overwhelming joy Natasha would feel when she saw her son again, and these thoughts, and her hatred for Barinsky, sustained her through the long day.

Finally they arrived at the Kolcluleys' mansion, where they were received with delight and enormous pleasure. Countess Elizabeth asked her chef to make a special broth for Alexei, and as soon as he had eaten he was taken up to bed by his great-grandmother and his aunt. After prayers, and partway through a story, the little boy fell asleep.

Over dinner the whole tale was related to Count Nikolai and Countess Elizabeth, who were horrified. Then the discussion turned to Natasha, and the dreadful ordeal she had suffered. What could be the Prince's motives, they wondered? And what was the best way for Countess Nadia to handle him? Natasha must get a divorce immediately, they all agreed. The Countess Nadia's friendship with the Empress Catherine would help there, as she was sure the Empress would expedite the process when she was told all the facts.

They had all been struck by how composed and adult little Alexei had sounded as he told his story, and they hoped he would not break down now that his ordeal was over. What a fine young man he would grow into. Countess Elizabeth swelled with pride when told how Dmitri had Alexei laughing shortly after they left the fort.

As everyone's attention turned to Dmitri, the Countess said sombrely that she also had some news. She had not wanted to mention it straight away because she did not want to spoil Alexei's release from bondage, as she put it, but while they were at the fort a courier had come from General Suvorov calling Dmitri back to the Crimea. Dmitri looked startled and slightly dismayed at this news, but his natural sunny nature soon asserted itself. In an effort to cheer up his mother and sisters, he said he was probably being called back to accept his promotion to major. Jestingly he added that perhaps they had decided to jump a couple of promotions and make him a colonel. 'No, no,' cried his mother, 'there are sixteen other officers on leave in Kiev and they too have been called up.'

'Well, then,' said Dmitri, 'it must be that Prince Potemkin's siege of Ochakvo is about to end and the assault about to begin. What a battle it will be, the Ochakvo Fort is said to be impregnable.'

As soon as he said this he realised that he had made a mistake, as his mother immediately flew across to put her arms around him, saying she had had a presentiment the previous night and dreamt he would not come back.

Count Nikolai promptly said, 'Lizzie, my dear, you have had the same dream every time Dmitri has left home. Remember, you even had it when he went to the Pages school as a cadet.'

Not at all mollified, the Countess Elizabeth went on to say that Suvorov was brutal, not a gentleman, while Dmitri was just the opposite, and wonderfully kind, with no malice in him. Count Nikolai responded that Dmitri took after her in character, at which the Countess suddenly stopped and said to him, 'Nicky, how good you are to me, and how I love you.' Then she went to where he was sitting and kissed him on the cheek.

David, feeling a sense of loss for the parents he never knew and the sisters and brothers he had never had, made up his mind that when he married Gisela they would have lots of children and bring them up to love each other, just like the Kolcluleys.

No wonder Countess Volonskaya would be happy to see Tatiana marry Dmitri, he thought. Once again he felt a pang of regret at the thought of Tatiana marrying, and he wondered why. After all, he now thought of her as a sister, and if she married Dmitri he would really have a sort of brother. What was wrong with him? Perhaps it was because, though he deeply loved his grandfather, and had been greatly loved in turn, he had never experienced the spontaneous love and warmth of a family.

Shortly after dinner they retired to bed, as Countess Volonskaya wanted to leave at first light in the morning. She apologised for leaving so early, but the Koluckeys well understood the need to get back to St. Petersburg as quickly as possible, especially when Countess Nadia admitted she was now desperately worried about Natasha. Dmitri said he would ride alongside them for a couple of hours, which immediately led Sophie and Daria to say they would do the same. David thought Dmitri had probably hoped to spend some time with Tatiana on his own, but he agreed willingly that his sisters should accompany him.

The Countess said that once the other horses caught up with them, she was determined only to spend six hours a night at each tavern, and that was only so that the horses could be rested. She would have thirty-two horses for one coach when the other two teams arrived, and each team of eight horses would do six hours each. It would still be hard going for the horses, but she must reach St. Petersburg in as short a time as possible.

They set off with the Countess and Alexei in the coach, since the boy was still too weak to stay long in the saddle. They all knew too that his great-grandmother wished to cosset him, and could not bear to let him out of her sight. David and Tatiana rode, and for two hours were accompanied by Dmitri and his sisters. Dmitri rode beside Tatiana quite often, but what they talked about David didn't know, as he had Dmitri's charming sisters beside him most of the way. He knew they liked him and even wanted to flirt with him, but he had no heart for flirting as it reminded him of Gisela and his love for her. However, he enjoyed their artless chatter and talk of their family. They told him how they missed Dmitri when he was away, how he played jokes on them all, and the funny letters, often with drawings in them, that he used to send them from the Crimea. Sometimes his letters were hilarious, but other times they were sad, particularly if the army sacked any town or city needlessly. If any of the officers mistreated their men Dmitri became very angry. That was one of the main reasons he liked Potemkin so much, they said.

'Did you know that in this terrible last winter when the troops were laying siege to Ochakvo and lying in dug-outs, Prince Potemkin made sure the men were all supplied with a fur coat, hat and felt cloth to go over their boots?' Sophie asked. 'Some of the officers thought this was pandering to the rank and file, but those who did not take such steps lost men to the cold and to sickness. Prince Potemkin had also moved out of his palatial headquarters, turning it into a hospital and living in much smaller quarters. That is the sort of man he really is, under all the pomp and grandeur.'

The sisters obviously adored their brother and took everything he said as gospel, but well they might, thought David.

Finally Dmitri said that they must turn back to Kiev, so they halted to say their goodbyes. Everyone was sorry to part, and there were lots of last minute ideas for what they would do when they all met up in St. Petersburg. The Countess crowned their suggestions by saying that if Dmitri arrived on leave during the festive season she would give a grand ball. She would find out when the Empress was free and ask her to honour the ball by her presence.

'What if Dmitri cannot come during the season?' asked the irrepressible Sophie.

'In that case, I will give a skaters' dance and supper on my estate up near the Peterhof.' Dmitri said he would hate to miss that, so the Countess laughingly asked Alexei what she should do. Dmitri was already a hero to Alexei, so he said she should do both.

'Agreed,' said the Countess, with fond indulgence, then it was time to go their different ways.

Two days later the extra horses arrived from the south, and their travelling pace, already a cracking one, further increased. Two horses were lamed on the way, but it made no difference to their speed. They were simply retired with a groom, who was told to bring them home slowly, and other horses rotated to take their turn in the harness.

Finally one evening they arrived in St. Petersburg. It was ten o'clock, but the Countess was determined to call at the Barinsky Palace immediately. Alexei was taken inside the Volonski Palace, where he was welcomed with amazement and delight by all the servants who remembered him. As most of the Countess's servants seemed to stay forever, almost everyone knew him. He was allowed to take Minnie up to bed with him, fussed over and served some broth in bed, then quickly fell asleep.

In the meantime, David and the Countess, taking six servants and guards, left for Barinskys Palace. Tatiana had pleaded with her grandmother to let her come, but was told she must stay behind with Alexei in case he woke and was frightened. While this placated Tatiana, David knew the Countess was really trying to keep her out of danger, since she didn't know what would happen at the palace. She had earlier, privately told David, Dmitri and Count Nikolai that she thought Barinsky must be mad. Count Nikolai had said there had been a dangerous streak in Boris's father, and suggested that perhaps it had degenerated into madness in the son. This frightening thought had been growing in the Countess's mind ever since they had left Kiev.

When they arrived at the palace they found it shuttered up for the night. Leaving the guards mounted on the coach behind them, David, who carried a pistol hidden in his coat pocket, and the Countess walked up to the door. David knocked vigorously and the door was cautiously opened several minutes later. The Countess announced that she would like to see her granddaughter, Princess Natasha, and Prince Boris immediately. The servant hesitated, then said he would have to ask Prince Boris.

'Don't ask,' said the Countess, 'just tell him I am here while showing me the way to Princess Natasha's room.'

The servant then said that the Prince and Princess had gone into the Prince's study around six and had not yet come out. Alarmed, the Countess asked if they had had dinner, or been seen by anyone? No, the servant said, the Princess always dined in her room, and one never asked the Prince when he wanted dinner. He informed the servants when he required a meal, as he often went out quite unexpectedly.

The Countess then ordered the servant to take them to the study. The man, who knew the Countess and was clearly in awe of her, took her upstairs to the study. They knocked but no one answered and no sound was coming from the room. They found the door was locked, with no key in it, which meant someone inside had locked it. The Countess told the servant to force the door, and when he was unable to open it

David joined in. After several runs at it, the lock gave and the door burst open, taking David and the servant with it.

They entered to an incredible scene. Prince Boris was sprawled on the ground, shot through the head, a dreadful mess. On a couch on the far side of the room Princess Natasha lay as if sleeping. The Countess and David both ran across to her and the Countess took her hand. David felt for her pulse and found there was none. She was dead. In death, David thought, she seemed even more beautiful than she had in life. With her perfect skin, lustrous hair and classical face she could have been the model for any statue requiring timeless beauty. He felt a deep despair that he had never known her and now never would.

The Countess was kneeling and praying over her, while tears ran down her cheeks, fell onto the Princess and gently washed over her face. Then an almost primitive cry came from the Countess and she slowly rose, walked over to the Prince, bent, and spat on his face. Coming from Countess Nadia the act seemed terribly defiling.

She was moving slowly back to Natasha when David noticed a letter on the writing desk. He crossed over and picked up the first page. The letter was addressed,' Dear Grandmother.'

David turned to the Countess and said, 'This is for you, from your granddaughter.'

As if in a dream, the Countess slowly went to the desk, sat down and began to read.

The tears gradually became a watercourse as the Countess, now looking very old and frail, read her granddaughter's letter. Every so often she made a little cry or a sob would burst out. When she had finished she wordlessly passed the pages to David, then she went and sat beside Natasha, stroking her face, her hair and her hands, and repeatedly kissing her.

As David read the letter he began to conjure up what a horrifying eighteen months Princess Natasha had had since her marriage. Her letter to her grandmother told the whole horrifying tale of her marriage.

'After we had married quietly, at Barinsky's insistence, while Countess Nadia was in France, Prince Boris had changed. Before that he had been the soul of consideration, and very helpful after my husband's death, and during my grandmother and Tatiana's sojourn in France I had begun to lean on him.

'The first night of our honeymoon,' she wrote, 'he virtually raped me. There had been no need for this, because although I knew I could never love him as I had loved Sasha, I certainly intended to let Boris have his marital rights. I was shocked, but hoped that it wouldn't happen again.

'At Prince Boris's request, because I had expected Alexei to stay at home with his nanny while we were on our honeymoon, he had suggested that we should bring Alexei with us. I was delighted. But the day after the rape Boris said Alexei would have to go to Branka, a dreadful old fort in the country, and days away from St. Petersburg. I vehemently protested, but he insisted, and then said if I did not agree to Alexei going he would kill him. This was like a horror story and I couldn't believe him.

'It was then that he virtually paralysed me with fear,' Natasha wrote, 'by telling me, with obvious relish, how he had killed my brother, my father and my husband. In growing horror I finally panicked and tried to run to Alexei's room, but Barinsky caught me, knocked me to the ground, and forced me to hear in detail the killings.

'He had found out where my brother was going to be, and had gone ahead and climbed a tree on the opposite bank of the river. Then, when he came into sight, he shot him. No one dreamt of looking up a tree, and it was decided it must have been a hunting accident. This had been so easy and successful it had given him confidence to continue.

'He had apparently used a combination of bribes and threats with father's coachman and footman,' Natasha continued. 'After they had jammed the coach doors and forced the horses to bolt they disappeared to a house he had told them to go to. When they arrived his serfs slit their throats.

'My husband, Sasha, was easily handled, Barinsky told me laughingly. All he had done was walk up to him and say, 'Good morning, Count,' and admire his gun. He asked if he could feel the weight of it and her husband passed it over. He then pointed the gun at Sasha, who told him to be careful since it was loaded, but Barinsky laughed again and said that he should be careful. He then shot him, laying the gun in such a position to make it look an accident.

'He said he would do the same with Alexei if I did not do exactly what he said. I pleaded to no avail, and ended up terrorised. I was never to speak to my grandmother or Tatiana again. I could attend no functions except essential ones, but even there I was only to nod and not say a word. When we returned from these functions he would laugh and say how they all thought I had had a stroke, and how impressed with his kindness and goodness to me they all were.

'On returning, she continued, I was always locked in my room. I was never allowed in any other room without a sadistic maid being with me. The maid he imposed on me was simply terrible and was really my jailer. On my return from our honeymoon I was forced to sack all my staff. Boris made out I was doing the sacking and pretended he disapproved.

'Then one day I had tried to slip out to see you grandmother, sure that you, and only you, had the power to free me. But I had not got far before I was caught and brought back to my room, where Boris whipped me. He then told me he was going to visit Alexei and would bring me back a present. By this time I knew I was dealing with a madman, but one who appeared perfectly sane when he wished to create a certain impression. He was away for three weeks, and during those three weeks I was never allowed out of my room. I spent most of those days either praying, or in despair.

'Then Barinsky reappeared and asked me, in that frightening voice of his, if I had been looked after, whether the staff had behaved well, and if my food had been to my satisfaction, all the time knowing that on his orders I had been locked in my room for three weeks, the food was virtually slops, and the staff were nothing but jailers. After asking me these questions, in the mocking tone I now both hated and feared, he said he had a present from my son. I was terrified by the way he said this and looked, and I went rigid with terror. He then passed over to me an ornate little ivory box. Trembling, I opened it, and fainted. I came to when I was slapped several times on the face. Boris then picked up the box, which I had dropped, and there again I saw Alexei's finger smeared in blood. I then vomited, while he laughed and then snarled that if I ever disobeyed him or tried to escape again I would receive a bigger box and in it this time would be Alexei's head.

'From then on he continued to mentally torture me. At the ball where the Empress was so kind and offered her own doctor to me, I did not dare talk, and he took great pleasure in pretending to be concerned for me. Then, when as we were leaving he took me up to you and suggested that Tatiana visit us in the country, as this might cheer me up, I knew he was planning to kill Tatiana as he had killed the other members of our family.

'Terrified of what would happen to Alexei if I said anything, and since Boris had convinced most people that it was I who was unbalanced and he the protective husband, I was sure that if I tried to warn anyone they would not believe me. Boris wanted to kill Tatiana for her fortune.

'Under father's will, if Tatiana died unmarried before she was twenty-five, all her inheritance passed to me. Therefore, Boris intended Tatiana to have an accident while she was staying with us in the country. Then, once I turned twenty-five, which is only months away, control of both inheritances would be transferred from the trustees to me.

'Boris controlled my money through my fear of what he would do to Alexei. The only time I was allowed out without Boris was once a month when I had to go in person to the bank to receive the allowance the trustees paid me from the income on my fortune. On these monthly visits I was accompanied by the maid, who was to ensure that I spoke to no one. She even came into the banker's office with me.

'Frantically trying to find a way to warn Tatiana without endangering Alexei, I remembered how each Friday morning at eleven Tatiana always used to attend the Academy. I normally went to the bank on a Thursday and collected my allowance, which Boris took from me as soon as I arrived back at the house. Boris was away for several days and so, taking a great risk, I pretended I was so ill I could not move, and could not visit the bank that day. The next day, Friday, I said I felt well enough to go to the bank. I saw the banker, received the money, then, once back in the coach I hid the bag in my dress and told the maid I must have left it at the bank. The maid, openly furious, went to find it.

'I waited anxiously in the coach till I saw Tatiana coming along the road. It nearly broke my heart when I saw the look in Tatiana's eyes when I told her not to come to the country, or ever to see Boris alone. The maid stormed back very angry, and I then said I found my bag; it was on the seat covered by my dress.

'The next day, Boris returned. When he came up to see me he knew I had seen Tatiana and wanted to know what she had said. The coachman had seen Tatiana near the coach, and was sure that I had spoken to her, although he could not hear what I said. I told Boris that all I had said to Tatiana was 'Go away.' Knowing how frightened I was of him, Boris believed me.

'Some time later the maid dragged herself into the room. Boris had had her severely beaten by one of the menservants and she could hardly walk. Now, instead of just despising me, she actively hated me, blaming me for the beating.

'Another day Boris came up to gloat, and told me he had just had Baron Llov killed because he had planned to betray him. He told me how he had used Baron Llov to front for him in a gambling den he owned.

David, mesmerised by the shocking account Natasha had written, abruptly realised why the voice he had heard on the night of Monty's death had been familiar. It had been Barinsky's.

'Then, Natasha wrote, 'three days ago Boris gloated that I had over the last few months been slowly poisoned, and that I would only live for about a week or so, after my twenty-fifth birthday.' The poison was irreversible. It was when Boris said he was going to visit Alexei shortly, I became positive that he intended to murder him before I reached twenty-five. Alexei's money, inherited from his late father, would then be inherited by me, and when I died Boris would inherit it all.

'I had no choice but to kill Boris before he left for the south. I decided on a plan that required me to write a new will, which meant Boris would have to take me into the study. I was praying that Boris had left Sasha's pistols in the desk, as he seldom used the study and was unlikely to have changed much. If the pistols were not there I intended to try and kill him with a paperweight.

'When we went to the study, I asked Boris for some writing material. While he was getting it I pulled a drawer open and grabbed one of the pistols, praying it was still loaded. I pointed it at Boris's head and fired. He died immediately. I have written, grandma, this long letter to you so that you will know what really happened to me. I intend shortly to take a large quantity of the poison they have been feeding me, which I believe will kill me painlessly within a few hours.'

Natasha's last words were that she had never knowingly hurt anyone or anything in her life. She had prayed and prayed to God in these last terrible months, yet when she had needed help none was available. She had no idea why this should be her fate. Perhaps she had had too much when she was young. She was heartbroken at the thought of dying before she could see her beloved Alexei, her grandmother and Tatiana once more, but she couldn't bear to bring the scandal of her husband's murder on the family and she had so little time left to live anyway. She knew that with her dead, her grandmother would be able to hush it up.

When the time was right grandmother would be able to tell Alexei that what she had done was only because she so loved him and wanted to save his life. She finished by writing that God had given her great happiness for twenty odd years. She did not know why these last eighteen months had happened to her, unless it was for the peace she now felt. The letter finished with an outpouring of love for her family, and grief at parting from them so soon.

As he finished reading David gazed across at Natasha's beautiful face and saw there a serenity he had never seen before. He saw too that the Countess had become calmer but looked terribly drained. He became bitterly aware that they had only missed seeing Natasha alive by a few hours.

He gently raised the Countess to her feet and they left the study, leaving the bodies where they were. David propped up the broken door, and told the servants not to try and enter the study. They would return in a short time, he said.

When they reached the waiting coach, the Countess instructed the coachman to drive to the home of the Chief of Police. It was now after midnight, but the Chief of Police swiftly came down realising that the Countess would not be calling on him unless something serious was wrong. After quickly introducing David, the Countess briefly told the Chief what had happened, and gave him Natasha's letter.

The Police Chief's face sagged as he read the letter. When he had finished, he asked quietly what she wanted him to do. The Countess said that firstly it was important that Natasha was buried with the full rites of the Church. Therefore, she had not committed suicide, but had simply died of an illness. Secondly, to avoid a scandal, Barinsky must to be thought to have committed suicide on the death of his loved wife, Natasha. Hateful as she found this, she said she believed it was the best way. The Police Chief agreed, and said that he would make the appropriate arrangements.

The Countess then added that she would like Princess Natasha's body to be brought back to her palace where, after embalming, she would lie in state for two days. She then said she would seek an audience with the Empress and tell her the true story, but that she would like the Chief to keep all he now knew secret.

As she turned to leave the Countess asked David if he would come back to the palace with her and stay the night, which he readily agreed to. On their arrival at the palace, Tatiana, who had been anxiously listening for their return, rushed up to them. The Countess briefly told her that Natasha and Boris were dead, passed Tatiana the letter, then sat down and called one of the staff to bring in a tray of drinks. David poured them each a glass of vodka while watching Tatiana read the letter. The tears began to flow down her cheeks, but she seemed unaware of them, as she made no move to wipe them away. When she came to Natasha's description of how she had tried to save her from Boris, Tatiana was overcome with remorse. How could she have ever thought Natasha was jealous of her.

Once she had read the letter, she rose and put her arms around her grandmother, who was looking older than David had ever seen her look. The two women sobbed together, as David poignantly reflected on the dreadful last months of Natasha's life.

The next morning the three of them breakfasted, leaving Alexei to sleep on in peace. Countess Nadia was looking drawn and haggard, but she had resolved that to take her mind off Natasha she must concentrate on Alexei. They discussed whether to tell Alexei about his mother immediately, or to wait. After discussing the pros and cons of telling him the truth it was decided to tell him that his mother had died saving him from Barinsky. They reasoned that they could not hide the fact that Barinsky was dead, and they would have to explain why he could not see his mother. It was agreed to give him a censored version, but to keep his mother's letter, and give it to him when he was older so he would know how courageous she had been and how much she had loved him.

The Countess began to consider the people she would need to tutor Alexei, since he had had no lessons for eighteen months. Tutors in history, writing, French, Russian, English and maths were essential, and he would also need teachers for fencing, riding, music, dancing and athletics. She became busy mapping out his future, the future she believed his mother and father would have wished him to have.

When David left the palace a little later it was with a somewhat abridged version to tell Lord Malvern. In confidence, he told the Ambassador that Barinsky had been the owner of the gambling den.

The Ambassador was scandalised that a man of the Prince's standing, who was married to one of the richest heiresses in Russia, could stoop to such a level. However, he said, 'At least we know that with Barinsky dead we will have no more trouble from that quarter.' He went on to say how shocked the Prussian Ambassador would be when he returned to St. Petersburg, but they agreed that he too would be relieved that the mystery had been solved.

Mention of the Prussian Ambassador brought David's thoughts back to Gisela, for even she had been pushed to the back of his mind during the events of the last few days. With the Countess's early return to St. Petersburg he found himself back three weeks before the Hertzburgs.

His attention was drawn back to the Ambassador as he congratulated him on the information he had supplied in his reports.

CHAPTER SEVENTEEN

DAVID WAS NOW SPENDING A GOOD DEAL OF TIME AT THE VOLONSKI PALACE. While the inhabitants of the palace were in deep mourning, there was still some laughter centred round Alexei. In fact, he wondered what would have happened to Countess Nadia if Alexei had not been there to give her something to live for.

A stunning portrait of Natasha, painted when she first went to Court at the age of seventeen, was brought down from the Countess's bedroom and hung in the dining room. Another portrait, showing her in riding habit with her favourite horse, was brought over from the Barinsky Palace, and hung in the blue drawing room. Both portraits were by the same painter, and he had caught a vitality in Natasha that David had never seen. She looked amazingly lovely, and one would swear she was just about to step out of the frame and speak to you.

Except when Alexei was around, Tatiana seemed unable to rise out of the deep depression she had fallen into. David had always seen her as beautiful, but previously her beauty had been lit up by her vivaciousness. Now that her gaiety was gone, her beauty was unexpectedly heightened by what he could only describe as a sadness constantly drifting over her face.

One day a letter arrived for Alexei from Dmitri. It was so like Dmitri, said Countess Nadia, to think of a little boy, even in the midst of preparing for battle. The letter was full of jokes and funny little sketches which everyone laughed at. It conveyed such charm and goodwill that each felt as if they could see the debonair, laughing Dmitri with them.

To David's pleasure, Alexei asked if he would help him write a letter back to Dmitri. They sat down and spent a pleasant hour writing a reply to Dmitri, then they read the letter to the two Countesses or rather David did, since Alexei had a great deal of schooling to catch up on. The women laughed with delight, and then suggested a postscript to the letter. This was done, again with much laughter and fun, and David felt happy that Tatiana and her grandmother might be beginning to throw off some of their sadness. Thank God, he thought, that Alexei is here for them to love and plan for.

The following day a letter for Tatiana arrived from Dmitri while David was there having lunch. When the servant brought the letter in on a silver tray and placed it beside Tatiana, Alexei became very excited and asked his aunt to read it out to them. 'I must read it myself first, Alexei,' Tatiana said.

The little boy, always so logical, replied, 'Why? I read you mine straight away,' quite forgetting that he could not have read it properly himself. In fact, David reflected, that was probably one of the reasons Dmitri had drawn all those funny sketches.

Alexei pestered Tatiana in such an appealing way that she, who had been busy reading it to herself, said she would read out the funny pieces. When she did, it was again, as if Dmitri was in the room with them. Several parts were so funny and described so well, they could almost believe they saw it.

On the third day, Alexei was looking much more rested and showing the benefit of good food. He had also settled in securely at the palace, so his grandmother decided to tell him about his mother. Prior to this they had told him she was sick but would see him soon. That afternoon she took Alexei on her lap and told him the wicked Barinsky was dead, and that his mother had loved Alexei so much that she had died making sure the he could never hurt him again. Oddly enough, the little boy simply said he thought he would never see his mother again, the people at Branska had told him that. So had the Prince at the time he had cut off his finger.

Alexei's tone was so matter of fact, everyone in the room was appalled. It simply didn't seem natural that a child of his age should show so little feeling on such a highly emotional subject as his mother's death. He then left the room, and when Tatiana went to look for him a few minutes later, a servant told her the young Count had just gone into the blue drawing room. When Tatiana quietly opened the door she saw Alexei lying on the floor in front of his mother's portrait, his shoulders shaking with sobs as he cried as if his heart would break. She went and sat down beside him and put her arms around him. Alexei immediately responded by throwing his arms round his aunt.

Tatiana told him again and again how much his mother had loved him, and how much she and her grandmother had loved her. Then she told him amusing stories about Natasha when she was younger, and the tricks she would play. She told him how beautiful his mother had looked at her first ball, when Tatiana was too young to go, and how she had brought home for her an icing figure of a skater off the special cake that had been made for the ball.

Looking at the portrait, Alexei asked what had happened to the horse. Tatiana told him it was leading a life of retirement at Grandmother's stud outside Moscow. The horse was now twenty-two, and the next time they visited Moscow she would take him to the stud and introduce him to 'Falcon,' as he was called. Falcon had been a great hunter and, like all her family, his mother was a great horsewoman. Alexei asked if his aunt thought he would also be a great rider. She assured him that he would have inherited the ability to ride from both his mother and his father, and so he would become a great rider. This pleased him very much.

Countess Nadia, wondering where Tatiana and Alexei were, peeped in, then closed the door silently, seeing all was well. As she returned, unobserved David studied her closely, and realised that while her patrician beauty remained the Countess had drastically aged. She seemed tormented by the thought of the last months of Natasha's life, and the knowledge that she might still be alive if only they had realised what a madman Barinsky had been. There were great shadows under her eyes, as under Tatiana's, and he knew neither was sleeping well.

The Countess's audience with the Empress had been very poignant. The Empress recalled how she had asked Natasha why she was not seeing more of her at Court, and if she could send her own doctor to her. The Empress declared that she had never liked any of the Barinskys. She felt deeply for her old friend, Nadia, and said she would speak herself to the Chief of Police to ensure the matter was kept secret. If it had not been for the potential problem of Princess Natasha's suicide, and a Christian burial, she would like the world to know what a monster and madman Boris Barinsky had been. The Empress's kindness and support lifted Nadia's spirits somewhat.

As a young girl Nadia had been a maid of honour to the late Empress Elizabeth, and when she died Nadia was one of the few maids of honour the Empress Catherine had taken on from the old Empress's household. Although Nadia was older than Catherine they had gradually become good friends, and Nadia was one of the few people who was in Empress Catherine's confidence.

Having heard the story of their journey to Kiev, the Empress invited the Countess to bring Tatiana and David to a small party at the Winter Palace the following evening where a new play was to be performed. She said she knew the Countess was in mourning, but she felt she needed some pleasure to take her mind off her great sorrow. 'If I say I have invited you, despite your being in mourning, no one will dare condemn you, my dear.'

When the Countess relayed to Tatiana and David the invitation they were thrilled, and particularly for Nadia. They also both looked forward to seeing the new little theatre in the Winter Palace, since they had heard stories about how lovely it was. The Empress was known for great taste, and like her recent predecessor, was never short of funds to achieve what she wanted. The wonderful collection of great paintings and statues she was building up in the Hermitage was an example of much money spent with great knowledge and taste.

The next evening David called for the two Countesses and together they drove to the Winter Palace. They were ushered into an entrance hall through a side door, and then into an enchanting little theatre. The theatre was built to seat around a hundred, but there were only about thirty people present, most of whom were known to Nadia and Tatiana, while David also knew some of them. The play was a French comedy, witty and well acted, and deserving of the applause the audience gave it.

Supper was served round little tables, followed by an hour's game of cards. Nadia was seated at the Empress's table, while Tatiana was seated at a table that included one of Count Alexei Razumovsky's handsome and dashing sons. The Razumovskys were fabulously wealthy. The father, who had been a favourite of the late Empress Elizabeth, was given incredible wealth and rose from being a Ukrainian Cossack to a Count of Russia. He was a delightful old man and a good friend of Countess Nadia from the days when she had been a maid of honour to the Empress Elizabeth, so Tatiana knew and liked the son. David, who was sitting with an older group, watched Tatiana and Razumovsky conversing easily and began resenting Razumovsky's attention to her.

On the way back to the Volonskaya Palace David told Tatiana that he thought the Count was a little forward in his attentions to her. She replied that she didn't mind, as he was so wealthy that when he flirted with her she knew he wasn't interested in her money but only in her. She then gave David a cheeky smile, which made him think she was implying he was interested in her money. He told her, sharply, he certainly wasn't interested in her money, to which she smilingly replied that she knew that, but she also knew he wasn't interested in her at all. Countess Nadia laughed, but David was upset. He replied heatedly that of course he was interested in her as a very good friend. 'Haven't we spent a great deal of time in each other's company over the last few months?'

Smiling, the young Countess said she wondered how much time he would spend with them over the next few months, as she had heard that the Prussian Ambassador returned the next day, adding 'I'm sure, now, diplomatic pressure will keep you very busy.'

David's heart lurched. He had thought Gisela was not returning until early the following week, but at the thought that she might be here tomorrow, his heart now began to sing. Still, he wondered what had made Tatiana say that. It was too provoking. He was certain she didn't know about his relationship with Gisela, but some of her remarks were very enigmatic and they often carried what could be called a double entendre.

When they arrived at the palace David saw the ladies in and said good night, then he continued on to his apartment. His mind and body were seething with lascivious thoughts of Gisela. The following morning he could scarcely concentrate on his work, as his thoughts continually turned to Gisela. She must get a divorce, and meanwhile, they could live together. If Malvern threatened to sack him, he would leave the diplomatic service. He would take Gisela to Scotland, to meet his grandfather, she would win the old man over. The Earl could not help but love her.

Of course, they would never be able to go to Court again, but what did Court really matter? After all, he would have the estate and his investments to look after. His grandfather was getting on and would surely welcome David taking over some of the workload, though he couldn't be sure on this point. He knew his estate and business interests were his only consistent pleasures.

He waited impatiently to receive a message from Gisela, but none came that day. Perhaps she was not yet back, or had arrived too late to send a message to him. David spent the night thinking about her, anticipating with enormous pleasure and excitement the future he and Gisela would have together.

Baron and Baroness Hertzburg had indeed arrived back at their residence late that night, and retired almost immediately, as they were both exhausted from all the travelling. It had been a successful journey and the Baron had secured most of the information his King wished to learn. The Baroness had been a great success wherever they had stayed. Max was now so enthusiastic about everything that he now carried a distinct warmth with him and that, combined with his old-fashioned courtesy, gave him a very appealing personality.

Gisela had found she was growing to love Max, not with the passion she felt for David, but love of a gentler, less demanding sort. There could never be the exhilarating sex that caused every nerve in her body to tingle when David touched her, but she had chosen her path, and she was determined to be faithful to it.

She steeled herself to face David, hoping that her love for him would not lead her to break her decision. She decided she must not let him touch her. That would be fatal. She had asked herself time and time again why she had been put in this position. Why hadn't she met David before she married? Why, after being married, should she have met and fallen in love? There was no fairness in this world. Then she would remind herself how very fortunate she was, and think about what she had that so many others hadn't: a loving, distinguished husband, an abundance of luxury, a prominent social position, and now a coming child. This must steel her resolve to part from David. She would also be saving David's career with the choice she was making, and this thought gave her added strength. But although she could convince her mind she couldn't convince her body, which still ached for David's touch. She decided she must see him the next day before she weakened.

In the morning she had breakfast with the Max and told him she was sending David a note, saying that if it was convenient she would call on him at his apartment at four that afternoon. 'Then, Max,' she said, 'I shall explain I can never see him alone again. I shall make no mention of the baby. I shall ask him in future to treat me simply as a friend, as I shall do with him.'

Max replied that he knew whatever decision she took today she would remain committed to it. He wanted her to know that he loved her as he had never loved before, he said. For this reason, he said, although he had told her he would never agree to a divorce, if after her meeting with Mountforte she felt she must go to him, he would arrange a divorce, making it as easy as possible on her.

Gisela looked at her husband speechlessly, and tears sprang to her eyes. She knew how much it had meant to him when she had invited him into her bed, and she also knew how dearly he loved her. To offer her a divorce was the greatest sacrifice he could make. She stood up and walked round the table to him, and kissed him lovingly on the head, putting her arms around his neck. Looking at him tenderly, she asked how she had been so fortunate to marry such a gallant and saintly man. Today would see the end of her relationship with Lord Mountforte, she assured him.

Max then said that he would be home by five and would be in his study if she wished to see him when she returned from meeting Lord Mountforte. However, if she preferred some time alone he would understand, as he could well imagine the stress she would be under.

Gisela sent an unusually formal note to David, requesting a meeting at four that afternoon. She then occupied herself getting the Embassy residence in order, planning meals, writing menus, answering the correspondence that had been awaiting her return, and generally keeping as busy as possible. She wanted no time to dwell on the coming farewell.

When David received her note he was so overjoyed that he did not notice how stilted it was compared to the other notes he had received from Gisela in the past. He left his office early in the afternoon, and at the apartment he had numerous vases of flowers placed throughout the rooms. Champagne was put on a silver tray with two flute glasses, ready to be opened. The flowers and Gisela's favourite potpourri in silver bowls transformed his bedroom into a lover's boudoir.

By three-thirty David could not restrain himself from hopping up and looking out of his second floor window every time he heard a carriage on the road. Then, just on four, he heard a coach and horses and peered out to see the coach from the Prussian Embassy, its doors emblazoned with the coat of arms of the King of Prussia. For a moment he was shocked. Gisela always came in a small, anonymous carriage. Was the Baron coming to see him?

Then he saw the footman hand Gisela out of the coach and he knew she must have told her husband, and he had agreed to a divorce. David was exultant. He sprinted down the stairs to the ground floor entrance just as Gisela was admitted. Heedless of who was watching he rushed to pick her up in his arms. To his surprise she stepped back, hesitated momentarily, and then held out her gloved hand to be kissed. Wondering what sort of joke this was, he bent and kissed her hand, then he began moving his lips up her arm, all the while teasing the palm of her gloved hand with his fingers.

Gisela, whose face he suddenly noticed looked very pale and taut, jerked her arm and hand away, and asked if they could go into his drawing room. David felt a cold shiver tingle through his body. 'Of course,' he said, and moved to put an arm around her shoulder. Again she rebuffed him, and when he sat down beside her on the sofa she moved away to sit in a chair. Dismayed, David asked her what was wrong. In a very formal, clipped voice that he had never heard before, Gisela told him she could never see him again alone.

David was momentarily stunned, then his heart began to heave and pump so rapidly that he thought it might explode. With a sickening feeling he asked her, 'Why? Why?'

Gisela replied that after all this time the Baron had come to her bed. He wished for another child, and she had therefore to give up David.

For a moment David could not take in what he heard, then he began to plead, to storm and shout, and finally to plead again, but to no avail. Gisela sat like stone throughout, merely reiterating that it was over. Inwardly, she was on the verge of giving in when faced with David's handsome face, his virile body and, perhaps most, his misery. Finally David, virulently, accused her of never loving him and simply using him for her own pleasure. She had tired of him and found someone else. At this Gisela blanched, then she stood up and said she had loved David with all her heart, more than he would ever know, and that she knew she would never have another love like she had felt for him.

David then lost control and began shouting that he knew she had found another lover and that he would find him and kill him. She would be responsible for murder. Gisela replied simply that whatever David thought, her only lover from now on would be her husband. She then began to move toward the door. David tried to kiss her, but she again rebuffed him, shielding her face with her fan.

Regaining himself slightly in front of the footman, he could do nothing but see her out to the coach. She waved briefly and then closed the curtain that covered the window. As the coach began to move Gisela burst into deep, soul-rending sobs, and she did not stop until they reached the residence. She took a few moments to recover herself, then she stepped out of the coach and entered the embassy.

Once inside she went straight to Max's study. He turned round, looked at her, then rose from his desk and took her into his arms. Through her tears she told him all was finished between David and herself. Max, who had been tense with worry all day in case she had changed her decision, relaxing with relief, comforted her as best he could. He would do everything in his power to make her happy, he said, and he reminded her of the joy she would have with the coming baby.

After a time Gisela gently withdrew from his arms and said she thought she would go upstairs to rest. If Max did not object she would not come down to dinner, and she would prefer to sleep alone that night. He agreed, and Gisela, now exhausted, slowly went up to her room. She wept until she felt she had no tears left in her. All she could see was David, distressed, angry and throwing bitter accusations at her, while all the while her whole body was desperately yearning for him.

David, meanwhile, was shattered. He paced the drawing room, one minute planning to give up his position and return to Scotland, the next asking himself why he should give up anything because of a treacherous woman. One minute he wondered if he had not been a good enough lover, the next he thought what a beautiful snake Gisela was, a real Delilah. Finally he went upstairs to his bedroom, where he opened the bottle of champagne and rapidly drank glass after glass. He then threw the flowers and potpourri out of the window, flung himself on his bed and wept in misery.

The next day he managed to drag himself to work, but he found it impossible to concentrate, and found fault with everyone and everything. When someone joked that he must have had a lovers' quarrel he said nothing, but savagely glared at the unfortunate person, flung on his coat, and left.

He decided he didn't want to go home, and turned his steps towards the Bear, a restaurant and high-class bordello. After several drinks he asked for a girl, went upstairs with her and left twenty minutes later, vowing he would never go to a brothel again. He had used the girl without any feeling at all, merely slaking his lust in a matter of minutes. He had stood up, feeling unclean, and rapidly began putting on his clothes. As he had turned to mutter goodbye he had seen the gentle, pretty face of a young girl in her teens. It was filled with such utter hopelessness that he suddenly felt terribly, and deeply ashamed. He found himself foolishly starting to apologise, until she said in a weary voice, 'Don't — that's what I am here for.' For a moment a wistful expression touched her face and she said, 'You were much nicer than most.'

Despising himself, and not knowing how he could help the young girl escape from a life he would not wish on anyone, he thrust his hand in his pocket and drew out all the money he had on him, pushed it at her, and stumbled out of the room. Then he turned for home, feeling loathsome and unclean both in mind and in body.

The following day he was a little more himself, and he apologised to the staff for being so bad-tempered the day before. He was popular in the Embassy, and normally a considerate and affable colleague, and his uncharacteristic boorishness was quickly forgiven. He was still puzzling over Gisela's behaviour, however, and every time he thought he had found an answer another question would enter his mind.

Just after midday an invitation arrived from the Prussian Embassy, inviting him to a reception at the Ambassador's residence in two days' time. So, he decided, Gisela must think she can parade me around like a bear on a chain. Well, he thought, we shall see about that. His first thought was to decline the invitation, deciding the Baron must know about Gisela and himself. He was still ashamed of deceiving the Baron, but he was sure Gisela must now have told her husband the truth. He didn't want the Baron either glaring at him for cuckolding him, or gloating because he had won. After a little thought, however, he changed his mind and decided he would go. It would be cowardly not to, and if Gisela or the Baron tried to mock him he would reciprocate. It would also be better to get this first meeting over as soon as possible, since he could not avoid meeting them at other Embassy and diplomatic functions.

He still couldn't believe that Gisela, who had professed so much love for him, could have dropped him the way she had. He would never trust another woman again. He waxed between wanting Gisela and hating her, but deep down he knew he would accept her on almost any terms. This set him wondering if the determination he had expressed in wanting to marry her, or to live with her, had frightened Gisela. He wondered if he should try to see her again and say that he would accept the situation as it had been before she had gone back to Berlin, even though he did not like the dishonesty.

On his way home that evening he decided to call and see if the Volonskis were in. They were, and with them were the Kolcluleys, who had arrived in St. Petersburg the previous afternoon. After hearing the news of Natasha's death they had come around to express their deepest sympathy to their friends.

When Countess Nadia asked after Dmitri they all started talking at once, until Count Nikolai said to his daughters, 'Would you both please let your mother tell Aunt Nadia the news.' Countess Elizabeth then began to tell how Dmitri had played a significant part in the taking of Ochakvo. He had been one of the first officers to reach the top of the ramparts and, with his men streaming behind him, had dealt a devastating blow to the Turks. Apparently the Russian soldiers, having been vilified by the Turks and seen many of their fellow soldiers die, briefly ran amok. Dmitri had personally intervened, at great risk to his life, and saved several Turkish women and their children from being slaughtered. 'Wasn't that marvellous, and so like Dmitri?' the Countess finished proudly.

'Just like the gallant Dmitri,' echoed Tatiana.

The Kolcluleys were not yet positive, but they understood from a friend of theirs, another major who had been at the battle of Ochakvo, that Dmitri was being promoted again. However, since Dmitri was so modest they had not heard it from him. This caused a lot of speculation, with Tatiana commenting that she thought Dmitri would end up as the youngest field-marshal in the Russian Army.

Count Nikolai said he had heard that Prince Potemkin was developing even more Cossack regiments, and since they were such good warriors he intended to make them the backbone of the Russian Army. They guessed from Dmitri's letter that he might be one of the officers sent to train them in the Russian style.

Countess Elizabeth said their friend had told them that if Dmitri was sent to help with the training it would be because of his humanity as much as his valour. This was because Prince Potemkin wanted the Cossacks to be won over by kindness as well as military style. 'Isn't that a wonderful recommendation?' asked the Countess.

Just before they left, Countess Elizabeth put her arm through her husband's, and said that they were planning a party to celebrate their twenty-five years of marriage, and would be sending an invitation to each of them. They hoped both the Countesses would come, and David as well. Countess Elizabeth said she was sure Natasha would have understood, and would want them to celebrate the happiness of their old friends.

Sophie, who was always laughing and teasing, added that David must certainly come because she had told all her girlfriends about this rich, handsome English lord, who was unmarried and ripe for the picking. Countess Elizabeth pretended to hush her, but everyone laughed. David blushed a little and replied that he would be pleased to come, but that if all her girlfriends were as lovely as Sophie he would have to convert to Islam and begin a harem.

The delighted Sophie and Daria immediately proposed that the party should be fancy dress, and instructed everyone to come as Ottomans. This time the Countess Elizabeth's 'What nonsense!' was not pretended, it was very definite. She had already been to the dressmaker and her gown was almost ready, and she believed she was going to be the belle of the party. Countess Nadia said that she was not sure she would come, being in mourning for Natasha, but as it was a private party Tatiana could certainly go.

Finally the Kolcluley family said their goodbyes, with lots of kisses and waves, and Countess Nadia asked David if he would stay to supper. He agreed readily, as he always enjoyed both women's company, and felt almost one of the family. The Countess Nadia now asked David if he had heard of or met Princess Maria Zinoviena. David had not, so the Countess told him she had been the fiancee of her late grandson, Sergei. She was not only a beautiful girl, but an extremely intelligent and loving person. The Countess was very fond of her. Well, the Princess had been to see her that morning and told her that after months of praying she was going to enter a convent. She had never really recovered from Sergei's death, and she wished to retire from the world. Countess Nadia thought that at twenty-two Maria was too young to commit herself to a convent, but the young woman was adamant.

The Countess had then put to Maria the following proposal, which she had been thinking about since Natasha's death. If Maria would take some other nuns or laywomen and form an Orthodox Order, Countess Nadia would build and endow an orphanage called The Dolgurky Orphanage, after Sergei and Natasha, and pass it over to Maria to run. Countess Nadia said she would take some of the wealth she had been going to leave to Sergei and Natasha and endow the orphanage. The endowment would be a large one, enabling the orphanage to employ good teachers, and if any of the orphans wished to learn a trade, become a musician, or attend university, the necessary funds would be available. The Countess thought the orphanage should start with forty orphans, then take in ten more each year. She was pleased to say that Maria had leapt at the idea, and Nadia had asked Barsov to begin planning the financial details. Tatiana, Barsov, Maria and herself would be trustees.

The Countess wondered, in view of what David had told her of his British education, if while he was living in St. Petersburg he would also become a trustee and thus add his knowledge of English and Scottish teaching to the Board of Trustees. David was honoured and delighted, and accepted immediately. Then the Countess began an intense discussion about what she proposed for the school curriculum.

David suggested they should certainly include some sport, and while Tatiana made some suggestions, she mainly smiled gently at David's and her grandmother's intensity. It was not until he had returned home later that night that David remembered he was considering giving up his diplomatic career and returning home to Britain.

Two nights later, after drinking two glasses of vodka, David arrived at the Prussian Embassy. He knew he was looking stiff and haughty but he could not help himself. His heart was pumping at high speed, and he began to wish he had not come. As he climbed the stairs he didn't see anyone he knew until a hand touched his sleeve and he turned to see Princess Dashkova, who said she had just returned from Moscow but hoped to see him soon. She was holding a small reception at her palace in two weeks' time, and would be sending him an invitation. David thanked her, made way for her to precede him to greet the Hertzburgs ahead of him.

When David approached the Baron he was surprised at how kindly the Ambassador greeted him. He went on to ask David about his journey south, commiserated with him over Montague's death, and congratulated him on his part in exposing the owner of the gambling den. David was stunned, and decided that the Baron must know nothing about his relationship with Gisela. Then his temper began to rise. So Gisela had not thought enough of their relationship to even mention it to the Baron. What a fool he had been, loving her so deeply while she used him as a toy to satisfy her desires until she found someone else. He felt sympathy for the old Baron, who obviously had no idea what an unfaithful wife he had. How diabolically clever she must be for her husband to be so blind to her goings on.

Meanwhile Gisela had been watching him without appearing to do so. Her heart had almost stopped when he had entered the lobby at the bottom of the stairs. She saw how stiff and haughty he looked, but if anything the haughtiness only added to his handsomeness and she felt her knees beginning to tremble. She had wondered if he would come. One part of her wishing he would not arrive, and one part urgently hoping he would. Then he had reached the Baron, and she was filled with admiration for the way Max handled him. What a wonderfully courteous and kind man he was to make David feel as much at ease as possible.

She had planned how she was going to greet David, pleasantly but very formally and correctly. Now he had left Max and was approaching her. God, how she loved him. Her knees began quivering and she had forgotten what she was going to say. He bowed over her hand and then kissed above it, as if it was the first time he had met her. She was sure she would collapse, but instead she heard herself saying that it was very good of him to come and that she hoped he would have an enjoyable evening. Then with one searing look he passed on.

She thought she was going to faint. Who was standing in front of her? She knew the person but could not recall the name. Oh God, what was wrong with her. Max must have been watching because suddenly he was at her side, telling the guest that his wife had not been well that morning, a touch of the flu, so could they excuse her for a moment while she sat down. A few minutes later she resumed her place and continued receiving the guests.

David had gone into the large reception hall, his thoughts in a turmoil. One moment he felt he hated her, and in another moment felt he couldn't live without her. Her pathetic greeting was imprinted on his mind. Savagely he could still hear her saying, it was good of him to come and that she hoped he would enjoy himself, when she knew she had wiped out any chance of his happiness now or in the future. Just then a young lady he knew slightly came up and spoke to him, and by her startled face he realised he must have said something abrupt. Goodness knows what he had said, but he must pull himself together. With that he took his young acquaintance's arm and escorted her across the room to her friends.

For the rest of the evening he really felt as if he wasn't there and that someone else was talking and acting for him. He left early, telling the Baron he had a daybreak appointment in the morning. The Baron thanked him for coming and said he was sure he would see more and more of him at diplomatic functions — he hoped so anyway. David then moved across to where the Baroness was standing talking to some guests. He had intended to avoid saying goodbye to her, but she drew him like a magnet and he found himself crossing the floor to where she was standing. As he bowed and said his farewell he felt a piercing pain shoot through his body as he contemplated the beautiful woman whose body he knew every part of but now would never be able to touch again. He left feeling sick with grief and an overwhelming sense of utter loss. When he arrived home he drank what was remaining of a bottle of vodka then passed out, fully dressed, on the bed.

The next week everyone was busy at the British Embassy and David had to put in a great many hours in the evenings drafting and polishing reports for the Ambassador. Britain's Russian policy was now in a shambles as Charles Fox and Edmund Burke attacked William Pitt and almost brought down the English Government. Lord Malvern was being asked by Pitt for more and more information even though, as the Ambassador said, by the time the report reached London any decisions would already have been made.

The Empress and Potemkin were now greatly enamoured of Charles Fox, as he had destroyed Pitt's anti-Russia policy. In fact, the Empress had had a statue made of Fox and placed it in one of her palaces. The Empress and Potemkin had been worried that in the event of a war with Britain, their British officers, and there were many in leading positions in both the army and the navy, might refuse to fight. The Empress had tried to put the American, Paul Jones, in with the Russian Baltic Fleet. Jones had fought Britain in the American War of Independence and led the rebel navy. But Admiral Grieg and the other English officers serving in the fleet had offered their resignations if Jones, who the British regarded as a dreadful renegade, joined the Baltic fleet. The Empress had then sent Jones south to the Crimea, where he had also caused problems.

In view of all this, the British Embassy was pulling out all the stops to try and alleviate, and hopefully reverse, the rising antipathy toward Britain in response to what the Embassy privately thought of as a stupid policy by Pitt's administration. Leading members of the Empress's Council did not personally place much blame on the British representatives in Russia, but her advisors who favoured the Austrian Alliance were pleased to see the British representatives somewhat humbled.

David was glad of the extra work, as it left him less time to think about Gisela. He was by now a very popular bachelor and any free nights were usually taken up with invitations. He continued to see a good deal of Countess Nadia and Tatiana, whom he now regarded as family, and he believed they felt the same about him. Tatiana's infectious laughter and mischievous remarks were less in evidence now, and he knew that both she and her grandmother found it hard to forget the terrible last months of Natasha's life, and regretted they had not found Alexei earlier. But Alexei was now beginning to blossom, and unconsciously kept both his great grandmother and his aunt's spirits up, giving them something to care about and live for.

He also saw quite a lot of the Kolcluleys, who kept open house for him. He was aware that Sophie and Daria were both interested in him, and that with a little encouragement, could easily fall completely in love with him. Although it was a tightrope act, he managed to keep their feelings on a brotherly and sisterly plane. One evening Sophie confided to him that she expected that when Dmitri came home on leave he would propose to Tatiana. For some reason this upset David, just as he became upset when he saw so many of the young and eligible bachelors flocking round Tatiana. He had watched Tatiana and had never seen her show any preference, but he was not sure how she felt about Dmitri.

He knew that Dmitri wrote regularly to Tatiana, because she often quoted news from his letters. In fact, Countess Elizabeth had told Tatiana that she thought she received more letters from Dmitri than all the members of the Kolcluley family combined. Tatiana had laughed and said she could not believe that, but David had noticed that she also blushed.

David knew he was being selfish, but he really didn't want Tatiana to marry Dmitri. He didn't understand his feelings, because he liked Dmitri very much, and he knew that in many ways they were ideally matched. It came as something of a shock when one night he was dining at the Volonski Palace and a footman entered and said Count Dmitri Kolcluley wished to be announced. Countess Nadia immediately told the man to show him in, and greeted him warmly and enthusiastically. Tatiana invited him to join them for dinner, saying they had only just started, but Dmitri declined, saying he had not yet seen his family.

They then noticed that in contrast to his usual smart appearance he was looking a little worse for wear and Tatiana remarked on it. Dmitri at once replied that he had been asked to courier some letters from Prince Potemkin to the Empress as rapidly as possible. He had gone straight to the Winter Palace, where the Empress had granted him an immediate audience. She was thrilled with the news the letters contained, which included the capture of an important Tartar position and the surrounding territory. The Empress had then eagerly asked him many questions, so he had been at the Palace for about two hours.

Since he had to pass the Volonski Palace on the way to his parents' mansion he thought he would just call in and say hello. He wondered if they would be free to come to luncheon at his parents' house the next day. He generously included David in this invitation although David was sure it was really only Tatiana he wanted, but was too polite to say so. David was in two minds whether to accept or decline. He was still extremely busy at the Embassy during the day, but on the other hand he didn't want to give Dmitri the chance of being alone with Tatiana. He was sure that if he wasn't there Countess Nadia and Dmitri's family would see there was an opportunity for them to be alone, so he said he would be delighted to come.

If Dmitri was disappointed he didn't let it show, and in fact expressed his pleasure that David could get away from the office. Tatiana, with an arch look at David, then said she was very surprised that David could find time to come to lunch as he had been working such long hours. She studied David for a minute, then turned to Dmitri and said he must take it as a great compliment that David could be called away from the Embassy, at such short notice, to dine with them at lunchtime. Dmitri again expressed his appreciation, and David felt rather guilty. He was also not quite sure what the enigmatic Tatiana meant by her remark.

He saw Countess Nadia was looking somewhat speculatively at her granddaughter. However, all she said was that it might be an imposition on his parents if they were to come to lunch, as they didn't even know he was in St. Petersburg yet. But Dmitri said that Aunt Nadia knew his mother, and that nothing would stop her cancelling everything to give a luncheon for him when he was only in the city for one night and a day. They all laughed, knowing how true this was.

'So why are you returning to the Crimea so soon?' asked the old Countess. Dmitri explained that he had been instructed to return to the Winter Palace at three the next day, where he would find letters awaiting him from the Empress to deliver to Prince Potemkin. He was then to leave immediately for the south.

'Well, you must then hurry home, see your parents and sisters, and go to bed,' said Countess Volonskaya. Dmitri smiled, told Tatiana how lovely she was looking, and, including them all in his open smile, repeated that he looked forward to seeing them the next day. Tatiana then showed him out, and it seemed to David that when he left it was as if the candles had dimmed, such was Dmitri's personality. Tatiana came back a few minutes later looking pink and a little flustered, but happy. It made David feel a little lonely suddenly, although he tried to shake off the feeling.

As they continued their dinner they discussed what Dmitri's letters would mean for the continuing expansion of the Empire. David asked the Countess if, now that Russia had conquered new territory, she would petition Potemkin for more land to develop. She wouldn't ask for more land, she told him, because she already had well over a million acres, and any more would be far too hard to handle. This was particularly so as developing her Crimean estates was going to take up a great deal of time and money.

David wondered if she would have said this prior to Natasha's death. Now she only had Tatiana and little Alexei to provide for, having lost Natasha and her only grandson, Sergei. However, Nadia said she had recently begun to feel her age, and her estates and her other investments were now taking up more of her time than she liked. Smiling at Tatiana, she told her that soon she would have to take over more responsibilities.

Tatiana quickly told her grandmother that she shouldn't talk like that, she was sure she would still be looking after the family affairs in twenty years' time. The Countess only laughed, leant across and ruffled Tatiana's hair, saying she was a good girl. Tatiana smiled back to her with a face full of adoration. David thought what a lovely portrait that would make.

He began to tell them how he had written to his grandfather about the widespread range of the Countess's interests. His grandfather had been absolutely fascinated, and had replied asking lots of questions. The old Earl had also wondered if he thought the Countess would consider supplying timber from her Russian forests direct to his shipbuilding operations. This, he said, would cut out the middleman. The Countess looked interested in the idea, and said they should have a talk with Barsov, and with Bibikov when he returned from the south.

Tatiana then asked if David thought his grandfather would visit him in St. Petersburg. He replied that although he had asked him, he was sure the old Earl would never again leave his castle in Scotland. Most people that he wanted to see went to visit him there. Of course, David wished he would come to St. Petersburg, and he would keep on asking him. Perhaps in his next letter he would suggest to his grandfather that he should travel to Russia on one of his ships that came to take timber back to England. 'What a good idea,' said the Countess. 'Inform him that he could visit my forest, which has excellent stands of timber growing.'

CHAPTER EIGHTEEN

Dᴀᴠɪᴅ ꜰᴏᴜɴᴅ ʜᴇ ᴡᴀꜱ ɢʀᴀᴠɪᴛᴀᴛɪɴɢ ᴍᴏʀᴇ ᴀɴᴅ ᴍᴏʀᴇ ᴛᴏ ᴛʜᴇ Vᴏʟᴏɴꜱᴋɪ Pᴀʟᴀᴄᴇ ɪɴ ʜɪꜱ ꜱᴘᴀʀᴇ ᴛɪᴍᴇ, ᴀɴᴅ ɪꜰ ʜᴇ ꜰᴏᴜɴᴅ Tᴀᴛɪᴀɴᴀ ɴᴏᴛ ᴀᴛ ʜᴏᴍᴇ ʜᴇ ꜰᴇʟᴛ ꜱᴜɪᴛᴇ ᴅɪꜱᴀᴘᴘᴏɪɴᴛᴇᴅ. He also saw a great deal of the Kolcluleys and the two families began to provide the family he had never known. He now called on them without invitation, and was always welcomed with open-armed pleasure.

Sure enough, first thing in the morning the Countess, Tatiana and David received invitations to come to lunch at the Kolcluleys, with firm instructions to arrive at eleven for an early luncheon as Dmitri had to be at the Winter Palace at three, after which he had immediately to leave for the Crimea. The invitations were written by Countess Elizabeth, and they were more like letters since she bubbled over with happiness at having her son home, even if only for a short time. She also said in the invitation that she had a surprise for them that she could hardly wait to tell.

When David read this he wondered if Dmitri had proposed to Tatiana and been accepted. The thought caused him to lapse into a fit of depression which hung over him like a dark cloud, even though he knew he should feel congratulatory.

Although they had driven separately, the two Countesses and David arrived at the same time the next day. As they approached the door it swept open and Countess Elizabeth kissed them all and drew them inside. Then she stopped and proudly drew back. They saw why. In the centre of the hall stood a table, and on it lay the Order of St George IInd Class, St George being the Empire's highest honour. Standing behind the table were Count Nikolai, Sophie and Daria, and in the middle an embarrassed-looking Dmitri.

'Isn't it wonderful? On the recommendation of dear Prince Potemkin, the Empress has awarded Dmitri the Cross of St. George for valour at the taking of Ochakvo. Oh, I am so proud of my son,' said Countess Elizabeth. 'And would you believe it? He said nothing to us, even though he knew yesterday. We only found out when a package addressed to Count Dmitri Kolcluley arrived this morning.'

At this stage Dmitri began to gently remonstrate with his mother, saying that he was taking back with him the Cross of St. George Ist Class, which the Empress had awarded on the recommendation of Prince Potemkin to Count Suvorov. 'But he's a general and an old man,' said his mother, 'and you, dear, are only young.' In fact, she went on, in some ways she couldn't think why Suvorov got first class and her son only second class. After all, Dmitri had looked after his men and still achieved a victory.

General Suvorov won victories and was becoming a hero but every mother knew he wasted his men and didn't care how many died, so long as he won. She was sure no mother would want her son serving under him.

Dmitri said that the general also risked his own life. He was deeply moved to be so honoured, he said, and thought his men deserved a medal, as they had fought so well. 'There,' said his mother, 'Dmitri is always thinking of others.'

At this stage everyone could see that Dmitri was becoming very embarrassed and his father, with gentle irony, said, 'Elizabeth, don't you think that we should all go into the salon and drink a glass of champagne to Dmitri, Russia's greatest hero since Peter the Great?'

Everyone, including Countess Elizabeth and certainly Dmitri, laughed and eagerly went in to drink a toast. It was a wonderful luncheon. Drinks flowed and the company was in high spirits. At one-thirty Dmitri said he must go and change for his appointment with the Empress, and then he would be leaving for the south. He said goodbye to Aunt Nadia and David, and bid a very tender farewell to Tatiana.

Then he greatly surprised them all by telling them he had another secret. Everyone guessed wild and improbable ideas, only to find that the secret was that he had been promised one month's leave in two months' time. The Kolcluleys were overjoyed and so, noted David, was Countess Nadia. More ominously, he thought, so was Tatiana. David, who normally wasn't a jealous person, couldn't understand why he resented it when Dmitri gave Tatiana an intimate glance. He found it disturbing. After some happy chatter about his news, Dmitri went upstairs and the three guests made ready to depart. Countess Elizabeth then almost broke down, saying to Aunt Nadia that every time he went back to the army she lived in real fear it would be the last time she saw him. At that point the Count took his wife in his arms and said that God would look after him, and that Dmitri was fighting for Russia and to secure her future so the Tartars and Ottomans could never again terrorise them. The Countess, still upset but determined to be a good hostess, waved her friends off, still tucked gently in Count Nikolai's arms.

David thought again what a lovely, uncomplicated family the Kolcluleys were, and how fortunate he was to have been accepted like a family member. He saw Countess Nadia and Tatiana into their carriage and then returned to his apartment.

That night he found himself yearning again for Gisela, wishing she was in bed beside him. Every time he weakened and let his thoughts run along this track his whole body ended up being racked with an unfulfilled desire that he knew could only be calmed by having Gisela beside him. It was during this tossing and turning that he again knew he would accept Gisela on whatever terms she demanded.

CHAPTER NINETEEN

THE FOLLOWING DAY LADY MALVERN CAME DOWN TO THE OFFICE TO CONFER WITH THE AMBASSADOR, WHO WAS DUE TO LEAVE THE FOLLOWING DAY FOR MOSCOW, AND WOULD BE AWAY FOR THE NEXT THREE WEEKS. David was called in while she was with the Ambassador, who asked that he escort Lady Malvern to a dinner dance at Count and Countess Sheremetev's palace the following evening. He said it was necessary for the British Embassy to be represented there, even though he was away, as the Sheremetevs were one of Russia's oldest families and very powerful.

David liked Lady Malvern, as all the Embassy staff did. She was always concerned for the welfare of the staff, and although they knew she had more money and a greater position by birth than her husband, she never alluded to these things. David thought that as long as she did not have too much to drink she would be excellent company, and he replied that he would be honoured to squire Lady Malvern in the Ambassador's absence. Lady Malvern smiled at him and said, 'I am sure, Lord Mountforte, we shall have fun.' At the word 'fun' Lord Malvern looked sharply at his wife and said she was to remember that this was a duty dinner and not a 'fun' dinner, as she put it. The Ambassadress smiled slightly mockingly at her husband and said that doing her duty was always a pleasure.

The following night Lady Malvern arrived in the Ambassador's light carriage to pick David up at his apartment. She was in a happy mood, and had obviously had several drinks. She asked Lord Mountforte if he minded her calling him David, as he was about the same age as her eldest son. David said he would be honoured, and they chatted companionably on the way to the Sheremetev's palace. Lady Malvern said she did not know the Count very well but she had met the Countess Sheremetev quite often and that she was a nice woman and not at all difficult or stuffy.

Personally, she said, she became a little tired of all the Embassy functions, many of which were so dull, but of course she had to entertain and be entertained in order to support her husband. Without actually saying so, she indicated that her husband was a very clever man of great integrity, but a little on the dull side. She then gave a small sigh and said that he was a good man but their children, fortunately, had her light touch and sense of humour. All except the eldest, but then, she went on, if you were a peer it really didn't matter if you had a sense of humour or not and her eldest son would eventually inherit his father's peerage. She did, however, feel sorry for his future wife, as having a dull husband could be quite depressing.

She then gave another sigh and changed the subject. 'Look, we're here. Doesn't the palace look lovely, lit up so beautifully with all those wonderful torches?'

As they entered the palace David noticed how striking Lady Malvern looked, with an impressive tiara, necklace, earrings and bracelet of diamonds, emeralds and pearls. She had the figure to carry off such grand jewellery. However, she nearly tripped going up the stairs, and was only saved when David managed to catch her arm and steady her. Much as he liked her, he hoped she would not have too much to drink.

As they were discarding their furs and cloaks Lady Malvern whispered to David that if there were any attractive young women there he should not worry about her, except when they were going in to dinner and when leaving for home, and to have a good time. However, if the party was a dull one and he saw her for any length of time on her own or looking harassed, would he please come over and rescue her. David thought how charming she was, and asked if she would give him the first dance. She was delighted, and told him what a chivalrous young man he was, but added that there would be plenty of people to ask the British Ambassadress for the first dance. It was later on that she might need a dancing partner, she said, so he should just enjoy himself, but keep an eye out to see how she was faring. It was very hard for a lady to ask a man to dance and she didn't fancy being a wallflower halfway through the evening. David was greatly amused at her frankness and said he would certainly keep an eye on how she was placed during the evening.

They greeted their hosts, Count and Countess Sheremetev, who said how sorry they were that Lord Malvern had had to go to Moscow, but how good it was to see Lord Mountforte at their home. They had heard many good reports about him from their old friend Countess Volonskaya, who was here tonight with her granddaughter, Countess Tatiana Golvinka. David felt flattered that his friends had mentioned him to the Sheremetevs.

Lady Malvern spied several acquaintances at the far end of the salon, and asked David to take her over there. Then, she said, he should look round and see who he would like to talk to. At that moment she spotted Tatiana and said to David, 'Why don't you go and speak to the young Golvinka Countess? She looks especially exquisite tonight.' David looked over to where Tatiana stood, surrounded by young men, and agreed that she was certainly looking very beautiful.

Baron and Baroness Hertzburg had already arrived, and Gisela saw David come in with Lady Malvern. Her heart turned over as she thought yet again how youthful, handsome and virile he looked. She hoped he would not come over to her. She couldn't stand it. Just seeing him caused her pain. She was still not sure she could withstand him for any length of time, no matter how good her intentions. She knew now that her husband was always alert and that he would also have noted David's entrance. She knew too that if she showed any signs of panic or agitation he would unobtrusively come to her aid. Sometimes she felt that Max was too good to her. She must concentrate on that, her husband's goodness and how fortunate she was to be married to him, and on her coming child.

She saw David look around the room, and then his eyes fastened on her. She was too far away to read his expression, but she trembled as he began to come toward her. She felt trapped, since her feet seemed stuck to the floor and wouldn't shift. His long, athletic stride as he relentlessly made his way toward her caused frissons of heat to run through her body.

David, meanwhile, was determined to find out who the lover was who had supplanted him in Gisela's affections. He didn't believe for one moment her story that her husband had now begun to join her in bed. Not after all those years when he had left her alone. David knew she had a lover, and he wanted to find out who it was.

When he reached her he bowed and said, 'Good evening, Baroness,' and she smiled and held out her hand for him to kiss. He looked up into her face and thought how lovely she was, she seemed even more beautiful than before. He trembled with a violent surge of rage against the new lover who had inspired this look. He starkly remarked that she was looking extremely well, and as she was acknowledging his comment he impetuously asked if she would keep one of the dances for him. There was desperation in her voice as she apologised and said that she was not in the best of health. The few dances she felt up to had already been booked, she said. Then she smiled at him and turned away to join her husband.

David felt as if he had been pole-axed. He didn't for one minute believe she wasn't in the best of health. It was a cold, deliberate snub. He was completely humiliated. Even though he now knew Gisela was only a cold, calculating, pleasure-seeking woman, the knowledge didn't help salve his pride or calm his emotions.

Gisela had turned away to join her husband only because she felt she would collapse if she stood looking at his dear, impassioned face any longer. As she reached Max she took his arm to steady herself. He turned, patted her arm and said that if at any time she wished to go home she should let him know and he would make their excuses. She knew, as she thought, Max had been observing everything in that quiet way of his.

David had momentarily stood immobilised, and for a minute couldn't see anything, then he too turned and moved away. There was Tatiana, still surrounded by young men. He would go and join them. No, by God, he would cut them out and ask Tatiana to keep two dances for him. When he reached the group around Tatiana it was obvious that she was flirting outrageously, and equally apparent that the young men were loving it and responding. This fuelled the banked up fury he was feeling against all women. He forced his way in unceremoniously, much to the surprise and annoyance of the men around her, and surprised even himself by the vehement way he practically demanded Tatiana keep two dances for him.

Tatiana paused and looked at him. She then said that Lord Mountforte had the appearance of someone who had been badly let down. She was sorry if that was so, but she couldn't help because she was not dancing at all that night. As he glared at her she asked if he had already forgotten she was mourning her sister and would not be dancing in public for another month.

David felt an even greater fool than before, realising how stupid and ignorant he looked in front of Tatiana and her followers. Silently damning all women, he abruptly apologised and left the group. He then made his way across to Lady Malvern, who was in the centre of a group of friends and acquaintances, hoping he could recover his equilibrium there.

He couldn't understand why he had been so rude to Tatiana and the group around her. It was quite out of character. He was well aware that he was noted for his courteous manners. It was the fault of getting entangled with that Hertzburg woman. Still, he must make a point of apologising to Tatiana before the evening was out. There was absolutely no excuse for the way he had spoken to her.

Lady Malvern greeted him with her gracious smile, asked him if he knew everyone, and then introduced him to several people he had not met before. Such was the state of his mind that he immediately forgot their names, and while he was trying to recall them he heard one of the ladies asking whether they had heard the delightful news about Baroness Hertzburg. One of her friends said no, she had not heard anything — what was the news? The first said the Baron had told her husband that they were going to have a baby. They were both overjoyed.

'I would think so,' said the second lady, whose name David could not recall. 'They have been married nearly eleven years. He has a son by his first wife, but none by the present Baroness.

'I have thought he has been different since they returned from Berlin,' she added. 'He has always been pleasant and courteous, but very formal. Now he positively overflows with warmth and charm.'

David was stunned. Perhaps Gisela didn't have another lover. Perhaps she had been telling the truth when she said the Baron was now sleeping with her regularly. How he wished he could leave the reception and go to his apartment and get drunk. He could not, of course, since he was here to escort Lady Malvern. He snatched two glasses of vodka from a passing footman and downed them quickly. That soothed him a little but he still felt as if he had been viciously kicked in the stomach. God, what a ghastly evening!

Seeing that Lady Malvern was all right, he decided he would find Tatiana and apologise. Finding her was not hard, and although she was still surrounded, this time it was by ladies. As David approached the ladies smiled at him, well aware of his background and what an eligible catch he would be for any single girl. The only one not smiling was Tatiana.

He greeted the ladies and chatted with them pleasantly for a few minutes, then at the first opportunity leant over and whispered in Tatiana's ear that he was sorry for his apparent rudeness earlier in the evening. To his mortification Tatiana moved her head away from him and said coldly that he was not 'apparently' rude, but quite definitely, aggressively rude. With that she turned her back on him and began to talk to someone else.

Despite his attempt to whisper, this exchange had been overhead by several of the other ladies, and he could see that they were all agog. Obviously the incident would be a major topic of conversation for some time to come. Well, he was not going to add to the speculative gossip, so he bowed and smilingly left the group. Inwardly, he was raging, at himself and at Tatiana.

Just then his opposite number from the French Embassy appeared and David managed to compose himself as they discussed the Russian moves in the Crimea. Finally it was time to go in to dinner, so David excused himself and went to seek out Lady Malvern.

The rest of the evening, despite the sumptuous dinner and the magnificent surrounding, dragged agonizingly slowly for David who couldn't wait to go home.

When they left, some hours later, Lady Malvern commented on what a delightful evening it had been. David agreed, but privately thought it had been one of the worst evenings of his life. He couldn't wait to get home, but even there sleep eluded him as he tormented himself about Gisela. Then, if he managed to put her out of his mind for a few moments there was the problem of his having needlessly upset and offended Tatiana.

When he arrived at work the next morning he felt tired and depressed, but his mood improved when he received a note at lunch from Lady Malvern asking him if he would be kind enough to be her escort this evening at a concert to raise funds for charity. The concert was to be given by Count and Countess Samoilov. Count Samoilov, he knew, was a nephew of Prince Potemkin, and the Countess was by birth a Trubetskaya. David was confident the concert would be excellent as both families were renowned for their interest in music and the arts. One of the many things he loved about Russia was their wonderful singers — he did not believe there was anywhere in the world that had basses with the same depth and quality of voice.

The Embassy carriage picked him up that evening, then returned to the Residence to pick up the Ambassadress. Lady Malvern had been out to a ladies' luncheon party and was in fine form, leading David to believe there must have been quite a lot of wine drunk. Sometimes after drink Her Ladyship could be amazingly indiscreet, and David quite looked forward to these disclosures. However, tonight there were no indiscretions, although she did regale him with some amusing stories.

When they arrived at the Samoilovs Lady Malvern was greeted warmly, and David welcomed. They were then ushered into their hosts' private theatre where a number of other guests were standing round in an anteroom drinking wine and having canapes. David saw Countess Volonskaya and Tatiana on the other side of the room, and once he had established the Ambassadress with some friends he moved across to join them.

Countess Volonskaya greeted him warmly, but gave a rather wry smile as David bent to kiss Tatiana's hand. Tatiana's greeting was considerably less warm than her grandmother's, in fact it was downright chilly. David was a little nonplussed, so he began asking how little Alexei was faring. Countess Nadia burst into an enthusiastic account of his activities, and even Tatiana began to unbend a little as she told him of the progress her beloved nephew was making.

A few minutes later a gong was struck to indicate that the guests should take their seats for the concert. David excused himself and went to rejoin Lady Malvern, glad that Countess Nadia was pleased to see him, and that there was a slight thawing in Tatiana's coldness towards him.

As he had expected, the concert was well worth attending. Like Count Sheremetev, the Samoilovs had an orchestra and singers taken from the ranks of their serfs, and while the group tonight was not as large as the Sheremetev's, the performers were equally skilled.

After the concert he escorted Lady Malvern home, feeling he had regained a little peace of mind. It had been a good night, and for a brief time David had forgotten Gisela, or at least put her to the back of his mind. He also felt he had made some headway in regaining his status as Tatiana's good friend after his disastrous conduct the previous night.

Lord Malvern returned from Moscow after a successful trip, and the weeks began to fly by. They were now entering autumn, and the weather was growing noticeably colder. David had found some distraction in the performance of his racehorses, which had done reasonably well, but racing was now over for the season. He had found the racing quite exciting and had made several new friends among the other owners. He had also enjoyed talking with the various owners and studmasters about their breeding ideas and techniques.

In recent weeks he had not seen Countess Volonskaya or Tatiana, as they had taken Alexei to Moscow.

By the time they returned to St. Petersburg the ball season was under way, and Countess Volonskaya had already issued invitations for the ball she was giving. This was the ball she had promised to hold when Dmitri came on leave to St. Petersburg. Tatiana regularly received letters from Dmitri, and Nadia had already had two letters from Countess Elizabeth telling her of Dmitri's further promotion and the recent highlights of his service in the Crimea. Elizabeth said proudly that it was no wonder Russia's Empire was expanding so fast when there were such good and fine young men as Dmitri serving the country's interests. While in Moscow the Countess Nadia had also received a very newsy letter from David, telling her what was happening on the St. Petersburg scene. He expressed himself well on paper, she thought. Tatiana had also received at least one letter from David, but was somewhat uncommunicative about its contents.

Tatiana still seemed annoyed with David, although her grandmother was not sure why this was, as it was not like her to hold a grudge. She wondered if Tatiana would accept Dmitri's proposal. She was sure Dmitri was going to ask her permission to offer for Tatiana, and she would be delighted at the match. However, she was a little puzzled about how Tatiana felt about Dmitri. She knew Tatiana was very fond of him, but she wondered whether she regarded him more as an adored brother than as a lover. She knew Tatiana missed Sergei desperately, and she thought she had grown even closer to Dmitri after his death.

She was aware that Tatiana had become very fond of David, despite their recent disagreement. The Countess also had a great deal of affection for him and thought he would make an excellent husband for Tatiana, but he had the disadvantage of not being Russian, and he would ultimately want to take his wife to live in Britain. She would not like that, but her own life was gradually drawing to a close and she would not stand in Tatiana's way. However, she did not believe Tatiana would be happy if she could not spend at least some of her time in Russia.

The main thing, she thought, was that she would like Tatiana to marry for love, and if he was a suitable man she would not object, whoever he was. But she did hope that whoever she married would be capable of managing the estates and property she would leave Tatiana on her death. Provisions would also have to be made for trustees for Alexei while he was a minor. There would also be his late father's affairs to manage. That monster Barinsky had been interfering with them as Natasha's husband and Barsov had told her there was a lot to sort out.

Ironically, since Natasha had died after Barinsky she had inherited all his wealth. This had grown from virtually nothing to a sizeable estate, mainly through illegal dealings like the gambling den he had owned. Although his money had now been left, through Natasha, to Alexei, the Countess was determined to try to find out who had been cheated, and if possible repay them or their families. She still could not think of Barinsky without shaking with rage. She could not bear to think of his hypocrisy, and how taken in she, and everyone else, had been.

In an effort to shake off her despondency, the Countess went to take a last look at her recently built stables.

The following day they left for St. Petersburg. They called in to see various friends on the way, so it took them almost three weeks to reach St. Petersburg. There were a number of invitations and letters awaiting them, including an invitation to lunch with the Kolcluleys the following day, if they were back. They accepted happily, as they always received a warm welcome from their old friends, and their house was always filled with kindness and laughter.

When they arrived the next day they were met almost immediately by Countess Elizabeth, who told them that her husband's nephew, Count Lev Kolcluley, had arrived to spend a week with them as his parents were currently in France. He was about Dmitri's age, and a delightful fellow. They had not seen him for years, not since he was about sixteen and had come back to school for one of the Guards regiments. His mother had preferred France because it suited her health, and the whole family spent most of the year there. So, she said, they were very pleased to make his acquaintance again, and he was so good with her daughters.

However, the exciting news was that he had served as an ADC to Field-Marshal Rumiantsev-Zadunaisky and was able to tell them much more about Dmitri. After Ochakov, Dmitri had been recommended for additional promotion, because of his leadership qualities and the personal courage he had shown in three battles. Lev believed he was going to receive the Order of St. Vladimir.

Count Nikolai had by this time arrived in the entrance hall to see what was holding them up, and was not surprised to hear his wife in full flight on the brilliance of their son. He let her finish then, as she drew breath to continue, he smiled. 'Elizabeth, don't you think it would be more comfortable for our guests if they were sitting down while you told them your news?' The Countess was immediately contrite and ushered her friends into the drawing room.

Sophie and Daria came forward quickly to kiss their Aunt Nadia, then they flung their arms around Tatiana and took her over to meet their cousin. Tatiana saw a tall, slim, very good-looking young man in his early twenties. When he greeted her warmly, she saw he had inherited in full measure the Kolcluleys' winning smile and charm.

Lev in turn saw a beautiful, poised young woman who was the epitome of elegance and beauty, and complimented her to that effect. At that moment David, who had been standing in the background unseen by Tatiana, stepped forward and kissed her hand, saying how good it was to see her and Countess Nadia back in St. Petersburg. They had been badly missed, he said. Tatiana gave him such an enchanting smile that he believed he must have been forgiven at last, and his spirits rose accordingly.

He then went with Lev to greet Countess Nadia. The old Countess told Lev she had known his mother when she was a young girl and used to come and stay with the Countess's daughter before she married. She liked his mother very much, and had seen her in France about two years ago, but she gathered that Lev had been studying in Russia at that time. She hoped he would call on her while he was in St. Petersburg, she added, and with a glance at Tatiana Lev replied that it would be a great pleasure.

The Countess greeted David warmly and began to talk of her Moscow trip, her horses and the plans she had for the stud. Normally David would have been highly interested, but he kept seeing Lev sparkling with the three girls and he wanted to join them, although he did not want to appear rude. The Countess, with a twinkle in her eye, then told him he should go and join the younger members of the party while she caught up with what had been happening in St. Petersburg from Count and Countess Kolcluley.

Meanwhile, David's favourable opinion of Lev was fast being replaced with resentment as he watched the young man flirting with Tatiana. Really, he thought, Tatiana was a consummate flirt. But he had to admit she looked ravishing, and Lev was obviously smitten. Daria and Sophie were also joining in the fun and teasing, and attempting to include David, but he felt quite wooden and knew he was not responding in his usual natural manner.

What was wrong with him, he thought despairingly, although he knew he had never been the same since Gisela had dropped him. When he had seen her at a diplomatic function two weeks earlier, he had felt certain she was avoiding him. He wasn't able to talk to her because he could never get close enough.

Lunch was announced, and they went into the dining room, where David was seated with Countess Nadia on one side and Sophie on the other. Opposite him was Tatiana, with Count Nikolai on one side and Lev on the other. Countess Elizabeth sat on Lev's other side, and David noticed how well-mannered he was as he flirted lightly with both ladies. Even Countess Elizabeth, who was happily married to the man she loved, was obviously enjoying his attention and teasing him in return.

But it was Tatiana David was really interested in, and he was sure she was encouraging Lev. She could be extremely funny at times, and before long had the whole table laughing as she flirted with Lev, who she said she suspected had a whole harem of ladies hidden away in the Crimea. Lev responded in kind and everyone sparkled except for David. This didn't seem to disturb Tatiana, who said that Lord Mountforte apparently didn't approve of light-hearted conversation and perhaps they should all listen to his more profound thoughts, of which she was sure he had many.

At that the conversation stopped and everyone looked at David, who could cheerfully have throttled Tatiana. However, he managed to respond lightly, saying that his mind had slipped back to a minor problem at the Embassy, but he was thoroughly enjoying the conversation. Everyone nodded happily, and the jokes and laughter soon returned. David thought he saw Tatiana give him a mocking smile, but she was as quick as quicksilver and he couldn't be sure. What he was sure of was that he did not enjoy seeing Lev and Tatiana flirting. She almost seemed to be trying to provoke him, although he did not understand why, as there was no reason for her to do so.

Suddenly Dmitri's name came up and the Countess was asking Lev to tell her friends all he knew about her son's progress in the south. As Lev began talking about his cousin it was very clear that he really admired the reputation Dmitri had.

According to Lev, Dmitri's men loved him because of the care he took of them. He tried to make sure their wages came on time, although this wasn't always possible because the army was notoriously late with its payments. He also made sure they had adequate clothing, something many officers did not do, despite Prince Potemkin's express instructions, and they received the best food he could procure.

He also made sure care was taken of any men who were wounded, and tried to get word back to their families. In battle, the men trusted him, as he always led from the front and never asked his men to do anything he would not do. The officers serving under him liked him for his decency, his sense of humour, and the fact that whatever his men and officers achieved he always shared the credit around fairly.

Lev said he had heard Prince Potemkin tell Field-Marshal Rumientsev-Zadunaisky that if all the Russian officers looked after and led their men as well as Count Dmitri Kolcluley, Russia would not lose so many soldiers as it had been doing. He also praised the way the officers serving under Kolcluley were taking him as their example of how to look after their soldiers. Lev concluded by quoting Potemkin who had said Dmitri Kolcluley could go to the top of the Russian Army if he remained with it.

Everyone at the table was impressed, and the Kolcluleys were filled with pride for their son and brother. Count Nikolai thanked Lev for what he had said about Dmitri, and Countess Elizabeth addressed all the table with tears of joy in her eyes, and again reiterated how proud she was of her son. Everyone then drank a toast to Dmitri, then another to Lev, wishing the latter luck when he went back to the south.

When the lunch was over David returned to the Embassy. That evening he was to attend a reception at the French Embassy, which turned out to be a very grand affair with masses of people milling around. He was glad there was a large crowd, as he had been delayed at his own Embassy and by the time he had gone home and changed he was nearly two hours late. As a result, the Ambassador and his wife had finished receiving by the time he arrived, so after entering the hall and giving his coat, gloves and hat to a footman he thought he would slip along the terrace and enter through one of the side doors.

As he went toward the terrace he saw a woman standing by one of the potted shrubs with her back to him. Suddenly he realised it was Gisela. With a feeling of excitement, and some trepidation, he crept up behind her and said hello. She whirled around, and exclaimed, 'Oh, no, I was just out here thanking God that you weren't at the reception.' Then she put her hand to her mouth as if she wanted to take back the words.

David was shocked. 'Why were you so concerned whether I was at the reception or not?'

Slowly Gisela reached out and took both of his hands in hers. David felt a rush of exultation swim through his body and felt his hands trembling. Gisela looked hard at him, then said she couldn't bear to see the look in his eyes when he saw her. She said she saw detestation, agony, love and hatred in his glance.

David tightened his hands on hers and endeavoured to pull her to him, but she held herself apart. Then he said that try as he would he could not detest her, and that he still loved her desperately. He stammered that he wanted her and would agree to any terms she suggested, just as long as he could keep meeting her and loving her.

Gisela drew a deep breath, then she said, 'Let us sit down on that bench where no one will see us.'

Catching his breath, David took her arm, escorted her to the bench and sat down close beside her. He couldn't believe the wonderful feeling that engulfed his body.

Gisela took another deep breath. 'I have received the flowers you have been sending, and the notes, and it has to stop. I'm sorry, David, but this must be the last conversation we ever have alone.' As he gasped she went on, 'The only reason we are having it is because you have caught me by surprise.' She sighed softly. 'But now I am glad you are here, because perhaps I can explain the position a little better, so that you understand.'

She then turned and faced him, her body taut, and in a flat voice said she loved David still, and would never love anyone as much as she had loved him. But for her sanity, her future, the future of her child, for his future, and the happiness of her husband, this was the last time she would ever be alone with him.

As David began to protest she hushed him and said that he must realise, whatever he felt, that she had duties to her husband, who loved her deeply, and to her unborn child. If David continued, by his presence, to haunt her she could easily become ill. Did he not realise that? If he really loved her he must leave her alone to live the rest of her life in as happy a manner as she could contrive. She hoped he would not hate or despise her, but realise that she was taking the best and most honourable steps she could, for all their sakes.

Although David hated hearing what she was saying, he was also very much aware of how she too was suffering, just by sitting beside him and talking to him. Only then did he realise what strength and courage she had, and he was once again overwhelmed by a feeling of terrible loss. Gisela then stood up and falteringly said she hoped David would soon find someone else he could love, and that she would always wish him happiness. She dearly hoped he would wish the same for her. She then touched him on the cheek with her gloved hand, turned and went back indoors.

David felt like crying. He knew now that Gisela had no new lover, that it was he she loved, but it was because she and the Baron were having this child that she would never leave her husband and jeopardise the child's future. He realised she was taking the most honourable of positions, and he now knew she would maintain that stance whatever he did. It was the end, and no matter how he felt, he would never win her back. If he persisted he would only cause her harm, and because of the strength of her feelings he might even cause her to have a breakdown.

David walked slowly back along the terrace to the entrance hall. He asked for his coat, hat and gloves, called for his carriage and went home. He took a full bottle of vodka, slumped on a chaise lounge and slowly drank himself to sleep.

The next morning he took an oath. Knowing that he would never meet another Gisela, he would find an attractive woman with a pleasant personality and marry her within the next twelve months. He would never find great love again, the alternative was a vegetable kind of happiness and he must provide an heir. He would have five or six children, treat his wife considerately, run his future properties and console himself with his hobbies.

These dismal thoughts pursued him for the next few weeks, during which he didn't see Gisela, except once at a distance. He spent much of his spare time with the Kolcluleys, and in particular with Lev. From their discussions David was able to pick up a lot of information about the south, which the Ambassador was pleased to include in his reports home to Britain. David never felt he was spying on Lev, because the latter spoke so openly. He found Lev's descriptions of the battles, and of the Ottomans, the Tartars and the Cossacks, quite gripping. He was also continually amazed at the genius of Prince Potemkin, who seemed to crop up in almost every incident in the south. Potemkin may have had enemies at Court in St. Petersburg, but in the south he was revered almost without exception. Since the Prince had such power, and was also such an anglophile, David again thought Britain was foolish to antagonise Russia.

Countess Nadia said there was a great deal of jealousy and even hatred by some of the aristocracy against Prince Potemkin, but as long as he continued to perform in the south and retained the Empress's confidence, no enemies could harm him. She commented that she did not like some of his morals with certain women, but that was a price to pay for genius. No one since Peter the Great had expanded the Russian Empire as Potemkin had. Nor had anyone, not even Peter the Great, been so sensitive in their dealings with Russia's new subjects, or brought such countries as Georgia under the sway of the Russian sovereign as he had managed to do without any fighting.

When Lev left for the south again David found that he missed their conversations and his amusing wit. The day before he left, Tatiana, Sophie, Daria, Lev and David had all gone ice-skating. David once again thought how striking the Russians looked on the ice. Their furs were so rich looking, and the other garments so colourful. Even the poorer classes, who may not have furs, still appeared gay and colourful in their felt coats and the hats they wore, which were of so many colours.

His four Russian friends were excellent skaters and they all had a lot of fun. When the orchestra or band played, as it did some weekends, the music heightened the rhythm of the skating and gave one a great sense of exhilaration that even David could not withstand.

With Lev's departure David's social life became a little quieter, but for the Kolcluleys the excitement was building up as they began planning what they would do for Dmitri when he came home on leave. The invitations to Countess Volonskaya's ball had gone out several weeks earlier, and David thought it would be one of the highlights of Dmitri's leave. Then, from hints that Sophie and Daria began to drop, he began to wonder if Dmitri had already proposed to Tatiana and they were going to announce their engagement at the ball. He had tried tactfully to find out more, but Tatiana gave nothing away and Sophie and Daria just giggled and gave him amused, knowing looks.

Countess Nadia who was looking forward to Dmitri's arrival, was also wondering what might transpire between Tatiana and him. She had also noticed that David was paying very close attention to Tatiana. But like David, the Countess had no idea whether Tatiana was serious about Dmitri or not. She knew her granddaughter liked him very much, but that was not the same as being in love with him.

Never before had Tatiana been so unforthcoming with her. Of course she had not asked Tatiana outright, but she had given her plenty of opportunities to let her grandmother know what she was thinking. Sometimes, she noticed, when Tatiana thought no one was watching, she looked at David in a speculative way. However, she doubted that Tatiana was looking at David as a future husband. And as much as she liked David herself, and he certainly qualified in terms of breeding, title and above all character, she knew she would miss Tatiana terribly if she were to marry David and go to live in Britain.

On this thought her mind went back to Alexei. How the boy was growing up, and what a lovely disposition he had, just like his father, Sasha. She still trembled when she thought how close they had come to losing Alexei, how close he had come to being put to death by that monster Barinsky. He was a bright child and doing very well at his studies. Princess Dashkova had recommended sending Alexei to an English school later, as she had her son, Prince Pavel. It could be a good idea. The Countess had discussed it with David, who agreed, but not until Alexei was fifteen or sixteen.

David was so good with Alexei, she reflected, and Alexei was very fond of him. She was glad she had made him a trustee, even if it was only temporarily, while he was in Russia. She wondered if it would be practical to keep him on as a trustee after he left Russia, and if he would agree. She would miss David when he left Russia, since they had a great deal in common, and she respected his judgement. She was also in regular correspondence with his grandfather now they had begun to do business together. Timber was the main commodity they had a mutual interest in, but they were also looking at what products his ships could bring to Russia when they came to collect a cargo of timber. She hoped the ship might be able to bring some woollen goods.

There were wonderful opportunities for business in Russia now. If only she were twenty years younger. She had begun to feel her age lately, and she noticed that almost unconsciously she was passing over more of her responsibilities to Tatiana and her senior staff. If Tatiana married Dmitri, she wondered if he would leave the army and look after the estates. She was sure his parents would like that, no matter how high he rose in the army or how great his prospects were. His mother in particular was always afraid of something happening to him in battle. Of course when his father died, there would also be the Kolcluley estates to manage.

As she thought how her business interests had grown the Countess reflected that she really should get at least two young assistants for Barsov. He would certainly need them if the timber business kept expanding at the current rate, let alone her other interests. She thought back to when her husband had died, when she was just twenty-three, leaving her a very considerable fortune and one daughter. No one had expected her to do anything about the estates except draw the income, but despite being devastated with grief at his early death she had begun to take an interest in the properties. She found she had a natural flair for business and soon began to instigate changes. She read widely and was not afraid to adopt some of the agricultural reforms that were being developed overseas, particularly in Britain.

She began to enjoy implementing her plans and watching the results. In time she built up a skilled team of experts around her, and she paid them well, significantly above the usual rate. Some of her friends had warned her that she was unwise, but her investment in good people had paid off handsomely. Now she could look back with pride on her achievements. Her estates were some of the best run in Russia, not that she would ever say so herself.

Of course, when Tatiana married and had children she would not have as much time as Nadia had had, so it really was important that she married a good practical man, and not one who squandered his time and money, like some she could name. No, Dmitri would be ideal, particularly if he gave up the army. Meanwhile, she must make sure the heads of her various businesses were training enough young people to take over their positions when they eventually retired. It was imperative that she left Tatiana and Alexei with good, sound stewards, financial managers and advisors.

She decided she would take Tatiana with her when she went to visit her timber mill the next day. They would be away for four days, but there was nothing requiring them to stay in St. Petersburg. She got up to go and find Tatiana to tell her they would leave early in the morning, but before she could find her granddaughter a footman announced that Lord Mountforte was here and enquiring if the Countesses were at home. Nadia went to meet him, sending a servant to fetch Tatiana. She invited David to join them for a light dinner, then as an afterthought added, 'David, could you spare the time to come to the Smirsk Timber Mill with us? We are leaving early tomorrow.'

'I'm sure I could make it,' he replied. 'Britain's trade in timber with Russia is very important, and I am sure the Ambassador would encourage me to learn all I can about it.'

Finding that the Countess intended to leave at nine, he decided he would try and see Lord Malvern at breakfast. The Ambassador breakfasted at eight, so if he was packed and already dressed for the road, and His Lordship agreed, he could be at the Countess's by nine. As they were agreeing on this plan Tatiana came into the room, and she looked pleased to see David. Once again it struck him what a beautiful girl she was. She always dressed with style, had beautiful manners, and was intelligent and often very witty. Dmitri was a most fortunate man. Why, David thought, did he always have a pang of jealousy when he thought of Tatiana married? Why didn't he want her to get married? Since he regarded her almost as a sister, he wondered if all brothers resented the thought of their sisters marrying. Surely not?

After dinner they went into the music room where David and Tatiana sang several duets, with Tatiana playing the piano accompaniment. Their voices blended perfectly, and Countess Nadia always enjoyed listening to them, finding it a restful way to spending an evening. David enjoyed it too, and it was with some reluctance that he announced he really should leave if he was to have his packing organised that night. Contingent on the Ambassador's approval, he would meet them the following morning at nine.

Lord Malvern thoroughly approved of his visit to the timber mill, and readily gave his permission. He praised David for developing such good relationships with the Russian people, adding that any information he provided was usually inserted into his reports to the Foreign Office, where it was of considerable interest.

When David arrived at the Volonski Palace he found to his delight that little Alexei was coming too. The little boy was very excited, as this was his first visit to Smirsk. He was now so different from the self-contained, quiet child they had rescued from the Branska fort. These days he laughed, continually asked questions, and absorbed information quickly. He loved games, and now that he felt secure he was very spontaneous in his actions. There was already a slightly whimsical charm about him, which David envisaged would make him most attractive to women when he grew up.

Once they were seated in the sleigh they were joined by the Countess's maid, Tanya, who Tatiana said she and her grandmother were going to share. Like all old retainers Tanya spoke her mind, and she now said that since they were going into the country and were going to stay in a peasant's hut and eat peasant food, she couldn't think why they would require a maid. Countess Nadia laughingly told David that Tanya always complained when they went to Smirsk because she thought the cottage they stayed in wasn't grand enough. Tanya then muttered that the Countess shouldn't have all these business responsibilities, and should leave them to her stewards.

David always enjoyed listening to these encounters. He felt the easy relationships between good Russian employers and their staff was rather like those of a large family. Certainly the longstanding servants would think nothing of giving advice, praise or criticism. Sometimes it was heeded and sometimes not, but it was always listened to. It was such an unusual situation — here were employers who had almost the power of life and death over their servants and serfs, yet the best households ran along lines that made everyone feel part of the family, with differing degrees of responsibility.

Once they set off Alexei chattered non-stop, commenting on everything he saw out the window and asked what he would see when he got to Smirsk. Tanya told him there were many savage wolves around the area and that if he wasn't in bed by eight o'clock the wolves would break in by coming down the chimney. 'What would the wolves do then?' Alexei asked with wide eyes.

Tatiana, seeing that he was a little nervous, laughed and said, 'Tanya was only trying to frighten you so you will go to bed on time and not bother her, because she has too much to do.' Alexei was quite indignant at this and said that he never bothered Tanya, and that his nanny, Marfa, always looked after him. Tanya promptly said she would never let any wolves hurt Alexei, and that of course she knew he wouldn't bother her.

A truce having been drawn, the Countess began telling them the story of how she had come to acquire the Smirsk estate some twenty-odd years earlier. For some reason Tatiana had never heard this, and David always found the Countess's tales fascinating. She could see the estate had enormous potential, but it was run by a merchant who never visited it and spent most of his life living in France or Italy. He drew all the profits as they were made and invested nothing in new plant and machinery, or in training his employees and serfs. When she bought it, she called in experts who helped her draw up a plan for the estate, which she then put into effect with the help of her stewards. For the first six years she drew no profits out but invested every rouble back into Smirsk. Eventually, of course, it paid off and now she drew a very large income from the estate. Like Prince Potemkin, and unlike many other forest owners, she was replanting the areas that had been logged.

Looking at Tatiana and Alexei, who would each inherit half the estate when she died, the Countess told them that as long as the trees were replanted, the logging would never diminish the life of the estate. She hoped they would always remember what she had done, particularly in the Smirsk area, as the land there was only good for trees. David asked how big the Smirsk estate was, and was impressed to find it covered over three hundred thousand acres of forest.

They finally arrived at the estate just before dusk. The sleigh trip had been a delight, and it was amazing how warm they had kept. Snow covered the ground and the roofs of the buildings, but David was impressed with his first glimpse of the layout of the mill and the surrounding cottages. The cottages all appeared to be in good order, and smoke was issuing from their roofs. They were all quite solid buildings, and not the usual shacks or huts he had seen in so many villages in Russia. He wondered if all the Countess's estates catered so well for her servants, and from his knowledge of her he was fairly sure they would.

When he expressed his surprise at the quality of accommodation provided for her servants and serfs, the Countess replied that she had found that the more dignity and respect you gave people — whether stewards, tutors, servants or serfs — the more you benefited. Good living conditions were part of giving people dignity and respect. On all her estates the children of her servants and serfs received rudimentary schooling between the ages of six and twelve years old. During that time they were taught to read and write, and given a preliminary introduction to some trade. If a child was particularly bright, and recommended by a schoolteacher, she would pay for higher education for the child. She told David, with some pride, that eleven of her middle managers had been educated at university, paid for by her, and that five of them had been serfs. She had others who were currently at university, and still others who were now musicians and painters.

They trotted past the cottages and the mill, then down a drive lined with shrubs and trees until a larger house came into view, somewhat removed from the other buildings. 'This is our house,' said the Countess.

'House!' snorted Tanya, adding that it was nothing but an overgrown cottage and not fit for Countess Volonskaya. Countess Nadia laughed and David could see that she was thoroughly enjoying herself.

The house was built of wooden logs and shingles, and fitted right into the scenery. When they had stepped down from the sleigh they found a soberly dressed man and two serfs were standing at the steps. The serfs knelt in the snow and the other man bowed. The Countess and Tatiana greeted the man happily, and he appeared very pleased to see them. The Countess smiled at the serfs and then introduced the man to David, saying this was Bashoff, her Smirsk steward. The man accompanied them inside the house and after making sure they were comfortable, he turned to leave, saying he would meet them again at nine the following morning.

The inside of the house was surprisingly warm. They entered a large room that combined a dining area with a sitting area. There was a large porcelain stove at either end of the room, a table to seat ten, comfortable sofas and chairs, and a scattering of rugs on the floor. In addition to this room there were five bedrooms, a large kitchen and a small back hall.

After David and Alexei had been shown around they all retired to their bedrooms to rest briefly and change for dinner, Tanya accompanying Alexei. When, thirty minutes later, they gathered for a drink before dinner, David was amazed at the transformation of Countess Nadia and Tatiana. They had cast off their conventional travelling clothes and were now wearing colourful peasant dresses. As Tatiana saw

David's appreciative expression she twirled around, showing off her dress. Then she came over to him, seized his hand and, humming a melody, began a peasant dance. Countess Nadia, in high spirits, took Alexei by the hand and they joined in the dance, while Tanya tried to look disapproving. She could not help but look proud, however, and finally burst out laughing and began clapping in time with the dance. This brought in the two serfs from the kitchen, where they had been preparing the meal, and they too joined in the clapping. This encouraged the dancers to keep going for another few minutes, although David and Alexei were not the most gifted of peasant dancers, especially as they tried to keep up with Tatiana and the Countess's increasingly fast steps. Finally they all collapsed amid much laughter.

It was obvious before the evening was over that Countess Nadia loved being in the woods at Smirsk, and that she enjoyed pretending to be a peasant. David wondered how his grandfather would have reacted if he had been here to see his newly acquired timber partner dancing in peasant style then sitting back with a glass of vodka. He realised that he really didn't know whether there was a side to his grandfather that might have enjoyed the evening. Perhaps the old Earl would have surprised him as much as the Countess had.

Over dinner, which was basic peasant food but pleasantly seasoned and well-cooked, David was told the programme. The Countess said he was welcome to join in all or any part of it. First thing in the morning she would go through the quarterly reports, after which she would have lunch with Bashoff and two of his assistants. Then at one-thirty she would take a tour of the mill and yards. At three-thirty she planned to take Alexei for a ride through the woods for an hour or so and let him see a tiny part of his inheritance. In the evening, Bashoff, his wife, the two senior assistants and their wives would join them for drinks and dinner. That night would be a social occasion with no business talk.

In the morning of the second day she would again meet with Bashoff, then at noon she would be giving a lunch in the main shed for all the workers, their wives and children. After a short rest they and some of the men would take Alexei over by sleigh to see where a bear was hibernating. That evening they would have dinner by themselves, and the next morning they would leave for St. Petersburg.

It sounded a strenuous few days, especially for a woman of the Countess's age. David wondered whether she should not have planned a rest before returning to St. Petersburg, although he was not entirely surprised that she had not, as by now he was well aware of her determination and stamina. Both Tatiana and she seemed to thrive in the countryside, and he remembered what excellent company they had been on the trip to Kiev.

The next morning they had a tasty breakfast of local fare: eggs, bacon, black bread, dried mushrooms fried in bacon fat with onions and various herbs, some oat cakes, tea and milk, plus sugar from their own beet. There was plenty of everything and much left over, but leftovers were never a problem in Russia. There were always servants, serfs and their relatives to eat it.

David, Tatiana and even Alexei joined the Countess for her nine a.m. meeting with Bashoff, and he was again surprised at the breadth of her knowledge. At times Bashoff listened earnestly to the Countess's more informed suggestions, and she in turn absorbed all the practical information he offered. They made a good team and each appeared to appreciate the value of the other's contribution.

Tatiana was clearly keen to learn all she could, and from time to time contributed slightly hesitantly to the discussions. But what he found particularly interesting was the way they all encouraged little Alexei to ask questions, and went out of their way to provide answers he would understand. Countess Nadia later told David that it was important to instil as much information as possible in a future landowner, at as early an age as possible. She had done that successfully with her three grandchildren, she said, and he could see how it had benefited Tatiana. David was completely sincere when he said he could see that she had raised her grandchildren well.

Lunch was a working meal, but Bashoff and his two assistants obviously enjoyed it. After the normal courtesies the assistants were soon immersed in discussing the problems and opportunities of increasing the productivity of the estate. David had to admire the adroit way the Countess and Tatiana made them relax, gained their confidence, and drew them out. Equally interesting was to see how much the men had to offer once they knew they had the confidence of the proprietor.

Just before lunch ended, Nadia told Bashoff that she would like both of his young assistants to go abroad, as soon as he could spare them. Not at the same time, of course, and to different countries. She had made contact with what she believed was the most modern mill in Poland, and they were prepared to let her send a foreman there for a couple of months. She had also contacted one of the most modern mills in the Grand Duchy of Finland, which was owned by a very distant relative of her late husband's, and they had also agreed to take a foreman for several months.

She asked Bashoff to work out the best time to send them, and to let her know. Her financial steward in St. Petersburg, Mr. Barsov, would make all the necessary arrangements. She did not wish to inconvenience Bashoff in any way, nor, she added with a smile, did she wish to see Smirsk's profits fall.

The young men were too overcome to laugh at that remark, being mesmerised by the thought of travelling abroad, but Bashoff said with a smile that he would take the Smirsk's profits into account. Shyly, the two young men began to ask the Countess what she wanted them to learn and how they would travel. How would people understand them, they asked; did they know Russian, and so forth. The Countess enjoyed answering their questions and was pleased with the excitement she had created.

After lunch they toured the mill and its yards, and David was again impressed when he saw that it had the most up-to-date machinery and some of the best working conditions he had seen. At his grandfather's request he had visited two Finnish mills on his way to St. Petersburg, and Smirsk was a considerably better operation than any he had seen there. The Countess had also been breeding horses to suit the timber work and Smirsk's weather conditions. Her breeding programme had proved very successful.

Around four o'clock they all changed into riding clothes and mounted some local ponies, on which Alexei enjoyed plodding through the snow. Tatiana began to tell him about how she had come here at around his age and looked for wolf lairs and hibernating bears. In the summer, she had gone looking for all the animals, deer, bear cubs and wolf cubs, and hunting for beehives. Then she named all the birds in the area, described where they lived during the summer, where they lived during winter, and what they ate in the various seasons. Alexei was fascinated, and David, listening, found himself quite beguiled by Tatiana's chronicle of life in the countryside.

The difference in attitude between the beautiful, elegant and much sought-after heiress of St. Petersburg, Kiev and Moscow, and the beautiful, charming, nature-loving peasant girl of this trip was extraordinary. As they plodded along on their ponies, he listened to Tatiana and Alexei and abruptly realised that Tatiana was not two separate people but rather one of those rare persons who could accommodate herself to her surroundings and the people inhabiting those surroundings. Yet he also realised that she would never lose her dignity in a crisis or under pressure. What fun she was when she was enjoying herself. Like Countess Nadia, Tatiana seemed to be comfortable in any strata of society.

Just then the Countess, who had been riding behind with Bashoff, called out that they should turn back or it would be dark before they arrived back at the house. There were also the final arrangements for the dinner to be seen to. Although Tanya had said she would oversee these, and the Countess had every confidence in her, she also wanted to make sure everything was just as she envisaged, since she only came down to Smirsk twice a year. She liked to see something of her managers' wives, and she wanted to ensure they had an enjoyable evening.

The dinner was a great success. The Countess and Tatiana soon had everyone at their ease, helped by little Alexei, who eased any tension by telling everyone all about his day's activities and what he was going to do the next day. Despite his enthusiasm, Alexei was a naturally courteous little boy, and the women in particular were charmed by him. After dinner the Countess encouraged everyone to dance, joining in herself and again making sure everyone was at ease. Her enjoyment of the music and the rhythm was obvious, and even the most retiring of her guests found it infectious. The music was a surprise to everyone except Bashoff, since Countess Nadia had asked him to bring several gypsy musicians over from the settlement, which was on her property and not far from the mill. They were delighted to come, because she was known for her generosity and made sure they were never harassed on her property.

As David got ready for bed that night he reflected on how much he had enjoyed the evening. He fell asleep on that note and, for the second night in a row, he slept well and did not dream of Gisela.

The next morning the Countess suggested that Tatiana, David and Alexei should go for a sleigh ride in the woods. Perhaps Tatiana would show them the lake which, though it would be frozen over now, was lovely in the summer. This was agreed on and the horses were ordered to be harnessed to the sleigh. They decided not to take a driver, but Tatiana and David would take turns with the reins. With an admonition not to be late for lunch at the mill, the Countess set off for her meeting with Bashoff.

Three plump ponies arrived pulling a troika sleigh, and once they were all seated Tatiana took the reins. She was a very competent driver, and told David that she often drove a wheeled or sledge troika on the estates, depending on the season. She loved having three horses to handle, she said, and they always seemed so fast.

It was an idyllic ride. The snow on the ground and the icicles that hung from the branches created a beautiful scene. As the sun's rays struck icicles the woods took on a mysterious beauty, leaving one feeling as if anything could happen. As the troika trotted through the woods Tatiana began to tell Alexei the fairytales her old Matushka used to tell her as a child. Some of them were happy and told of fairies, princesses and princes, while others were frightening and told of monsters, devils and giants.

Tatiana was a natural storyteller. Often David saw Alexei furtively glancing round at the trees as if expecting a monster to appear, and he acknowledged that he was also caught up in the atmosphere created by the almost fairyland forest and Tatiana's stories. Sometimes, despite the stillness, her voice floated away as the ponies plunged forward over a slight bank, but this only enhanced the magic of the story.

When David offered to take a turn with the reins Tatiana said no, she was happy driving if he didn't mind. David sank back contentedly into his seat, and he and Alexei continued to listen raptly to the wonderful old fairytales Tatiana narrated with such feeling. As he listened, David began to be aware of an indescribable feeling for Tatiana. It certainly wasn't the passion he felt for Gisela, but he suddenly knew with certainty that he didn't want anyone else to become intimate with Tatiana. When he thought of Dmitri he felt ashamed. Kind, brave, generous Dmitri, whom he liked immensely, but he now knew he did not want him to marry Tatiana. Why, he thought, when he still wanted Gisela? Was it because now that he knew he could not have Gisela he had become jealous of Tatiana and Dmitri? He had always despised jealousy. Had his character changed as much as that?

Finally the troika pulled up on a snow-covered bank and they looked down on the frozen lake, which glistened with sparkling blue lights where the sunlight hit the icy surface. It looked so tranquil, with a pristine beauty. After spending a few minutes absorbing the peace of the scene, Tatiana said they had best turn and head for home if they were to be back and changed by noon. Alexei reported that Great-Grandmother had told him they were not to change but to come straight from the sleigh to the mill. She said she did not want the serfs to think they were not well-dressed for the lunch.

Tatiana agreed this was a good idea, but thought it was still time they started back. At precisely fifteen minutes before twelve the sleigh drew up at the mill. A groom came and took away the horses, side-stepping and prancing as they were led away for a rub down, and later a warm meal of mash.

The Countess had supplied a great feast for all the men, their wives, sweethearts and children. A bullock had been killed and roasted, along with dozens of fowl and ducks, two pigs, and masses of potatoes and onions. When the vodka appeared they all realised the Countess didn't expect them to return to work that day. After a while they began singing, while others danced, and it became a very happy, if slightly inebriated, afternoon.

At about five the Countess announced that she was going back to the house, but before leaving she thanked them for all they had done since her last visit. With that, someone among the revellers called out for six hurrahs for the Countess. The cheering sounded loud and clear and very genuine, if sometimes a little tipsy, with one or two of the men still cheering as they left. Nadia then took David's arm and said goodnight to Mr. Bashoff, who assured her he would see her before she left in the morning. Now, she said, she would have a short rest before dinner and the others may do what they wished, but to remember they were dining at eight.

They were all pleasantly tired after their busy day, so Tatiana and David sat down with Alexei and taught him a game of cards. David noted that once Alexei had mastered the rules and could play the game, Tatiana subtly warned him against ever gambling for money with cards. She told him in a most chilling manner how so-and-so had not only lost his money and estates through gambling, but also his wife and children. The picture she built up for Alexei would, David suspected, reform any gambler, her stories were told with such conviction. What an actress Russia's stage had lost in Tatiana!

Tatiana was beginning to occupy his thoughts more and more. As he couldn't have Gisela, and knew he could never love anyone else as passionately, perhaps he should consider Tatiana. After all, she was very lovely, and they got on well. He was convinced his grandfather would love her on sight, and could easily imagine her taking London society by storm. He began to visualise Tatiana giving a luncheon for his Scottish crofters in the Highlands and performing the Scottish dances with the same zest as she did the Russian peasant dances. He began to see a different future for himself. Then he thought of Dmitri. Was he being unfair? Of course he wasn't, let the best man win.

Dinner that night was a pleasant, relaxed meal, with Alexei monopolising the conversation, to everyone else's amusement, and in some cases pride. At nine o'clock Tanya came and took him to bed, and he went off happily retelling some of the more frightening stories he had heard that morning. Tanya obviously made a good audience, as she let out pretended shrieks of terror and gasps of fright. The others were amused as they listened through the partly open bedroom door.

Tatiana was especially amused as Alexei embellished the stories, and when Countess Nadia laughingly asked if her stories were really as gruesome as the versions she was hearing, replied she had better ask David. David assured the Countess that they were worse, and that Tatiana had frightened even him so much that he spent most of the sleigh ride hiding under the furs, fearful of a monster. He had not been able to see any of the scenery, he said. At that, Tatiana called him a shocking liar, and in pretended anger threw a cushion at his head.

Shortly afterwards, Countess Nadia said she was going to bed, and since Tatiana said she would follow suit there was nothing for David to do but to retire also. He lay in bed thinking over his idea of marrying Tatiana. The more he thought about it the more he liked the idea, and he began to plan a campaign to win her hand. He knew the Countess liked him, but he was also sure she had set her mind on Tatiana marrying Dmitri. On the other hand, he also knew that the Countess would ultimately agree to Tatiana marrying him if she believed she loved him. Now what he needed to know was how keen Tatiana was on Dmitri. In the midst of puzzling this out he fell asleep.

In the morning, David awoke pleasantly happy and began to think over his ideas for winning Tatiana. He decided he must not be too obvious, as the Countess was an intelligent and shrewd observer. If she suspected what he was up to she was quite capable of deciding to visit her estates in the Crimea and taking Tatiana with her, or even going right into the Crimea and visiting Dmitri. He decided he would have to work quickly and try to win Tatiana before the Countess's ball. He was sure she was expecting an engagement announcement at the ball, as the Kolcluley daughters certainly were. He began to feel pressured for time. Was not Dmitri due back shortly?

They left early the next morning, and as they travelled David began to tell the Countess about the British estates he would inherit. He described his grandfather's business interests and the coalmines he was involved with, and spoke of how he would like to increase the number of ships his grandfather owned. The Countess was interested to know what he thought the future would be for trade with India. David said he saw huge potential there, particularly now the East India Company was becoming so strong in that area. His grandfather was a considerable shareholder in that company and though he was not on the company's board, because of the size of his shareholding, notice was usually taken of his views when and if he expressed them.

David was disappointed to find that while the Countess Nadia was extremely interested in what he had to say, all Tatiana's attention was being given to Alexei, who was telling her some stories he was making up. He decided to change tactics, and began asking Tatiana if she had been to France and if she had enjoyed it.

Tatiana replied that she had accompanied her grandmother on her last visit to France, but had not been before that, even though the family had owned property there for more than forty-five years when her maternal great-grandfather had married a French heiress. She had enjoyed it, but the state of France was so uncertain that Grandmother had spent most of her time inspecting, and in some cases selling, family properties.

'I was presented to King Louis and Queen Marie-Antoinette at the Tuileries Palace in Paris, which was a grand affair, but to be frank I didn't find the French Court as grand as the Russian Court. Of course, I have never been to Versailles, but I did not see anything in France to equal the Winter Palace or Tsarskoe Selo.

'But I did enjoy visiting the French dress designers, and the hat and shoe salons,' she added, 'and Grandmother allowed me to spend an extravagant sum on clothes.' She added that the news coming from France now was not good, as there was much unrest internally and the King was being badly advised, they had been told.

At this stage Countess Nadia entered the conversation to say that her old friend the Duke de Richelieu had suggested that unless she was very attached to her French properties, she should sell them and deposit the proceeds with one of the private banks in Switzerland. French Protestants had established these banks in Geneva years earlier, after persecution by the Catholic Church and the government in France. She was contemplating following Richelieu's advice, as he had privately told her that some of the shrewder members of the French aristocracy and upper middle class were already doing so. It was very difficult, she said, looking after property that was so distant. She was thinking that if she sold her French properties she might invest some of the proceeds in a timber mill in Poland or Scandinavia. This would spread her timber interests and give her greater bargaining power with buyers.

As they discussed the economic prospects of France and its political instability, it became clear that the Countess was much better informed than David. Even Tatiana seemed to have followed French politics along with her grandmother, as they had regularly entertained people like the Duke de Richelieu, Prince de Lignes, Comte de Segur and Comte de Damas. There were also many Jacobites, mainly Scots, in the service of the Empress, who kept up with their relations in France, Italy and Scotland.

Yes, thought David, they are very well-informed. He asked them what they thought would happen in Russia after the Empress died and the Grand Duke Paul succeeded to the throne. Both agreed that it was worrying. Paul would change the alliances Russia currently had, and bring in a strongly pro-Prussia policy. He was known to hate Prince Potemkin who, being younger than the Empress, would naturally expect to outlive her. If he did, there is no knowing what Paul would do to him.

The Countess knew that Potemkin was well aware of the Grand Duke's hatred of him, and had tried unsuccessfully to appease him. That, she added, was why the Prince was acquiring estates in Poland, in case he had to flee there. There were strong rumours that he was interested in becoming King of Moldavia, or Dacia as the whole area was called. If this were to happen, said the Countess, Russia would lose a great patriot, a brilliant statesman and a natural genius. She was sure, however, that Prince Potemkin would never let the Empress down. He would only become the King of Moldavia or Dacia, or head of a Grand Duchy created out of the vast lands he had acquired in Poland, if the Empress agreed.

The Empress was also worried what would happen to her great statesman and, as everyone knew, her former lover, when her son succeeded her. The Empress loathed Paul, despite the fact that he was her son. She disliked his proposed policies, and the people surrounding him. On the other hand, she adored her grandchildren and was taking great care to see that they had the best education possible. Alexander, the eldest grandchild, was very bright and the Empress and the Court had high hopes for him.

Tatiana then said most of her friends were worried about what would happen when the Grand Duke succeeded to the Imperial throne. Dmitri, she said, was anxious, as almost all the officers in the south admired and respected Prince Potemkin, both for his patriotism and for his vision for Imperial Russia. He even thought there could be trouble in the army if Paul, on becoming Tsar, made his preference for Prussia too great, and as some feared, sacrificed Russia's interests.

This mention of Dmitri, and the knowledge that Tatiana had been discussing these controversial subjects with him, brought David swiftly back to his plan to captivate her. However, he was now at a disadvantage because both the Countess and Tatiana proceeded to muse out loud about what could happen if Dmitri was right about trouble in the army. The Countess thought he could well be correct in his summation of the situation, but added that one never knew what would happen in Russia if a strong man intervened.

The Countess thought Paul intelligent but stubborn, and she liked his wife very much. However, she also believed Paul was very sensitive and nervous. These days he was very frightened of his mother and those who surrounded her. He would, as a consequence, deal very harshly with anyone who opposed his wishes once he was in control. She was glad she was on good terms with his wife, who was a kind, intelligent and good woman, the Countess said. She worked with the Grand Duchess on two charities, and as a result was in reasonably regular contact with her.

In fact, she went on, she thought the Grand Duke's wife would be a better ruler than her husband. However, since she was totally loyal to her husband there was no chance of that, and naturally she was not advocating it in reality. Russia must now have legitimacy with the throne. She hoped, she said, that the Grand Duke Alexander, Paul's son, would in time prove to be another great Tsar in the mould of Ivan the Awesome, Peter the Great, and the Empress Catherine.

Then she said that if any of the Court spies had been listening in to her conversation she could be in serious trouble, Countess Volonskaya or not. She asked David to keep her comments to himself, and please never to jeopardise her or even potentially Tatiana by passing them on to the Ambassador, or disclosing them in any letters to Britain. She said this very seriously, and David willingly gave his word.

By the time they reached the outskirts of St. Petersburg it was around four o'clock and David felt frustrated that he had not managed to make any emotional impact on Tatiana. They had continued to discuss the political situation, which was very interesting, but it did not advance his cause with Tatiana. They were now trotting into the centre of St. Petersburg, and had just turned into the Nevsky Prospect when the sleigh came to a halt. As they looked out to see why they had stopped they noticed an open sleigh alongside and quickly recognised Countess Kolcluley and Daria struggling out in their furs, muffs, hats and boots. The Countess's face was wreathed in smiles. It was part of her considerable charm that all her thoughts and feelings were always expressed on her face — as Nadia had once commented dryly, it was just as well most of Elizabeth's thoughts were good, as she simply could not dissemble.

'You must have good news about Dmitri,' Tatiana called to her as the Countess reached their sleigh. 'No, no,' said Elizabeth, 'we are not expecting him back until later in the week.

'I do have good news though,' she added. 'It's about Sophie.'

Daria tried to remonstrate with her mother, telling her she should not say anything until the following day. Countess Elizabeth replied that telling Aunt Nadia was quite different, and when she spotted David in the sleigh she added, 'And we all regard David as part of the family, don't we?'

Daria again tried to persuade her mother not to say anything, saying she had promised not to. However, Countess Elizabeth said that the promise certainly wasn't meant to include close family. After all, Aunt Nadia had been her mother's greatest friend and she had known her all her life. Anyway, she said, it was fortuitous that she had recognised the Countess's sleigh when she had and been able to signal the driver to stop.

She then added, 'I will follow you home and tell you the secret there.' Then, as

Daria almost dragged her mother back to the sleigh, Elizabeth managed to turn her head and mouth, 'Sophie is engaged.'

This was a complete surprise, and as their sleigh moved off again Tatiana began to speculate about who her fiancé might be. 'I have no idea how it has been kept so quiet,' she said, smiling broadly in anticipation of the news. 'We all know that part of Aunt Elizabeth's charm is that though she always intends to keep a secret, she never can.'

Sophie had always said that if she really wanted to keep something quiet she usually told her father but not her mother. Her father never let on to his wife that he was in on the secret, and it was always amusing to see him express complete surprise when the secret was revealed. Dmitri did the same, because though they dearly loved their mother, they knew she was incapable of keeping news private.

Countess Nadia said that surely Tatiana would have noticed if Sophie was being courted — after all, they saw so much of each other. Tatiana agreed, but reiterated that she had not seen any indication of Sophie being courted, and wondered if perhaps it was an arranged marriage. Nadia did not think this was likely since, unless it was at the Empress's express command, Elizabeth would want all her children to marry for love.

Suddenly Tatiana said, 'I didn't think anything of it until now, but Sophie has been going skating for the last few weeks with only a maid. The last time I went skating with her about six weeks ago Felix Shuvalov asked her to partner him. They came back laughing, and she looked a little flushed, which at the time I thought was just due to the skating.'

'Well,' said her grandmother, 'he would be a fine catch for Sophie. Apart from their wealth, they are an influential family at Court. I do not know Felix very well, but Princess Shuvalov's mother was a great friend of mine. She is dead now, but was a most forceful woman in her time.'

She then asked Tatiana what she thought of Felix, and after pondering for a moment or two Tatiana said in a surprised voice that she supposed he was rather like Sophie's father.

'Well, then,' said Countess Nadia, 'let us hope it is Felix she's engaged to. One would go a long way to find a better husband and father than Nikolai Kolcluley.'

They arrived at the Volonski Palace, and Nadia insisted that David should come in. She asked her major-domo to bring in tea and drinks as soon as Countess Kolcluley and her daughter arrived. A few minutes later Countess Elizabeth and Daria were announced. They had obviously been arguing, since Daria looked a little put out and Countess Elizabeth's face wore a rather stormy expression.

In no time the Countess had told them that Sophie was indeed engaged to Felix Shuvalov, but they were not to tell anyone else until the following evening. Daria immediately said that was because Princess Shuvalov wished to tell the Empress first, and Mama had agreed not to tell a soul other than her husband and daughter.

'Well,' said Elizabeth, who was looking a little nervous now that she had told them, 'I said I would tell only the family, and of course I have always regarded Aunt Nadia as family. And I could hardly be rude and leave David out, since he has been staying with Aunt Nadia,' and here she beamed at David, 'and as he is the soul of tact.' Nadia, Tatiana and David all hastened to assure her that indeed he was.

Now that the secret had been disclosed, Daria was as keen as her mother to regale them with all she knew. Sophie had been meeting Felix every Saturday when she went skating, and they spent the whole of each Saturday morning together. Then again on Wednesday, when she went to the Academy, Felix would slip away from his office and spend another two hours with Sophie. At this point her mother intervened to say that it was all done without her knowledge, but while she pretended to be cross she was clearly thrilled with the outcome.

Later, Elizabeth turned to Nadia and said that her only worry was Felix's mother.

'Why are you concerned about Felix's mother?' Countess Nadia asked.

'Well, of course I've known her for years, but we have never been more than acquaintances — well, perhaps a little more, but certainly not close friends.' Here she adopted a slightly conspiratorial voice and explained that she had always thought the Princess too bossy, and in fact was a little frightened of her. Nadia reassured her by asking Elizabeth to remember how autocratic and bossy she had thought Nikolai's mother was, and yet she had managed to tame her and ultimately to love her.

'I hadn't thought of that. You're right; I'm sure I'll manage to win her over somehow.' Countess Elizabeth smiled and appeared to relax.

After they had all had tea Countess Nadia asked David to fill the champagne glasses and then all toasted Sophie and Felix. Nadia next proposed another toast to Dmitri, and after that Elizabeth's floodgates were opened and all the wonderful news about him gushed forth. He was to be further promoted. Lev Kolcluley had told them that after his next leave Dmitri was to be transferred to become an aide to Prince Potemkin.

'Do you realise what this means? He will no longer be in the forefront of battle but sitting further back helping Prince Potemkin plan the strategy, out of harm's way. Now I will have no need to worry about him endlessly.

'Do you realise that Felix hopes to follow his father into the inner Government circle that administers Russia?' she added, with the air of a conjurer, as if she had personally directed Felix into this role and kept him out of the army.

The subject then returned to Sophie's engagement, and Countess Elizabeth told them that Prince and Princess Shuvalov would be sending them invitations to attend a dinner-dance in a fortnight's time to celebrate the engagement. However, next Monday the Kolcluleys would be giving a dinner to welcome Dmitri home and they would be inviting Felix, and his parents, and of course all present were naturally invited.

Then a cloud passed over Elizabeth's face and she turned to Nadia and said, 'I'll sit you on the other side of Prince Shuvalov, and perhaps between the two of us we can keep him happy and the dinner will not be dampened by the Shuvalovs',' she paused, and added, 'rather weighty presence.' She then said she thought she would put Dmitri on the other side of the Princess, for between dear Nikolai and Dmitri the Princess couldn't find better company. Turning to Tatiana with a happily expectant smile she added, 'I will put you on the other side of Dmitri.' Then she turned to David with her charming smile. 'And David, you can sit on the other side of the Princess.'

Having conferred this honour, she turned to Daria and said they really must be going. Nadia gave her friend a warm hug and told her to pass on their sincere congratulations to Sophie. David said he should be leaving too, and after saying farewell to Countess Nadia and Tatiana, and thanking them for allowing him to accompany them to Smirsk, he left for his apartment.

As he made his way home David mused that he would much rather have been sat in a less auspicious place at the dinner, that is, on the other side of Tatiana. However, he must not let Dmitri have a clear run. He would have to make some moves this week, before Dmitri returned to St. Petersburg.

The next day David drafted a report on his visit to Smirsk for the Ambassador. He knew Lord Malvern would be keenly interested, as it was vital for Britain to know as much as possible about Russia's timber industry. When he had finished the report to his satisfaction he took it in to the Ambassador who read it immediately, every so often stopping to ask David to elaborate on a point. When he had finished the report, the Ambassador asked if he had any other observations that might be of interest. David then told him about the Countess's relationship with the workers, including the schooling she provided for their children, and went on to describe the dinner and lunch the Countess had put on for her people. The Ambassador was impressed, and asked David to join him for lunch, saying he knew Lady Malvern would enjoy hearing about the peasant dresses and the dancing.

Lunch was a very amusing meal. Lady Malvern had already indulged in what she said was a couple of thimbles-full of vodka, putting her in a receptive and amusing mood. If they were only thimbles-full, the thimbles must have been made for a giant's hand, David thought. Halfway through lunch, when David was regaling them with stories of the peasants' dancing, a footman came in with an urgent letter from the French Ambassador. After reading the letter Lord Malvern excused himself, saying he needed to go and write an immediate reply.

He had hardly left the room when Lady Malvern said they should have a toast to the King's birthday. David, bewildered, asked which king. 'Our King, of course,' replied Lady Malvern, in a voice of deep reverence. 'His Britannic Majesty.'

'I thought his birthday was several months ago,' David said, still confused.

'So it was,' said Lady Malvern, 'but nothing is more patriotic than starting early on toasting the Sovereign's health.'

No sooner had they raised their glasses and toasted the King when Lady Malvern asked the footman to bring some larger glasses and to fill them up, as they would now toast the Queen.

'Is it the Queen's birthday?' David asked. 'I haven't the faintest idea,' Lady Malvern replied, but I have always thought it very bad form not to celebrate the King's Consort's birthday, particularly considering what they have to put up with at times. I know something of this, simply by being Consort to the Ambassador.' After that comment she clinked glasses with David and they both drank.

David began to feel a trifle alarmed when suddenly Her Ladyship said her birthday was coming up soon and her husband would undoubtedly forget unless she reminded him, so they had better toast her health. The footman was sent to bring another bottle of wine, but before he was out the door Lady Malvern called that he had better bring in two bottles. Turning to David, she said, 'Toasts, like life, should be generous,' then fixing her eyes firmly on him, added, 'Never be mean in life.'

Then, wobbling slightly on her seat and leaning forward, she murmured that he could tell her in confidence — 'had he noticed that Lord Malvern was a little inclined to be mean?' David did not know what to say, so he simply replied that he had never been in a position to notice.

'I am not a mean person,' said Lady Malvern, with a smothered hiccup, 'so let's have another toast — this one will be for your birthday.'

'My birthday is not for five months.'

'Never mind,' said Lady Malvern. 'A good many people in our position are never sure what date their real birthday is. It all depends which side of the blanket they wish you to appear. Malvern was lucky, you know.'

David wasn't at all sure what she meant about the blanket or Lord Malvern's luck but didn't dare ask, as he felt it might be a delicate subject. Anyway, he didn't have time because Lady Malvern leant shakily across and banged her glass against his, saying, 'Happy birthday and good health.' They had scarcely downed the drink when she said to the footman, 'Hurry up and fill up the glasses before the old Trout gets back from his letter writing.'

David was beginning to feel light-headed, but there was no way Her Ladyship was going to stop toasting with him. The next toast was again to his good health, just for luck. David began to wish the Ambassador was a quicker letter-writer. They drank another toast then, as if she was a mind reader, Lady Malvern said David must have noticed long before this that the old Trout, as she called her husband, was something of a slow-top. 'In fact, when writing any serious report he usually reads a draft to me, and I often revise it.

Then, placing one elbow on the table for support, she leant at a dangerous angle towards David. Whispering confidentially, she told him that Malvern had only secured his position because her father controlled six seats in the House of Commons and the Prime Minister needed her father's support. Rotten boroughs, some called them, but my father said that while they were expensive to maintain at every election, they gave a good return over the years.

One minute David was sitting down and the next he found he was on his feet, for with amazing agility Lady Malvern had literally sprung up and seized him, at the same time saying, 'Show me how the peasants danced.'

David, appalled in case His Lordship walked in, started to protest, but Lady Malvern took absolutely no notice of his words and began what seemed to be a very vigorous tarantella. In fact, not only was Her Ladyship a vibrant dancer, he seriously wondered if she was not also double-jointed. She was able to swing her legs through the most extraordinary positions.

Then, snatching up her fan while at the same time downing another glass of wine, she took hold of David and began to perform a Spanish dance, wielding the fan with enormous gusto. David found himself being whirled around the floor at high speed, which was beginning to affect his stomach. However, he could not help thinking that Lady Malvern was a very fine dancer. At one stage, to avoid being hit in the face by a particularly high kick, he fell onto a chair, only to be vigorously pulled up again. Lady Malvern was beginning to take on several images in David's eyes, one of which was definitely that of an Amazon.

Fortunately, at that moment an English servant who had been with her family for many years, walked in and said his Lordship apologised but had to remain in his office, and he would see David there after lunch. Although this was said very politely, David sensed that the servant resented him and was blaming him for Lady Malvern's condition.

Turning to Lady Malvern, he reminded her that she had an appointment at three o'clock, and her maid was waiting to dress her. Reeling only a little, Lady Malvern then extended her hand for David to kiss. Graciously she thanked him for coming to lunch, and said she hoped he had enjoyed himself. She was sorry her husband had not been able to join them, but she was sure he would meet him later. They then moved toward the entrance hall, where Lady Malvern's maid was waiting. The maid took her elbow and the two women slowly ascended the stairs.

The servant then said gently to Lord Mountforte that Her Ladyship enjoyed good company. 'She was the kindest person he knew,' he added, 'but St. Petersburg can be a lonely place, can't it, Lord Mountforte?'

Although his face was impassive, his voice and eyes expressed the feelings of a good servant who loved his mistress and did not want anything unkind thought or said about her. David was touched by his loyalty. He suspected there was no three o'clock meeting; this was simply a ruse to get her Ladyship to bed. The thought of his own bed loomed invitingly, but he knew he had to return to his office and face Lord Malvern. He could feel his stomach turning unpleasant somersaults, and decided he had better make use of a chamber pot before he returned to the office.

When he got back to his office later he felt dreadful, and he was very relieved to find that Lord Malvern had decided to go and see the French Ambassador. David decided the only thing to do was to slip home and, after dunking his head in icy cold water, go to bed with the hope that when he awoke he would no longer have soldiers banging drums in his head.

Meanwhile Countess Nadia was busy with the final details for her ball, which was to be held in seven days' time. As she was a good organiser there was little more to do at this stage other than to check all the arrangements made. The ballroom was dazzling, and only awaiting the shrubs and flowers that would be brought in on the morning of the ball from her conservatory and her large hothouse. After inspecting the flowers and shrubs the Countess was satisfied that when they were transported into the ballroom they would look spectacular.

Her chef, Andrei, and his minions had been working all week on food for the ball. The food would be served on fifty tables that had been set up in two adjoining rooms. The white drawing room had thirty tables and the music room twenty. Each table would seat ten people. Twenty extra footmen had been summoned from her other estates so that each table would have a footman continually on hand to serve food from the two trolleys of delicacies that would be wheeled to each of them, and to make sure the guests' glasses were kept full.

The ball was somewhat more grand than usual just in case Tatiana and Dmitri announced their engagement that night. The Countess knew Dmitri would ask her permission to propose to Tatiana but equally, knowing Dmitri, he would not ask unless he was sure of being accepted. The Countess thought how she would love to see Tatiana married and have children before she died. An alliance with the Kolcluleys would be such a happy one, and Tatiana would not find a better and kinder father- and mother-in-law than Nikolai and Elizabeth.

She was contemplating this with some satisfaction when a footman brought her an envelope embossed with the Kolcluley crest. Wondering if it could be a written request from Dmitri requesting permission to propose to Tatiana, she opened it with pleasurable excitement.

The letter was brief. 'Dear Aunt Nadia, Dmitri died yesterday on his way back to St. Petersburg. Nikolai.'

The Countess stared unbelievingly at the letter. Lovable, vital, darling Dmitri, dead! She could not believe it. Dear, generous Dmitri, who brought a sparkling touch to any company or place he was part of. Nadia felt suddenly cold and very old. Why was she alive when young people like Natasha and Dmitri, who embodied all the graces of the time, were not?

She wept silently as she remembered Dmitri's christening and how he, only a few days old, had yelled so robustly each time the Bishop plunged him into the christening font that his grandfather had remarked that with lungs like that he would grow up to be a strong man. She remembered him on his first pony and as a young cadet at school, with his parents so proud of his results. So many happy flashes of the past raced through her memory that it seemed impossible that Dmitri was dead. Then, after taking a little time to compose herself, she rang the bell. When the footman appeared she asked him to find Countess Tatiana, and ask her to come to her grandmother.

When Tatiana arrived she was smiling. 'I was just in the kitchen. Andrei is excelling himself, but I doubt his staff will survive to see the ball at this rate. He is working them so hard.'

As she came close enough to see her grandmother's face her own expression turned to anxiety and she cried, 'Grandmother, are you ill?'

Nadia shook her head, patted the seat beside her, and as the bewildered girl sat down she silently passed her the letter.

Tatiana took the letter, read it, and froze, her face becoming ashen. The old lady gently clasped her granddaughter to her and they sobbed together. After a while they pulled apart and Countess Nadia said 'We must go and see the Kolcluleys and I will cancel the ball.'

Andrei was called for and told to stop any further preparations. The ball was being cancelled, as Count Dmitri had died. Like everyone in the Countess's household, Andrei liked Count Dmitri and, like so many, had hoped that he might marry Countess Tatiana. Andrei was extremely upset, since apart from liking Dmitri, all the servants knew he would be an excellent employer. Within minutes of his leaving the room all the staff in the palace were aware of the terrible news. When an hour later the two Countesses, dressed in black, came down the stairs to leave for the Kolcluleys most of the staff were waiting in the hall to offer their condolences.

As they drove to the Kolcluley mansion, the two women discussed what they would say to the various members of the family. Nadia said she would sit with Elizabeth, after speaking to Nikolai, since she would be the most emotional. Tatiana should go to Sophie and Daria.

When they arrived, Count Nikolai, dressed in black, greeted them with the courtesy of old. After they had expressed their shock, sadness and sorrow, Nadia asked if she might go and see Elizabeth. 'Please do,' Nikolai replied. 'You might be the only one who is able to break through her reserve.'

Nadia stopped and asked Nikolai what he meant. He replied that when the news had been received, some six hours earlier, Elizabeth had screamed and then fainted. Since being brought out of her faint she had behaved like a mechanical doll. Nikolai was desperately worried and had sent for the doctor. He said Elizabeth had answered the doctor very politely, declined all assistance, thanked him for coming, and then asked a servant to show him out.

'With me, and with Sophie and Daria, she is unfailingly polite but she shows no emotion. For all the real attention we receive from her, we might just as well not exist.'

Terribly worried now, the Countess said she would go to Elizabeth immediately. Tatiana should go straight away to the girls, she said. After leaning up and kissing Uncle Nikolai on the cheek, Tatiana left to find Sophie and Daria. Nadia, patting Nikolai on the shoulders, put her arm through his and they hastened to see Elizabeth.

Elizabeth was sitting, with an appearance of serenity, dressed in black. Nadia stretched her hands out taking Elizabeth's into hers and went to pull her into her arms but found that she couldn't since Elizabeth made no attempt to rise. 'I am so very, very sorry, my dear,' she said.

'Thank you for coming, Aunt Nadia, it is very good of you.'

Perhaps what frightened Nadia more than the flat, unemotional voice was the shock of not seeing even a flicker of emotion touch Elizabeth's face — this very attractive face that had once showed every thought or feeling Elizabeth had.

Noticing that Elizabeth was in a draught, Nadia said, 'Wouldn't it be better, dear, if we sat somewhere warmer?'

'Certainly. Where would you like to sit?'

Nadia suggested the small sitting room, where she knew there were comfortable sofas that Elizabeth could lie down on. Shocking her even more, Elizabeth rose stiffly like an old, old woman, then she straightened up and walked slowly to the sitting room, like a soldier on guard duty. Nadia suggested that she should perhaps rest by lying down on the sofa, but Elizabeth told her she did not wish to. Then, no matter how hard she tried, Nadia only received polite replies to her efforts to make conversation. Servants brought in tea and drinks, but Elizabeth took neither.

The servants were all red-eyed, and one was openly weeping. Nadia knew Dmitri had been truly loved by the household and that they had regarded all his victories and successes as theirs.

Finally, greatly disturbed, Nadia said goodbye to Elizabeth, who thanked her automatically, still showing no emotion at all.

Meanwhile Tatiana was sitting with Sophie and Daria. Felix was also there, trying to comfort Sophie. Both girls were shattered by Dmitri's death, but Tatiana could see that for the moment worry over their mother had blunted the edge of their grief for Dmitri.

'I feel as if Mother has left this world, she's acting so strangely. I just don't know what to do,' said Daria through her tears. Tatiana tried to comfort them both, but being so upset herself, mostly hugged them and murmured endearments.

She asked how Dmitri had been killed, thinking he must have been killed in battle. The girls started to tell the story, choking as they tried to hold back their grief, when Count Nikolai entered the room. In an emotional but controlled voice he said that his son had died trying to save a child. He had been riding back to St. Petersburg with two junior officers and fifty men, all about to take their leave in the city, or reporting for duty at their regiment's barracks.

Two days before they were due to reach St. Petersburg they had spotted a child of about four or five, out on the frozen river. The child, a girl, had apparently gone after her puppy, which had wandered out onto the river. The girl had caught the puppy but must have sat down to cuddle it and, not getting up, had begun to grow desperately cold. The men called to the child but she didn't respond, except to cry. Dmitri jumped off his horse and said he would go to her, although several of his men offered to go and try to get the child. They realised it was risky because in the centre of the river, where the child sat, the ice was not so thick.

Dmitri was renowned for never expecting his men to do anything he would not do himself. Swiftly he told them to get some rope from the packhorses, link it together, give it to him and he would rescue the child. The men protested, saying they would go. But Dmitri replied that he was lighter than most of the men, and that as a child he had been used to sliding over the ice. He took the rope, walked out over several hundred yards where the ice was still firm, and then where it was more fragile laid down his fur coat, stretched out lengthwise to spread his weight, and gradually inched his way toward the child and her puppy.

He reached them after about forty minutes of crawling and inching, and carefully tied the rope around the now shivering little girl, leaving the pup loose as he expected it to follow her. Then, still lying down, he slowly lifted his hand and signalled the men on the bank to pull the child back to them. This they did, while Dmitri carefully began to move round on his fur coat in order to crawl back.

At that stage the puppy, by now almost frozen, crept over to the fur coat and lay on Dmitri's arm. He tried to gently move it further down the coat since he needed his arm free to propel himself, but the pup apparently didn't want to leave what little warmth there was in Dmitri's covered arm and would not budge. As he tried to give the pup a stronger push away from his arm Dmitri cracked a section of the ice beside him. Then, as he tried painstakingly slowly to move back from the crack, he caused it to widen. Realising the danger, he made a lurch away from the widening cracks, but to no avail.

One of his men who had a rope moved out as far as he could on the solid ice and flung Dmitri the rope. It just missed him, and then the ice under him gave way. The man flung the rope again, but Dmitri was now in the water and though he caught the rope the second time, his long riding boots were filling with water. Despite his soldiers desperately pulling the rope, and Dmitri initially holding on, the weight of his water-filled boots and the pressing of the ice on his chest was too much. Dmitri was unable to pull up on to the surface of the ice.

Then, Count Nikolai said quietly, apparently seeing he had no hope and was now endangering those who were on the ice trying to pull him in, Dmitri gave a wave of his hand and let the rope go. He disappeared immediately as the weight of his water-filled boots pulled him under. 'I heard that from one of the officers who was returning with him,' the Count said.

'How very like Dmitri to die saving a child,' Tatiana chokingly said, tears streaming down her face. The Count, continuing in the same stressed but firm voice, then said that Dmitri's death was in vain. The child had been too long in the cold and had died shortly after on the bank, despite the soldiers lighting fires and wrapping her in warm clothing. So, the Count said, as if in a dream, it was all in vain. He tried to smother a gulping sound in his throat, then turned abruptly and left the room.

When Nadia went to make her farewell, she found Nikolai sitting gazing out the windows at the bare trees, their branches etched black and grey against a blue-grey sky. The ground was covered in snow and the only sign of life was a couple of birds perched on the wall by the gates. Somehow the bare branches of the trees and the snow seen through the windows seemed to Nadia to symbolise Dmitri's death. She wondered if she could commission Gavrili Derzhavin to write a poem about Dmitri. She would think about that and perhaps offer it later as a gift to Nikolai and Elizabeth.

Nikolai had not heard Nadia enter the room and when she touched his shoulder he stood up and apologised, then asked her what she thought of Elizabeth's condition. Nadia could only reply that she had not been able to penetrate past Elizabeth's innate courtesy. She had no idea what could be done, except to keep talking to her in hope that she would break down and cry and begin to recover something of her old self. She could understand how Nikolai felt, seeing his usually vivacious wife in such a state of shock.

Before she left, Nadia went to speak to Sophie and Daria, quietly congratulated Felix, whom she hadn't seen since his engagement, then left with Tatiana. On the way out they asked Nikolai to let them know immediately if there was any way either could help. Nadia added that she thought only time would heal Elizabeth, but she believed it essential that she broke down and cried instead of bottling her emotions up. Nikolai kissed them both then waved them off, looking a sad, shrunken figure as he stood in front of the massive door in his black clothes.

On the way home the two women were quiet, each engrossed in their own thoughts, but taking comfort from the other's presence. Count Nikolai had told them Dmitri's body was not able to be recovered, but a remembrance service would take place the following Friday in St Isaac's Cathedral. When they arrived home both went up to their rooms to rest. Countess Nadia called her secretary to her, and gave him all the instructions necessary for cancelling the ball. How up and down life was. Only this morning she had been planning the final touches for her ball, at which she was secretly hoping Tatiana and Dmitri would announce their engagement. Now Dmitri was dead and she was cancelling the ball. She felt desperately sad, deeply depressed and very, very tired.

She thought of the two wonderful young people Tatiana and she had lost. And not only them, but Russia itself. The Empire desperately needed people like Natasha and Dmitri, who understood the challenges that lay ahead, and could have played such a vital part in the future. How attractive they had been, each in their different ways. Nadia now thought of them as brilliant comets flashing through Russia then disappearing from view.

What a dreadful twelve months it had been, except for the one highlight of saving little Alexei. It was such a source of pleasure to her to see how he was improving, both physically and mentally. She could see that many of his attributes were inherited from his father, but there were also traits in him that reflected his mother.

Her thoughts turned to her other granddaughter. Who would Tatiana marry? Had she set her mind on Dmitri? There were plenty of suitors for her hand, but would she be interested in any of them? Of one thing she was sure — Tatiana was safe from being forced to marry that awful Swedish Prince. After hearing about Natasha's tragic marriage the Empress would certainly not try to push another of Nadia's family into a marriage they didn't want. The Empress was shrewd and at times ruthless, but in other ways kind, sentimental and generous. No matter how she had come to the throne, Nadia knew, as did most Russians who counted, that Russia was extremely lucky to have her as their ruler.

With these thoughts drifting back and forth in her mind Nadia fell asleep, and dreamt of Elizabeth's tragedy with Dmitri, and hers with Natasha. The two became muddled in her dream, and she tossed and turned restlessly.

It was the next day before David received the news, by which time everyone who mattered in St. Petersburg had heard. Shocked and overcome by a feeling of great loss, David decided to go and express his condolences to the Kolcluleys. Although he had been hoping to beat Dmitri to win Tatiana's hand, the undeclared rivalry between them had not diminished his affection for Dmitri. He had enjoyed his friendship, was proud of it, and knew he was going to feel the loss of Dmitri deeply.

As he arrived at the Kolcluley mansion he found a dozen or more carriages waiting outside the gates. The occupants of all but the last carriage had disembarked and entered the house, and he now saw Gisela emerge from the carriage, though she had not seen him. He jumped out and hastened to catch her, ploughing through the snow without thought to what it was doing to his clothes. When he called out to her she stopped and reached out her hand. 'How good it is to see you, Lord Mountforte.'

David kissed her hand. 'Couldn't we still be on first name terms?' he asked. She just smiled in response and began walking toward the entrance, saying how shocked she had been by the news of Dmitri's death.

For a moment David was too angry to even think of Dmitri. All he could think of was that Gisela, whom he knew better than any other woman, was now calling him by his title and not his Christian name. Then he thought, two can play this game, so he asked the Baroness when her baby was due. She stopped for a moment, paled, looked oddly at him, then walked on and said in about two weeks. What an odd woman she is becoming, David thought. Still, even pregnant she is beautiful, although with all the furs swaddled around her it was hard to tell she was pregnant.

When they reached the entrance a footman announced their names, and Count Kolcluley came up and greeted them. They made their condolences then looked for the Countess. David was shocked at how drawn the Count looked and how much he seemed to have aged. He wondered how the Countess was taking it, if her husband looked that bad.

Baroness Hertzburg had sighted the Countess standing talking to a group of people in a corner, and David followed her over. When he reached them he was staggered at how poised the Countess looked, and how calmly she was greeting people and talking to them. How amazingly stoic she is, he thought. It was hard to believe that the gushing, emotional Countess could be so controlled. Then he noticed that she showed absolutely no emotion in her voice or person; she was acting like a wound-up doll. Polite, pleasant, yet untouched by what anyone said. Somehow it was almost worse than knowing Dmitri was dead to see this formerly vivacious, loving, generous person walking and talking like someone who was not really there. David suddenly felt terribly depressed as he thought of all the happy times he had had with this family.

Looking across the room he saw that Gisela was now chatting with another group of people with apparently not a care in the world. He felt humiliated that what he had believed was the love of a lifetime had meant nothing to her. Just a passing infatuation. He felt sick.

Gisela, meanwhile, had been watching David unobserved, and her whole body ached for his touch. It took tremendous willpower not to run over and say she was carrying his child. That she loved him passionately. That she would run away with him. She wouldn't, of course, since the repercussions of such an action would harm the very people she loved. It would be cruel to her dear and honourable husband, whom she had grown to love in a totally different way from the way she had felt for David. Her child, the child she was so looking forward to, would be born illegitimate, with all that implied, if she left her husband for David. She herself would never be received again in the society she had been born in, and in which she had lived all her life. Above all, she knew, whatever David currently believed, eventually he would miss the life he had been brought up believing in and which he would, without a doubt, lose by taking her either as his mistress or his wife. She was overcome by such a feeling of loss that she felt ill, and decided she must leave and go back to the Embassy as quickly as she decently could. She must concentrate on the love she would be able to lavish on her child.

After speaking to the Countess, David went across to Sophie and Daria. They were holding up remarkably well, he thought, but he noticed how drawn their faces were. He wondered if this was partly due to worry about their mother, or whether, being with her all the time, they had not noticed how unemotional she was appeared.

He was introduced to Prince Felix, who he had not met before, and then he took Daria aside and asked her about her mother. Daria was only too eager to tell him how worried they were about their mother. She said that apart from giving one desperate cry, just before she fainted, on hearing the news of Dmitri's death, her mother had not cried or shown any emotion. They were all frantically worried about her, Daria said, and now she and Sophie were also desperately worried about their father. He had not changed from the lovable, kind father they had always known, but he was so concerned about their mother's condition that he was making himself ill. 'We are all in a horrible state,' she said. Realising that it was some relief to Daria to release some of her pent-up emotions by talking to him, David encouraged her to talk. When it was time to leave he said he would call in again the next day.

Just as he was saying goodbye to Count Nikolai a group of soldiers, marching three abreast and led by two officers, came round the corner and headed for the entrance gates. Seeing that David looked puzzled, the Count told him these were the officers and men who had been returning back to St. Petersburg with Dmitri. 'They are coming, I expect, to pay their respects.' Proudly but sadly, he added, 'All Dmitri's officers and men loved and admired him.'

As David drove back to his office he felt a mood of deep gloom descend on him. At the office he found a letter announcing the cancellation of Countess Volonskaya's ball, due to the unexpected and tragic death of Count Dmitri Kolcluley, whom the Volonski family had always regarded as part of their family. David decided he must visit the Countess Nadia straight away.

When he arrived at the palace he was shown into the small drawing room, where he found both ladies working on a tapestry. Countess Nadia looked up and welcomed David, saying they were working on the tapestry to try and take their minds off the tragedy of Dmitri's death. 'In fact, we are recalling all the funny scenes and anecdotes we can from the past, in which Dmitri played such a large part.

'The suffering from two terrible losses in twelve months, David, is rapidly ageing me,' she added.

Although she said this with a smile, David thought the Countess was indeed beginning to show her age. She had seemed to age overnight when Natasha died, but recently she had begun to regain some of her youthful beauty. Now, however, the effects of this second tragedy were clearly apparent in her face.

David realised the Countess had been hoping that Tatiana would marry Dmitri and that he would leave the army and slowly begin to take over the management of her vast properties. Admittedly she was well served by her employees and trustees, but when one considered that she was now directing not only her own affairs but those of the Dolgurkys, it was amazing what a success she had achieved. No wonder she was ageing. Few men could have managed as well. While she had been training Tatiana in the management of her affairs, she would also have been hoping that Tatiana would marry Dmitri, who was capable of taking over the management of all her affairs.

David turned to Tatiana, who though welcoming was very quiet. As David began to try and draw her out he realised that, like Daria, she was extremely worried about Countess Elizabeth. 'If she continues in this way she will have a total breakdown,' Tatiana said. 'If it wasn't that she looked the same, one could believe one was talking to a stranger.' She and her grandmother were also worried about the strain it was putting Uncle Nikolai under, she said. Everyone was so fond of Nikolai, and all knew how much he loved his son and wife.

David was invited to stay for the evening meal but declined, saying he had work still to do. This was not true, but he felt so encased in gloom and depression that he really wanted to be alone.

On the day of Dmitri's remembrance service St Isaac's Cathedral was full. The Empress had earlier sent a letter of condolence to the family, and was represented by one of the Princes. The Kolcluleys were a popular family, and Dmitri in particular had been highly thought of and admired.

The aristocracy turned out in force but there were also a goodly number of people from the middle classes there. This included people like the English family who ran a factory where guns were made. David had often visited their offices to talk about their designs and see if they could adjust them for different conditions. Similarly, Dmitri would originally have seen these people on business, but with his warmth and charm they would become lifelong friends. There were also many people from the charities that were associated with the Kolcluleys and, of course, the army was heavily represented.

The singing was glorious. The basses rose and fell sonorously, and the sopranos' voices soared to the heavens. Everyone present must have felt cocooned in the majestic, soulful singing. At times David was moved to tears by the intensity of the singing. During one of the Magnificats he felt he was hearing the soul of Russia. He visualised the Mongol hordes subjugating and destroying Russia's cities and villages, but underneath all that destruction, terror and violence, the people keeping faith with God and the Orthodox Church.

Although the service was long and elaborate, it still managed to touch every individual. David was deeply moved, and as he left the great Cathedral he hoped the Kolcluleys were similarly uplifted, especially the Countess. When he saw them later the Countess still seemed to be talking and acting like a mechanical doll, but the rest of the family looked more serene. Felix Shuvalov was there with Sophie. He was very protective of her, and David reflected that theirs would be a happy marriage. He saw Countess Nadia and Tatiana at a distance, but the crowd was so thick that by the time he managed to reach the spot where they had been standing they had gone.

Perhaps because of the dreadful conditions the ordinary Russian soldier so often lives under, they seem to sing whenever they have an opportunity. At about eight that evening an officer appeared at the Kolcluleys' door and told the Count that the soldiers who had been returning to St. Petersburg with Count Dmitri would like to sing some words they had written about him. Count Kolcluley asked them in, but the officer said no, the men would rather sing in the snow, because it was in the snow and ice that they had last seen him.

Count Kolcluley immediately ordered servants to bring out vodka, ground covers and rugs, to set out braziers for warmth, and to make soup to feed the men. Flaming torches were found, and chairs were brought out for the Kolcluleys. The Countess sat beside her husband, still in that doll-like trance, while all the servants who were free gradually came and clustered around the family.

The men made a marvellous sight as they began to sing. There were about fifty soldiers, sitting on covers in the snow, their thick felt coats wrapped around them and head encased in warm fur hats, lit by the light from the burning braziers and flaming torches.

The soldiers had taken old Russian melodies, love songs and marching songs and made up words about Count Dmitri. Sometimes the songs were light and sprightly as they told of Dmitri's sense of humour, some were martial as they told of his valour and courage. Then they sang of what his loss meant, and these songs were often laments, melancholic, often heart rending but always beautiful with the end of a song gradually fading away and slipping into the night.

People from the surrounding houses began to appear and often other voices joined in the harmony, even though they did not know the soliders words. As Count Nikolai sat lost in the singing, seeing his son through the eyes of his soliders, he felt a hand touch his. Turning, he saw his wife, with tears running down her face, gently smiling at him. For Nikolai it was a moment of pure joy. He leant forward, kissed her tears, and said, 'I thought we had lost you, and I could not have borne it much longer.'

He pulled off his gloves, took her hand in his and placed them inside her muff.

They sat together like this until the singing had finished. The Count and Countess then asked everyone into the hall where hot soup, meat, bread and vodka was produced.

Sophie and Daria watched, first in amazement and then with profound thankfulness, as their mother moved between the officers and their men talking in her former manner. Because Count Nikolai and his daughters were so pleased to see the Countess back to her normal self, the feeding of the soldiers became an almost festive affair. As the vodka was liberally drunk the shyer soldiers became more vocal and Dmitri's exploits and heroism became greater and greater. When they finally left, the whole household felt uplifted. It was with deep satisfaction that all heard Countess Elizabeth turn to her husband and, taking his arm, say, 'Niki, let us go up to bed.'

It would never be quite the same again in the Kolcluley household because Dmitri had been such a vital element in it, whether he was there or away. In the past they had always been waiting for his letters or anticipating his return.

Sophie's engagement to Felix helped bridge the loss, but there was never a time when the household, in whatever their capacity or position, did not at some stage think or say to themselves, 'Now, if Dmitri were only here.'

CHAPTER TWENTY

'WELL, WELL,' SAID LORD MALVERN; 'CONGRATULATIONS ARE IN ORDER. Baroness Hertzburg has had a daughter. The Baron is overjoyed, and is giving a christening party at the Prussian Embassy. We are all invited, David. Apparently there is a Prussian Priest here in St. Petersburg at the moment whom he knows, so the Baron is taking advantage of that.'

When David asked how was the Baroness? Lord Malvern said he had not heard anything special, so he assumed she must be all right. David thought about whether he should make his apologies and not go to the christening party. It would be hard to see Gisela with another man's child in her arms. God, he thought, Baron Hertzburg was such a lucky man. He would have liked to say something nasty about the Baron but he couldn't because the Baron was always so very pleasant and courteous to him when they met. David had never been invited to anything intimate by the Baron before.

David had no idea that this invitation had been the Baron's idea. Gisela had been frightened at the thought of inviting him, particularly after he had asked her when the baby was due. For a dreadful moment she had thought he was calculating the dates. However, her husband considered that it would be best to invite David and allay any suspicions anyone had. He promised to stand beside her when David first saw the baby.

David, unaware of the drama at the Prussian Embassy over his visit, decided he would go for a short while. However, that plan was stymied when he received a note from Lady Malvern inviting him to come with them in the Embassy carriage. He had seen Lady Malvern several times since their unfortunate lunch, and she had been as cordial as ever, saying how nice it had been to see him at lunch. She had never mentioned peasant dancing or toasts. One could not help but like her because she was never anything but cheerful, sometimes very funny, and always interested in you, no matter how junior your position. She was also, David knew, very popular in diplomatic circles. Even the Empress was known to enjoy dinner at the British Embassy because of Lady Malvern's light, deft touch and her amusing style, and would laugh heartily at some of Lady Malvern's reflections on life. So, overall David was pleased to be attending with the Ambassador and his wife, as she would brighten the christening party.

As they set off the Ambassador asked if David knew Count Seivers. When David said he did not, Lady Malvern remarked that he was lucky not to know him, as his wife had a poisonous tongue and the Count was too much of a smooth flatterer to ever be truthful. Lord Malvern, fixing his eyes firmly on his wife, said that despite her dislike of the Count and Countess, which he agreed with, they still must have them to dinner as Seivers' support was needed over an important issue with the French.

'Why can he not be invited to a small reception, rather than a dinner where we will be forced to sit with him all night?' Lady Malvern asked.

'That will not do,' said the Ambassador. 'I have received a strong hint from the French Ambassador that Count Seivers is surprised that although we have been here for so long, he had not been invited to a dinner at the British Embassy.'

'What a snob!' retorted the Ambassadress.

'Well, I agree, but you will have to ask them,' Lord Malvern replied. 'We can include them in the dinner party next Tuesday.'

'We have Countess Bruce coming. Her husband is away in the Crimea. The Seivers will be delighted to find her at the dinner table; Countess Seivers is always trying to butter up Countess Bruce knowing she is one of the Empress's closest confidantes. I am not sure Countess Bruce will be as pleased. Unless you have thought of somebody else, perhaps David is free and could partner Countess Bruce'.

Lord Malvern agreed that this was a sound idea, so David found he was also to attend the dinner party.

When they arrived at the Prussian Embassy the Baron immediately took them over and proudly showed his daughter to them. Lady Malvern thought she could already see a resemblance to the Baroness. The Baron agreed, but said that his sister's daughter had looked very like this one when she was born, but now at 28 she looked more and more like his mother when she was young. Yes, he said, the eyes and mouth were Gisela's, but the rest had the look of his mother.

David barely glanced at the baby, all his attention on Gisela. After greeting him she said that her husband flattered her, as the baby was going to be a beauty like Max's sister. She could distinctly see the same shape of head. With her heart pounding, Gisela watched David, but he paid no attention to the baby. She was again grateful to Max first for insisting it was best to invite David to the christening, and second for standing beside her and commenting on the baby's resemblance to his mother. She felt the danger was now past, and to her surprise she found she didn't hunger for David as she had only a week ago. The arrival of the baby had brought about a great change, and more and more of her love was being channelled to her daughter.

When David moved on, after making the usual complimentary remarks about the baby, Gisela reached out and squeezed her husband's hand. As he smiled down at her she thought again how steady and thoughtful he was, and how lucky she was to have him as a husband. It was at that exact second she knew she could live with happiness without David. There would always be some love there for him, but it would never rule her or destroy her. She caught her husband's eye and gave him the loveliest of smiles.

As he crossed the room David could not help thinking how heartless Gisela was to treat him with such indifference. He decided he would never again allow himself to fall for a woman as he had for Gisela. Never again would he expose himself — he would make a calculated marriage, and he would treat his wife courteously. He would never ever let a woman use him and then, when it suited her, discard him without the slightest sign of remorse. His thoughts turned to Tatiana. There was no Dmitri to rival him now, and although he knew there were dozens of other suitors there seemed no front-runner amongst them. He felt he was on the inside track.

Just then Lady Malvern said to him, 'See the Seivers over there? Let us go together and I will invite the dreaded couple.' Then she chuckled. 'Watch her face when I tell her that when your grandfather dies you will be one of the richest men in Europe.' Before David could say anything, he was being introduced as Lord Mountforte.

The Seivers smiled politely, then Lady Malvern went on to say that she knew they would not gossip, but David's grandfather, the Earl, had been ill. David noticed that the Seivers' faces perked up at the mention of the Earl. He was not aware that his grandfather was ill, and then he realised that, for her own reasons, Lady Malvern was making it up. The Seivers began to express their sympathy, and the Ambassadress added quietly that when the old Earl died Lord Mountforte would inherit one of the largest fortunes in Europe. The Seivers then began to purr over David, who was now very embarrassed, but as Lady Malvern said later, to everyone else but himself, he simply looked very modest.

Then David heard her say that the Countess Bruce was coming to dinner the following Tuesday and that although she had combed through her friends she could not find anyone to invite whose friendship with Countess Bruce was on the same footing as the Seivers'. The Seivers accepted the invitation with alacrity, particularly appreciative of why they were needed. In fact, David thought he detected a slight look of condescension appear on Countess Seivers's face.

When he later remembered to tell this to Lady Malvern she said it was quite likely. 'But did you appreciate my cleverly worded invitation to the Seivers, when I said I knew of no one on the same footing as they were with Countess Bruce?' Lady Malvern winked at him. 'Now, dear David, I know for a fact that Countess Bruce finds their fawning manner secretly objectionable, and once this Polish problem is solved she will give that French couple a great set-down. However, I have carried out my husband's wishes and I know you will be a great help at the dinner. Now they are aware of the enormous inheritance you will come into they will be inviting you to all their receptions. Of course, if they had had an unmarried daughter I would not have put you in that position, as they would never let go of you until you had married their offspring.'

She then assured David that he would be a great asset at the dinner. Between their trying to impress Countess Bruce and wanting to make friends with him, she would not be bothered by the Seivers at all. This was not much comfort to David, but still she was his chief's wife, so there was little he could do about it.

As they left the party and took their leave of the Hertzburgs, the Baron and his wife were both very gracious. While David thought Gisela's smile seemed rather enigmatic, the Baron was very kind and jovial. In fact, the few times he had seen him since his wife had become pregnant David had noticed that the Baron's whole personality had changed. He seemed more approachable and much happier than he had formerly.

After the carriage had dropped him off at his apartment David decided he would finally go round to the Volonski Palace. It was time he began in earnest his campaign to win and marry Tatiana. Changing into less formal attire, he rode round in his new light carriage, thinking that perhaps Tatiana would like to go for a drive. However, when he reached the palace he was informed that Countess Nadia and Countess Tatiana had gone to the Kolcluleys, and that Countess Tatiana would be staying there for the next two weeks.

Just as he was leaving the Volonski coach arrived, and he turned back to see Countess Nadia. Nadia was pleased to see him and asked him in for tea. He accepted, explaining that he had brought his new fast carriage round for Tatiana to see, hoping she would come for a ride in it. The Countess suggested that after tea he should go to the Kolcluleys and see if both Tatiana and Daria would like a ride. She explained that Tatiana was staying there while Sophie was visiting her fiancé's parents. Count Nikolai thought Tatiana would keep Daria's spirits up while Sophie was away.

Happily, Countess Elizabeth had totally recovered from her collapse, but Dmitri's death had not unnaturally dampened her personality. It was early days yet, however, and Countess Nadia hoped that time would partly heal the loss. Sighing, she said one could never totally heal a loss like that of Dmitri. Even now, she said, she often grieved at the loss of Natasha and had difficulty shaking off the depression which always followed.

After tea the Countess retired to rest and David set off to visit the Kolcluleys. He was warmly greeted by the Count and Countess, who immediately offered him tea. He declined, saying he had already had tea with Countess Volonskaya. They then told him that both girls had gone skating in the park with some other friends. After chatting with them for about fifteen minutes, David headed off to the park.

There were several hundred people skating, so it took a little while to find them. When he did, all six girls were skating together, attempting to outshine each other with their stylish skating. David wished he had some skates with him, though he could see he would not equal the tall, slim man who was currently jumping round

Daria and Tatiana. He watched them for about forty minutes then decided that as they showed no signs of leaving their skating, he would go home.

Just as he was walking back to his carriage to go, he heard a voice calling out to him. It was Daria, who had spotted him and skated across to the edge of the park. He ran down to her, and she said they would be finishing skating in about fifteen minutes.

'Why don't you come back and have dinner with us?' she asked. David accepted happily, and promised to be there at around six-thirty for drinks, and the music Daria promised before dinner. He then headed home and changed yet again.

When he reached the Kolcluleys and was shown in, he found the family, Tatiana, plus five other friends already playing charades, with much excitement and laughter. Watching, David thought how good it was to hear laughter again in the house, even though the laughter from the family might be a little fragile. He was introduced to the three girls and the two men.

The girls were attractive, and all three promptly began to flirt with him gently. The two men were also good-looking and, to David's annoyance, Count Ivan Vorontsov was making no secret of his interest in Tatiana. The other, Prince Nikolai Trubetskoi, was very amusing and seemed to lavish his undoubted charm on all the girls, who flirted with him and teased him. However, as the evening wore on David began to wonder if the Prince was not playing a deeper game and if he, too, had his eye on Tatiana. Though enjoying himself, David felt a stir of rivalry that helped sharpen his wit. Soon he was one of the centres of attraction.

Dinner was a very jolly affair, with all three men trying to outshine each other without appearing to do so. Tatiana, David noticed, seemed to be paying a lot of attention to Vorontsov, and try as he might to catch her attention and hold it, he could not. She would respond to him momentarily, but then Vorontsov or Trubetskoi would make a remark and Tatiana would switch her attention to them. This meant, of course, that no matter how amusing and interesting the others all found him, the one person he wanted to amuse did not seem as impressed.

After the Count and Countess had retired, Tatiana's behaviour began to create a feeling of pique in him that manifested itself in the odd, slightly sarcastic remark directed at her. Since he had seldom used sarcasm before he was initially surprised at himself and rather ashamed. Tatiana looked startled, but soon gave at least as good as she got, but with greater subtlety. At first no one else noticed, but before long the rest of the party was taking sides, except for Daria, who was bewildered. When no one else was listening she said quietly to Tatiana that she had thought Tatiana and David were good friends. Tatiana simply shook her head and muttered something about David being a stiff old fogey, and that she preferred more amusing friends like Ivan Vorontsov.

When Daria asked David why he was being so cutting in his remarks toward

Tatiana, she was shocked when he said it was because Tatiana was spoilt. As he said this he knew he did not mean it, but he just did not seem able to help himself. Instantly he was very upset and angry with himself, particularly when Daria drew herself up slightly and said with dignity that she had known Tatiana and her family all her life and had never considered Tatiana to be spoilt. Daria said this gently, but it was a firm and definite rebuke.

David felt ashamed and embarrassed because both the Volonskis and the Kolcluleys had given him their friendship and asked for nothing in return. The least they could expect of David was good manners. He tried to explain away his rudeness to Daria, but for someone normally so sweet, fun-loving and gentle, she was surprisingly resolute and did not accept his explanation. Now David, knowing he was in the wrong and that no one but he had put himself there, began to feel, unreasonably, angry with everyone. He covered it up to a certain extent, by, saying he did not feel well and would they please excuse him, he left early.

As he left he heard a peal of laughter from Tatiana and gleeful shouts from the other guests, and he felt they must be talking about him. Probably Tatiana had made some witty comment at his expense. Why had he indulged in sarcasm? He had always rather despised sarcasm, and thought it was something to use sparingly.

In an attempt to console himself he began to consider that he was hard done by with women. First Gisela used him, and now Tatiana. However, by the time he got into bed he had to admit to himself that none of the evening's contretemps had been caused by Tatiana, but rather by himself. He fell finally asleep, depressed and wondering what had gone wrong with him.

The next day he was informed at the Embassy that he would be required to work for the rest of the week and over the weekend on the Polish problem. It was essential to try and have it resolved as soon as possible, and the Ambassador wished to limit any damage it could cause. Therefore David had no social life until the following Tuesday, when he attended dinner at the Embassy. This meant there was no chance of seeing either Tatiana or Daria and trying to expunge his rudeness.

The dinner was a success. David had never met Countess Bruce, but she had been pointed out to him several times so he knew her by sight. Although she was more than fifteen years older than David, she had considerable charms and he sensed that her reputation for taking younger men as lovers was not just malicious gossip. She was witty, intelligent and politically astute, and he found himself enjoying her conversation.

The Seivers were a different story. They acted as if he was an old friend, and they had certainly checked up on his background, telling Countess Bruce about his potential wealth, the Earldom and what it meant in Britain, and also myriad other details they had gleaned from their enquiries. Inwardly, he resented their attentions, but he was conscious that both Countess Bruce and Lady Malvern were aware of how he felt by the slightly odd replies they made to the Seivers' statements. In fact he felt they were enjoying themselves, not at his expense but at the expense of the Seivers, who seemed unaware of the real impression they were making.

There were about twenty people at the dinner table, and to David's pleasure he was placed between two middle-aged ladies who both had a dry sense of humour. He found himself laughing a great deal and enjoying the evening. Lady Malvern was not so well placed. Protocol and the Polish problem required some delicate seating. Unfortunately for the Ambassadress, duty had required her to place Count Seivers on her left hand, and a very fat, stuffy and bigoted Court official, Baron Zhukov, on the other. Lord Malvern was better placed, because although he had Countess Seivers on his left, having Countess Bruce on his right saved him.

Towards the end of the dinner Lady Malvern started to become bored and to consume her wine at a faster rate. When the Ambassador noticed this he indicated to the footman not to refill Her Ladyship's glass so quickly, although only David noticed his subtle action. It had no effect on Lady Malvern, however, and she simply asked the footman to make sure everyone's glass was kept full, including hers.

At this remark, which was made during a lull in the conversation, Lord Malvern glared down the table at his wife. Unperturbed, she turned to answer Count Seivers's question. Yes, she said, Britain had suffered from the American War of Independence. The Grosvenors and her family had lost their plantations. Her great-uncle had gone out there over a hundred years ago to help develop the country. Count Seivers asked, 'What did your great-uncle do when he went there?' Lady Malvern meant to say he had gone out as a cotton planter, but instead said he went out as a cotton picker. This caused the Count to cough, and Baron Zhukov to ask if he had been sent out as an indentured labourer, as aristocrats had been sent out as such before.

The Ambassadress, who was taking a quick gulp of wine as this question was asked, thought the Baron had asked if he had been sent out with dentures. Lady Malvern's family were very proud of having excellent teeth, and she replied stiffly, 'Certainly not; my family are famous for their good teeth.'

With that, she opened her mouth wide and leant over to show off her admittedly fine and strong set of teeth. The Baron however thought for a moment that she was trying to bite him, and leant back quickly on his chair, which promptly snapped. To everyone's horror, Baron Zhukov fell to the floor.

Lord Malvern, who had been trying to control his wife from the other end of the table by glaring or sending ferocious facial signals to her, looked aghast. Lady Malvern, seeming completely unconcerned, took another swallow of wine and said to Count Seivers, 'Let us pretend it hasn't happened, so we do not embarrass him.'

Then, hearing a scuffling sound on her right, she looked down to see the Baron trying to get up, but his legs were stuck through the chair's complicated leg structure. Pretending he was not there was naturally not possible with the Baron lying on his back and trying to kick his legs out. Lady Malvern remarked, 'Goodness, doesn't the Baron look like one of those turtles you hear the sailors talk about, which they used to turn on their backs to stop them getting away when they were captured?'

At this Countess Bruce was unable to control herself and burst out laughing. Since she was known to be so influential at Court the others relaxed and began to laugh too. Not so Lord Malvern. He was already tense from wondering what his wife would do or say next, and now he was in a rage, made all the worse because he had to try and stifle it. He rose from his chair and made his way rapidly down the table to the Baron. However, by the time he arrived two footmen had raised the Baron and put out a new chair, and Lady Malvern was placating him.

It was an extraordinary scene. First the Baron looked nervously at the Ambassadress, muttering that he did not wish to be bitten. She, somewhat puzzled by this remark, said no one wished to be bitten and there were no dogs in the dining room. With that, she leant over and patted the Baron gently on the back, thinking perhaps that being so large he had had a seizure. The Baron, seeing the Ambassadress looming towards him again, leant back, and only Lord Malvern's quick action in grabbing his chair prevented him falling over again.

Appearing totally unconscious of her husband's wrathful presence, Lady Malvern addressed the table at large, saying, 'It is amazing how agile the Baron is. If I had not seen him so gracefully disappear, I would not have believed it.' Then, with enormous aplomb, she thanked the Baron for so kindly entertaining them all. The Baron, red in the face from his exertions, for a moment did not know what attitude to take, but when Countess Bruce called out to him, saying 'Well done!' and clapping, which everyone other than the Ambassador joined in, he decided to take it as a joke.

Lady Malvern then turned round and, appearing to see her husband for the first time, asked him what he wanted. Feeling positively violent inside and finding it hard to dissemble, he glared at his wife and said he had come to see if the Baron was all right. 'Of course he is, my dear,' she said; 'in fact, the Baron rolled so gracefully I should not be surprised if it isn't a party trick he does often.' The look her husband gave her as he returned to his seat was totally malevolent. Ignoring this completely she called down to David that she might have some Shakespeare later. 'What was that piece about "full of sound and fury"?'

David, who thought the whole scene hilarious, nearly exploded with laughter because he knew Lady Malvern had absolutely no intention of having any Shakespeare. She was simply quoting from *Macbeth* and slyly remarking on Lord Malvern's state of mind, and the row that was likely to occur after the guests had gone. God, thought David, how I do like her.

Oddly enough, after the chair incident everyone began to laugh and make jokes, and the party ended on a very high and enjoyable note. Countess Bruce had been a great asset, particularly by saving the disastrous scene when the Baron disappeared under the table. As she was leaving the Countess told Lady Malvern that it had been one of the funniest dinner parties she had attended in a long while, adding in a whisper that the Empress would roar with laughter when she heard of Baron Zhukov's disappearing trick.

CHAPTER TWENTY ONE

DURING THE WEEK DAVID BEGAN TO THINK OF WAYS TO TRY AND SEE TATIANA AGAIN AND PUT HIMSELF IN A MORE FAVOURABLE LIGHT. He decided to call on the Kolcluleys and offer to take Tatiana and Daria out in his new light carriage, which converted from a wheeled carriage to a troika sleigh in the winter. He had purchased three wonderful grey Alkal-Teke two-year-old geldings from Countess Volonskaya some six months earlier. They were remarkably swift and had the greatest long-distance stamina of any horses he had ever owned, being able to travel at the same fast trot for hours on end. They were marvellous to handle and he was immensely proud of them.

Knowing how Tatiana loved first-class horses and how interested she would be to see how horses bred at her grandmother's stud were performing, he was sure she would jump at his offer. He decided he would take them to the gypsy encampment outside the city. Some weeks ago he had saved the young son and daughter of the gypsy leader from a savage beating that was about to be inflicted on them by a soldier, and their father had pledged his eternal friendship. If he arranged it in advance he could engage a couple of their best singers and several musicians.

The more he thought about it, the more he warmed to the idea. Realising he would not be able to take Tatiana alone, since she was staying with the Kolcluleys to keep Daria company until Sophie returned, he decided he would make up a party. He would invite the Countess Volonskaya and Count and Countess Kolcluley as well, and take out a late afternoon meal. It would take some planning, and he would need to arrange another sleigh to cope with the extra numbers and food, but he was sure it would be worth it.

As he rode toward the house he felt happier at the thought of seeing Tatiana than he had been feeling since he had last seen her and Daria. His light-hearted mood received a jolt, however, when he arrived at the Kolcluleys to see waiting outside a carriage emblazoned with the Vorontsov arms. Even worse, when he was taken in and announced he saw Tatiana and Daria sitting playing cards with Ivan Vorontsov and Nikolai Trubetskoi.

'I hope you are in a better mood than last time I saw you,' Tatiana said, then she clutched Vorontsov's arm as if she feared some violence. David felt himself flush. Vorontsov put his hand over Tatiana's in a proprietary manner, and smiling, said he would protect her. Inwardly seething, outwardly smiling, David asked how anyone could be in a bad temper with ladies as lovely as Daria and Tatiana.

Daria, smiling, said, 'Truly, David, we are pleased to see you.' Tatiana released herself from Ivan and said that was true, but only as long as he remained in a good mood.

Damn her, thought David, I have never been in a bad mood with her before, and because of one instance she is going to prolong it for her own amusement. So, ignoring her remark, he said he would like to take the girls out on Friday, as well as Daria's parents and Countess Volonskaya. He had thought they might enjoy going out to the gypsy encampment to hear some singing, and to have a meal he would provide. Both girls were delighted and Daria immediately went to ask her parents if they were free, although she said she was sure they would be, as they did not venture out of the house much yet. David said if they were able to come he would call on Countess Volonskaya and ask her on the way home.

While Daria was out of the room Tatiana said it was such a lovely idea that she was sure Ivan and Nikolai would also like to come. Both young men assented enthusiastically. Daria arrived back laughing and saying her parents would love to come. From then on, to David's scarcely hidden anger, Tatiana somehow high-jacked the planning. Yes, of course Ivan should take his sleigh. That would give David more room in his for her grandmother and Daria's parents, and the food. She and Daria could ride in Ivan's sleigh.

Feeling totally outmanoeuvred, David could only agree smilingly and pretend he was delighted. He knew without a doubt that Tatiana guessed how furious he was really feeling, because every now and then, when no one else was looking, she gave him an impish look. He had never felt like hitting a woman before, but he did now, particularly as he was positive she had asked Vorontsov and Trubetskoi simply because she knew it would annoy him. However, the more he reflected the more he began to wonder if, now that Dmitri was dead, she was considering Vorontsov as a husband.

There was no doubt Vorontsov was keen on Tatiana. David began to form an even greater dislike of Vorontsov than he had the other day, although when he tried to analyse why this was he could not honestly decide. Vorontsov was good-looking, well-educated, good-mannered and had a sense of humour, all combined with breeding, background and wealth.

Having arrived at the Kolcluleys in a happy mood, he left feeling depressed, wishing he had never thought of going to the gypsy encampment. When he arrived at the Volonski Palace he received a warm welcome from the Countess, which lifted his spirits somewhat. He explained his idea for the expedition to the gypsy encampment, and she said she would be delighted to come. When David added that of course she was welcome to bring Alexei along, the Countess said she would confer with his tutors. She asked him not to mention the plan in front of Alexei in case his tutors convinced her not to take him. Then she added, twinkling at him, that they would have to put up some strong arguments to persuade her not to bring him.

David's spirits dropped again when Countess Nadia asked if that nice Ivan Vorontsov had been at the Kolcluleys. David said that he had been, as also had Nikolai Trubetskoi. The Countess said she was glad, since Tatiana and Daria needed cheering up and those young men were just the ones to do it.

David asked her some more about Ivan Vorontsov, saying he knew the family were great anglophiles. 'Oh, yes,' said Countess Nadia, 'Several of them were educated in Britain. In fact, we always consider Prince Michael Vorontsov a very English Russian, as he has some of your countrymen's phlegmatic nature and less of our more melancholic one.'

David could not help himself and asked her if she thought Ivan Vorontsov would be an appropriate suitor for Tatiana. 'Certainly,' she said. 'He has a good character, is very wealthy in his own right and so does not need to marry Tatiana for her inheritance, and he has fine and powerful parents. He is a very well-bred and cultured young man and a good sportsman. Yes, all these qualities I would like in someone interested in Tatiana.'

'Mind you,' said the Countess, 'I believe Tatiana is still hoping to marry for love.' Her shoulders drooped and she sighed as she said she had held out great hopes for a marriage between dear Dmitri and Tatiana. David took the opportunity to ask her if she believed Tatiana had been in love with Dmitri, because he was sure Dmitri was in love with her. This was a fairly daring question to ask Countess Nadia and he half feared a snub. However, the Countess was in some sort of reverie and simply said she had hoped so at the time but could not be sure. For once in her life Tatiana had not confided in her, despite being given plenty of opportunities to do so. This unusual reticence on Tatiana's part had surprised her, she said, and she had not known what to think.

She went on to say what a delightful young man Dmitri had been, and how he had been the same as a child. His family background was also such a good one, and just as she had been exceedingly fond of Dmitri, so the Kolcluleys were as fond of Tatiana. What a great waste Dmitri's death was, for all who knew him, and indeed for Russia. The Countess swiftly wiped away a tear that had briefly appeared and continued to expound on the great prospects Dmitri had had.

Suddenly she looked very old and vulnerable. She told David that while her life might look grand and wonderful to him it had in fact been full of sadness and tragedy. First her beloved husband had died young. Her only daughter had also died young. Her son-in-law, her grandson, her grandson-in-law, and she faltered, even her granddaughter, all murdered by that mad monster, Barinsky. And now Dmitri was dead too. Sometimes these days, she said, she almost feared loving anyone too much in case they were snatched from her.

For a moment David wanted to go across to her and put his arms around her. Then she straightened up and became the redoubtable old Countess again, saying how very lucky she was to have Tatiana and Alexei, and that every night and morning she said prayers for them. Just then Alexei came into the room, having been told David was in the Palace. After joking with Alexei and commenting on how smart he looked, David said his farewells to the Countess and got up to leave.

Late the next afternoon David received a note from Lady Malvern saying she had met Countess Volonskaya at a fundraising event that morning and the Countess had mentioned that David was taking some friends to the gypsy encampment. She wondered if there would be room for her as well. David immediately sent a note back saying he would be delighted if she could come, and told her he would pick her up. He really was delighted because he knew she would enjoy herself, and her happiness always overflowed onto her friends. Since he would not be able to have Tatiana all to himself he might as well have a jolly party, and Lady Malvern would certainly contribute to that.

He had decided to provide a sumptuous meal, and accompany it with the best of wines. It didn't really matter how much one drank at these winter parties. So long as you drove back in an open sleigh, wrapped in furs but with your face open to the weather, you never experienced a hangover and woke up totally refreshed in the morning.

After lunch on the day of the expedition David picked up Countess Volonskaya and young Alexei, then went on to collect the Count and Countess Kolcluley. He was very pleased they were coming, as he knew from Daria and Countess Nadia that they had not been going out since Dmitri's death. Both had a look of pleasant anticipation, and they made much fuss of Alexei, who was very excited since he had never seen a gypsy encampment. Alexei's constant barrage of questions about the gypsies kept them all amused, and Count Nikolai further entertained them with stories about gypsies in earlier times.

When they arrived at the British Embassy to pick up Lady Malvern her footman, who had been told to keep a look-out for the sleigh, came running out with another footman, carrying between them a large container. When David asked what was in it one of the footmen said it was contained champagne, oysters and caviar, and Lady Malvern had asked them to put it in the sleigh.

Then Lady Malvern appeared, looking very formidable in a tall fur hat, long fur coat and large fur muff. However, when she smiled at the sight of them looking at the box the whole picture changed. She really could be somebody's wonderful godmother, David thought. Laughing, Lady Malvern told them that since she had invited herself to the party she thought she ought to contribute something.

When David began to protest she told him to say nothing, but an English visitor had arrived via France and brought some especially good champagne for her husband. Well, as she had never thought champagne agreed with him, and as he was out and didn't know anything about it, she had purloined six bottles and left him six. And of course oysters and caviar went so well with champagne that she had to include them too.

'But what huge amounts of caviar and oysters,' said David. 'There must be at least three kilos of caviar.'

'Well,' said the Ambassadress, 'someone is bound to eat it; maybe the singers will sing even better if we give them some.'

By this time Lady Malvern had settled herself comfortably in the sleigh. She remarked that provided she was well wrapped up she preferred a sleigh like this without any cover as it always seemed so magical. She went on to praise David's horses, and he was impressed at how much she knew about them. When she learned that David had bought the horses from Countess Nadia's stud, the two women quickly became engaged in a lively discussion of the merits of various horses, in which Count Nikolai joined enthusiastically. It turned out that Lady Malvern's father was a horse breeder of note, and she was very well-informed on the subject.

Meanwhile Countess Elizabeth was getting some bittersweet pleasure in having Alexei to herself, and she began to tell him some of the wonderful Russian fairytales she used to tell her children when they were small. On hearing the tale of the firebird in the woods, Alexei asked Aunt Elizabeth if they would see the firebird today. 'Once we enter the woods, keep your eyes open and maybe you will see it,' she replied seriously.

There are few things as attractive as a perfectly matched trio of horses pulling a sleigh troika, and the three Akhal-Teke geldings kept up a spanking pace. David loved driving them, and it wasn't long before they overtook Prince Ivan Shuvalov's sleigh, which had left about ten minutes earlier than they had. David was secretly proud that his horses were outpacing Shuvalov's Orlov trotters, especially as he saw Ivan making a subtle attempt to increase his horses' speed. As he skimmed past, knowing how superb his horses looked, David waved his whip and smiled. Everyone in his sleigh waved and Count Nikolai called out jocularly that they would eat the meal before the others arrived.

Countess Nadia was, of course, thrilled to see her horses outstripping the horses bred by Count Orlov at his relatively newly established Stud Khrenov. She admitted that he had in a short time built up a reputation for producing the top trotters in the world, so it was even more exciting to see hers overtake his. Mind you, she thought, while Ivan was a good driver, David had beautiful hands for bringing out the best in the horses.

She was even more gratified when Lady Malvern turned to her and said that her father, the Duke, had asked her to purchase a couple of mares, and a stallion if possible, from Count Orlov. After this afternoon, however, she would write and suggest that he consider buying Akhal-Tekes instead from the Countess's stud. Would the Countess agree to sell them if he wished to buy? Countess Nadia, who kept her breeding stock under tight supervision and never sold a stallion, only selling mares and geldings, thought for a moment. Then, as England was so far away, and if the horses proved successful it could increase the demand for her progeny, she decided there and then that she would.

Lady Malvern began to tell Countess Nadia and Count Nikolai about the stud that King George II of Britain had set up in Celle, in his kingdom of Hanover. This stud, she said, was now producing excellent all-round horses called Hanoverians. Since their average height was about a hand taller than the Akhel-Teke, they might make an interesting cross.

By now they were in the woods, and Alexei was busy keeping a sharp look-out for the firebird. Countess Elizabeth, who David noted was another great storyteller, kept Alexei's imagination soaring. His party in the sleigh was such a success that David had for the moment forgotten how annoyed he had been with Tatiana for inviting the others. His mood was further improved when they arrived at the encampment seven and a half minutes before Ivan. He noted the time so he could tell Countess Nadia.

The gypsies sent out several men to help them and their belongings into a large tent, and to take the horses out of the harness. The horses were tethered on long ropes, watered and brushed down, then covered with blankets David had brought with him.

Alexei looked around with wide eyes, thinking of the stories about gypsies that he had heard on the ride out. He was excited at their carts and caravans, all painted with faces, animals or scenes, and David asked one of the gypsies if there was a responsible boy of about Alexei's age who could show him a little of the encampment.

Meanwhile, the food, rugs and cushions they had brought were taken into the tent. When Ivan's sleigh arrived he very decently congratulated David on his horses. Tatiana was obviously delighted that her grandmother's horses had outdistanced Count Orlov's. Her eyes sparkled and her face was lit up with smiles as she too congratulated David and then went to congratulate her grandmother. What a difference it makes to her when she is in a good mood, thought David, quite forgetting that it was he who was usually in a bad mood with Tatiana, not the other way around.

They sat on benches and couches covered with rugs and cushions, and the food and wine was placed on low tables that David had brought with him. It was laid out by Tatiana and Daria, while Ivan and Nicky Trubetskoi poured Lady Malvern's champagne and David found the bread that had come with the oysters and caviar. Soon they were all merrily waiting for the gypsy performance to start, agreeing that they would enjoy David's bountiful food after this.

It was not long before several gypsy women and men came into the tent. The women wore colourful blouses, over which were beautifully embroidered felt jackets. Around their necks they either had heavy gold jewellery or brilliantly coloured scarves, and there were large gold earrings dangling from their ears. On their heads they generally wore a mantilla. They had plain, full, ankle-length skirts of heavy material embroidered around the waist and at the hem. Under the skirts, they wore knee-high black boots. The men were equally colourful. They wore Persian lamb or red and green felt caps on their heads, and coloured blouses with embroidered felt or leather jackets over the top, with wide coloured leather belts. Underneath they wore loose-fitting trousers or pantaloons of red, black or green, and on their feet they had black half-length boots.

The women carried tambourines, castanets or a type of wooden rattle, while the men had a variety of what looked like mandolins and zithers. The women had a swinging, loose walk, which emphasised their hips and enhanced the attractions of their skirts as they flared out. The men had a more arrogant stride that gave the impression of a scarcely suppressed virility. Their entrance was very impressive, and everyone's expectations heightened.

The men with zithers sat down cross-legged on skin rugs on the floor, while those with mandolins stood behind them. Then the men struck up a song of welcome, and after they had been singing for about two minutes the women began to glide forward with a most enticing movement. Just as their audience became absorbed in that movement, a sudden change in the music sent the women into a dance in which they seemed to go wild, with high kicks, heads and shoulders thrown back, arms raised high, as castanets, rattles and tambourines clacked and rattled. It was so exciting, and the music had such a pulsating rhythm, that all the guests felt the urge to move some part of their body to the music.

Abruptly the music stopped and the gypsy women sank down beside the men. Lady Malvern, who despite her rather large size had been moving most gracefully, broke the awed silence by saying she wished she could dance like a gypsy. Touching David on the shoulder she thanked him again for letting her come, and said what imagination he had to have arranged such an afternoon.

Suddenly everyone began to talk at once, and as if the dancing had whet their appetites they began to replenish their glasses and to partake of David's food. While they were thus occupied in came six young men of about eighteen, dressed in a similar fashion to the musicians but with longer boots, and six young girls of about sixteen or seventeen, dressed like the other women.

There was complete quiet from the performers, and then the slow, soft beat of a drum was heard. Slowly, to the beat, the six girls glided out into the centre of the tent where they began to perform a peculiarly graceful movement involving their legs and hips, while their torsos remained motionless and their hands appeared to float ahead of them. It was mesmerising. Everyone stopped eating and drinking and just watched the dancers, with rapt eyes.

Suddenly, like a clap of thunder, so sudden and loud that several of David's guests dropped the glasses or plates they had been holding, the drum struck one great note. Then the musicians began a fast beat on the drum and all the other instruments were called into play with highly spirited music. At the first loud drumbeat the six men sprang high into the air and twirled around, and as soon as they landed they sprang in a long mid-air stride and each landed alongside one of the girls. Then with their partner they began to dance a type of gypsy mazurka. It was amazingly graceful and polished, with the feet and hands in perfect precision, the clicking and clapping exact. Gradually the pace of the music began to quicken, finally reaching such a speed that it seemed incredible the dancers could keep upright. Then there was one sharp, short thump on the drum. The music stopped abruptly and the girls fell in splits in front of their partners, who stood like triumphant bullfighters over them, absolutely motionless.

David's party were also motionless. Suddenly someone broke the spell by beginning to clap. Such was the effect that when Nicky called out 'Bravo! Bravo!' all the men began to call out. The women clapped and clapped. David noticed Lady Malvern wiping away some tears quite openly, and he thought he caught Countess Nadia surreptitiously brushing a few away. Then in one movement the dancers rose and moved out of the tent, the girls in that sensuous glide and the men with their extraordinarily sexual swinging stride.

Everyone began to congratulate David, with both Ivan and Nicky saying they had been to gypsy entertainment for fun and some drinks at a tavern on the other side of St. Petersburg but they had never seen anything like this. They asked him how he had arranged it. Before he could answer, the slow, captivating beat of the drum was heard again. In expectation all stared to see what was about to happen.

The musicians were still in the tent, as were the original women with the tambourines and castanets, all sitting on the floor on colourful floor coverings and cushions. The drum kept up its slow but insistent beat, and then slowly, walking in time to the drumbeat, there entered a large, fat woman dressed in black. When she stretched her legs to take a step the skirt opened to reveal a vivid red pleat beneath it. On her head was a black mantilla, its colour alleviated by a red comb, and in her ears were large gold earrings. Large and fat as she was, there was an immense dignity to her carriage and a curious aura of sadness seemed to drift round her. Just before she reached the centre of the tent one of the girls glided out and placed a stool for her. Because of her size and her dress the stool seemed to disappear as she sat down, and she gave the impression of sitting on nothing, as if she was suspended.

So impressive was her entrance that David's party had scarcely said a word, just watching her as she advanced into the centre of the space, carrying with her an air of some indefinable, timeless grief. As she sat down, the drum ceased. Suddenly the gypsy girls, still sitting, began to hum, sometimes with their mouths shut, at other times with them open, thereby regulating the volume. They hummed a sad air, hinting of loneliness and sorrow, and then a valdimir horn slowly began to counterpoint the humming of the girls, while the woman sat in the centre of the tent as if made of stone.

As the horn sank into a deep timbered tone, the woman, still without moving, took the same note. With the horn accompanying her, very slowly and softly she let her voice drift up into the clouds, or so it seemed to her listeners. It was a beautiful voice, and in that opening flow it was heartbreakingly so. With the horn now at counterpoint, she dropped down to an unbelievably low note and then gradually came up the register and began a lament, which made the listeners convinced that no one had ever known the sorrow she had. The lament took place without any movement from the singer. Had they not seen her walk in they could well have believed she was a statue. It seemed as if the sublime song would last forever, although it was really only about ten minutes.

Then the singing stopped and the drum began. The woman slowly rose and, with the same dignity, and trailing her sadness around, and behind her, moved across and out of the tent without acknowledging a soul. Everyone, gypsies and guests, remained spellbound, not daring to make a single movement. Even when she was out of sight, for seconds no one moved. When David's party looked at each other, most were in tears. Countess Nadia and Elizabeth were openly, quietly crying, and it was obvious that Lady Malvern, Daria and Tatiana had also shed tears. Count Nikolai was looking deeply moved, and even the younger men were affected to varying degrees.

For a while no one felt like talking. The singer and her song had had a profound effect, touching a deep, vulnerable chord in each of them. Lady Malvern told David she had never experienced anything to compare with what she had seen and heard that day. One by one they all began to describe their feelings, while David went over to the gypsy group and thanked them. He asked the leader if they could be left for an hour while they had their meal, and if he could then bring back the dancers for another one or two items before they left for St. Petersburg.

David did not ask for the singer to return, partly out of consideration for her, since he felt she gave so much of herself that singing again so soon might be too much for her. The second reason was that Countess Volonskaya and the Kolcluleys had experienced such sadness recently that he was not sure how much more emotion they could take. Anyway, he wanted the party to finish on a happy note. He was resolved to double the payment he had made. Never had he expected such dancing, playing and singing.

Joining his guests again, he found that although they were still subdued they were not only eating the food but drinking the wine and champagne, and so the party was beginning to bubble again. At one stage Tatiana came over, and taking David's hand in both of hers she thanked him with absolute sincerity for giving her a day that she would remember forever.

Alexei returned with his young gypsy friend soon after, saying he had had a wonderful time and asking if his friend could have something to eat with him. 'Of course,' everyone chorused, and the youngsters were given plates and told to help themselves to as much as they liked. Once the two boys had filled their plates they went to a corner, sat down together and were soon talking and eating with enthusiasm.

All the adults knew, however, that marvellous as the afternoon had been, they would go home, think about the day, and their thoughts might well conjure up something deep inside them. They were disquieted, but not necessarily unhappy. Perhaps, they each thought in different ways, they needed to re-evaluate their lives.

It was nearly an hour later when the musicians came in with the original group of women. They had on the same clothes and with that sexually provocative glide they were a stirring sight. They touched the senses and aroused almost unknown desires in David and his guests. They seated themselves cross-legged and the music began. The women sang an ancient song of the endeavours and trials of the gypsies of the past. The voices ebbed and flowed between a deep guttural sound that gave off connotations of pain and sorrow, and a purity of virtually coloratura notes that faded so softly it left their audience wondering if they had really gone. When the song ended none of the listeners knew whether it was finished or whether the last note had simply faded and would be taken up again.

Just as they were about to clap, the women emitted a harsh cry, the musicians followed and then began some marvellously vibrant singing. It was so exciting that everyone, excepting Alexei and his little friend, who were lost in their own world, wished they were participating. Then from the side of the tent came a whirl of legs and skirts as the six young girls they had seen earlier cartwheeled into the centre of the tent. As they came to a halt they burst into song, the six young men reaching them in seven spectacular leaps. The singers and the music reached a crescendo as the men landed by their partners.

Then, as the dancers were standing looking haughtily at their partners, the drum started a slow beat. Softly the mandolins and zithers joined in. The girls glided away from the youths and then, as the drumbeat quickened, and the music followed the drum's tempo, the youths with panther-like steps moved in to join the girls.

Then began the most intoxicating and erotic dancing and music any of them had ever seen. If any of David's guests had been asked to explain the eroticism the music and dancing caused, they could only have replied that you had to be there. There were no explicit or overt sexual gestures; it was simply the movement of the dancers' bodies and the throb of the mandolins and zithers, which now played counter to the drumbeat.

Such was the impact of the music and dancing that each member of the party felt washed over by emotions of desire they would hesitate to later acknowledge even to themselves. When the dancing finished, with the girls tossed in the air, caught and carried off without waiting for applause, even Countess Nadia did not look directly at anyone until they had composed themselves. Afterwards, with one accord they turned to David and could scarcely find enough superlatives to express their appreciation of the day.

David knew it had been a magic day and, still high on emotion, went to speak to the gypsy leader. When he rejoined the others he said he had a further surprise, but in the meantime they were to have some more vodka and wine.

What was the surprise? They all tried to guess. Most believed it would be the soloist performing again. David gave no clues, except to have them promise they would participate if necessary. This led to more excited speculation. Their emotions were on a higher and much more effervescent level than normal and as a result more drinking took place.

The singers and musicians, who had followed the dancers out, now returned to the tent. The drum struck and then, slowly and with a muffled sound, it began to beat. In glided and stalked the young dancers. But now, instead of heading for the centre of the tent they seemed to be prowling on the unsuspecting victims: David's guests. With the youths taking the ladies by the hand, and the girls taking the men, they led the way to the centre of the tent. As the music picked up a slightly faster tempo they began leading their partners in another slow but beautifully graceful dance. David was so lost in the pleasure of the dance movements, the music and the lovely slim gypsy girl partnering him that he forgot about his guests.

Countess Nadia, always graceful, moved smoothly and elegantly through the steps, while Countess Elizabeth felt as if she was floating and for a time temporarily lost the dead weight in her heart that was Dmitri's death. Like David, Tatiana and Daria were absolutely immune to their surroundings, lost to all senses other than those the dance and the music caused to well up in them. The same was true of the three men, while Lady Malvern was in a state of near ecstasy, totally unaware of anyone or anything other than her partner, the music and her own emotions.

When the dance ended, their gypsy partners led them back to their seats, where Alexei and his friend were watching. Then, bowing and mutely accepting the flustered and profuse thanks of their partners, they moved out of the tent to the beat of the drum, with that same incredible action.

It was time to leave. All David's guests, and he himself, felt drained of all emotion. Wonderingly, his friends asked David again how he arranged the day, and if the gypsies would do this again if they were asked.

'I asked the leader of the gypsy encampment if he would arrange the finest entertainment they could provide,' he said. When pressed as to how he knew the leader he somewhat reluctantly explained how he had saved the man's two youngest children from a beating about to be inflicted on them by a soldier who had caught them stealing some trifle. 'I paid the soldier several times what the stolen goods were worth, after which I obtained the release of the children and, after finding out where they lived, had my groom drive them to the encampment. The next evening their father called on me expressing eternal friendship.'

What a wonderful story, said Lady Malvern, and leaning forward she gave David a motherly kiss on the cheek, saying the kiss was also for a wonderful time. 'Never have I experienced such a flight of sensations as I did today,' she said.

The others agreed, including, slightly to David's surprise, Ivan and Nicky. David found himself liking the two men more and more, although he was reluctant to develop a strong friendship with Ivan while they were both in pursuit of Tatiana. All the same, when Nicky invited him to come to the Vorontsov's St. Petersburg palace two weeks later for a concert his mother was giving, he accepted with pleasure. He knew Nicky's mother was famous for her concerts, and a lot of the inspiration she commanded came from her uncle and his famous serf orchestra. Ivan also asked David to keep certain weeks free in the shooting season since he would like David, who he understood was a crack shot, to come and shoot on one of the family estates. This David also accepted.

As they were getting into their sleighs Tatiana ran across to David and in a very touching manner thanked him for what she called a beautiful and never to be forgotten day. 'You have shown we Russians something of ourselves we never knew,' she said. David was consequently remarkably light-hearted when he took up the reins of the sleigh. The horses were well rested, and when the gypsies had harnessed them, were raring to go.

Once he released the brake and gave the command to start, his heart surged with pride at the incredible power and speed with which his trio of geldings sprang forward. The other sleigh, excellent though the Orlov horses were, had no chance of catching David's. It was a marvellous sleigh ride. The stars were out, and the ground and the trees, and later the houses, were covered in ice or snow. Alexei was asleep reclining against his great-grandmother's knees, and for most of the journey there was hardly a word spoken, as everyone remained locked in their own thoughts.

Since he dropped his passengers off in reverse order of picking them up, Lady Malvern was the first to reach her home. Her farewell was so sincere and warm that David was positive they would always have a firm and constant friendship. As he took Countess Volonskaya and then the Kolcluleys to their respective homes they each thanked him in such a manner that he again knew the day had been a special one. It had already formed another firm strand in the bonds cementing their friendships.

David went to bed that evening feeling relaxed and happy. The day had turned out to be an unmitigated success. On top of that he had, early on in the party, asked Tatiana if she would like to go for a drive in his sleigh and experience the speed of the geldings her grandmother had bred. He was aware how thrilled she had been that the Akhal-Tekes had beaten the famed Orlov trotters. Tatiana had accepted at once, and asked if she could handle the reins during part of the ride, which he had agreed to, knowing her to be a skilled driver. He was surprised at how much he was looking forward to taking the sleigh out with Tatiana, and he went to sleep wondering where he could take her that would be exciting or interesting for her.

In the morning all thoughts of Tatiana were driven from his mind by the news that the Polish question was under pressure. The Swedes were reported to be interested in taking a large swathe of Poland for themselves and a party at the Swedish Court wanted to gain part of the Baltic States. The Ambassador told David that Britain would oppose the Swedes' wishes.

The Ambassador had also heard from the British agent in Poland that Baron Hertzburg had been visiting and sounding out several of the leading Polish magnates on behalf of King Frederick. One never knew, he said, what those powerful magnates would do if Poland were to be invaded. The Czartosyski and their 'Familia' would firmly oppose any attempt to partition Poland, but the others? The Ambassador shrugged. He must speak with Baron Hertzburg today, or as soon as the Baron was free. He was very suspicious of the French, saying one never really knew what game they were playing. He asked David to stand by, as he would like him to be present at his meeting with the Prussian Ambassador.

Another problem was what the Potockis were going to do. 'Surely,' said David, 'Baron Hertzburg, having just visited them in Poland, will have formed an opinion?'

'Not necessarily,' Lord Malvern exclaimed. 'If Potocki is being influenced by his wife — that scandalous Sophie de Witte — who is still currently one of Potemkin's mistresses. Even if she is not his mistress she is still his creature.'

'Who is Sophie de Witte?' David asked.

'Surely you know?'

Seeing David shake his head, Lord Malvern gave him a brief summary of her life. She had been born near Constantinople, to a Greek vegetable trader. When they were about twelve or thirteen their mother had sold both Sophie and her sister — Sophie to the Polish Ambassador, who in turn sold her on to Major de Witte, who having bought her, then married her. He sent her to France to learn the French language and acceptable manners.

She then went down to the Crimea, flirting with Potemkin, and since leaving there she had married Felix Potocki. 'If she is Potemkin's pawn, now that Potocki has succumbed to her she will place him in Russia's camp. She is undoubtedly a very beautiful woman, but I am told by reliable sources that she is a cold, mirthless and calculating schemer.' Lord Malvern shook his head.

Understandable if she was originally sold, thought David, as she would have had to look after herself. The Ambassador went on to say that the sister was now married to the Pasha of Khotin.

'What an amazing story,' David said. 'It's incredible that she went from slave to catching the incredibly wealthy Potocki.'

The Ambassador then said that another major concern was that no one seemed to know which way Sweden would jump. 'Previously Pitt thought King Augustus was committed to us, but now he is to all intents and purposes offering his army up to the highest bidder. Britain had offered 200,000 pounds, but my sources cannot yet find out if Russia is going to outbid that sum.'

Just then the messenger Lord Malvern had sent to the Prussian Embassy arrived with a note saying that unless he heard otherwise from Lord Malvern, Baron Hertzburg would call on His Excellency at three o'clock, as he could come on from where he was lunching. Lord Malvern told David to come and see him about ten minutes after Baron Hertzburg arrived.

David then set out for home to have lunch, but seeing Tatiana and Daria going into the Academy he stopped and went in to see them. They both immediately repeated how much they had enjoyed the afternoon at the gypsy encampment, and said they had written to him to express their appreciation more fully. David was particularly pleased when Tatiana said her grandmother considered that one of the reasons his horses had beaten Ivan's was that he handled them exceptionally well. 'That is a great compliment, since my grandmother is an excellent judge,' Tatiana said, smiling. David knew this to be true, and wondered if it enhanced his standing in Tatiana's eyes. They then said goodbye, David on parting reminded Tatiana, 'I am taking you out in the sleigh tomorrow.' She replied that she had not forgotten.

Inwardly, Tatiana thought, how could I forget this devastatingly good-looking man with the handsome, chiselled features and athletic build? If only he loved her, she was sure she would be the happiest woman in the world. However, she knew he did not, and therefore she would never show her feelings to him or anyone, not even to her beloved grandmother.

After David had left them, Daria commented how much she liked David, since not only was he handsome but he was also very considerate of others and of course highly intelligent. As Tatiana heard this, she thought how typical it was of all the Kolcluleys to think of a person's character rather than their money and position. That was why they were such a lovable family, in her eyes anyway. Unless they were unfairly wronged, they were also so trusting and kind.

She hoped, however, that Daria was not falling in love with David. She therefore received a rude shock when Daria asked her if she was in love with David. Tatiana recovered quickly and retorted, 'What a silly thing to say.' Daria remarked that she had noticed Tatiana was often on edge when David was present, whereas with the delightful Ivan she was completely relaxed, as if with a charming and well-loved brother.

As she said this Daria suddenly remembered Dmitri's death and that of Tatiana's brother, Sergei, and burst into tears. Sobbing, she apologised to Tatiana, who had also begun to cry. However, she told Daria there was no need to apologise, she quite understood. They had both lost much-loved brothers and she knew that Daria's phrase had been quite unintentional. They hugged each other, the subject for the moment closed.

Daria, forgetting about David, put her arm through Tatiana's and together they went on into the Academy. Tatiana was greatly relieved that Daria did not pursue her original question. She certainly did not want to answer Daria as she had no prepared reply. She knew from long experience that Daria was far more perceptive than her gentle, fun-loving nature would indicate to those who did not know her well. All the same, she was not only surprised but also worried that others might guess her real feelings, which she thought she had kept well hidden. Tatiana decided she had better stop seeing David so often after she had been out on the promised ride in his troika.

The next day David picked her up in his sleigh for the ride he had promised her, with her maid coming along as a chaperone. He would not let her hold the reins until they reached the outskirts of the city, then he handed them over. Once she had taken over the reins she felt the thrill of holding the powerful, spirited horses and realised how excellent David's sleigh was. It responded so easily to the horses' turns. David explained that he had discussed with the builders certain modifications that he had read about in Bavaria, and had had the builders use some of them when building the sleigh.

Tatiana was so excited driving the three greys and experiencing their power and speed that she was almost able to forget the usual intoxicating feeling she had when David was near her. It was only to keep from succumbing to this feeling that she always teased him. She well knew that she would have behaved differently with him if she had not known about his affair with Baroness Hertzburg. She had known this from the day of the skating competitions, when she had watched them together and at one stage had skated discreetly behind them and seen the way they acted together.

The next day the Baroness's Russian maid, who served under the Baroness's personal maid, had visited her aunt, who was Tatiana's personal maid. She had asked her maid, Marie, to find out if the Baroness and Lord Mountforte were sleeping together. Marie was shocked, and asked why Countess Tatiana was even thinking of such a thing. Nevertheless, Tatiana had persuaded her to find out from her niece, and ever after she had had a regular report through Marie. This, of course, had depressed her and made her flirt more with the young male friends she liked, but it also meant that she never let David know she was the slightest interested in him.

Then she heard that the affair had been broken off, and that on her return from Prussia the Baroness had visited David and then come back weeping and gone to bed. She believed that David had broken with the Baroness. This gave her hope and she had felt elated, but when she saw David and the Baroness in the same room it was clearly apparent that David was still in love with Gisela. Then when she heard through her maid that after years of never visiting her bedroom the Baron now went regularly to his wife's room, Tatiana realised that the Baroness must have broken off with David. That he still loved the Baroness, she never doubted.

David, standing alongside her as the sleigh raced through the snow, had not the slightest idea of Tatiana's thoughts. Instead, he was wondering how he could prise Tatiana away from her maid so he could talk to her alone. He had decided to ask her if she liked him enough to allow him to ask her grandmother's permission to pay court to her. He needed to get rid of the maid for at least twenty minutes.

Shortly afterwards he took the reins from Tatiana and drove off to a little tavern in the woods. It was often frequented by the younger members of the aristocracy and the middle classes of St. Petersburg, who would drive or ride out for a meal. They had got there early, so there was no one there apart from the tavern staff. David asked Tatiana if she would mind if, while they went in to order lunch, Marie asked one of the kitchen staff whether there was any edelweiss growing near the tavern since he would like to take some back for Lady Malvern. David, in fact, had no idea if edelweiss even grew in Russia, let alone cared about it. But Tatiana said that of course Marie could go, and Marie was quite happy to do so. Then after finding a table and ordering food he asked for some wine to be brought immediately. Once the wine had arrived and they had chatted for a few minutes, David looked at Tatiana intently.

'Tatiana,' he asked, 'would you be agreeable if I were to approach your grandmother and ask her permission to court you?'

Tatiana, who had not suspected for one minute that this was David's intention in bringing her here, was momentarily flummoxed. Then, recovering, she knew she could never accept him while he loved another woman. He would be kind to her, generous and upright, but that would not be enough if, as she believed, he loved someone else. Slowly she said that of course he could approach her grandmother. At her words David relaxed somewhat, but he snapped up with shock when Tatiana added, 'But I would not marry you, David.'

Stiff and white-lipped, with a mouth that had suddenly become unaccountably dry, David asked her why she would not marry him.

'You don't love me,' Tatiana said coolly. David, feeling yet again humiliated and a fool, asked if she would be good enough to tell him how she knew he did not love her, and why she would never marry him.

If possible, Tatiana's answer was even more devastating than her first one. She simply said, 'Because you are in love with Baroness Hertzburg.'

'What on earth do you mean?' David spluttered, after he began to recover himself. 'I rarely see the Baroness, and that is usually only at diplomatic functions.'

Then, to his growing horror, Tatiana told him something of what she knew about David and the Baroness's relationship. David wanted to shout out that it was all lies, lies, lies, but he knew he could not. The fact that she had known all along explained those knowing looks and enigmatic remarks she would sometimes make. They flooded back to him and he understood. He now wished he had never mentioned marriage to her. In fact, he wished he were back in his apartment and had never come out today. What a disaster. What a laughing stock he was making of himself.

He looked, to Tatiana, such a picture of misery — white-faced, ramrod straight, but still so handsome — that she took pity on him. She knew that underneath that now cold, contained and haughty exterior he was distraught and humiliated. He could never again be even friends with her because he would always be ashamed that she knew about Baroness Hertzburg, and that he had spoken and been so abruptly refused.

So, loving him deeply and seeing him trying to control his emotions, she decided on a very generous, courageous gesture to put him more at ease. She did not wish to lose his friendship, even though it was sometimes torture to have him near her, knowing he did not love her. Therefore she replied, to his utter astonishment, that she loved him.

This, of course, did not make any sense to David. 'Why then, if you love me,' he said, hoping he had heard correctly, 'would you not want to marry me?'

Tatiana was now rapidly losing courage and beginning to wish she had not admitted she loved him. 'It would be heartbreaking to marry someone you loved and to know they did not love you, but someone unattainable. I would sooner marry a good man who loved me.'

David was now feeling less humiliated, but still bemused. Tatiana continued bravely, saying that if she married a man who loved her she would never let him know she did not love him as he loved her. Rather, she would let him believe she loved him, and it was very possible, she said, that this liking could well turn into love, especially if they had children together.

At this crucial point her maid returned, saying there was no edelweiss. Their meal had also arrived, and with Marie within earshot there was no further chance for talk on the subject. The open exposure of their feelings was now exercising both their minds. Tatiana was regretting her frankness, and wondering if she had been wise to expose her feelings to save his. She was confident, however, that he was such a gentleman that he would never repeat what she had said.

David's humiliation was lessened by Tatiana's admission that she loved him, but he was furious that she knew about Gisela. He began to feel hot and cold, wondering how many other people knew. And how did Tatiana know, and if she did, what about Countess Nadia? Had he been the subject of much gossip without knowing?

In a subdued atmosphere, they talked about what they each planned to do in the coming spring. They did not have their minds on spring, however, as each just wanted the trip to finish and to return home. When they had finished their meal, David asked if Tatiana would like to take the reins for part of the drive back to St. Petersburg. As she took the reins Tatiana felt some of the tension and depression that had been building up inside her ease. The horses were wonderful, but they needed careful handling since they wanted to race back to their stable, knowing they were headed for home, and this meant she had to concentrate on them instead of on David.

David, on the other hand, began to speculate that Tatiana was planning to marry Ivan Vorontsov. He had to admit he was a decent enough character, but he found himself disliking the thought of such a union. At one stage he thought it would serve Tatiana right if the Empress made her marry the Swedish Prince, then he knew he didn't really want that and was just being petty and he despised himself for stooping to such a selfish and rotten thought.

Watching Tatiana handling the reins so expertly, and with her furs looking extremely glamorous, he began to lose his feeling of humiliation and hurt. In fact those feelings were beginning to be replaced with a sense of loss. He had believed he had an excellent chance to win Tatiana's hand, but she had sounded so definite when she said she would not marry him. He was convinced he was no longer in love with Gisela, and he began to wonder how he could persuade Tatiana that this was no longer the case. Of course, he would then have to make her believe he loved her. He didn't, of course, but he liked her very much and had been finding her company very enjoyable. She would certainly make a lovely wife and mother. One only had to watch her with little Alexei to see the latter.

The whole day had been a mess. He should have planned it better. He should have wooed her more. He should not have spoken of marriage. He had been too sure of himself. All these thoughts raced backwards and forwards, round and about in David's mind. When he took the reins from Tatiana as they reached the approaches to the city, his head was in a complete muddle. He decided, love her or not, he was not going to take no for an answer. Since he knew he was never going to let himself love a woman again as he had Gisela, he would have to work out a plan.

He drove Tatiana home, and they rather stiffly thanked each other for the day. Neither had mentioned the business of marriage since lunch. David went home and changed and then, since it was five thirty, decided to go down to his club and see if there was anyone there with whom to box. He had taken up boxing again about four months earlier, firstly to keep trim, and secondly because he enjoyed it. He hoped

someone would be there. He wanted to box some of his frustration out and then go
and have a relaxing sauna.

David found the sauna particularly good for relaxing after a busy day at the office
or a bruising day on a horse.

Over the next few weeks, David made sure that whenever possible he was at the
same party or reception as Tatiana. At first she was a little stiff in his presence, but he
hoped she would get over this in time. There were always people milling around her
and usually much laughter. He also called on the Kolcluleys often, partly because he
genuinely liked them, and partly because Daria was always full of news about Tatiana,
even after she had moved back to the Volonski Palace. The Count and Countess were
still their warm, delightful selves, and made him very welcome. It was, however, a
shock to see how the Countess had gone grey in just a couple of weeks after Dmitri's
death. Her face wore a slightly wistful expression in repose.

Plans were now being made for Sophie and Felix's wedding, which was to be held
in six months' time. Despite Dmitri's death they were obviously very happy together.
It was delightful to see and David was glad for them, but a little envious that two
people in love could be so openly happy together.

One day after work, he thought he would call on Countess Nadia and Tatiana.
He was greeted by the major-domo almost as if he were part of the family, and
immediately announced. To David's embarrassment he found Prince Potemkin
talking to Countess Nadia and Tatiana. He had not been told that they had visitors,
let alone one as illustrious as Prince Potemkin. He began to back out of the room,
but Prince Potemkin waved a hand and beckoned him forward and Countess Nadia,
smiling, asked him to join them.

After greeting David warmly, the Prince explained that he was about to leave for
the Crimea. Before he left he had wanted to see his old friend, Nadia, and discuss how
her estates in the south were performing. He praised her energy and ability to make
things happen, and commented that if Russia had a dozen more women with her
qualities it would be controlling not just a large part of the east, but a larger chunk of
Europe. His words were accompanied by much laughter from the Countess, who said
that her dear old friend was a great flatterer, but it was clear she was pleased.

They then returned to discussing what they were each doing on their estates, and
the problems and successes they were having. When the Prince mentioned that the
Countess of Craven, an Englishwoman, had asked him for land in the south, David
expressed surprise that foreigners were able to take up land grants. The Prince then
told him grandly that as the Empress's Viceroy in the south he had the sole power,
apart from the Empress, of course, to allocate land to whom he wished.

However, he only gave land to people he knew would immediately begin to
cultivate it. People like Countess Volonskaya, for instance, or the Count of Parma,

who had begun silk production. When there were worthy landowners, such as Countess Volonskaya, he would grant tax holidays to encourage further investment.

David was astonished at how enlightened the Prince was, and began to wish he was participating in the Prince's very progressive scheme. Perhaps seeing his thoughts reflected in the expression on his face, Countess Nadia suddenly turned to Prince Potemkin. Sitting with them, she said, was a prime candidate for a land grant, and before David could say anything she went on to tell the Prince all about his grandfather and his family interests. Although rather embarrassed by the Countess's glowing description, David leant forward eagerly to hear what the Prince's response would be.

The Prince appeared interested. 'If you were given a large estate in the south, where the black soil is probably the most fertile in the whole world, what would you do?' he asked.

David's imagination was fired up now, and so he said he had been impressed at what Countess Nadia had achieved and was planning. He told the Prince he had seen part of the south with the two Countesses, and if he had the land he would immediately write to his grandfather and, with his blessing, import cattle, sheep, men and women to work the estate, buy the most modern equipment available to plough the land, and begin planting. He would look at setting up a tanning factory to tan the hides of the cattle and sheep.

Before he could go any further the Prince stopped him and said that if David would commit himself to using the land well he would grant him the equivalent of one hundred thousand acres of land adjoining Countess Nadia's. He had, he said, just taken this piece of land back from the landowner he had given it to, because he had done nothing to exploit its rich black soil in the three years he had had it.

The Prince's sudden offer made David slightly nervous, but on the other hand the thought of being given 100,000 acres of some of the most fertile, flat, clean land in the world was too marvellous an opportunity to miss. So he told the Prince that if he was sincere he would accept his offer gratefully, and do his best to bring the land into production as soon as possible.

'What if your grandfather doesn't back you with the necessary funds?' the Prince asked.

David replied that he had money of his own in the bank since his grandfather gave him a large annual allowance. He had never had to touch the surplus income from the estate his mother had left him. That income had been progressively used to improve the estate and the balance invested in British funds.

'Right,' said the Prince. 'I will have my secretary, Vasily Popov, arrange the details of the transfer. However,' he went on, 'if within three years you have not made significant progress in carrying out the plans you describe, I could just take it back.'

David smiled and said that he hoped to have achieved all he had spoken of and more.

Shortly afterwards the Prince took his leave, and David warmly thanked Countess Nadia for making this incredible opportunity possible. She, ever practical, said that perhaps he would like to meet two of her men of affairs and discuss the arrangements they had made for the further development of her estates in the south. Then perhaps the following day he should come to the palace and they could discuss matters together. Tatiana, who had been listening to the conversation but not saying much, now said, 'How fortunate our two estates adjoin, we will be able to help each other.'

David was so excited when he left that evening that he went back to the office and immediately began a letter to his grandfather. After telling him about the grant of land and describing what Prince Potemkin and Countess Volonskaya were doing on their estates, he spoke of the mulberry trees Potemkin was planting, and how he was establishing a mill with the intention of producing silk from his own trees. David said he would like to do the same with the skins and hides from the sheep and cattle he raised, and would like to establish a tannery.

He then asked his grandfather to convert the government funds he held into cash and to place the money on deposit with his other funds, as he intended to buy the latest equipment for ploughing and reaping. In the same diplomatic bag, he said, he was sending a list of all his requirements to old McNabb, his grandfather's chief factor, with instructions to order them for him. There would be sheep, beef cattle and dairy cattle, and he would also need people such as artisans to work the land. He would be much obliged if his grandfather could keep an overall eye on the project and, using David's money, make the necessary payments as bills fell due. He then went on to describe the quality of the land he had acquired in the Kuban, and the plans he had for the estate.

When he had finished the letter he still felt charged with excitement and he decided to walk home, taking a roundabout way to his apartment, since he was sure he would never go to sleep in his present state. It was now about eleven-thirty, and he set off walking briskly through the back streets running roughly parallel to Nevsky Prospect. He was about thirty minutes from home when he heard swearing, muffled moans and sobs, and turning a corner came across three young officers of the crack Preobrazhensky Regiment, one of the Guards regiments, beating up a figure lying on the ground. This person was fruitlessly trying to fend off the attack, and there was blood running down his face.

David called out to the officers to stop, then ran toward them. The attackers took no notice except to tell him to mind his own business, or else! They then continued to kick and hit their victim, which was too much for David, who seized the attacker nearest him and with one well-placed punch knocked him out. The others were so startled that they briefly stopped their attack, then they turned on David. With a quick side jump he avoided the first, then he hit the second man such a blow that he went reeling back. Meanwhile the figure on the ground, a youth, had struggled to his feet and was trying to grasp one of his assailants by the back, but he was too weak and was quickly thrown off.

The two men then charged at David, who again sidestepped one, but managed to inflict a punch that winded him, and then had time to plant a rock-like fist on the other's jaw, which knocked him to the ground. Before any of them had time to recover he grabbed hold of their young victim and half-dragged him down the road, as fast as he could, and then dodged into a side street. After what seemed a safe distance he slowed down so the youth could keep up more easily, and they made their way to David's apartment.

When they reached the apartment David's manservant was waiting for him, and after taking a quick look at his companion he went to heat water for the bathtub. In the meantime David sat the exhausted youth down and gave him a large shot of brandy. Observing his unexpected guest as he drank the brandy, David estimated he was only about fifteen or sixteen. Normally, he thought, he would be good-looking, but now his face was bloodied and swollen, and a number of bruises were beginning to appear. The brandy appeared to revive him, and after putting the glass down he stood up and introduced himself as Prince Mikhail Viazemsky. As David explained who he was, the young man bowed and shook his hand, at the same time thanking him for intervening and probably saving his life.

When David asked him what had happened the young Prince explained that he was with the Noble Cadet Corps. He had been returning to the Menzhikov Palace, which houses the Noble Cadets, when he heard screams and saw the three men holding a struggling girl, who was attempting to pull away. The men, who appeared to be drunk, were laughing and trying to tear her dress off. Affronted at seeing the men attacking a girl, he had tried to intervene. When he grabbed one of the men the others loosened their grip on the girl to concentrate on him, and the girl broke away. The men became infuriated when she ran off, and they began beating the Prince.

At this stage David's manservant appeared and informed David that the bath was ready for the young man. While Mikhail cleaned himself up, David asked the servant to find some clothes for the Prince to wear home. He also asked him to have horses harnessed to his light carriage so the Prince could be taken in comfort back to the Menzhikov Palace.

When Mikhail was ready, David said he would drive him to his quarters. He asked him if he knew his assailants, and the Prince said no, he did not know them, but he would be able to recognise them again. After David had left Mikhail at the palace he returned home and, by now exhausted, promptly fell asleep.

Around noon the next day a letter and a largish box arrived at the Embassy for David. The letter was from Prince Mikhail, formally thanking David for, as he said, saving his life, and asking David to please accept the accompanying gift as a very small token of his gratitude. He further asked David if he would dine with him at the Nobles Club the following evening. He apologised for the short notice, but he and five other cadets were being posted to Moscow for two months.

When he opened the box David found twenty-four magnificent cut-glass wine goblets. The base of each goblet rested in a beautifully wrought gold holder inscribed with the Viazemsky crest. They were obviously family heirlooms, and as well as being extremely valuable they were very beautiful. David was very touched at receiving such a gift from a youth in his teens.

He sent a letter in return, thanking the Prince for the wonderful but completely unwarranted gift, and saying he would be very happy to dine with him the following evening. Remembering a pair of lovely carved crystal glasses that he had bought not long after he had arrived in St. Petersburg, David decided he would give these to the Prince, since he felt the Prince's gift to him was far too generous. He sent around to his apartment and had the glasses wrapped, then he wrote another note saying they were a gift for a brave young man who was prepared to risk his life against overwhelming odds to save an unknown young girl.

Having to some extent eased his embarrassment at receiving such a valuable gift, he then concentrated on his work. This was not easy, since he found it hard to keep his mind off his plans for the Crimea estate. On the way home that evening he called at the Volonski Palace, as he wanted to tell someone about his letter to his grandfather, and who better than the two Countesses. Countess Nadia was at home but said that Tatiana had gone to a dance party at the Sheremetevs' and would be staying there the night.

David was disappointed at this news but pleased to have the chance to discuss his plans for the land in the south with the Countess. She made some practical suggestions, and commented that lack of water could be a problem at certain times of the year. She suggested that perhaps, between the two of them, they could dam a small stream, which she understood never went dry, and form a system of small channels from it to irrigate the land in the valley immediately below. As her steward had sent up designs for a dam to water her land, she suggested they should look at it together. Seeing the plan, David was again surprised at the level of practical interest the Countess took in her properties. It was an excellent plan, and if the dam was increased in size it would not only irrigate Countess Nadia's land but some of his adjoining land as well.

Between them they had over nine thousand acres that could be irrigated. Fodder crops could be grown there and in the dry season the sheep, cattle and dairy cows' feed could be supplemented. This would allow both estates to increase their stock levels. David gratefully agreed, and said he was prepared to start work on the project as soon as Countess Volonski wished. He would write to his grandfather the next day, asking him to try and locate a man skilled in dam and irrigation construction and send him out to Russia.

That evening David met Mikhail at the Noble's Club, and was very pleased that he had sent his glasses and the note to Prince Mikhail. Although he was a modest young man, David could see he had been thrilled by David's description of him as someone fighting against odds to save a young girl. Mikhail had invited two other friends to join them for dinner, but had asked them to come half-an-hour later so he and David would have a chance to talk first. Mikhail's friends were also pleasant young officers in the Noble Cadets, and the evening was a very merry one. When they parted, Mikhail took David aside and told him that if there was ever anything he needed in Russia and they could help, his parents and he would deem it a favour , if he would ask them.

Two evenings later, David went to a small dinner party the Kolcluleys were giving for Daria's name day, an important occasion. There were about twenty guests, a small number for the Kolcluleys, but the shadow of Dmitri's death still hung over them and their entertaining was consequently very curtailed. No sooner had David walked in than Tatiana approached him. She said she had heard about how he had come to Prince Mikhail's aid, and that everyone who knew about it was full of praise for him since the Prince was very popular amongst his set. His sister was the Princess Maria who had been engaged to her brother. Also, Tatiana said, his father's cousin was the Empress's Procurator-General, a powerful figure in the Senate, so David had made some influential friends through his action.

'I did very little, really,' David said, flushing slightly. Tatiana went on to say that they were looking for the three Preobrazhensky officers involved, but with Mikhail having gone to Moscow it was proving difficult to identify them.

Tatiana was looking particularly lovely, he thought, in a gown with a soft waist, with an aigrette of diamonds and emeralds in her hair. Ever since he had raised the question of marriage there had been something of a barrier between them, or at least some constraint. He found to his surprise that he rather missed her teasing, and wished they could resume their old footing. He had since acknowledged in his mind how generous she had been in telling him she loved him, realising it was because she did not want him to feel humiliated. There were not many women, he thought, who would sacrifice their pride to save another's.

With time he found he was becoming more and more enamoured of Tatiana. She certainly had courage, and in his eyes seemed more beautiful each time he saw her. He liked it less and less when he saw young suitors around her. While he didn't believe it was jealousy, he had to admit to a possessive feeling. He put this down to his having travelled to the south with Tatiana and her grandmother, and acquiring a feeling of belonging to the family.

The evening was a very jolly one. Everyone toasted Daria, who positively sparkled as young Count Voinovich paid obvious attention to her. David was pleased to see this, as he liked Daria a great deal and thought of her as one of the nicest people he knew. She was a staunch friend and someone who was always kindly in thought and deed, and never malicious.

The Kolcluleys were delighted with the news that David had acquired land in the south, telling him that whenever he visited his estate he must stay with them in Kiev if they were in residence. Count Nikolai said that they expected to be there for several months each year, partly to oversee the sowing of the grain in spring, and then to oversee the harvesting towards the end of summer. David was delighted to accept the offer of their hospitality, and in return said that once he had built a suitable dwelling he hoped they would all come and allow him to repay a little of their hospitality and to enjoy their company.

Count Nikolai confided sadly that now Dmitri was no longer with them, once their two daughters were married he and the Countess intended to spend more time on the Ukrainian estate. They would keep their St. Petersburg mansion for visiting their daughters, but later might sell it and buy a smaller residence. They no longer felt the need to keep a strong presence in the capital and he, and particularly his wife, would prefer the country. There were fewer memories of Dmitri in Kievan society, and he felt they would not feel his loss there quite so much. David admired their attitude to their tragedy, and was aware again of how much their friendship meant to him.

As he made his way home later that night, he thought how time had flown since he had first arrived in Russia nearly eighteen months ago. He did not feel so bitter about Gisela now, though he had only seen her on her own once since the day she called on him to tell him their affair was over.

When he thought about that last meeting, he still became angry thinking how she dropped him as soon as she had tired of him. How different Tatiana was from Gisela. Tatiana never led people on as Gisela had done. To think he had once believed Gisela loved him. What a fool he had been. No, he thought, he did not love Tatiana as he had Gisela, and he never would love any woman again that way, but he was very fond of her and he respected her greatly. He resolved that if he did marry her, he would not exploit the fact that she had told him she loved him. He reached home with these rather smug thoughts in his mind, and went to bed.

The next few weeks flew by. The Embassy was busy with work and preparing for the arrival of William Fawkener, who was coming to represent the British Government. His purpose was really to report back to the British Prime Minister independently of the reports he received from the Ambassador. What was causing a problem for the Embassy was that the Opposition party in Britain, at Charles Fox's instigation, had unofficially sent an envoy called Adair, and it wanted him to be given the same treatment as Fawkener.

In addition to his work David was still attending a number of parties and receptions. He always kept an eye out for Tatiana and watched to see who she was with, and if she was favouring any man in particular. Tatiana was always the centre of attraction in some group or other, and David noticed how she sparkled and there was always laughter around her. He found he was missing the way she used to make gentle fun of him, and he once said to her that she never teased him now. She stopped for a moment, and then said they had passed the teasing stage when they had had that discussion at the tavern in the woods. Then, smiling, she changed the subject, saying that her grandmother was eagerly awaiting his grandfather's opinion of the estate Prince Potemkin had granted David.

David began to sense a more formal barrier rising between Tatiana and himself. She was always charming to him, but she never let her guard down or revealed any of her intimate feelings. This had the effect of increasing the attraction he felt for her and, of course, making him more frustrated. He could not be certain, but she seemed to be ensuring they were never able to be alone, even for a few minutes. How different it was now from when he first met her and she had tricked him into dancing with her. Now every time he asked her to dance with him she was already booked.

Then came the day when the diplomatic mail bag was opened and among its contents were two letters addressed to Lord Mountforte. One was from his grandfather, the other from McNabb, his steward. Eagerly he opened his grandfather's first. It was the best of news. The old Earl said David need not touch his own money, but that the old Earl was forwarding 20,000 pounds from his family estate for David's use in Russia. He had made another 50,000 pounds available for his steward, McNabb, to use for the purchase of the animals and equipment David had requested.

This was a colossal sum, and David was stunned at his grandfather's generosity. His grandfather was obviously delighted at David's success and initiative, and he informed him that to save him time and expense he was sending seventy-two people, plus nine children, to Russia on board his next two timber ships. Reading on, David became even more excited. Twelve of the adults coming were wives, and the other sixty were men. Apart from two, one a blacksmith and farrier and the other a surveyor, the men were all under thirty-five. Among these fifty-eight men were carpenters, good agricultural labourers, cowmen, shepherds and foresters. McNabb had apparently screened them all for their character, health and abilities.

Then came a startling sentence. All the men were convicts and due to be transported, but now America was no longer a colony but independent, there was a shortage of places to send them. He had done a deal with the Scottish law courts and taken over the convicts on the condition that he removed them from Britain. He assured David that none of the men were evil, and their convictions were mainly for stealing game from estates or crimes of that sort. McNabb had also found out who was married and who had children, so their families could come with them.

He had told the men that they would not be treated as convicts once they reached Russia. However, they must work for at least five years on his grandson's estate, and they would receive a fair wage. Here his grandfather said he had no idea of workmen's wages in Russia but he knew he could depend on David to treat them fairly. He also said he had promised them reasonable accommodation.

David was truly staggered. This solved the language problem for him, and above all he was sure his grandfather and McNabb would have chosen good workers. Another bonus was that he would not now have to purchase so many serfs. There was a scarcity of serfs with the opening up of the south, and this was enabling their owners to ask higher prices for them. Even if one could afford to buy them, they were usually from deceased or bankrupt estates, otherwise they were hard to come by. There was now rapidly becoming a scarcity of labour throughout Russia, as the empire expanded. David could have jumped for joy. What imagination his grandfather had to think of sending convicts.

The letter went on to state that McNabb would be writing a separate letter with all the other details. He added that he only wished he was twenty years younger, or no, ten years younger, so he could come and visit the property. Asking David to keep him informed of progress and to let him know of anything he needed, the old Earl closed off, gruffly sending his regards. David smiled at the ending, knowing how hard it was for his Grandfather to show his affection in words but he knew how much he was loved, by his grandfather's continuing munificence to him.

It was such wonderful news that David felt like hugging the first person he saw, but as the first person he saw through his office window was a drunken Kalmack, he changed his mind about the hug. The equivalent of 20,000 thousand pounds here, plus another 50,000 pounds in Britain: his grandfather had provided him with a fortune. He decided to contact Russia's most powerful banker, Richard Sutherland, who was also a Scot, and have him handle the transactions on his behalf. This sum was too large not to be put in the most capable of hands.

McNabb's letter was also exciting. He wrote he was chartering several ships to bring the beef cattle, sheep and dairy herd and the tools and equipment over. He further wrote that the Earl had doubled the number of animals Lord Mountforte had originally asked for. When McNabb had protested that there might not be enough feed for the animals, the Earl had said he was sure Lord Mountforte only ordered that number because that was all he thought he could afford using the money he had in government funds and on deposit. David smiled, thinking how much his grandfather would have enjoyed the argument with his much-trusted steward. McNabb added that the Earl had requested that Lord Mountforte try and find return cargoes for the chartered ships.

Then more good news. McNabb wrote that at the last minute he had been able to secure the services of four talented men whom he had been interviewing just before the ships sailed. One was an agricultural foreman, one was an excellent manager of cattle and sheep, one a first-class builder, and the last an engineer. McNabb said apologetically that he had had to offer them wages and conditions superior to those they would receive in Britain, but he had consulted the Earl on the matter of the wages and had been ordered to go ahead and secure them. McNabb wrote that he hoped Lord Mountforte would agree. When he saw the terms and conditions offered to each of the men David was overjoyed; McNabb had done a marvellous job if the men were as good as he suggested. Perhaps the best news of all, however, was that McNabb said the Earl was now so interested in the Russian project that he appeared totally rejuvenated and looked ten years younger.

David was now itching for the ships to arrive so that he could get underway. He decided he would ask the Ambassador for two months' leave, promising to report back on the state of the south and the Crimea in particular if leave was granted. He decided to go straight round to see Countess Nadia and let her know he was now underway. The Countess was impressed and congratulated him, and then she mentioned that there was a Hungarian here in St. Petersburg in whom David might be interested. He had been employed by an acquaintance of hers, a very difficult man to work for, she imagined, to manage the planting of grapes and later the production of wine on his Moldavian estate. The manager and the landowner had a falling out, and the manager had since been to see her steward asking for a position on her Crimean estate. Her steward recommended him but she did not have an opening for him. She wondered if David would like to interview him for his estate, if he was seriously considering growing grapes. David thanked the Countess and said he would, so she said she would ask her steward to arrange a time later in the week.

Just then Tatiana arrived brimming with the news that a plot to assassinate the Empress had been uncovered. Countess Nadia and David were both very concerned, since neither could see Russia without the Empress and both secretly thought Grand Duke Paul would be a difficult Emperor. There would also be a major shift in Russia's foreign policy, as Grand Duke Paul, who was also hereditary Duke of Holstein, favoured Frederick the Great of Prussia. David knew this would suit Britain, but personally he much preferred the Empress.

Countess Nadia pressed David to stay to dinner, over which they discussed what they would have done if the Empress had been assassinated. As David listened to Countess Nadia's assessment of the situation if Grand Duke Paul acceded to the throne he was struck, as always, by the intelligence and lucidity of her thoughts. Fortunately the plot to assassinate the Empress Catherine had not succeeded, but it did raise worries in people's minds about what would happen if she was to die. The immediate outcome, needless to say, was that her popularity soared.

The next day David went to ask the Ambassador if he could have two months' leave to visit his southern estate. To the Ambassador's credit, he showed no jealousy over his junior receiving such a magnificent gift from Prince Potemkin. Rather, he saw it as further support for Britain in Russia. He was willing to grant David leave, but only after Fawkener and Adair had left St. Petersburg. When Lady Malvern heard, she too was delighted, and she made David promise to invite her to visit the estate once he had built a roof over his head. Then, she added, laughing, that of course she could come almost immediately if he took those famous tents of his.

The days flew now, as in his spare time David made preparations to move his animals and people down to the estate. He was busy ordering timber and fittings for housing, and he had already employed an Italian architect to design a mansion for the estate. Though he wouldn't start building it yet. He also hired a Russian architect to design prefabricated wooden houses for his English employees, knowing that the wooden houses and buildings were burnt so regularly in places like Moscow that Russia led the world in producing prefabricated housing. David had decided that since his grandfather had provided so much more money than he had expected he would build model quarters for all his employees. Now it was spring and the rivers were navigable, he was having all the precut timber for the houses barged down the river. It gave him real pleasure to think of how happy his employees would be when they saw their accommodation.

He had also asked the Earl and McNabb to find a schoolteacher who would teach all the children on his estate to read and write English. He also intended to find a Russian teacher to teach the children Russian, so that both English and Russian children would go to the school and become bilingual. In addition he was contemplating a night class for the adults once or twice a week. The English could pick up basic Russian, and the Russians could pick up basic English.

He had employed the Hungarian and was now using Countess Nadia's contacts to secure up to 1000 thousand grape stock. When he found that the work involved in establishing his estate was encroaching on his official working hours he asked his grandfather to endeavour to find him a good overall manager, a competent secretary and a good financial clerk.

He was now writing letters to his grandfather and to McNabb to coincide with every diplomatic bag sent back to Britain. Sometimes the bag contained two or three letters as new thoughts arose after he had closed off a letter. When he received letters from his grandfather these days he was amazed at the Earl's new enthusiasm and vigour. He thought that if nothing else came of his estate, it had had the benefit of revitalising his grandfather. McNabb had commented that he was now hard pressed to keep up with the Earl.

So the letters raced back and forwards between Russia and Britain, and all the while David was kept extremely busy preparing and organising the movement of supplies down to the Kuban. He was ordering seed grain, hoping to get it planted in time for harvesting at the end of summer. He was considering planting potatoes, and he had already acquired the best strain he could find of oats and barley, as he would need those crops for feeding his workhorses. Countess Nadia and he had some interesting sessions on the breeding of the best heavy workhorses. They knew they would both require several hundred draughthorses to work their lands; consequently they were considering setting up a joint stud in the Kuban.

Tatiana did not appear very often now when David was at the Volonski Palace. He was always disappointed if she was not there when he arrived, but his discussions with the Countess became so intensely interesting that it was not until he left that he pondered over her absence.

Finally the ships chartered by the Earl arrived and David's plans to take the people, animals, equipment and seeds south, was activated. He liked the look of the people his grandfather and McNabb had sent, and when the convicts were assembled on the deck he had the leg irons struck off them.

Then he addressed them and said that in Russia they were free men. This was greeted with astonished silence, but after they had recovered from their surprise the bolder among them began to ask questions. They would be paid better than the average Russian pay, David told them, but he expected them to work better and produce more than their Russian counterparts. He told them he could not come down with them immediately but they would be travelling with the sheep and cattle, so it would be a slow, leisurely trip. There would be covered carts and wagons to take them part of the way and later they would go by barge from Kiev, a city in the Ukraine, to the estate.

The carpenter, and any other men who had carpentering skills, would travel on horseback as this would be much faster. This was so that they could assemble the houses which had been prefabricated, a term he had to explain, and just needed to be put together. He left them to disembark and march to a field where he had had some military tents erected for them to spend the night in, and where they would have their dinner and an early breakfast, since there would be much to do the following morning.

Almost all the animals had survived, partly, David thought, because there were so many men to look after them. He was particularly surprised to see twenty-four Tamworth sows and three big boars, which he had not ordered. They turned out to be a surprise from his grandfather. Although most of them were not in the best of condition after their trip, David could still see that they generally had well-shaped bodies. In fact, he thought McNabb had made an excellent job of his purchases.

He then took the management team of four back to his apartment, where the Hungarian was also waiting. Over dinner David explained what he wished each of them to do. The Hungarian had a little English, but for anything that was difficult to explain David used French, in which the Hungarian was fluent. The four English managers were to travel with the carpenters, while the Hungarian was to wait for the grape vines and travel down with them.

David stated that he wanted all his men to be well treated and regarded as free men. He emphasised that unless he personally ordered it, no one employed by him, Russian or English, was ever to be flogged. Whatever crime they had committed in the past had been minor, and he wanted it forgotten. He also told them about his plans to educate the children of the estate, and provide night classes for the adults, which impressed the managers. Two of the managers, being married, asked if they could take their wives down with them, or whether they would have to journey down with the others. David replied that he would prefer them to go with the others, so that by the time they arrived their accommodation would be ready. He explained that their own houses would be larger than those of the men working under them, and said that on the wages he was going to pay them they would be easily able to afford Russian servants to help in the house or garden.

After the men had left, David sat down and wrote to both his grandfather and McNabb, congratulating them on all they had done and expressing his gratitude. He expressed the wish that they would come and visit in about six months' time, and see what their efforts in finding the people, animals and equipment had achieved. He wrote that he was particularly pleased to have received the Newcomen steam water pump, and even more so the latest Watt steam water pump. He said he had spoken to Countess Nadia and she wondered if they would purchase six for her. She would transfer the funds to pay for them through David's banker, Richard Sutherland. Both the Countess and he anticipated the pumps would help with circulating water around her estates. Coal was not a problem, as coal already arrived by barge from the Donets Basin. David asked if they could also send him four more pumps of the latest Watt design.

The animals had been transported by canal barge overnight to some fields on the outskirts of St. Petersburg, and it was not until two the next afternoon that the journey south was able to begin. This, however, was breakneck speed by Russian standards. Countess Nadia and Tatiana jokingly called David 'young Potemkin' since, like many others, they believed only Potemkin in the whole of the Russian Empire could make anything speed up.

That night David had dinner with Countess Nadia and Tatiana. They drank champagne to toast the venture, and afterwards enjoyed a particularly good Hungarian Tokay wine produced from the same vine stock that Countess Nadia had located for David. It was a happy evening. That night David felt closer to Tatiana than he ever had before, and he believed she too had enjoyed their companionship. It was therefore in a very happy frame of mind that he went back to his apartment and bed.

The next month passed quickly, with David working hard during the day and enjoying the round of receptions, dinners and parties that was the norm for St. Petersburg at this time of the year. Finally Fawkener left, and Adair went south with Potemkin and his people. Fawkener's visit had not been a success as he was representing the British sovereign and therefore seen to be representing the Prime Minister, William Pitt. Charles Fox, on the other hand, had supported the Russians and opposed the Turks, and he was regarded as a hero in Russia. As Adair was believed to represent Fox, he was everywhere treated as a great friend of Russia, including at Court.

Now that the two envoys had left St. Petersburg, Lord Malvern agreed that David could take two months off. He made a series of farewell calls and gave a dinner for the Countess Nadia, Tatiana, the Kolcluleys and Lord and Lady Malvern. The next day he left for his estate, taking with him letters and instructions to be delivered from Countess Nadia to her steward on the adjoining estate.

David was enthusiastic and impatient as he headed to his estate, and his only nagging problem was Tatiana. He had achieved no encouragement from her on the subject of marriage. Whenever he came near to bringing the matter up she adroitly managed to switch subjects or avoid him. He had kept a careful watch on the young men courting her, but he had not noticed that she favoured any over the others. Still, two months away was a long time, and Tatiana would shortly be twenty. Most girls were married by then. He made an effort to shake off these gloomy thoughts, and turned to contemplating the success he knew he was going to make of his estate. Since he was only travelling with four male servants he expected, with fast travelling, to reach the estate in ten days.

CHAPTER TWENTY TWO

SOME FIFTEEN DAYS LATER, AN IMPERIAL COURIER DELIVERED A LETTER FROM THE EMPRESS TO COUNTESS NADIA. It was a charming letter, as the Empress had a style of writing that conveyed her thoughts exceptionally well. However, after the usual pleasant salutations, the reason for the letter became clear. The Empress wished Countess Tatiana to marry the Swedish Prince Karl. She said it would be a great honour for Countess Tatiana to marry into the Swedish Royal Family. She invited Countess Volonskaya to come to Tsarskoe-selo, where the Empress was presently residing, at noon the following day. She stated that Countess Golvinka was not to be told of this great honour until after she and the Countess had met.

Countess Nadia knew this news would be a terrible blow to Tatiana, and she was thankful that she did not have to tell her straight away. Nadia wondered how or if she could persuade the Empress to change her mind. She knew the Empress realised Tatiana did not wish to marry the Prince, and she found herself wishing her friend Prince Potemkin was in St. Petersburg. He was the one person who might be able to change the Empress's mind, but he was down in Jassy. She would just have to try herself.

Thank heavens, she thought, Tatiana was weekending with Daria Kolcluley and would not see her preparing to go to the Palace. Tatiana was very quick at sensing things and she would almost certainly guess why her grandmother was being summoned. Nadia began to try and think of some way of saving her granddaughter from the marriage. She knew Tatiana would hate the cold, formal Swedish Court, and that to have to spend her life there would crush her.

She remembered the days when as a young girl she had been a maid of honour to the Empress Elizabeth, who delighted in luxury and sumptuous living but had been a capricious mistress. At times she could be very kind and generous, but if crossed she could be very vengeful and everyone feared her temper. She shuddered when she remembered that dreadful day when one of Empress Elizabeth's ladies-in-waiting, a very pretty young Countess, was found to be maliciously gossiping. The Empress, furious, had ordered the girl's tongue to be cut out, and the girl to be sent into exile. What a mercy that the present Empress was not so barbaric.

Setting out early the next day, Nadia rode in her fastest carriage, drawn by her beloved greys, to the Catherine Palace in the Tsarskoe-Selo complex. Catherine had remodelled the Palace superbly with the help of a Scotsman called Charles Cameron.

Originally, Empress Elizabeth had employed an Italian called Rastrelli, who built in the Rococo style. The exterior of the Palace was magnificent, as she drove along the facade, which was the longest in the world.

To try and control her nervousness, the Countess tried to concentrate further on the Palace. The great staterooms created by Elizabeth and Rastrelli were stunning, but Nadia preferred the more restrained Palladian style of Cameron. His rooms were more comfortable and somehow more intimate. She still remembered when she had first seen the Great Hall and had gasped. First there were the wonderful carved golden doors to the vast hall, which was itself all decorated with gold, Rastrelli having used over a hundred kilograms of gold throughout the suite. Then the beautiful floor, 846 square metres, made of inlaid precious woods; the huge windows, and the magnificent painted ceiling depicting 'The Triumph of Russia'. As a young girl she had been totally overawed. The wonderful Amber Room was considered to be the eighth wonder of the world with its marvellous amber panels. The Jasper Room and the Agate Room each had walls and pillars made of lovely shades of green jasper and red agate from the Urals. Then there was the splendid lapis lazuli furniture and ornaments, and the other rooms with incredibly beautiful, intricately inlaid wooden floors that almost rivalled the Great Hall.

All these thoughts raced through the Countess's mind as she tried to allay her fear at the summons, even though she had known the Empress ever since she had arrived in Russia as a shy young German Princess to marry the Grand Duke Peter.

Finally she arrived and was shown to the Blue Snuff Box Room, where the Empress was sitting writing. The Empress greeted Nadia warmly, saying she did not see enough of her old friend these days. Then, after this pleasant welcome, the Empress said she was delighted to be able to inform Nadia that a great honour was coming her way. A letter had arrived from the Swedish Palace requesting the hand of her granddaughter, Countess Tatiana Golvinka, in marriage to Prince Karl. The Empress said she had been delighted to receive this request, as the marriage would strengthen Russia's ties with Sweden and weaken Britain and Prussia's interests there. She was sure Nadia would be honoured to have her granddaughter marrying into the Swedish Royal Family.

Both the Empress and Nadia knew this latter statement was not true. When the idea of such a marriage had first been mooted Nadia had tried to forestall it, knowing that Tatiana was appalled both by the Prince and by the idea of having to spend most of her time in Sweden. However, Nadia saw that beneath her warmth there was a very determined look on the Empress's face and in her eyes. Seeing this, Nadia thought that for the moment there was nothing she could say that would help Tatiana, so she smiled and thanked the Empress for the honour offered to her granddaughter.

The Empress, who had been expecting at least some token resistance, relaxed somewhat, and asked the Countess to bring Tatiana to the Peterhof Palace in five days' time. She then changed the subject and invited Nadia to join her for lunch, which was starting shortly. If Nadia had not been feeling sick with worry over the proposed marriage, lunch would have been a very amusing affair.

After lunch, Countess Nadia drove back to St. Petersburg with a heavy heart, wondering what to do. She finally decided to send a message to the Kolcluleys asking Tatiana to come home. Several hours later Tatiana rushed into the Countess's study to find her grandmother looking tense and upset.

'Grandmother, is everything all right?' she asked.

Gently Countess Nadia told her about the Empress's summons, and the reason for it.

'No,' Tatiana said, an expression of horror on her face. 'I will never marry the Prince.'

Her grandmother explained that such a refusal would only incur the wrath of the Empress and her advisors and nothing would be gained. Indeed, depending upon the Court's determination, Tatiana could be forced to marry the Prince, simply by being put under house arrest until the wedding day. Such things had happened before.

Tatiana replied angrily that she would rather give up everything and enter a convent than marry the dreadful Prince. Alternating between helpless rage and despair, her thoughts ran the gauntlet of such fantastical ideas as suicide, taking to a convent, and eloping. Seeing her genuine horror of the marriage, her grandmother asked her to sit down and they would see if they could devise a plan to avoid the marriage without having to resort to such foolish ideas as suicide or the convent.

After considering various ideas the Countess finally said that Tatiana must find somewhere safe to hide for a month or two. She must keep the place a secret, and not even tell her grandmother where she had gone. Nadia said she would draft a letter, which Tatiana would write and leave with her, and this together with her absence might save the day. The Empress, she said, was basically a kind and sentimental person, but where Russia's interests were concerned she was totally ruthless. Her advisors, with the possible exception of Prince Potemkin, would not for one minute reflect on Tatiana's position if it suited them to have her marry the Prince.

'No,' she said finally, 'we must somehow gain the Empress's sympathy.'

'But how do we gain her sympathy?' wailed Tatiana. 'There would not even be anyone willing to elope with me if they knew they would face the rage of the Empress and the Court.'

This was a State matter now, and no one in their right mind would risk becoming involved against the wishes of the Empress.

The Countess, however, was now writing, and she asked Tatiana to be quiet until she had finished the letter. Tatiana lay on a sofa and dramatically planned how she would kill herself rather than marry the Prince, then, knowing she would never kill herself, she tried to think of some other way of escape. She well knew that if she blatantly defied the Empress and her advisors there was a possibility of her estates being confiscated. Empress Catherine had never done this, but it had happened in earlier reigns and it was still in the sovereign's power to so do.

Finally Countess Nadia stopped writing, and asked Tatiana to listen as she read out what she had drafted. The letter began by saying that since she, Tatiana, knew her grandmother would never lie to the Empress, she was not telling her where she had fled to, but that it was safe. Putting the letter aside for a moment, the Countess said that she would have to let Tatiana find somewhere safe, and she emphasised 'safe,' to hide, and she would not be able to tell her where it was, otherwise all her interests could be at stake.

She then returned to the letter, which continued by saying that her grandmother had told her what a dreadfully sad marriage the Empress had had forced on her as a young girl, and how only her courage and intelligence had saved her, and how her children had been taken from her by Empress Elizabeth. She knew she would never have the courage or strength that the Empress had shown in her time of trouble. This, she said, was the reason she had run away.

Would her grandmother please try and mediate on her behalf with the Empress, the letter continued. Everyone believed the Empress had a kind and generous heart, and her grandmother had often assured her of this from her long friendship with the Empress. Could her grandmother not suggest someone else who would be honoured to marry into the Swedish Royal Family, as there must be many families ambitious for such a connection. The letter was signed 'Your loving granddaughter, Tatiana.'

Having finished the letter, Nadia said that in this way she would be exonerated and would avoid the direct wrath of the Empress, and by citing the problems of the Empress's own marriage, it appealed to her sympathy. Tatiana agreed, and after throwing her arms around her and kissing her she began to copy out her grandmother's letter. 'You're a wonder, Grandmother. Thank you,' she said.

Her grandmother said that if she could think of a safe place, and she kept repeating 'safe place,' then Tatiana should leave as soon as possible. Since the safe place would have to be outside St. Petersburg, she must take her maid and at least three of the men-servants with her.

Tatiana replied that she would leave early the day after tomorrow, which would give her time to outfit herself and those going with her. She also asked her grandmother to send a messenger to bring four of the homing pigeons back from the estate outside St. Petersburg. The Countess had long ago established relays of homing pigeons at all her estates, and it was four of these that Tatiana decided to take with her. She could let one go periodically and it would fly back to St. Petersburg with a note attached to its leg, letting her grandmother know how she was. Countess Nadia congratulated her, saying this was an excellent idea. She should take six of the pigeons, and send one back every week.

Tatiana then sat down to make a plan and calculate what she would need. Countess Nadia, of course, could not involve herself in the planning, but her anxiety was lessened as she watched Tatiana make lists and plans. By mid-afternoon the following day Tatiana had assembled everything she wanted. That evening, she gathered her maid, a footman and two grooms, and told them they were to be ready to leave at five-thirty the next morning. They were not to discuss their plans with anyone else in the household, she said. The grooms were to have five riding horses and three packhorses ready, and to have all the baggage evenly balanced and packed on the horses.

The next morning, when her maid went in to dress Tatiana, she was shocked to find a man's riding habit laid out for her mistress and another for herself. She was even more shocked when, after putting on the outfit, Tatiana suddenly tucked a piece of cloth in either side of her jaw and another up under her upper lip. She then blackened one of her teeth with some paint, tucked her hair up in a bun under a man's hat, and urged her maid to do the same. She then went downstairs, quite unrecognisable as Countess Tatiana. At first none of the men recognised her, and it was only when her maid came alongside her and spoke to them that they realised who she was. The maid had earlier been surprised that there was no sign of Countess Nadia, who always came to see Tatiana off if she was going on a journey without her. Now everyone was mystified, but Tatiana told them she would explain once they were outside St. Petersburg.

CHAPTER TWENTY THREE

They left St. Petersburg without mishap, and when they later stopped for lunch Tatiana told them she was going into hiding. As she was disguised as a man, they were to call her Baron Ropsha. She also told them she was fleeing from a forced marriage arranged by the Government, and that she had not told her grandmother she was running away, otherwise she could face trouble. She told them they would be some weeks on the road, but she would not tell them where they were heading in case someone recognised them and forced them to talk. Hearing this, the servants promptly became very protective of Tatiana, and resolved to do all they could to safeguard her. They were also relieved when she told them about her plan for the pigeons, and their fears about letting Countess Nadia down were allayed.

They made good progress during the day, and that evening they slept in two small army tents, which Tatiana had had put in with the baggage. They were up early the next morning, breakfasted quickly, and broke camp by five-thirty, as Tatiana wanted to be as far away as possible from St. Petersburg when her disappearance was discovered by the Court. Although her maid and the footman were stiff from the unaccustomed riding, they made no complaint, as they were all anxious to help their mistress escape.

On the third day they stopped at a farmhouse and Tatiana sent one of the men to buy eggs, milk, black bread and, if possible, some bacon. They were able to buy everything they wanted except the bacon. Tatiana had brought food for the pigeons, and it was relatively simple to purchase oats and barley. Of course there was also plenty of grass for the horses, which were hobbled at night to feed, but the oats and barley kept their energy up.

One night they were woken by the sound of the horses whinnying. One of the grooms got up to see what was happening and was just in time to see a man trying to take the hobbles off one of the horses. Tatiana had given each of the men a pistol but the groom had left his in the tent, not expecting to face horse thieves. He rushed back to get it, calling out to the others that there was someone trying to steal the horses.

Everyone shot out of the two tents but it was too late. The thief left the horse whose hobbles he was trying to remove, but jumped on the back of another that had already been freed, and raced away. This was a serious blow. The horses were some of the pick of Countess Volonskaya's stable and one horse short meant they would have to jettison some of their pack. It had already been kept fairly light as Tatiana had wanted to travel as quickly as possible. It was decided that in the future the men would take turns at night watch, doing three hours' duty each. This meant no one would be too tired to ride in the morning.

As it was now three o'clock, Tatiana decided there was no point in going back to bed, and breakfast was made straight away. After they had packed up they tried to reduce the amount of baggage, but Tatiana had calculated so well when ordering the equipment and provisions for the journey that nothing could be left, so the two packhorses had to carry extra weight. This concerned Tatiana, as she did not want any of the horses to carry too much. However, there was nothing to be done, except to leave behind the pack harness that had belonged to the stolen horse, hoping someone would find it and put it to good use.

They rode steadily for the rest of the morning, stopping at eleven for an early lunch since they had eaten breakfast at such an ungodly hour. When they set off again one of the packhorses began to act strangely, whinnying and looking back, falling back and halting, then cantering to catch up to the others. The packhorses had not been led once they had left the city, as they were happy to run alongside the other horses. Apart from stopping briefly to snatch a succulent branch or clump of grass, they kept up with the group. No one could understand why the horse was behaving so strangely.

After this had been going on for about thirty minutes one of the grooms took a rope and tied it to the horse's halter and tried to lead it alongside the horse he was riding. The packhorse kept pulling at the rope and trying to halt or turn back. Neither groom could make out what was wrong, so the other groom rode his horse up behind the led packhorse and endeavoured to push it forward. This only resulted in the packhorse lashing out with its hind legs, so the groom riding behind had to fall back.

Everyone was trying to think what could be wrong with the horse when suddenly they heard a triumphant neigh from behind them. The packhorse that was being led reared and half lost its pack, which caused it to buck and unsettled the two horses nearest to it. This, combined with the sound of a horse galloping up behind them, upset everyone, horse, man and woman.

Suddenly into their midst came their stolen horse, with a snapped rope hanging from its neck. At last they realised why the packhorse had been behaving so oddly. It and the stolen horse were close friends, usually pulling the light chaise together, and it had scented the other horse as it tried to catch up with them. A great fuss was made of the stolen horse, which had obviously broken away from where it had been tied and followed their trail.

Of course, now they had no pack harness for it, so it was decided that the packhorses could take turns carrying the packs. Everyone was pleased that they had not lost such a valuable horse. The grooms, who were very attached to all their charges, made a great fuss of it, telling it how courageous it was to get away from the thief, and how clever it was to find them.

It was a long day, and by the time they stopped for the night everyone, including the horses, was tired and looking forward to their rest. Night watch was something of a bind, but when Tatiana offered to take a turn the men objected and said they would prefer she slept so she could make all the right decisions in the morning. Tatiana agreed, smiling, but knew they really wanted to keep her out of danger.

Back in St. Petersburg Countess Volonskaya had already had to face the Empress's anger. The day after Tatiana had slipped away the Countess pretended she had only just found the letter addressed to her and said she had come immediately to the Empress. When the Empress learned that Tatiana had disappeared, she turned red with rage and then poured out her sarcasm on Nadia.

Countess Nadia kept a cool, composed profile but inwardly she was trembling and wondering what punishment the Empress would order. She had asked Countess Nadia in the iciest of tones if she had any idea where Tatiana had fled to. The Countess, truthfully and thankfully, said she had not. With that the Empress instructed her secretary to order an immediate manhunt for the Countess Golvinka. No effort was to be spared, she was to be found and brought to the Empress as soon as possible.

The Empress then began to berate Countess Volonskaya for not bringing up her granddaughter to respect and obey her Sovereign, and Tatiana for not being a patriot and thinking only of herself. How did the Countess expect her to explain away this humiliating affront to the Swedish King? If they were humiliated like this the Swedes would have every reason to take the British bribes and join the British, Prussian, and French Alliance. Who did the Volonskis and Golvinkas think they were to turn down a royal suitor? How grand did they think they were? Well, the Empress would show them how grand they were when she had finished with them.

By this time the Empress's rage had shown no sign of abating, in fact just the reverse, and Countess Volonskaya was not only inwardly quaking but outwardly trembling. Then, shouting at the Countess, the Empress said angrily, 'Surely she left you a note or a letter.'

The Countess had originally intended to give the letter to the Empress, it was for that reason that she had drafted it, but in the face of the Empress's fury she had quite forgotten it. Now, with a sense of partial relief and a shaking hand she found the letter and mutely passed it to the Empress. The Empress, who had been pacing up and down the chamber since she had heard the news of Tatiana's disappearance, took the letter and suddenly sat down, leaving the Countess standing.

As the Empress read the two pages of the letter her face underwent an astonishing change. When she had finished she began to read them again. All the while the Countess stood, her heart pounding, wondering what Tatiana's and her fate was to be. Then the Empress said in a totally changed voice that Nadia should have given her this letter immediately. She was sorry she had shouted at her old and dear friend, Nadia. The difference in the Empress's tone of voice and the softening of her face nearly caused Countess Nadia to faint, so great was her relief. Seeing this, the Empress asked her to sit, and then she ordered one of her footmen to bring in some tea for them both. She then said that this was a very tricky situation, but if Tatiana truly felt this way she should not have to marry the Prince.

Nadia's relief was so great when she heard these words that she stood up, curtsied, then took the Empress's hand and kissed it. The Empress, visibly touched, patted her, told her to be seated again and said with consideration, 'We shall have to think of a solution to this problem which will not humiliate or embarrass the Swedes.'

Softening further, she looked at Nadia and said, 'So you still remember those terrible days of my marriage to the Grand Duke, and the awful fear I had, of which way the Empress Elizabeth might move? Yes,' she continued, 'and you, even though a maid of honour to the Empress, were always kind to me, even when you didn't know I would succeed Empress Elizabeth.'

With that, she began to reminisce, and Nadia knew the danger to Tatiana and herself, so real half an hour earlier, had vanished.

After a few minutes the Empress grew silent, before stating that Countess Nadia was to announce that Countess Golvinka was in the south on her grandmother's estate and was not due back in St. Petersburg for two months. 'That,' she said, 'will give us time to plan what steps to take to avoid a problem with the Swedes.'

When Countess Nadia at last left the Empress, she felt she had somehow strengthened her ties of friendship to Catherine, the woman. The letter she had drafted for Tatiana to write had been a godsend, and had saved them both. Nadia sank into her carriage with a mixture of exhaustion and contentment, something she had not felt since the spectre of Tatiana's marriage had arisen. Now, if only a pigeon would arrive to let her know that Tatiana was safe. If all was well, and how she prayed it was, one of the birds must arrive within the next few days. She hoped it would come soon, as she was not sure she could take too much more strain.

Meanwhile, David had arrived at his estate, and already much had been accomplished. The workers had all arrived safely and settled in, and the animals looked in good condition. The houses had all been erected, including the four-bedroom house he intended to use for himself until he could build a larger mansion. The men were delighted with their houses. None of them had ever had such fine accommodation before, and already some of his foremen had employed local women to keep house for them.

The foremen told David that the men all appeared to be excellent workers and the fact that they had been granted their freedom and were earning good money had given them all new enthusiasm. They had started to clear and plough the ground, and in some areas seeds had already been planted. David was delighted with the cheerful, hard-working atmosphere he found. Among the things he had brought down with him were some flower seeds and cuttings, which he had intended to plant to beautify the area near his mansion. However, when he saw the efforts the women, and some of the men, were making to tidy the areas around their cottages he decided to offer the plants to those who wished to have them. He was surprised at the enthusiasm with which they responded, and touched by their efforts to truly make the cottages their homes.

David now began to work with his manager and foremen. He had always enjoyed estate work, but opening up and developing a new estate was obviously something he had never experienced. He found it exhilarating. They started work straight after breakfast, almost at the crack of dawn. He insisted the men had two hours for lunch, then work through to dusk. To the amazement of his employees he ordered that only essential work be done on Saturday afternoons and on Sundays, and that this work be rostered so that everyone had time off. He also encouraged them to organise games on Saturday afternoons if the weather was good, and the women to arrange picnics. The work was hard, but the positive atmosphere and the freedom from tyranny had a strong effect, and they all began to bloom under this new regime.

At night David would retire to his house, where his key men would often join him for a drink as they discussed the day's work and plans for the future. He was looked after by two serfs, Peter and Olga, whom he had bought in Kiev. They were a couple in their late twenties, and had been put up for sale when their owner had died. David had gone to the auction simply to assess the price of serfs, but when he saw Peter he thought he might be useful on the estate, as it was said he was skilled with horses. When the serf, who was relatively expensive, was brought over to him, David was surprised to find that he spoke some French. When questioned, the serf said in his halting French that until his mistress died he had worked in the house. She had taught all the household servants basic French, as this was the only language she and the master used in the house.

When David said he needed a housekeeper, the serf told him that his sweetheart, who was also being sold that day, was an excellent cook, and spoke better French than he did. This persuaded David to bid for the girl, and although she also went for quite a high price it was worth it to see the pleasure on her face when she realised she had been purchased by her lover's new owner.

Now David did not regret a rouble of what he had paid for the pair. They were both eager to please, and Olga was a good cook, having been well trained by her late mistress. She was also clean and more refined than many serfs. They were to be married in a couple of weeks, although they were presently living together. To their amazement, David told them that if they continued to work well he would free them in twelve months' time.

After dinner David often wrote to his grandfather and McNabb, telling them about what he was doing, and sometimes asking McNabb to arrange for more animals to be purchased. His mail was sent to a garrison about sixty miles away to wait for a courier who went through weekly to Kiev or Nikolaev, from where it would be forwarded.

David also wrote to Countess Volonskaya and Tatiana, regaling them with his achievements. He sent back a favourable report to Countess Nadia on progress on her adjoining estate, which was flourishing. He found he loved the country more and more. Now that he was often out working with the men his torso was a golden brown, and he did not think he had ever felt fitter in his life. To his surprise, he also found that the hard work wiped out his bitter thoughts about Gisela.

The dairy herd was due to begin calving in another three months, and he was sorry he would not be there to witness it, but by then he would be back in St. Petersburg. However, he had negotiated with the garrison to supply them with butter and cheese once the cows were milking. Milk, butter and cheese were always in short supply in the south, so there was a ready market for his produce.

He was also considering the possibility of using water transport to convey his produce to Nikolaev, where there was a good potential market developing. He had decided in future to barge live sheep and cattle to town and sell them in the local market. Soon, he told himself, he would build an abattoir there.

One day towards the end of his fourth week he was sitting on his verandah after lunch when he saw a small posse of riders coming over the horizon. As they came closer he saw that there were five riders and three loose horses. He wondered what they wanted. They did not look as if they intended trouble, but one never knew. He called to Peter to bring him a gun and take one himself, and to stand just inside the doorway in case he was needed.

As the horsemen came nearer one of them waved. David waved back, although he had no idea to whom he was waving. The horses looked familiar, however, and he realised they were Akhal-Tekes: he would recognise their trot anywhere. Good heavens, he thought, Countess Nadia must have sent these men. As he began to speculate what this might mean, one of the riders cantered up to him. It was not until the rider dismounted and he went to greet the stranger that he realised the man was Tatiana. What on earth was Tatiana doing here, he wondered, but it was wonderful.

He ran down the steps to greet her, took her hand and kissed it, and said how happy he was to welcome her as his first guest. He noticed that although her face was tanned, she looked thinner and very tired. As the rest of her party came up and joined them Tatiana told him they were her servants; she would tell him all about it if she could come inside, she said. They went inside and David asked his servants to bring food and a cool drink for the men, and for Tatiana.

He was intrigued as to why she was here, but Tatiana said she would tell him everything as soon as she was clean and changed. David then realised that one of the other 'men' was in fact her maid, as she came forward and ordered one of the men to bring in the pack that carried some of the Countess's dresses. When she reappeared David could see that Tatiana had lost weight, which made her look more like her late sister, Natasha. There was also a worried look about her, which made him feel anxious on her behalf.

She came and sat down beside him and slowly told him the whole story, how the Empress had virtually ordered her to marry the Swedish Prince; about the letter her grandmother had drafted and she had written, and her escape from St. Petersburg. She described the exhausting journey, all the time worried about being found and arrested, so that they had always slept on the road and never in an inn or tavern.

The only place she thought she could safely hide was on David's new estate, since no one would dream of her going there. On the way, she had begun to realise that she was putting David at great risk of incurring the Empress's wrath. However, she thought if everyone believed that David knew nothing about the Swedish affair he could not get into trouble. She then looked at him, and asked if she could hide here. He thought he had never seen her appear so uncertain and vulnerable and loveable. Deeply touched, he immediately replied that of course she could stay here; he was honoured that she had come to him.

At this Tatiana, who had been hiding her fears and worries from her servants, burst into tears of relief. Her fear of being discovered and arrested, her worries about her grandmother's safety, and the terror of robbers on the road had all taken their toll. She threw her arms around David and cried on his chest.

Warmth and desire flowed as he put his arms around to soothe her, and felt her warm, slender body. After Tatiana had stopped crying and wiped her eyes, he suggested she sit down and eat while they made some plans. He proposed that Tatiana should live in his house with Olga as a chaperone, plus her maid. He would sleep in the house of one of the single managers, but would continue to have his meals here.

Tatiana asked if there was something useful she could do on the estate, as she needed something to keep her occupied. David suggested that as he had no schoolteachers yet, perhaps Tatiana could take on the role of teacher, giving the British workers lessons in basic Russian, and the Russians basic lessons in English. The men could be taught at night, for just an hour, as they would be tired after working all day. The women and children would have four hours of lessons each day, four days a week. Tatiana agreed enthusiastically to this proposal, and after a moment's thought suggested that she and her maid could also give lessons in sewing one day a week. Tatiana would interpret for her maid, who spoke no English. David thought this an excellent idea, and said if she told him what was needed he would make arrangements to have sewing materials brought from the nearest town.

That settled, David returned to the subject of the proposed marriage with the

Swedish Prince. Had not Tatiana told him that she would marry someone she did not love?

'No,' said Tatiana, very promptly, and with a blush. 'What I had said was that I could marry someone I did not love provided he loved me, because I believed I could make him happy. I know the Prince only loves himself, and if I married him and went to the stiff Swedish Court, the rest of my life would be one of misery.'

David then said he would leave her to rest while he went back to work and found accommodation for her men. Olga showed Tatiana to the room she would share with her maid, where she settled her clothes and the few possessions she had brought with her. Then she sat down to write a brief note to her grandmother to let her know she was safe, and arranged for one of the carrier pigeons to be released.

When David returned that evening he found Tatiana in a sparkling mood, relieved to be able to relax at last, and waiting expectantly for tomorrow to dawn so she could establish her classes. As they ate dinner together Tatiana enthusiastically expounded on the best methods of teaching, while David watched her beautiful face, its vivid expression constantly changing as she emphasised one point or explained another. David reflected on how wonderful it was to have such enchanting company after being out of touch with society for the last few weeks.

Tatiana's classes were a great success, and David looked forward to coming home from the fields each night to her company. She nearly always had a humorous story to tell about something that had happened during the day, and sometimes she would regale him with an impersonation of someone who had made a faux pas. She was never inhibited, he noticed, and she took a surprisingly broad view of life considering the society she had been brought up in.

As the days passed, David realised his feelings for Tatiana were becoming more intense. He would watch her when he thought she was not aware of him, and think how tender and loving she was with the children, and how charming with the workers. She affected him physically too. Sometimes it was just the curve of her arm as she stroked some hair off her forehead. At other times it was the soft contours of her breasts as she leant back in her chair. He began to be aware of desires he had not associated with her before.

Each morning he was excited anew about the speed with which he and his men were opening up the estate. There were odd difficulties, such as when one of the pumps broke down, which meant they could not send water to one of the areas where they had planted seed. Several heifers had aborted after eating the leaves of a certain shrub, but once the cause was discovered the bushes were dug out and destroyed. Some sheep had died after being savaged by wolves and David had the shepherds patrol the animals, armed with guns. There had been no major reverses, however, and every day he counted his blessings as he watched the estate developing.

One of his immediate successes had been with the man Campbell, who was a blacksmith. Campbell, who was in his late thirties, was a genius. He had the knack of making practically anything from iron. David had originally bought equipment to set up a good-sized smithy but almost immediately Campbell began to extend it. Within his first week on the estate he had persuaded the manager to allow him to engage two young Russians whom he was now teaching to do the basic work while he concentrated on the objects that called for greater skill. By the time David had arrived he was presenting ideas for producing their own spades, shovels, picks and many other similar items. Campbell was now working on a system to expedite the watering of the larger fields of grain. He had already made a slight adjustment to the new ploughs David had imported, making them easier for the horses to pull, and enabling them to dig a little deeper.

If he had not been convicted of a crime, for which, he convinced David he had been framed by his employer, Campbell would without doubt have had his own business in Scotland. He was a jovial, good-hearted giant of a man, and despite the language barrier he and his two Russian assistants seemed to understand each other, although there were some comical mistakes made occasionally. The young assistants already seemed to idolise him. David also enjoyed his company as he had an excellent and lively mind, despite his lack of formal education.

Earlier in the week one of the shepherds had climbed a small hill and found the thin switch in his hand begin to move. The shepherd, who had a natural gift for water divining, had then held the switch between both his hands and watched it vigorously rotate. He later told the manager that he guessed there was a good stream, spring or river of water about fifteen feet below the surface. He estimated the hill to be about sixty feet at its highest which, if there was water in quantity, would be a godsend for irrigating the surrounding land. After consulting David the manager had sent up two men to dig a well to the required depth. At fourteen feet the water burst through, rapidly filled up the hole and then overflowed, running down the hill. Since water was the one ingredient that had been short in the area, this find was the equivalent of discovering gold.

That night he told Tatiana that he would be away for about a week as he was taking up all available men to dig a dam and a series of irrigation ditches from the water source through the fertile plains for several miles. He would be taking thirty-five men, leaving seven to do the essential work at headquarters, and a number of others who were out patrolling for wolves. It was roughly a six-hour ride to the site, where the men had built improvised shelters for sleeping, and enough provisions had been sent out to last the week.

David intended to work with the surveyor on planning where the irrigation channels were to run. He could hardly wait to get up there and see for himself the water bubbling out of the ground. He wondered if there were any other underground sources of water on the estate. Once they had worked out the best method of utilising this water he would have the water-divining shepherd travel over other key areas of the estate, where water was in short supply, in the hope that other sources could be located.

The next morning, after saying goodbye to Tatiana and asking Peter and Olga to take special care of her, he left full of anticipation for the project ahead of him. For anyone interested in farming it was like a dream to see the water cascading down the hill. Already, in the few days since it was opened up, the water had cut a stream averaging four to six feet wide, which disappeared into the distance. Not only David but all the men were thrilled at the sight, knowing how this water would enhance the productivity of the estate.

Once up on the hill, David spent the rest of the day with the surveyor and a couple of the foremen considering how to manage the irrigation to achieve the maximum benefit from the water. David began to think he should bring Campbell up and let him see the site, and find out if he could think of better ways to irrigate the land. He decided that he would send one of the men back the following day to fetch him. He had begun to consider that if Campbell could be further educated he might make a suitable manager for the entire estate. The more he thought about it, the more feasible it sounded. He was well-respected by the other men, he was liked by all, and he had proved he could delegate.

The next morning he asked Joseph, one of the cattlemen, to ride back to headquarters and fetch Campbell. Joseph left early, and David reckoned he should arrive by about one or one-thirty, so that if Campbell had a horse saddled up immediately they could be back before it became dark.

Joseph made good time, and at around midday, when he was about a mile from the outskirts of the settlement, he noticed smoke coming from what looked like Lord Mountforte's house. Spurring his horse on, he rode forward quickly, and soon saw a woman's figure dash out and run towards him. He recognised Marge, the wife of one of the shepherds. He realised she was crying, and as he dismounted she sobbed, 'The men are dead, and the women taken.' Then he heard horrifying news.

At ten o'clock Marge had taken all the children down to the river about a quarter of a mile from the homestead to teach them to swim, this being Lord Mountforte's wish. She had only been away about twenty minutes when she heard shooting, then shouting, yelling and screaming. Hurriedly she told the two oldest children to look after the others and on no account to let them make any noise, but simply to lie on the ground and wait until she returned. She ran up the brow of the hill above the riverbank and saw around thirty Cossack horsemen yelling and brandishing their sabres.

Dick, who had been working on the water pump, saw them and shouted out to the other men to get their guns, then began running to his cottage to get his. Two of the Cossacks rode after him, and one leaned over and sliced Dick's head open while he ran. None of the men had their guns with them, which were all back in their cottages. Campbell and his two young assistants ran out, each armed with a long iron bar. Roaring with rage, Campbell pulled one of the Cossacks off his horse and cracked his head with the bar. As he reached for a second, however, his arm was cut off by a sabre.

By now Marge was almost incoherent, telling the story between sobs and being ill. Joseph tried to soothe her, and she went on a little more steadily. There was a shot, she said, and then another shot, and as the Cossacks turned to see who was shooting, Campbell, with his good hand, hauled one of them off his horse, jumped on him and, grabbing his iron bar, killed him. One of his assistants ran to Campbell's aid, but was cut down. Then another Cossack leant down and sliced through Campbell's throat. The other assistant was saved by shooting that came from Lord Mountforte's house, where Peter and Olga had taken up their guns. Marge said she thought they had shot at least three of the Cossacks before the house was fired, forcing them out, when they were then shot themselves. Campbell's surviving assistant sprang up behind a Cossack on horseback and attempted to strangle him, only to be cut down a minute later by another Cossack.

Jed, who had been working at the back of the newly built dairy, trying to complete the race, must have managed to sneak back to the nearest cottage and now came out shooting. He killed one, and wounded two, before he too was killed. Then the rest of the women, who had been at a sewing class in the barn, tried to sneak to the cottages for the guns. But the Cossacks saw them, and whooping and yelling, immediately kicked their horses into a gallop and, running alongside the women grabbed them and tossed them over their saddles.

Countess Tatiana and Maude were two of the women she saw fighting back, until they were clubbed over the head by the handle of a sabre until they were unconscious. Norma, Dick's wife, had kicked, bitten, scratched and punched the Cossack who had grabbed her, until the Cossack suddenly stopped whooping, drew his dagger and cut her throat. The rest of the women were then trussed up in front of the riders. The Cossacks who had the women spoke to the man who appeared to be their chief, then they turned to ride off toward the west.

Some of the Cossacks looted Lord Mountforte's house and attempted to set fire to it, but as Joseph could see, it was only partially burnt. The remaining Cossacks had then picked up their dead and wounded, rounded up the fifty-odd heifers and the dozen horses that were in the homestead paddock, and driven them out west.

Joseph asked where the children were, but before Marge could say they were in the barn he saw them coming out. They began to run towards him, crying and looking absolutely terrified. They all knew their mothers had been captured and taken away. Norma's little five-year-old, Janet, had seen her mother with her throat cut, then running screaming toward their cottage, had stumbled over her dead father,

Dick. She was in a state of severe shock and did not seem able to stop shaking, while all the time making unintelligible noises.

Joseph told Marge that she and the oldest two children should give all the children a hot drink and some food. If they could find any of the whisky Lord Mountforte kept in his house, they were to lace the hot drink with that, so the children would soon go to sleep. If there was no whisky she was to use vodka. He would ride immediately back to the hill and tell Lord Mountforte. Marge was to put the children to bed, all in one place, and stay with them until he returned.

Marge, who was clearly in a state of shock herself, flung her arms around him and cried through her sobs that she was so frightened. Joseph told her she must be brave in front of the children, and that he was sure the Cossacks would not return. He also spoke reassuringly to the two older children, ten-year-old Jonny and twelve-year-old Elsie. He was amazed at how resilient and courageous they had been in looking after the younger children, but they were both showing signs of strain now. He told Marge to keep them busy helping her, otherwise they too might break down, and to take Janet to bed with her that night. Even with hard riding both ways, he did not think Lord Mountforte and the men would be back before midnight.

Marge decided to take the children's mattresses into the barn. Once that was done Jonny was left to try and entertain the younger ones, distracting them from the tragedy as far as he could. Marge and Elsie then began to prepare hot drinks and food.

To find the whisky Marge had to pass the bodies of Peter and Olga. Olga had been shot in the head, and Peter in the chest. Marge wept again as she looked at the two bodies. Only yesterday Peter and Olga had been at the English class in the barn, and the two were so in love. Peter had been making fun of Olga's English accent, and had had them all in peals of laughter.

Marge moved on and found a full bottle of whisky in a cupboard, which the Cossacks, in their hurry to fire the house and go, had obviously overlooked. It was then that she heard a groan and nearly dropped the whisky in fright. Standing motionless, she waited in fear. Then she heard it again, a soft, low moan. Suddenly she realised the sound was coming from Peter.

'Oh, thank God, he is alive.'

Rushing over, she spoke to him, but he did not hear her. Gently opening his bloodied shirt, she discovered the bullet hole. Fortunately, the shirt, being made of a coarse material, had helped staunch the flow of blood. Marge had little knowledge of health care, but she knew enough to find some of Lord Mountforte's handkerchiefs and gently stuff them into the wound, then she put some cushions behind Peter's head. Next, she opened his mouth and poured some whisky in, hoping this would help revive him. Peter groaned again and, moving his head slightly, tried to spit the liquid out. He was too weak, however, and Marge was able to get at least a couple of mouthfuls into him.

Rushing back to the cottage where Elsie was making the meal, Marge told her the good news that Peter was alive. This meant that one of them would have to sit with him. They called Jonny over from the barn and it was decided that he was best with the children, and Elsie would have to look after Peter. They then went back to where Peter lay. Marge decided it was too dangerous to move him, so they took a mattress from a bed, with sheets, blankets and pillows, and made him as comfortable as they could.

Elsie was to stay with him, and at dinnertime Jonny would come and stay with her through the night. Marge said that in the cupboard where she had found the whisky there was also brandy, vodka and gin. She believed the doctors used spirits to clean wounds, but she didn't know what spirit. Elsie thought she had heard her mother say brandy, so they cleaned Peter's wound with brandy and put clean handkerchiefs into and around the hole. Peter groaned when they were swabbing the wound with brandy, but still did not regain consciousness.

Then, feeling they were going to be ill, Marge and Jonny dragged Olga's body out onto the verandah so that if Peter did become conscious he would not see her body. They had not tried to bury anyone, as they were far too stretched already, trying to look after the younger children, and now Peter. That would have to wait until Lord Mountforte returned with the men.

When Joseph finally arrived at the hill camp he found everyone was sound asleep, having been at work since early that morning. He went straight to Lord Mountforte's hut and called out to him. David, thinking he had brought Campbell back with him, called out a greeting and said that bedding had been arranged for Campbell in Joseph's hut and that there was also a cold meal there. He would look forward to seeing them in the morning.

Joseph then said that Campbell was not with him, and blurted out that Campbell was dead. For a moment there was not a sound from the hut, then David bounded out in his nightshirt. Joseph had had to call quite loudly to wake him, as he had been deep in sleep, having worked manually all day. So by the time David sprang out all the occupants of the nearest huts were awake, and when Joseph shouted that Campbell was dead more men appeared. David asked Joseph what he meant, but as the man began to tell him Lord Mountforte stopped him, saying all the men must be woken to hear this dreadful news.

Once the men had assembled, Joseph told them about the Cossack raid. They were all shocked and horrified, and those who had wives and children were becoming distraught. David was sickened by the thought of the deaths of his men, especially Campbell, a man he had come to think of as almost an equal, and the faithful Peter.

Then a feeling of panic washed over him at the thought of what might be happening to Tatiana and the other women.

Plans were already forming in his mind. Joseph was clearly exhausted, and his horse would not be able to keep up with the others' fresh horses, so he was delegated to stay at the hill to look after the draught horses and equipment, along with Bill. The rest of the men were told to saddle up their horses, as they were to ride immediately to the homestead.

Three of the men were delegated to divert to a valley about two miles from the homestead and drive up the thirty-odd riding horses pasturing there. They would be needed as fresh mounts, since David said he intended to ride after the Cossacks as soon as he had assessed the situation at the homestead. The Cossacks must be one of the several small gangs who had not accepted Potemkin's offer to join the army, and had become terrorists.

He tried desperately to maintain an air of total control as he spoke to the men, but underneath he was worried sick about the women. Had they been raped? Were they still alive? Feeling almost beside himself with fear for Tatiana's safety, he tried to concentrate on what he would need to do.

After riding hard they reached the homestead just before dawn. The men were sickened at the sight of the bodies. Norma's dress had been virtually torn off as she had fought to escape, and there was blood all over her face. The men who went to bury her felt it a blasphemy to see the kind, fun-loving Norma like this. They covered her up quickly, and buried her beside her husband, Dick.

There were seven bodies in all, and the men buried them on a slight rise behind the barn where, as one of them said, they would have a good view come the Resurrection. David said prayers over the graves. Later they would make crosses or headstones. These were the first deaths they had experienced in their new land, which now felt a long way from home, and most wondered what the future held for them. All the hopes and expectations they had held had gone. David realised that their youthful ardour would never be the same again, no matter how positive their future became. Their spirits would always be tempered by this massacre. As he looked down on the body of Campbell, the man he had held such hopes for, and on Olga, whom he had intended to free at the end of twelve months, tears slid down his face.

He decided to leave three men at the homestead, including Davy, who was instructed to look after Peter. Davy had a very gentle way with animals, and could set birds' wings and tend to cattle or horses that had sprained legs or fetlocks. David asked him to try and extract the bullet lodged inside Peter as soon as there was enough light.

Arming themselves, they mounted the fresh horses, which had now arrived from the valley, and rode off in pursuit of the Cossacks. David hoped that by riding hard they could catch up with them by the evening. He counted on the fact that driving the heifers meant they could not travel at any speed, and that the captive women would also slow them down. Unless the women had told them differently, he imagined the Cossacks probably believed they had killed all the men on the estate. He was fairly sure they would not expect to be pursued. The army post was too far away, and anyway, there was no one left to alert the army.

As they rode, all the men were thinking of the frightful things that could be happening to their women. David was literally praying that God would let nothing happen to Tatiana. He thought of her humour, her intelligence, her compassion and her beauty. Suddenly he knew he loved her, a good, clean, full-bodied love. Even if she had been violated in some way, he would still want to marry her. What a fool he had been, not recognising that his feelings had changed so much, and that he wanted to marry her, not because she was suitable, but because he truly loved her. The way she sat, the way she stood, her wit, her courage, that courage, she would need now, he thought. He pushed his horse on faster, his feelings for Tatiana jostling for the grief he felt for his lost men, and for Norma and Olga.

They had been riding for about five hours, following a clear track that had obviously been made by a number of horsemen and animals, when they came upon an almost fully formed calf that had been aborted by its mother. This made them think the Cossacks were pushing the cattle at too hard. If they intended to keep the cattle they would have realised by now that they would not be able to keep up the same pace.

Sensing they were gaining on the Cossacks, David instructed one man to ride ahead until he caught sight of them, then to return and report to him. Approximately three-quarters of an hour later the man rode up a slight rise, stopped, turned round, and rode back to David. He was flushed with excitement and tension.

Just over the hill, beside a river and under some sparsely placed trees, the Cossacks were sitting eating. The animals were drinking or lying in the water, the heifers clearly exhausted. The women were sitting apart, but were not bound, as they were using their hands to eat. David asked how far the women were from the Cossacks, and was told around 300 yards. How far away were the horses, and were they hobbled? They were not hobbled, the man said, and they were some 500 to 700 yards away from the Cossacks.

There were two men at least, that he could see, sitting on the far side of the horses, separate from the mass of the Cossacks. Presumably they were to round the animals up when required. It looked as though the Cossacks had not long arrived, and as though they had settled in for a couple of hours. David thought they were probably resting the heifers and would not move them on until late afternoon when the sun had lost its heat. His man had spotted no sentries, which probably meant the Cossacks were confident no one was pursuing them. However, one or two of the Cossacks at least had their guns lying beside them.

David now began to plan their approach to the Cossacks. All his men had been taught to shoot, and had had regular practices, which gave them an advantage now. Before they left the homestead he had given them all strips of cloth, and he now instructed them to wrap these around their horses' nostrils and mouths to prevent them neighing and alerting the enemy.

Next, he delegated twenty men who, on his signal, were to dismount and in unison crawl up the hill. When they were all in position Jim, one of the foremen, would give the word to fire. Before firing they must each pick out a Cossack to shoot. They were only to fire twice, then race back and mount their horses.

Two more men were instructed to crawl up and sight the two men minding the horses. When they heard the first shot they were to fire and try and kill the two sentries, then run back to their horses and mount. Six men were to hold the horses belonging to those crawling up the bank. The moment the firing began, the other fourteen would follow David up over the hill and, firing, race between the women and the Cossacks. As soon as the snipers had mounted their horses, they were also to ride over the hill and at the Cossacks. One of the six men holding the horses would then take control of all the horses, and the other five would race up the hill and become snipers.

David was hoping the confusion would be so great that they would kill or capture all the Cossacks. He believed the Cossack horses would stampede at the sound of the gunfire, and the Cossacks would not be able to get to them in time.

Once the horses were all muffled they rode on to the foot of the rise. Then quickly the twenty-two men dismounted and began quietly but swiftly to crawl up the rise. Suddenly the firing started. They heard yells coming from behind the rise. David immediately gave the command and the fourteen men raced after him, and once over the hill, began firing at the Cossacks, preventing them from seizing the women hostages.

David could see about twenty-five Cossacks dead or wounded on the ground. It was a complete rout, and with no horses to escape on the Cossacks were easy targets. David's men dismounted from their horses, which were trained to stand when given the command, and the men knelt down and kept up a steady fire while the five snipers on the hill came into play and picked off more.

Suddenly there was a piercing whistle. It was made by the Cossack headman, who had slipped behind a tree, not because he was afraid, but because he had no gun and knew there was no hope in the open. Now he had decided to escape. In response to the whistle there was a hair-raising neighing in the distance. He whistled again, and they heard the thunder of hooves. Suddenly a magnificent black stallion tore through the shooting, jumping or sidestepping obstacles and bodies. As it reached the Cossack it slowed to a canter. It had no bridle or saddle, but in a brilliant feat of horsemanship the Cossack leapt onto the cantering horse, which immediately switched back to a gallop. They made a wonderful sight. The Cossack, holding the stallion's mane, was like a centaur. It was a spectacular act and they nearly got away, but as they came within gunshot of David and his men there was a volley of fire. The Cossack fell to the ground and lay still.

David was aware of screaming. Then he realised it was Tatiana, calling out 'Don't shoot, don't shoot,' but it was too late. They watched in disbelief and then in awe as the great stallion stopped, then slowly turned and trotted stiffly, neck and tail arched, back to his master. He stood, lowered his head and sniffed, then lifted his head and let out a low, heart-rending neigh, which was immediately echoed by the stampeded horses now at the end of the valley. Slowly the great stallion's legs bucked under him and he fell, partially covering the Cossack.

David and his men all rushed down to the horse. The Cossack was dead, with three bullets in him. The horse had five bullets in him but still lived, his breath coming in rasping sobs. He knew he was dying, and David felt he was pleading with his eyes for death. He placed his gun at the side of the stallion's head and shot him. He wanted to weep.

Everyone who had witnessed the episode felt a great pall of grief engulf them, that such a magnificent horse and rider should be dead. But their grief lifted quickly as they came back to the present and remembered their own dead and wounded. They still did not know what suffering their womenfolk had endured, and they turned to greet the women.

David ran towards the women and Tatiana ran straight into his arms, tears running down her cheeks. David clutched her to him and whispered again and again, 'My love, my love.' Tatiana just kept stroking his neck with her head buried on his chest. Then David asked gently what the women had suffered. Tatiana drew back, looked at him, and then, smiling through her tears, said they had not suffered. Certainly not what he feared, she told him.

When they were captured she had been clubbed for resisting, she said, then trussed up. Later, when they had stopped to give the horses and men a break, the women were untied and she had approached the headman, who they called the Ataman. Tatiana asked what he intended to do with them. He replied that he would give them to his men. They would provide some pleasure for the Cossacks.

Tatiana was inwardly terrified at the thought that they were to be violated by these brutal, uncouth men. She decided she must do something. She then told the Ataman who she was, and said that her grandmother, Countess Volonskaya, would pay a handsome ransom for her granddaughter's release. The Ataman said he understood that, but he also understood that whether she was raped or not, her grandmother would still pay a ransom to have her back. Tatiana knew this was true, and decided on another tactic.

She asked him why he was a rebel and raider when most of the Don Cossacks, which was what he was, and the Zaporogian Cossacks, had joined the army set up by Prince Potemkin. Surely he could see he had no future as a rebel. The Ataman then told her that several years ago he had travelled from his village with his men to a meeting, called by the Hetman, with the leading Cossacks and other Atamans, to discuss whether or not they should accept Prince Potemkin's offer to become a separate force in the Russian Army. They had all agreed, and so he rode home with his men with the intention of telling their wives and families that they were joining the Russian Army. When he arrived at the village he found it burnt to the ground.

There was just one old man alive. He had been left to tell the returning men what had happened, as a warning to all Cossacks to obey the Russians. The old man said a company of Russian soldiers under a Colonel Subov had ridden in and raped the women, then massacred everyone left in the village, young and old. The Ataman, whose name was Bely, said his wife and children had been among those who had been raped and killed. He had then vowed revenge, and had been the scourge of the Russians ever since. He now had an enormous price on his head, offered by the Russian Government. He said that after five years he was tired of having to leave every village he made as the Russians came to find him.

It was then that Tatiana saw a possible way of saving herself and the other women. She told Bely of her grandmother's great friendship with Prince Potemkin, and said that if they did not harm any of the women she would make sure he and his men received a pardon from the Prince, who was always looking for more troops. In addition, she said, her grandmother would pay him a ransom of 1,000 roubles. At first the Ataman did not believe this possible, but gradually she had convinced him.

She told David that strange as it seemed she had come to like the Ataman. He had reduced the amount of vodka he gave his men, saying that when they were drunk they were not always responsible and could be difficult to control. The women also sat apart from the men on his orders, so they would not be harassed by them.

Tatiana said she had been trying to stop Bely being shot when she called out. She felt desperately sad to see the Ataman killed, as he had suffered much from the Russians. He had agreed to release them all once he received word of an agreed ransom and a pardon. Tatiana was to have written as soon as they found a pen and paper.

Listening to Tatiana, David thought of the tragic waste of life caused by one Russian Colonel's viciousness. There was Campbell dead, Norma and Dick dead, their child an orphan; Peter was wounded, and his great love, Olga, dead, fighting to save the British people she had only recently met. Campbell's two Russian assistants had been killed trying to save him; a group of Cossacks had been killed, and their Ataman, greatly wronged, a brilliant horseman and skilful leader, was also dead.

When he had arrived in St. Petersburg and found what his wages were to be, Campbell had asked David if it would be possible to bring his wife and three children out to Russia, and to have their passage deducted from his wages over time. He swore Lord Mountforte would never regret it. David had agreed and Campbell, overjoyed, had striven continually to show him how grateful he was. Now, Campbell's wife and three children were expected to arrive in Russia in about four weeks' time, and Campbell was dead.

David decided there and then to divide the bounty money he would receive for Bely among his employees on the estate. He would give Campbell's share to his wife and children. Norma and Dick's share would be put aside for their daughter. Olga's share would go to Peter, if he lived. He would find the nearest relatives of Campbell's two Russian assistants and give them their share. They would each receive a large welcome sum, but he knew it would never compensate them for the lives lost.

Having heard the story of the Ataman from Tatiana, he had a deep sympathy for him, and later found his sleep sometimes haunted by the Ataman and his stallion. They would ride into his dreams, the stallion rearing over him, teeth bared, nostrils flaring, and the whites of his eyes showing, while his rider, the Ataman, kept saying, 'Countess Golvinka promised me a pardon — why did you kill me, why did you kill me?' He always woke, sweating, just before the stallion's hooves pounded on to him. He also had dreams about Campbell, so willing, so cheerful, and so full of natural wisdom. After this dream he would always wake up sad, and found the sadness took an hour or more to shake off.

However, now the married men were joyously reunited with their wives, the women had been told their children were safe, and it was time to make camp for the night. They ate the food the Cossacks had left. There were several wounded Cossacks, and David told those who would survive that he would seek a pardon for them from Prince Potemkin if they joined the army. Those who were in hopeless pain and would not survive had already been shot on David's orders to save them further agony.

Before eating, virtually all the men had been delegated to getting rid of the corpses. As they had no spades this was a difficult task. Finally, after discussing it with the wounded Cossacks, they resolved to pile the bodies up, cover them with grass and burn them. Unfortunately the wind changed while they were being burnt and the sickening smell of burning flesh streamed over the campsite.

The next morning the heifers, several of which had lost their calves as they had been driven too fast and too hard, were rounded up. Four men were told to drive them slowly home, taking three days to do so. The Cossack horses were also rounded up, and although there was certainly some good horseflesh in the herd, which numbered over sixty, there was nothing to compare with the Ataman's splendid stallion. However, David hoped some of the mares might be in foal. Horses were selected from these for mounts for the women, and six men were to drive the remaining horses back to the estate over the next few days. David, with the womenfolk and the rest of the men, would now ride hard for home.

When they arrived home late the next day, Marge and the children rushed out with shouts of joy to welcome them back. Tatiana ran and scooped the orphan, Janet, up into her arms and held her. David soon realised how much those at the homestead had been worrying that they would not return alive. Davy had cared for Peter splendidly, and he was expected to recover quite quickly now the bullet had been cut out.

That evening David and Tatiana discussed their situation and their hopes for the future. David was all for sending a messenger with a letter to Countess Volonskaya, to find out whether the Empress's attitude to Tatiana had changed. Tatiana was terrified the Empress would find out where she was and send an armed escort to bring her forcibly back to St. Petersburg and make her marry the Swedish Prince. Now that she knew David really loved her, and wanted to marry her for her own sake, she said she would rather marry him now and write to her grandmother, telling her she was leaving Russia for Scotland through the port of Nikolaev. Although David was overjoyed that Tatiana had agreed to marry him, he thought they should examine every step they took together to see if they could not resolve the problem of the Empress and the Swedish Prince. He was determined to marry Tatiana whatever the outcome, as he assured her, but he would prefer to do so with the Empress's goodwill. If the Empress refused her permission, then they would marry and flee to Britain. But for her sake, and the sake of her grandmother, he believed they should first try and appeal to the Empress.

In the end David sent a messenger to Kherson, where Potemkin was endeavouring to accelerate the shipbuilding in the new town. David had written a letter to the Prince, telling him of the death of Bely and his men, and claiming the Government's reward. Knowing the Prince would be pleased with his progress, he also told him about the estate. Included with David's letter was one from Tatiana, who pleaded with him, for the sake of his long friendship with her grandmother, to intervene on her behalf with the Empress. She said she could not marry the Swedish Prince, but wanted to marry Lord Mountforte. As the Prince was aware, His Lordship's family was a powerful one that had Russia's interests at heart. The messenger was instructed to give the letter to Popov, the Prince's factotum and close confidant, and to no one else. Tatiana said she knew that if Vasily Popov was given the letter, it would definitely be given to Prince Potemkin.

Tatiana had sent another pigeon off to her grandmother, but made no mention of the Cossacks since she did not wish to cause her any alarm. Although David did not expect any further raids on the estate, to reassure the women and children he had arranged for at least six men to work near the homestead, and to always keep their guns nearby. This meant he had to rethink some of the work on the estate, so that the men could be used productively. He had originally intended the home paddocks, as he called them, to be used for the dairy herd, as well as the riding horses and the pigs. Now he decided to plant a larger orchard there, to order more grapevines and citrus trees, and plant more vegetables such as carrots, potatoes, cabbages, cauliflowers, peas and beans. If conveyed properly, the vegetables could be sold in all the towns they could be taken to within a week.

Slowly life returned to normal, with Tatiana teaching again, and David reluctantly returning to the hill. He really did not want to let Tatiana out of his sight, and he also missed Campbell, both for his skills and for his companionship. Before he left he wrote to his grandfather and to McNabb, telling them of the Cossack raid and its outcome, but also requesting further men and a replacement for Campbell. He also told them about the discovery of water on the hill, and assured them that overall the estate was prospering. To his grandfather he wrote a separate letter, asking for his blessing as he intended to marry Countess Volonskaya's granddaughter, Tatiana. He spent some time on this letter, describing Tatiana's beauty and her many qualities, including her astonishing courage in dealing with the Cossack leader. He knew his grandfather would love her, he said, and he looked forward to the day when they would meet.

CHAPTER TWENTY FOUR

SOME DAYS LATER, AFTER DAVID HAD RETURNED FROM THE HILL, A CAPTAIN AND A DOZEN TROOPERS RODE UP TO THE HOMESTEAD. The Captain asked for Lord Mountforte, and when they met gave him a letter from Prince Potemkin. David opened the letter, in which Prince Potemkin congratulated him on his brilliant defeat of the Cossacks, and said Captain Gorky would give him the reward. He added that he was recommending to the Empress that Lord Mountforte be given the Order of St. Alexander Nevsky.

David was thrilled with the recommendation for the Order, and he realised for the first time just how feared Bely must have been in the area. He was also delighted to receive the reward, and took pleasure in telling the astounded Captain Gorky that he intended to distribute it among his employees and serfs.

When he had recovered from his bewilderment, the Captain said that he also had a letter for Countess Golvinka, and David asked her to join them. The Captain handed Tatiana a letter from Prince Potemkin, and left the room. David watched Tatiana anxiously as she read the letter. Finally, white-faced, she told David the Prince said she was to go to St. Petersburg and plead with the Empress. At this David took her in his arms and said that if there were any doubts in her mind that the Empress would still force her to marry the Swedish Prince they would elope straight away and take the first ship leaving Nikolaev. As he held her in his arms he felt intoxicated at the thought of finally being able to take her as his wife, but his ardour was abruptly cooled when in a flat, desolate voice Tatiana said that an elopement would not be possible. The twelve armed troopers under the Captain's command were to escort her back to St. Petersburg and the Empress. No escape was possible.

At the thought of losing Tatiana, David became irrational and started to consider ways of escaping with her. She, anticipating what he was thinking, said she would not try to escape, neither was he to try to aid her. She must go back to St. Petersburg with the Captain immediately. After some heated discussion David asked the Captain to join them, and it was decided that he and his men would stay the night and leave with the Countess in the morning. How would she travel? David demanded. The Captain said Prince Potemkin had felt sure Lord Mountforte would be able to provide a suitable conveyance for the Countess to ride in.

Tatiana stated that if she was to return to St. Petersburg she wanted to travel as quickly as possible. She would travel back as she had travelled down, riding on horseback and camping out. Her maid would travel with her. The Captain, impressed by her resolve, said that this would certainly cut several days off the journey. Then David said he would travel back with her, and no argument Tatiana advanced would change his mind.

It was decided that the Captain would sleep in David's house, which had now been fully restored, and the troopers would sleep in the barn. The foremen who were working near the homestead were called in to a meeting with Lord Mountforte, who told them he would be leaving the following morning. He then outlined his instructions for what was to happen over the next four months before he or a manager returned.

That night it took all his willpower not to go into Tatiana's bedroom and take her in his arms. He could not sleep for tossing and turning, fiercely rejecting the thought that he might lose Tatiana, and trying to see a way of marrying her. He was aware that if he persuaded her to elope with him he would lose his cherished Kuban estate and the money he had spent on it, but that now meant nothing to him if only he could make Tatiana his wife. He recognised, of course, that Tatiana was right and they could never elope now that Potemkin had sent an escort. He was not worried about giving the escort the slip. That would be easy, but once it was known they had escaped they would become hunted fugitives and soldiers would search the country relentlessly for them. He now cursed himself for writing to Potemkin.

In the morning they left the estate for St. Petersburg. Captain Gorky was a decent enough fellow and tried to make the days as pleasant as possible. Once he had David and Tatiana's word that they would not try to escape he treated them not as distinguished prisoners but as distinguished travellers. He talked a lot about the south and the Caucasus, and at one stage mentioned Count Dmitri Kolcluley, saying he had served under him at the battle for Ochakov.

David and Tatiana were thrilled to hear him describe Dmitri's gallantry in battle, and the Captain was overjoyed when they told him they had been friends of the Count. He said what a marvellous officer Dmitri had been, and what a tragedy it was for Russia to lose such a man. There were only a few officers who looked after their men in the same way as Count Dmitri had, and Captain Gorky said he tried to emulate the Count in his treatment of his men. After this Tatiana and David both fell quiet and rode in nostalgic silence for the next mile or so, each thinking of the vital, fun-loving Dmitri they had known and loved.

Tatiana found her thoughts wandering to her own position. She wondered if she should not beg the Empress to let her enter a convent rather than forcing her to marry the Swedish Prince. She desperately wanted to marry David, whom she now loved with an urgency and passion she had never felt before, and she knew he truly loved her. But she also knew that if the Empress and her Council had set their minds on her marrying the Prince for the good of Russia, there would be no chance of her being allowed to marry David.

It was just possible that if she requested permission to enter a convent she might be allowed. She knew she did not want to enter a convent, she wanted to marry David. What would she do in a convent? Sit and sew, and kneel in prayer all day, every day, until she died? She would hate it. No, she would seek permission to enter the orphanage that her grandmother was establishing with Princess Marie as its head. Yes, that was it. There she could do some good and would not be totally cut off from the world. Oh, what misery it was to be born to a position of consequence, she thought as they rode steadily towards St. Petersburg.

When they were within two days' ride of St. Petersburg they stopped at an army garrison post and the Captain requested a fresh horse on the orders of Prince Potemkin. A good, fast horse was produced, and Captain Gorky gave one of the troopers a letter, instructing him to give it to the Empress as soon as he arrived at the Palace. He was then to await the Empress's instructions regarding the Countess Golvinka.

When, two days later, they reached the headquarters of the Governor of St. Petersburg, there was a letter awaiting the Captain from the Palace. After reading it, Captain Gorky told them that a set of clothes had been brought for the Countess from the Volonski Palace to the Governor's headquarters. The Countess was to change into these clothes and then be taken straight to the Empress at the Winter Palace, no matter what time of day or night it was. This sounded so ominous that Tatiana began to tremble with fear of the Empress's wrath. She told David he must leave her now, and that whatever the outcome she would contact him.

David said he would immediately go and put her case to his Ambassador, but even as he spoke he knew it was useless. Even supposing the Ambassador could do anything, he never would, fearing that it would further jeopardise Britain's position with the Empress and her Court at this difficult time. They clung ardently to each other as they said their goodbyes, with David still vowing to Tatiana that he would rescue her from this marriage. Tatiana and her maid were then shown very courteously to a room where Tatiana's dress and other essentials were laid out.

The dress was loose on Tatiana, as she had lost weight since leaving St. Petersburg. Her nails were chipped, and her complexion, despite all her efforts to shade it, had been touched by both the wind and the sun. Feeling sick inside, her nerves at breaking point, Tatiana washed and changed. What would the Empress do to her? Had anything happened to her grandmother? Why had she been taken to the Governor's headquarters and not to the Volonski Palace? Why had the Governor not welcomed her, since their families were old friends? All these thoughts raced through her mind, causing her to feel faint as well as ill.

When she was finally ready and could delay leaving for the Palace no longer,

Tatiana was shown into an enclosed coach, surrounded by another escort of guards. Humiliated, but grateful that no one could see who was riding in the coach, Tatiana could only pray. It was not far to the Winter Palace and the coach arrived long before Tatiana wished it to. A footman opened the door and let down the steps of the coach. Another footman ushered her in through a side door. This was even more sinister, as in the past Tatiana had always entered through the main doors. In fact, she had never even noticed this side door. She began to wonder if there was a secret prison in the Palace, and if that was where she was being taken. Although she was walking with her back straight and her head held high, she felt so weak that if anyone had given her a gentle push she would probably have keeled over. What had happened to her grandmother, she thought desperately? How she hoped she had been spared, and not blamed for her disappearance.

Tatiana was now being escorted by two footmen, one in front and one behind, along a series of passages. She was too intimidated to ask where she was being taken. Finally one of the footmen opened a door on the right that was so well disguised she had never noticed it, and bowed her through. She found herself in a small sitting room, but she was feeling so ill now that she hardly took in the beautiful furnishings. She sat down in a chair and one of the footmen took up a position to her left. The other footmen went out through another door and disappeared.

Five minutes passed, then ten minutes, and still Tatiana sat there on edge, alone. Suddenly a door opened and the Empress emerged. She stopped and stared in a frightening and formidable manner at Tatiana. Tatiana hastily rose, and dropping a deep, deep curtsey, stayed down, until the Empress said in a stern voice that Countess Golvinka could rise. This use of her title, especially in this informal room, terrified Tatiana. Except on very formal occasions, the Empress always called her Tatiana.

Fearing the worst, but now urgently wanting to hear her punishment, since she did not feel she could stand the tension for much longer, Tatiana raised not only her body but also her pleading eyes to the Empress. The Empress asked in an exceedingly sharp tone what the Countess had to say for herself.

Somehow managing to gather her wits and her courage, and knowing that she would now have to marry the Prince, Tatiana said she was ashamed of putting her own selfish interests before those of Russia. Her only plea in mitigation was that she had been brought up knowing the Empress had had a dreadful marriage, and that she, Tatiana, knew she did not have the Empress's courage. She felt the proposed marriage would be a terribly unhappy one for her. She did not like the Prince or what he stood for. Gathering further strength, she said that, unlike the Empress, she did not feel she was clever enough to sway Sweden's policies in favour of Russia. This made her feel she had nothing to offer to the advantage of Russia in such a marriage.

When she had finished, the Empress smiled at her and told her she was to sit down. Was Tatiana cold, she asked? She was shivering. Was that because she had lost weight? The Empress was now full of concern. She ordered the footman to fetch a stole from her room for the Countess. The change in the Empress was so great that it was almost too much for Tatiana, who wobbled with relief and again nearly fainted.

The Empress then proceeded to tell Tatiana how her dear friend, Nadia Volonskaya, had come and told her about Tatiana's fears. Well, the Empress knew from bitter experience what a tortured time a wife could have if those fears were ever realised. She had therefore abandoned the idea of Tatiana's marriage to the Swedish Prince. Indeed, she had done better. The Zovodovksy family were extremely flattered at the thought of being connected by marriage to royalty, and their daughter, Countess Katrine, was now to marry the Prince. Both she and her family were delighted.

The Swedish Prince was not quite so delighted, as Katrine, although attractive, was not as beautiful as Tatiana, and although rich, not as rich. However, when the Swedish Prince heard that Countess Tatiana had gone down with smallpox and would probably be marked for life, if she lived, he had hurriedly withdrawn his request for her hand.

'There, then,' said the Empress, 'you are saved, but remember you have had smallpox, nearly died, and been miraculously saved. However, you had better appear at the play at the Winter Palace tomorrow evening. It is important, I think, that he sees you when you are so thin, as that will lend credence to the story Nadia and myself have put about.

'Your grandmother would make a marvellous actress,' she went on. 'She has been looking quite grief-stricken. When you come tomorrow night the Zovodovksys will be there too, and please, Tatiana, try and give the impression that you are upset at losing the Swede to Katrine. They, of course, being who they are, will gloat, but we will gloat in secret over our triumph. You had better wear a veil to hide your smallpox scars.'

Tatiana rose, her legs trembling. Then she almost ran to the Empress, fell on her knees at the Empress's feet, and fervently kissed her hand, pledging again her undying loyalty. The Empress smiled and said, 'And now I have another surprise for you.'

Although she knew the Empress loved giving surprises and pleasure to those she liked, Tatiana was so overwhelmed she could not even begin to guess what this could be. 'Follow me,' the Empress said gently, and led her through the door she had herself come through. As they entered the room Tatiana saw first her grandmother, looking radiant and oh so lovely, and then, on the other side of the small coffee table, David. Both had risen as the Empress came into the room.

Tatiana was stunned. She looked in bewilderment from her grandmother and David to the Empress. Before she could speak, the Empress said, 'I thought you would like to witness this.' Then, from a long box on a side table the Empress drew out the Order of St Alexander Nevsky. 'This,' she said, as David came forward and knelt, 'I am bestowing on Lord Mountforte in recognition of the singularly fine service he has done for Russia in cleansing us of the rebel Cossack, Bely. Prince Potemkin recommended you for your great valour. My Procurator-General, Prince Viazensky, has also told me how you saved his son's life in a brawl, so you have a high reputation at my Court, Lord Mountforte.'

As the Empress said this, with her charming smile, both David and Tatiana thought of Bely's last ride on his wonderful horse, and a flicker of sadness touched each of them. I must, thought Tatiana, tell grandmother the story of Bely, and then at an appropriate time she can tell the true, tragic story to the Empress.

The Empress then asked one of her servants to bring a bottle of champagne, saying they would toast Lord Mountforte's new honour. Then, after drinking a toast, she said she would have to leave them as she was due to see the Chinese Ambassador. Just as she was leaving the room she turned, smiling, and said to Tatiana, 'Don't forget to look suitably depressed tomorrow night.'

As soon as the Empress had left the room Tatiana put her arms around her grandmother and kissed her. She said how much she had missed her and worried about her, and thanked her again for her inspirational letter to the Empress. She then turned, and in front of her grandmother, put her arms around David, who bent over and kissed her full on the lips.

Releasing herself, Tatiana turned back to her grandmother, expecting to be reproached. Instead she found her happily smiling.

'David came straight to me as soon as he left you, Tatiana, and asked my permission to marry you. I gladly gave my consent.'

'Then,' said David, 'I went back to my apartment and found a messenger waiting to take me, as soon as I had cleaned up, straight to the Empress. When I arrived here I found Countess Nadia. The Empress told us that Prince Potemkin had written in glowing terms of my attack on the Cossacks and had recommended that she bestow the Order of St Alexander Nevsky on me.'

'At this stage,' interjected Nadia, 'the Empress told us that she would award it in Tatiana's presence, but first, for running away and disobeying, she was going to see Tatiana on her own and give her a fright.'

'She certainly did that,' said Tatiana, 'but she more than compensated later.'

'I have told the Empress that Lord Mountforte wants to marry you, and now that the affair of the Swedish Prince has been satisfactorily settled she is delighted. You know how generous and kind she can be. However,' the Countess went on, 'she insisted that you must make no announcement for at least a month. This is because she does not want the Swedish faction or those at the Swedish Court to know that one of Russia's leading families does not want the Swedish Prince.'

They returned together to the Volonski Palace where David and Tatiana, sitting close on a couch, between them described all that had happened since Tatiana had fled St. Petersburg. The Countess's expression and comments ranged from admiration for her granddaughter's courage and endurance, to horror at the raid, to satisfaction at the outcome. Nadia then said that when the Empress went to give Tatiana her so-called 'fright' she had been very nervous in case Tatiana said something by accident that would undermine the goodwill of the Empress. 'But,' she said, 'I should not have worried, Tatiana, as you have always had impeccable manners and timing.'

Tatiana responded by telling her how terribly fearful she had been when the Empress first came in and in a hard voice called her Countess Golvinka.

Countess Nadia then said they should discuss their strategy for dealing with the Prince and the Zovodovskys the following evening. She and Tatiana were to look upset at the news of Prince Karl's engagement to Countess Katrine Zovodovsky, and it would probably be best if David did not come near them, other than to say hello. The Countess went on to say that she had never liked Katrine's mother, considering her a very pushy woman who fawned on her superiors and was downright rude and hectoring to those she saw as her inferiors. Countess Zovodovsky had tried to become a friend of hers, she said, but she could never stand her malicious and cruel tongue. She also disliked the way she treated her servants.

'It will be interesting,' Nadia said, 'to see how she greets me, now that she is going to be related to royalty: probably condescendingly.'

It was decided that Tatiana would wear a heavy veil over her face, explaining to anyone who asked that she was wearing it until she had fully recovered from the smallpox scars. She was to say she was treating the scars with a mixture of honey, oil, vinegar and rosemary, and having some success. After all, when she did show her face there would obviously be no sign of smallpox, and they must prepare for this.

After a light-hearted dinner, tinged with the relief they were all feeling at Tatiana's escape, David returned to his apartment to prepare for his return to the Embassy the next day. In the morning he was greeted warmly by the Ambassador, who was pleased on two counts. Firstly, that David was back early, and secondly, he had heard via Lady Malvern, who had heard from her friend Countess Bruce, that David was being awarded the Order of St Alexander Nevsky. He said he was to come to lunch and tell Lady Malvern and himself all about the Cossack raid and its aftermath. He went on to say that David was regarded as a hero in Court circles, as Countess Bruce had told many people about the letter the Empress had received from Prince Potemkin praising him.

In the evening he changed in preparation for the performance at the Palace, thinking what a contrast it would be to his quiet evenings on the estate. When he arrived at the Palace he was swamped with people congratulating him and asking all about the raid, so he did not see Countess Volonskaya and Tatiana arrive. Her friends quickly engaged Tatiana, all expressing their sadness at her having caught smallpox and hoping she would not be too scarred. Tatiana felt rather ashamed at feigning such an illness to her friends and receiving their genuine sympathy, so she kept reiterating that she was using a special herbal mixture which seemed to be healing her skin. Most of her friends thought she was just being courageous, and they marvelled at how well she was taking her disfigurement.

Meanwhile, as Countess Volonskaya advanced into the room, Countess Bruce saw her and came over, smiling. She told Nadia the Empress felt she could not watch Nadia's performance, but had asked her to keep an eye on how it all went.

'What I am waiting for, Praskovia,' her friend said, 'is to see how that odious Countess Zovodovsky greets me. And believe it or not she is heading this way now. Oh, and so is Lady Malvern.'

'Good,' said Praskovia. 'I like Lady Malvern, she always livens things up.' Then she whispered, as she saw her take a glass of vodka off a tray, that it was amazing how much Lady Malvern could drink and still be marvellous company.

At this moment a booming female voice said, 'Good evening, Countess Bruce; good evening, Countess Volonskaya.' In the same breath, and looking triumphantly at Countess Volonskaya, Countess Zovodovsky said she was just trying to see where her future son-in-law, His Royal Highness Prince Karl of Sweden, was.

At this stage Lady Malvern joined them, having downed two vodkas as she crossed the floor. 'Good evening, Countess Nadia. Good evening, Countess Bruce, Countess Zovodovsky,' she said. Before anyone else could reply Countess Zovodovsky said she was just saying that she was looking for her future son-in-law, His Royal Highness Prince Karl.

The three women congratulated her warmly on her daughter's engagement. However, Countess Zovodovsky — very conscious that with her new royal relations she must be superior to that haughty Countess Volonskaya — decided to pay her back for what she perceived as past arrogance and disdain. So she went on to say that the Prince was totally enamoured with her dear Katrine. Of course, everyone knew that Countess Volonskaya's granddaughter and, with a sly smile, others had been hoping to attract the Prince. However, even if Tatiana had not contracted smallpox, and goodness knows where she had been to catch that, she was afraid Tatiana would have stood no chance against 'my dear Katrine.' Katrine had such a hold on him.

Hearing this blatantly rude attack on her granddaughter, Nadia was caught between fury at the Zovodovsky's insolence and a desire to burst into hysterical laughter because it was so untrue. Countess Bruce was astonished at Countess Zovodovsky's rudeness and was just about to make a cutting remark when Lady Malvern, having with the quickness of a conjuror whipped another glass of vodka off a passing tray, said, 'Yes, I can understand that.'

Countess Zovodovsky looked in some surprise at this unexpected but welcome interjection from the British Ambassador's wife, and beamed at her. The beam was promptly turned off when Lady Malvern went on to say, 'Your daughter has such strong teeth I can well imagine the strength of her hold on the Prince.'

Now, if one thing in particular marred Katrine's attractiveness, it was her unfortunately large and slightly bucked teeth. Countess Zovodovsky looked first astonished, and then massively indignant, whereas Nadia and Praskovia were struggling to conceal their laughter and not daring to catch each other's eye.

Lady Malvern had not yet finished, however, and went on to describe how her brother, who had been to the Cape in South Africa with Jan van Riebeck, told her about an animal called, she thought, a hyena. Apparently it had the strongest teeth imaginable, yet it only ate leftovers and did not catch anything itself.

Countess Bruce now had a severe coughing fit to try and conceal her mirth, while Nadia was covering her face with her fan. They need not have worried. Countess Zovodovsky, red-faced and almost choking with rage, had eyes only for Lady Malvern. To think she had once tried to turn her acquaintanceship into true friendship. Thank God it had not happened, for the monstrous woman was nothing but a drunk.

At that moment Lady Malvern noticed Katrine and the Prince heading their way, arm in arm. In a loud voice she asked whether they had noticed that the Prince had a rather awkward gait. Her father had had a horse like that, and despite its breeding it had had to be put down. There was an explosive gasp from Countess Zovodovsky, but not at all deterred Lady Malvern wondered aloud if Katrine was limping like that in sympathy or, poor girl, were her shoes too tight. She personally never worried about squeezing her feet into small shoes; it was far more pleasant to be comfortable.

With that, she bent forward and whispered, quietly but very clearly, did they think his shocking affair could be kept hushed up? The three Countesses looked at Lady Malvern, Nadia wondering if Margaret was teasing them, Praskovia wondering what she had missed and how she had missed it, and Countess Zovodovsky, who did not care what the Prince had done so long as he married her daughter, praying that the chandelier above Lady Malvern would fall on her head and kill her on the spot before she said another word.

So enraged was she that in a tone of suppressed violence she excused herself and tried to intercept her daughter and the Prince. As she steered them as far away as possible from the appalling Lady Malvern every bone in her body expressed her outrage.

The two Countesses, still trying to hide their mirth, then asked Lady Malvern what the shocking affair was. 'Oh, that,' said Lady Malvern. 'I just made it up, as I could see that the Zovodovsky woman was being even more vile than usual.'

'What about that animal with the big teeth, was that true?' eagerly asked Praskovia. 'Well, yes and no,' was the reply. 'My brother has never been to Africa, not even North Africa let alone South Africa, but we had to dinner at the Embassy a couple of nights ago a Dutch man who had. He was telling us some stories, and happily the hyena one came to mind when I remembered Katrine's teeth. I had no compunction about bringing up her teeth as she is going to be just as awful as her mother.'

With that, the three women could not suppress their hilarity any longer, and had to retreat to a corner where, laughing helplessly, they relived their meeting with Countess Zovodovsky. When they had recovered Countess Bruce said that the Empress would be in a fit of laughter when she regaled her with the incident. Plucking another glass of vodka off a fleeting tray, Lady Malvern commented dryly that she hoped Lord Malvern was not posted as Ambassador to Sweden.

She then turned to Nadia and asked her how bad Tatiana's scars were, as she had grown very fond of her since the gypsy party. In fact, she had been sending fruit and flowers regularly, and Nadia was ashamed that she had deceived such a good, kind friend. Looking first at Countess Bruce, she then said to Lady Margaret that she was to keep what she was going to tell her completely secret. Solemnly, with a hiccup, Margaret nodded her head, promising not a word would escape her lips. As it was well known that she was not a gossip, and was in fact very principled, the other two had no doubts and proceeded to tell her about the smallpox and where Tatiana had been.

Countess Bruce then said, 'Let us go into a private sitting room. You stay there and I will send someone for Lord Mountforte and another for Tatiana. Once we are all there I will go out and see if the Empress will come in for a few minutes. She will so enjoy all this.'

When they were all gathered in a little side room, Countess Bruce sent for refreshments and went to find the Empress. She was in a gay mood, and when she heard about Lady Malvern's conversation with Countess Zovodovsky she laughed until she was nearly crying. By then the three storytellers had had a good deal to drink and were so relaxed they each added their own piece to Lady Malvern's, with hilarious results.

The Empress loved it, and said if Sweden did not come in on Russia's side, completely ignoring the fact that Lady Malvern's country was trying to win the Swedes over to Britain, she would help them fabricate a story of some shocking affair that the Prince was involved in. The few minutes stretched into thirty minutes until finally the Empress left, still laughing. David and Tatiana both said they simply loved Lady Malvern's conversation with Countess Zovodovsky, and only wished they had been present.

Later in the evening David saw Baroness Hertzburg talking in a small group. Though Gisela no longer caused him any anguish, he now felt a great tenderness towards her, his first love. Hoping to establish a new platonic friendship, he made his way toward her. Gisela had not been able to watch David without feeling rushes of heat as she recalled some of their times together. She had carefully steered clear of him all evening, and now saw him approaching her with very mixed feelings. One thought was to run away, and the other thoughts were so erotic that she almost felt faint. She was practically mesmerised as he came over with his long, loose-limbed stride and devastating smile.

Reaching her, he took the hand she held out, bent over and kissed it. He then said how lovely it was to see her and that he hoped they could become friends now. With a wry grin, he said he had recovered himself. He meant it with the best of intentions, but inwardly Gisela was shattered. She had always said that this was what she wanted but, still desperately loving him, it was a bitter blow. She knew he must have found someone else. Just then Countess Bruce came up, and David, making his excuses, moved away.

Countess Bruce had been instructed by the Empress to gently prepare society for a marriage between Tatiana and Lord Mountforte. She was to hint that Tatiana was marrying David on the rebound from her disappointment at not catching the Prince. Countess Bruce now said to Gisela that she found young Mountforte rather dashing, adding that he had, along with every other apparent virtue, an Adonis-like figure. Did not the Baroness think so? Gisela not only thought so but also, of course, well knew so. However, she replied as nonchalantly as she could that she supposed so, now that the Countess had drawn her attention to him.

Internally Gisela was weeping, as she saw the love of her life walking away with no discernible regret. She wished Countess Bruce would go away so she could disappear. However, Countess Bruce chatted on, saying that she thought Mountforte could be interested in Countess Golvinka, if only she would give him a little encouragement.

Oddly enough, this comment lifted Gisela's spirits. Of course, David was so gallant that quite probably if he had been paying the Countess any attention before she caught the smallpox he would feel honour bound to make an offer for her. Not like that Swedish Prince, who had used all his Government's powers of persuasion to secure a marriage with the Countess then dropped the proposal like a hot coal as soon as he heard she had caught smallpox. No, David was a true gentleman. She then said, quite sincerely, that she hoped Countess Golvinka was not too disfigured by the smallpox. She had been such a beauty and had a delightful personality.

As Countess Bruce moved away Baron Hertzburg appeared at Gisela's side, and said with a lopsided smile that he knew she still loved Mountforte. Lifting her head, Gisela said there were many kinds of love, but that the love she felt for him was the finest kind of love. She knew she was one of the luckiest women in the world, and she wanted Max to realise and remember that. Slipping his arm through hers, the Baron said he was not one of the luckiest men in the world, but the luckiest. Smiling at him through moist eyes, Gisela squeezed his hand and said, 'Let us go home now; the Empress is about to leave.'

CHAPTER TWENTY FIVE

David had been extremely busy since he had arrived back in St. Petersburg, and although he had received two letters from his grandfather, and one from McNabb, he had put them aside until he was at his apartment and could read them at leisure. All were written before they had received his letter telling them about the Cossack attack. He read McNabb's first, and was again full of respect for his ability to handle all the requests David had been sending him. McNabb also repeated that the old Earl seemed to be rejuvenated these days, and he put it down to his interest in the Crimean estate.

Finally he read the two letters from his grandfather in the order in which he had written them. The first letter expressed his pleasure at the manner in which David was conducting himself, and was full of enquiries about the estate. No detail appeared too small to interest him. On opening the second letter, David had to read the last paragraph twice before he was completely certain he had read it correctly.

The first part of the letter was to advise that McNabb and he had found ten more suitable convicts, seven of whom had wives and children. He was shipping them all over. They were decent men, despite their convictions. What particularly pleased David was that one of them was a farrier, and only a young man. He went on to say that he knew David was delighted with Campbell but this man would, he felt sure, work very happily under him. Maybe it would free Campbell up to tackle some of the other projects David had mentioned. This caused David, again, pangs of loss as he thought of Campbell, dead and buried in the Crimea.

Then came the paragraph he could scarcely believe. His grandfather said that he was sailing on one of his ships, the *Scottish Lion*, which was coming to load timber in St. Petersburg for Liverpool. He further said that he would possibly stay for a couple of months, as he would like to see the estate and also visit some of the forests that were the source of the timber he bought.

David was absolutely delighted at this news. Reading between the lines he also thought that his grandfather was missing him but, of course, would never say so. This was the longest they had been apart. Even when he was at college he always went back to his grandfather in the holidays. Now he had been away for over twenty months.

David was so excited that first thing in the morning he went over to the Volonski Palace, where he found Tatiana and Countess Nadia breakfasting. Early rising was a habit that Countess Nadia had instilled in Tatiana, as well as her servants. Although they were surprised to receive a caller as early as eight o'clock, they were pleased to see David and both were delighted at his news.

David said his grandfather should arrive in about two weeks, and that Tatiana and he could be married within the month. Tatiana protested, saying that she could not marry for at least twelve months because she must not marry before the Swedish marriage. Anyhow it would look suspicious, and the Empress would not approve. David had not even thought about the Swedish Prince now that he was engaged to the Zovodovksy girl, and he began to argue.

Countess Nadia looked perplexed, and said she did not think the Empress would demand such a long engagement. If David and Tatiana wished, she said, she would go and see the Empress. Then suddenly Tatiana smiled impishly and said she was only teasing, and coming over, she sat on David's knee. Putting her arms around him, she said that as far as she was concerned the sooner they married the better.

The Countess began talking of possible dates for the wedding, and also asked where the Earl proposed to stay while he was in St. Petersburg. David said he would probably stay at the Embassy, to which the Countess replied that he might perhaps prefer to stay at the Volonski Palace. She could give him a suite of rooms and provide carriages and horses for him. That way, if he wanted to get away from people and retire at any time he could go to his own rooms and be comfortable. David thought this an excellent idea, thanked her warmly, and said he would suggest it to his grandfather.

Tatiana then said she was worried that his grandfather would not like her. David laughed, saying that was absolutely impossible. Tatiana persisted, however, saying he might not like a Russian granddaughter. To this Countess Nadia replied that she had not wanted an English grandson, but was now completely reconciled to the idea. Particularly, she admitted, now that David and Tatiana had decided to spend half their time in Russia and half in Britain. She said she might even visit them in Britain. This statement caused Tatiana to burst into tears and throw her arms around her grandmother. David was also thrilled, as he had a great deal of affection for Countess Nadia and was delighted at the thought that he might be able to show off his Scottish estates to her.

David had already declared that he was going to give up his diplomatic position in order to concentrate on running his and Tatiana's estates and investments, with Tatiana's help, of course, and if she approved. This suited everyone, especially Tatiana, who was looking forward to spending more time in the country.

Countess Nadia got up, saying she had things to do, leaving them together. David opened the door for her, then walked across to where Tatiana was sitting and pulling her up to him, kissed her for so long that she was breathless. Then he said teasingly that even though the entire world believed he had caught her on the rebound from a prince who had rejected her, and despite the terrible scars left by the smallpox, he still loved her madly. Tatiana put her arms around his neck and, as she pulled his head down to kiss him, said mischievously, that she did not mind at all being rejected.

They walked out into the garden, where the birds were singing and the sun was just rising. As they stood hand in hand by the pool, the sun suddenly touched them and as its warmth folded over them they knew the future was theirs.

ISBN 141206499-6

9 781412 064996